MORNINGSTAR
PRESS

THE HESTER STREET KIDS

ALSO BY ARMANDO MINUTOLI

FICTION

SCHISM

(Scheduled for: late 2015)

A Spiritual fantasy about the afterlife

NON-FICTION

MEDJUGORJE, A PILGRIM'S JOURNEY

Apparitions of the Blessed Virgin Mary in

Bosnia-Hercovinia

SCREENPLAYS

Mr. Minutoli is also the author of two screenplay

adaptations

THE HESTER STREET KIDS and SCHISM

THE

HESTER STREET

KIDS

ARMANDO MINUTOLI

Published by
THE MORNING STAR PRESS
Delray Beach, Florida

Armando Minutoli/The Morningstar Press
Delray Beach. Florida
www.themorningstarpress.com, email: aminutoli@earthlink.net

Publisher's Note: This is a work of fiction. Names, characters, places, and incidents are a product of the author's imagination. Locales and public names are sometimes used for atmospheric purposes. Any resemblance to actual people, living or dead, or to businesses, companies, events, institutions, or locales is completely coincidental.

Book Layout & Design ©2014 – Consuelo and Armando Minutoli

The Hester Street Kids/ Armando Minutoli. -- 1st ed.
ISBN: 978-0-9630544-3-2 Library of Congress Catalog Card No: 2014943119

For
My wife, Consuelo, our Children
And
Grandchildren
And
The Memory of My Parents

"A mirror reflects a man's face, but what he is really like is shown by the kind of friends he chooses."

– Proverbs 27:19-21

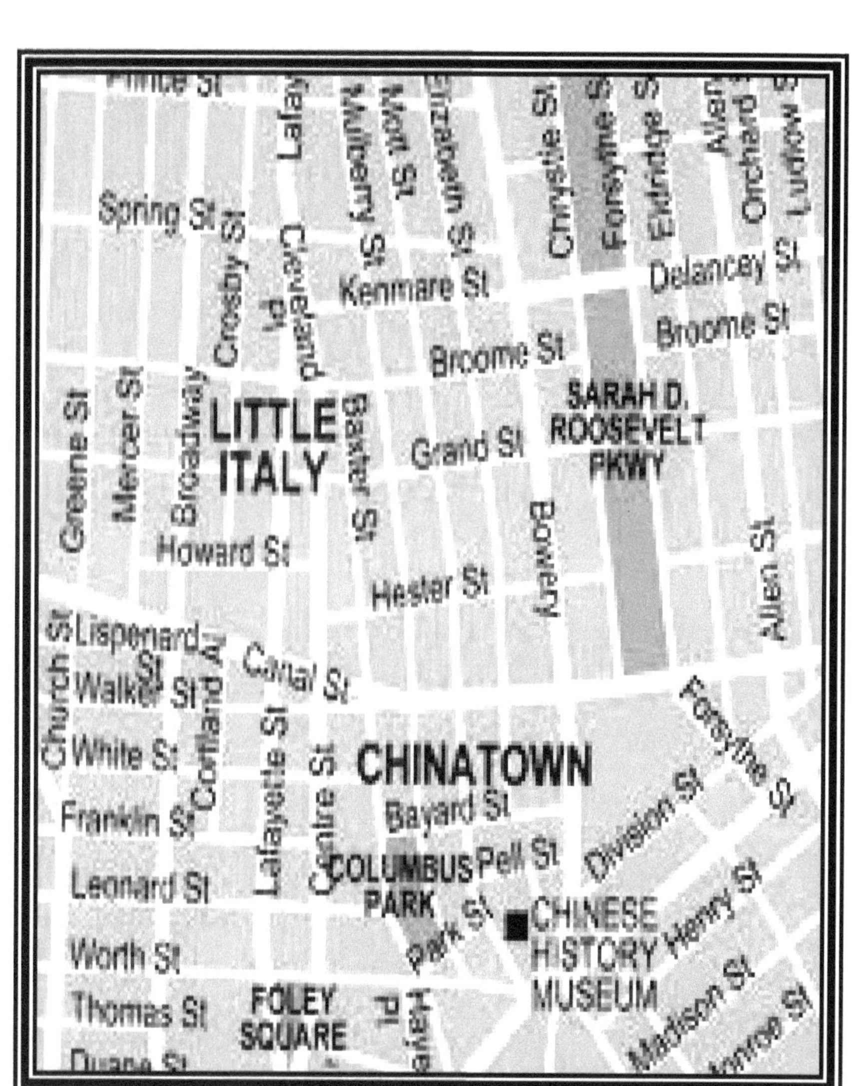

New York's Little Italy

1.

THE DAY OF DARKNESS – 1920

Immigrants spilled onto Hester Street, which ran through the heart of the neighborhood. Many were skilled tradesman on their way to work, while others opened shops catering to their cultures. The neighborhood was overcrowded and dirty and crime was a way of life, so it was often dangerous. The neighborhood streets bustled with the sounds of horses, carts, children playing, and the cries of street vendors peddling their wares. The attached tenement rooftops became crowded havens away from the noise and stench of the garbage-filled ghetto streets. These were places where mischief might be plotted and secrets made and kept ...

Concetta-Marie Maladesta, fifteen years young, had quit school to earn money for the household. She returned from her bakery job and found her father drunk and waiting for her at the door of their third floor railroad flat. He lunged toward her, ripping her uniform. In defense, she pushed him and he fell backward, hitting his head.

She flew down the steps to the second floor. There she stopped, fumbling nervously to raise her uniform in order to climb through the open window, which led to the roof of the adjacent building, which housed an auto repair shop. She sought out Birdie, her protector.

The roof for her and her friends was a magical space that served as their playhouse and sanctuary. As they grew older, it became their headquarters. She found her friends gathered around Birdie's makeshift table sorting a cache of coal, the day's haul from the horse carts of unsuspecting coal peddlers. The sound of Concetta-Marie's arrival interrupted the plotting of the coming night's mischief.

Embarrassed, she began to turn away but Carmella, the youngest, intercepted her, holding her tight in her arms. The others stood frozen as if posed for a snapshot, their senses filled by the dismal air, and laden with the pungent smell of the roof's asphalt.

The moment was broken by her father's drunken voice vibrating through the hallway.

"Come out here, you little whore! I'd like to make a woman out of you!"

He staggered out the window and stopped, startled by the six juveniles, who stood eyes wide, anticipating trouble. He called again to his daughter, this time with more restraint.

"Come on, Concetta, let's go home."

"Never," she yelled shaking her fist, "never again. I'll kill myself first."

With that, her father lunged at her. Tommaso shouted at him, "You bastard," and started for him, but Birdie held him back, saying, "Wait, Tommaso. Let me take care of this."

Birdie was the biggest and strongest of them. Six feet tall, although still fourteen, he approached the beastly man.

"Look, I think I can help. Let's walk over there and we'll talk about it."

The drunk, with a vile look, charged at him but stumbled. Birdie, with the confidence of a judo master seized him by the shoulders, and with cold surety led him right over the edge of the roof. To insure the success of his deed Birdie's eyes followed the man's fearful flight, and witnessed his head explode on the cobblestoned driveway below.

Birdie turned back to the group. With the calmness of a state executioner, he said, "It's over."

His eyes, without emotion, fixed on Concetta-Marie.

"Change your clothes, take Carmella home with you and stay there."

He turned to Carmella, "You didn't see anything, right?" Then with a glimmer of concern, "Carmella, you okay?"

Bewildered, in shock, she returned a fearful nod.

"Okay, go now, keep yourself busy. Bake a cake or something. We'll all meet by the lemon-ice store later."

The others stood frozen in place awaiting his next move. The stunned boys, full of fear, glared at him from under the brims of their tattered flat caps. The dark act energized them as if they were blanketed in the excited air of a lightning strike.

"You three, come down to the alley with me. We need to show our faces. People know we hang out here. If the cops ask you anything, we were walking up the block and heard the car mechanic's yelling."

Peppino Cortese, the undertaker's grandson, was accustomed to death, and he huddled them together and warned, "This is a secret that we must carry for the rest of our lives. He had it coming to him. All we have is each other. We're ... a family." His voice choked. "*Uno per tutti tutti per un,*" "One for all and all for one, like the Musketeers." He stared at them for a solemn moment. "I want to hear you all promise, or you're going off the roof, too." He pointed to each of them, one at a time.

"You?"

One by one, they promised, "All for one." Then, they each hugged Birdie as if paying homage to a newly appointed Mafia Don.

Concetta kissed and thanked him, and then said with eerie calmness, "You have sent the devil back to hell. My mother and I owe a lot to you. I will never forget what you have done for us."

He raised his hand as if blessing her. "Now go. Remember, you know nothing."

The cops were there within minutes, making their way through the crowd that had formed around the body. They looked over to identify the corpse.

Trying to read its face, Connolly, the rookie Irish cop, knelt beside the splattered body. He exclaimed, as his oversized officer cap slipped to the bridge of his nose, "Oh, shit, we hit the sweepstakes. It's Maladesta. Good riddance. One less drunken grease ball punk to worry about."

Connolly's partner approached Pete, the auto mechanic, and asked him what happened.

"I don't know, I was working on the old Chevy and I heard a loud thump. I thought a flowerpot had fallen. When I turned, and there he was," pointing a grease-stained hand at the lifeless body, "with his brains splattered all over my driveway."

The rookie turned to the crowd and saw the kids. He knew. He started for Anthony while Birdie inched his way to take his place. The cop asked him what he knew.

"We were passing by and heard the mechanic yelling. When we looked, holy smoke, he's lying there in a pool of blood." He supported his account with a disguising grimace.

The other three bobbed their heads in collaboration.

"You know this building?"

“Yeah,” Birdie responded. "I live up there.”

“You want to show me?”

“Sure.”

As he led with the cop, he turned to his friends with calm certainty, and signed off, “See you guys later.”

The group stopped as one. Peppino turned to the other two, “That is one cool *mamaluke.* He has always been there for us, gave us whatever he could, and never asked questions. So, mum’s the word, *Capiche*?”

2.

THREE YEARS EARLIER - 1917

"Nunzia, what's that noise?"

"It's the kids playing on the roof," she said with a puff.

"Those somma-bitches, they never stop," Ralphie vented, twisting his head.

"What do you expect, Ralphie? Their fathers and mothers, they always in the bar and God knows where else."

"Only one I think goes to school is the Burdino kid."

"Yeah, he's the only one got some brains."

"Well, he's very respectful," Nunzia, agreed. "Helps me up the stairs with the groceries and won't take no money, but don't let him fool you. That *ruffiano,* they're afraid of him."

"Yeah, and the udda one too," Ralphie said. "The undertaker's son. I wouldn't trust him as far as I could throw him. He's smooth like Burdino, but he has meanness in his eyes. If I chase him he doesn't talk back, he just gives me the look."

"And, the girls are worse than the boys, Ralphie. Do you hear the mouth on that Concetta-Marie? She takes no prisoners."

"She's the bossy one, alright. Treats her little friend Carmella like her slave and has that crazy, 'do anything' Tommaso wrapped around her finger. Am I right Nunzia?"

"Yeah, and that *stunad*, Anthony, follows her like a sheep, too."

"He's another one. You'd be dimwitted too, if your *Nonna* beat you like she does him. He always has the imprint of five fingers stamped on his face. She's crazy too, that old lady."

"Ralphie, do you think that Concetta-Marie has been a lot quieter since her father went to jail, that miserable soul? The only one she listens to is the Burdino kid."

Ralphie nodded in agreement.

"He's the brains, that kid."

"Please Ralphie, don't yell at them. They get a little bigger and they'll make our life miserable. The Jewish people on the block are afraid of them, too. Older people are like cops to them."

Concetta-Marie opened the large window at the end of the second-floor hallway, spied out and saw Birdie on the roof, banging away. Birdie was hammering scraps of lumber. As she made her way over the windowsill onto a makeshift step, she called out to him.

"Birdie, what you doin'?"

"I'm building a laboratory table."

"What you doin' that for?"

"I need room to do my experiments. My mother said I smell up the house. She's afraid I'll start a fire." He beckoned to her, "Hold the other end of the board while I nail it."

The 10-year-old, two years his junior, held the board in place. Birdie noticed her bruised arms.

"What happened now?" he asked. "You fall down again?"

He knew that she had not fallen. He knew that her father had beaten her and her mother again. When drunk, her father's usual condition, they became easy prey for his violent, irrational anger. He could hear their screams at night through his bedroom window, which also led out to the roof patio.

Concetta-Marie lived above him on the third floor. Her no-account father was a would be longshoreman who rarely worked because of his drinking.

Her mother supported the family as a seamstress sewing special occasion dresses for women in the neighborhood.

The neighbors were often awakened by the young girl's hysterical cries, begging her father not to hurt her or force himself on her mother.

Birdie hated him. It turned his stomach just to look at him. He appealed to his mother to do something. "I'm a woman alone with a child to raise," she'd say. "What could I do?"

He felt bad for Concetta-Marie and tried to compensate by being extra nice to her. He defended her violent outbursts and rough physical behavior with the other kids. He understood her anger. Why she provoked fights. Known as a tough cookie, she had the ability to take down a much older boy with a few quick punches.

She, in turn, held him in high esteem and was ever grateful to him. She knew Birdie would not allow anyone to hurt or embarrass her. She thrived on the attention he gave her. He took every opportunity to make a fuss over her. As the consummate gentlemen, he always offered her something, especially his mother's homemade cookies, which were her favorite. Sometimes, he would just quietly hold her hand in support. She felt protected and secure with him.

Deflecting the discussion and seeking his attention, she tapped on the table frame then pointed to the Porter chemistry kit sitting beside him on an old wooden folding chair.

"Did you get that from the firehouse?" she asked.

"Yeah. It's cool, isn't it?"

At Christmas and Easter, the local Hook and Ladder Company distributed donations of toys and clothing for the neighborhood kids. Birdie told her proudly that the fire chief had put the set aside specially for him. The firemen all knew him better than they knew the other kids. He ran errands for them, got them lunch and groceries, or placed bets for them with the local bookie.

A few minutes later, Peppino and Tommaso climbed through the window.

"Ah," Tommaso asked, "what the fuck ya doin'?"

"He's building a laboratory table and I'm helping him," Concetta-Marie answered.

"Geez," said Peppino, the practical one. "What're you gonna use for a top?"

Birdie pointed to an old tattered door that rested against the skylight that provided light to the auto repair shop below.

After driving in a few more nails, Birdie asked for help lifting the door. They placed it on the frame he had constructed, and he nailed the door to it. As he drove a nail into the last corner, Carmella came through the window with Anthony. "Birdie, what are you doin'? Nunzia and Ralph are making faces down there."

Peppino snarled, "They're pains in the asses, them two."

Tommaso, in a more sinister tone, chimed in. "Yeah, they always have something to say. Tell them to shut the fuck up. They should be glad that we don't break their windows or cop from them."

"Hey," Birdie said, "you don't shit where you eat. Leave them alone. They're old." That silenced everyone.

A clap of thunder and a sudden downpour sent them scurrying under the newly constructed table, squeezing together in a row. When Peppino shouldered in next to Concetta-Marie, he noticed the bruises on her arms. His face turned stern.

"What happened to you now?"

Tommaso also demanded, "Who did this to you? Did someone do this to you?"

Concetta-Marie flushed, and then counter-attacked. "Shut the fuck up, both of you." Carmella and Anthony did not say a word. They knew. They lived in the building and had heard the terrifying commotion at night. They had often prayed for her.

"Don't look at me," Concetta spat, "look at Nino. He got five fingers stamped on his face."

Birdie yelled at Anthony, also calling him by his pet name, "Nino. You just stand there and let her hit you?"

"What am I supposed to do? She's my *Nonna,*" – grandma – he answered, his head bowed. "And I have to show respect."

"Respect, my ass!" snapped Peppino. "I'm cleaning out the guts of dead people in the funeral home and gettin' nothin' for it. When Carmella says something or does something, they put her out the door like a dog and leave her alone in the hall. Tommaso works in the store and can't go to school because his stepparents are old and he needs a place to live. What the fuck respect do any of us get?"

They all nodded their heads, forlorn.

Tommaso Fingarro, orphaned under suspicious circumstances, never learned what had happened to his natural parents. A childless elderly Jewish couple had taken him in. The Shapiros ran a small grocery and hard goods store that catered to the Jewish immigrants in the neighborhood. They took pity on him and treated him well but they also depended upon him to do much of the physical work because of their late age. It was hard for him to connect at an emotional level with them or, in fact, most others, but he always remained respectful and protective of them.

Peppino started, "Concetta-Marie–"

"Shut up, alright. I don't want to hear it," she cut him off.

Birdie listened, boiling with anger and frustration at his life, too. Abandoned by his father in Italy at the age of three, he watched his mother battered by her second husband who had brought her to America. That husband was murdered, leaving her in a strange country with a son to raise on her own. Yet Birdie knew, out of all of them, he was the luckiest. His stepfather had accidentally left a lot of money and jewels. His mob associates had rubbed him out in the classic way: a single .38 gunshot to the back of his head. They'd also cut out his tongue as a warning to other would-be informers. But the booty remained.

The kids gravitated toward Birdie, who had assumed a fatherly role as if born to it. He would patch up their wounds and provide leadership for survival on the tough neighborhood streets. Bigger, older, and naturally street-wise, he defended them against the threats of the other clans of kids. He gave them advice but never expressed judgment of them.

That rainy afternoon, huddled under an old door, they did not foresee that Birdie's worktable would not only be a meeting place, but also a central base from which they designed their life paths.

A few nights later the shelter received the first wounded. Birdie, awoken by a noise coming from the roof patio, opened the window and saw a shadow of someone or something rustling under the table. He thought it was the rummaging of an alley cat. He squinted to identify it and discovered Concetta-Marie, with pillow and blanket in hand, preparing to spend the night.

Although summer, the evening air had a cool dampness to it. Birdie sat down under the table next to her. With gentle care, he wrapped a blanket around her and then put his arm around her shoulders. He did not ask her why she was there, but reassured her, "Relax. It's going to be all right. Come inside." He gathered her bedding and helped her up.

Beaten, she wobbled to her feet. His hands shaking, his teeth clenched, he restrained his emotion and lifted her through the window into his room and guided her onto his bed. He searched out a washcloth and rubbing alcohol to bathe her cuts and scratches, evidence that she had fought back. He always respected her for that.

After cleaning her wounds, he covered her and slipped a stuffed monkey he had won at the neighborhood Italian Feast under her arm. She held it close and scrutinized him steadily, her eyes reflecting her recent fear. He kissed her on the forehead as a father would kiss a daughter. She held him burying her head against him. He patted her on the head and reassured her that he would not leave her alone. He would sleep beside the bed on the floor.

She lay back as he turned to close the window, hearing him whisper under his breath an oath of vengeance.

Birdie's mother found them the next morning, just as they had fallen asleep. She saw the cuts and bruises, then took in the bottle of alcohol and washcloth on the nightstand. She understood what had transpired, and it brought tears to her eyes.

With a proud smile, she whispered to him, "My son, you will grow to be a strong man, a respected man. You're tough and willful at times but you have a good heart."

She closed the door, dressed, and left for work. When Birdie awoke, he found the monkey on his chest and the bed made.

3.

"BIRDIE"

Birdie's worktable became not just a meeting place, but a haven to heal wounds. It became the gang's headquarters. There they planned and plotted their outings, stored stolen goods and weapons, and shared their secrets.

Many times in the pre-adolescent years, Birdie might find one of them sitting under the tabletop crying, or raging with anger. He knew when to leave someone alone. They each carried their own burdens, which he never questioned.

He listened, and when asked for advice he offered words of protection and support. As they grew older, tears naturally morphed into anger, and too often into vengeance and violence molded and solidified by their protector.

Deeper emotions gradually evolved, leading to a darkness that overshadowed their life views. These experiences became the foundation of who they were to become as adults.

Concetta-Marie's father did time in prison for a couple of years, convicted of armed robbery. When he returned, he continued to drink and abuse his wife. Concetta-Marie hated and feared him even more, possessed by thoughts of his brutal behavior. She wanted to leave but was afraid for her mother, who would be alone with him and defenseless.

Some nights she would crawl through Birdie's window but would walk through his room and go to his mother's room, where she would crawl in to sleep. Older now, she needed to feel the security of Birdie's room, but respected the social mores. His mother never broached the issue with Concetta. They just wanted her to be safe.

Things worsened. Her father's depraved sexual hunger persisted. He became, more vigorous in his pursuit of Concetta-Marie. She was a mature fifteen, and when she dressed up, she could easily be mistaken for an older girl–one of legal availability–especially when she wore her white dress that contrasted against her complexion, accenting her hips and breasts. Still a tomboy, her strut and manner revealed her youth.

Birdie was drafted, but thanks to the local Boss's connections, rather than shipped to the trenches of The Great War in Europe he was stationed at Ft. Hamilton in Brooklyn. There he'd spend time with his old friends in the neighborhood on days off and when on leave.

Birdie kept a low profile as he led the kids on Hester Street, planned their activities, negotiated with the fences and spoke for the group with the gangsters. His friends had a reputation as hoods in the neighborhood. To the outside world, he kept a reputation for being a young gentleman pursuing a professional career. The bosses, at times, were happy to utilize his medical skills to patch up Mafiosi who were injured in the line of duty. He became their medic who looked after their Sgarriste–the mob soldiers.

The local mob liked his low profile. He could do things for them without drawing attention. They paid him well and treated him with appreciation for the loyalty he and his friends showed them.

As the war progressed, the Army sent him to pharmacy training school. After which he was shipped to Italy because of his fluency in both English and Italian.

This post served his secret life well. While there under the tutelage of the Sicilian Mafia he learned to do contract hits while on leave and negotiated deals for the American mob and the Sicilians for black market goods.

On his return to America at the war's end, the local boss, knowing his value, helped establish him in the neighborhood with an elderly Pharmacist who provided help to the needs of the local men of "respect."

4.

Birdie's acquired surgical skill allowed him to perform life-saving procedures for these same men of respect.

After the war, the six childhood friends reunited. Don Peppino courted his future wife, the daughter of another connected undertaker from Brooklyn. Carmella had already married Paulo, then already a dockworker. They lived in a railroad apartment in Brooklyn.

Anthony's grandmother died in her sleep, leaving him without living family. He had worked for many years at Downtown Florists on Canal Street. He became the group's historian, an encyclopedia rich with inessential details on who had married or died from the neighborhood –information gathered from orders at the shop.

Birdie met his future wife, Maryann, through an Army friend who had invited him to a house party in White Plains. She held a college degree, uncommon for a woman at that time. Her family was not rich but they were educated and sophisticated. They were part of a rising class of Italians that had *made it* in America, and were housed in Scarsdale and Hartsdale, both affluent communities in the northern New York City suburbs.

Birdie liked being in their company, and was attracted to their legitimacy. He saw marrying Maryann as a step up. In order to introduce her to his life-long friends, Birdie decided to host a dinner party at a Little Italy restaurant, and told them that he had a secret to share with them, a surprise. When they got to the restaurant, he introduced Maryann as his future wife.

Concetta's eyes welled up in with tears. *I want to die,* she thought.

She left the table sobbing, scurrying for the door. She could not contain her devastation. Her deep love for Birdie had blinded her to the possibility of anyone else marrying him.

Birdie shook his head, excused himself from the table, and followed her out the door. Carmella, embarrassed by Concetta's explosive exit, tried to soften her antics with an apologetic explanation, "She's happy for you both, just taken easily with emotion. We all grew up together, and we've been through a lot. Our feelings for each other run deep."

Birdie caught up to Concetta-Marie

"Concetta-Marie, what is this?"

"I can't talk now."

"You can't talk now? You're my family. This is important to me."

She retorted in a flash of anger, "Important to you? You have been everything to me my whole life. I have waited for you my whole life. I have covered and stolen for you and now you have abandoned me."

Birdie looked around and motioned her to lower her voice. He was dumbfounded as her ugly words sunk in and he became tongue-tied and unable to speak. He was blindsided by her emotional outburst. He'd had no idea of the depth of her feelings. As a parent would a child, he reassured her of his love.

"Abandon you? You're my life also. I love you as my sister. You're my sister. I have shown you my love always. You're always with me, always there in my heart wherever I have gone. I would die for you." He took a deep breath. "My love is deeper than any love I could have for anyone. My love is the same love for you as for my mother."

Her glazed eyes scanned him with the fire of her love searching for a like-minded expression on his face. *Men are so dumb, didn't he know I needed his love? His love has sustained me through the worst of times, a trusted and proven love. What am I to do?*

She had lost him, and was torn inside with anger at herself. She understood she had never shown him, or guided him toward romantic love for her. She had accepted his fatherly attention, needing his stability, strength, and protection. This replaced his adult love for her and prevented him from loving her the way a woman wants love.

Conscious now that her childhood need for security had sabotaged a future she had longed to have with him, her thoughts raced. *Why did I not crawl into bed with him, instead of his mother? Why did I not make my passion known? How could he be so dumb that he didn't know? Am I so unappealing?*

She felt loss. The only real hope she had for a complete life was forever gone. All that was left was to hold on to the brotherly love he had for her, for she could not do without him entirely. She regained her composure.

"Birdie, you're right. I don't know what came over me. I'm happy for you. What makes you happy makes me happy. I'm your sister and always will be. And I will treat your wife as my sister, as family. Birdie, you're the best and I wish you the best. Please go back to the table. I will be there in a few minutes."

"Are you sure you're all right?"

"Yes," she whispered and forced a smile. "This is an important evening for us all. We're welcoming someone new to our family. Go. I'll be right there."

Don Peppino saw Birdie coming back into the restaurant and went to him.

"What's that about?"

"She's all right." Birdie covered, "It just took her by surprise. She'll be back in a few minutes."

His answer was cool and removed. No one realized what he actually felt. He knew he had broken her heart. He didn't understand why. She ranked only second to his mother as a most important person in his life and his family. He apologized to his fiancée who quietly recognized he had unfinished business, but she had staked her claim, thinking, *He's mine now.*

Carmella, accustomed to running interference for Birdie and the others had kept the conversation going by sharing some of their childhood exploits. Her husband, Paolo, had brought his mandolin. He tuned it for a sing-a-long after dinner.

Fingers, who had for years withheld his romantic interest in Concetta-Marie, quietly celebrated the rift between Birdie and Concetta. Out of character, he tried his hand at charm, endeavoring to make Birdie's new lady feel accepted and comfortable. "You're in for a treat, Maryann. Paolo can really play that thing."

When Concetta returned, she presented Maryann with six roses that represented the six of them. She apologized. "I'm sorry, I have been having a hard time of late and I guess it all welled up."

The evening from that point on went perfectly. The friends shared their childhood experiences with Maryann of how they tortured their neighbors, Nunzia and Ralph, and an assortment of other people in the neighborhood.

"We were famous," Anthony said. "We were known as *Hester Street Kids.*" But he did not tell Maryann why.

After the party broke up, Tommaso escorted Concetta-Marie to her car. As he opened the door for her, he stopped and stared into her eyes, "Concetta-Marie, I know this might have hit you hard. I know you have always been in love with him. I've known it all these years. I admit now that I have had jealousy for a long while, since we were kids. But I resigned myself because I love him, too, and I wanted you both to be happy."

Tommaso paused to find words. "I'm not a classy man, have little education and am shy with women, but after a time, maybe, especially now that you know what direction–"

"Don't say another word you dumb fuck. This is not the time." Realizing that she might have hurt him with her gruffness, Concetta-Marie patted his hand and said, "I'll think about it, okay?"

5.

Tommaso "Fingers" Fingarro gained a reputation for his brutality. He and Peppino followed in the footsteps of Mustached Pete's remnants of the *Black Hand* Sicilian immigrant gangsters.

As the years passed Peppino, Fingers, Concetta-Marie, and Birdie had become involved in small time street crime. Birdie, however, always remained behind the scenes. Peppino and Fingers had an arrest record for petty theft and battery from their teens. Peppino's father or grandfather always bailed them out. They grew confident that their offenses would disappear with their police connections.

As they got older, they stole cars, broke into stores and houses, shoplifted, and sold what they harvested to people in the neighborhood.

When they became more adept and better trusted by the local mobsters, they used their fences to offload higher value items like jewelry and silverware, always with a kickback to the bosses. They assisted the neighborhood wise guys running numbers and hijacking trucks and they worked enforcement for the loan sharks. They built a reputation as moneymakers.

Peppino and Fingers became *made men* not long after Birdie's return from Italy and the war, but not before making their *bones* as button men.

After Peppino rose to the rank of Capo Regime, family members began referring to him as Don Peppino, a sign of respect for his underworld accomplishments.

Peppino being now powerfully rooted in the mob's ranks paved the way for Birdie's secret induction. Birdie had proven himself with his mob work in Sicily. A few senior Mafiosi and a few of his *made* friends knew that he had become one of them. The others saw Birdie as a close friend of the *la famiglia*, an associate, intimate but not *la famiglia*. They had perceived his education and status as more useful, having a cloak of legitimacy. In their words, he spoke the American's language.

Fingers adopted a more sinister approach to getting what he wanted. He believed that long lasting power came from instilling fear in people. *La famiglia* called upon him regularly to ply his skill as a hit man and contracted him out to other Mob families.

After waiting a respectable year, Birdie married Maryann. Concetta-Marie and Fingers were spending more time together. Concetta-Marie accepted that Birdie could never be hers and acquiesced to Fingers. They secretly married on a mob business trip to Sicily, where the local Sicilian Don, his face flushed from wine, dressed in a straggly suit with his belly flapped over his belt, raised her veil, kissed her on both cheeks, and gave her hand to Fingers. Mafia well-wishers applauded and shouted support for his grandiosity, which broke the solemnity of the small church.

When they returned, they renovated a cottage by the shore in the New Dorp section of Staten Island. Nevertheless, she kept her apartment in the City. With the movement of time, she became more and more involved in the criminal pursuits of Don Peppino and her husband, who had formed a partnership.

They protected each other, planned and plotted together and built widespread rackets. They controlled brothels, construction businesses, funeral homes and carting businesses. They were moneymakers who rose through the ranks of *La Cosa Nostra.* Concetta-Marie kept the madams in check and was often called upon for her skill with poison.

She could also be physically brutal. She shared her husband's thirst for money and power. As treacherous as he could be, he remained devoted to her as he had always been. He forgave her everything and anything. He idealized her, was amazed by her underworld acumen, and believed her skills exceeded those of most of the 'made' men he knew.

Before their trip to Italy, the boss gave Concetta-Marie her first opportunity to do a mob hit on a gangster known as Herald "Harry Connors" Conorocco, who had stolen money from the bosses' end of the proceeds on a stock caper. Given instructions from the Boss, she and Fingers accepted the assignment to eliminate Harry, a gregarious gangster noted for throwing big parties with excesses of food and drink. He was well-liked by fellow mobsters.

He frequented the best restaurants in New York. He also had a sweet tooth for Concetta-Marie. Playing on that, Concetta invited him to dinner at her house on a Saturday night. He had danced with her a few times at a party but he knew of her reputation and was openly suspicious of her sudden interest in him. Still, he was intrigued, and he accepted her invitation driven by his attraction for her.

Harry arrived at her house with a cautious anticipation. She welcomed him to her home, and they sat in her living room, a well-ordered space appointed with Italian provincial furniture, marble-based lamps with brass cherubs, and lampshades with tassels. She poured glasses of wine from a crystal decanter that rested atop an imported black Italian marble coffee table.

They sat next to each other on the plastic covered couch and she raised her glass to his and toasted, "I'm really glad you could make it." Then, she excused herself to check on the food in the kitchen. In her absence, he switched glasses. She knew he would do that. She also knew that he needed to feel comfortable. Therefore, when she returned to the room she sat next to him on the couch. She had changed her clothes and now wore heavy eyeliner and bright red lipstick. She had on a low cut black dress, which showed the depth of her cleavage and the firmness of her round, full breasts.

He talked up a storm, as often gangsters do, boasting about their exploits, who they screwed and conned. They wholeheartedly made fun of the reactions of their victims - how long they took to die, if they prayed, or peed their pants - thinking it comical.

Concetta-Marie began to massage his leg then moved to his manhood. With his face registering a mixture of surprise and pleasure, he accommodated her gentle caresses by spreading his legs apart. She unzipped his fly, and then buried her head in his lap demonstrating her oral skill. She laughed to herself, thinking, *Wow, he's going out good. A proper send-off if I must say.*

He moaned with pleasure and within a few minutes completed with an excess that escaped her mouth and soiled her dress. *He's relaxed now,* she thought. *Any suspicion is dispelled by his anticipation of what treats I may bestow on him later.*

"Harry, I hope you enjoyed that?"

"Are you kidding?" he told her, "You were great."

"Let me go in and clean-up. Pour yourself some more wine and have a seat at the table and I'll serve dinner."

A few minutes later, she came out with an antipasto, complete with all the finest ingredients - salami, prosciutto, provolone, mozzarella, encircled by fresh ripe beefsteak tomato slices and fresh basil on a bed of romaine lettuce.

"Wow, this looks great."

"So dig in. Here's the semolina bread," she said, handing the wire breadbasket to him.

"Hey, Concetta-Marie, tell me something. I thought you and Fingers had something goin'. Some of the guys even thought you were married."

"Fingers! Please don't let him hear you call him that. We go back a long way. We grew up together, and he's like a brother to me."

"Well, the way he looks at your ass is not like a brother would look."

They both laughed.

This is a shame. He's really a good guy, nice personality, a sharp dresser, respectful, well equipped.

The meal progressed and he seemed to enjoy each course, the classic broccolette –broccoli rabe–with sausage and particularly the stuffed mushrooms. After dinner, they made their way back to the couch in the living room. Concetta served espresso and special Italian pastries called *suspiro,* which translated to "takes your breath away." They were appropriate to the occasion.

As Harry bit into the fresh cream filled pastry, he winced at a sharp pain in his abdomen. She told him to sit back.

"You... you," he accused reaching to her.

"Yes," she said calmly. "Don't worry. It won't take long." She patted his arm.

"Who?" he asked with a tremor in his voice. His hands clutched his belly.

"The Boss," she responded with a sympathetic frown.

"I guess he found me out."

He rattled with the pains getting sharper as a force of heat consumed his body.

"The broccoli-rabe?" He mumbled to her.

"No, the stuffed mushrooms," she said with an endearing smile.

He shook his head, let out a gasp and expired.

As she closed his eyes in a respectful gesture, she said with admiration as if mourners were present, "What a nice guy and a true *Sgarrista.* He accepted his fate like a man."

Concetta-Marie called Fingers, who was waiting at a telephone booth on the Bowery.

"It's done," she reported.

"I will be there within the hour with the cleaning crew. How did it go?"

"Nicely, he went with dignity, a class act," she said looking with admiration at Harry's lifeless body.

A short time later, Fingers pulled up in front of her building in a station wagon borrowed from the funeral parlor. The windows had curtains for concealment. Two members of his crew exited the car with him. They entered the apartment without knocking on the door and rolled out a body bag. Fingers shut the door behind them and instructed them to remove all Harry's personal belongings. He'd leave nothing to identify him.

Concetta-Marie handed them a paper bag to collect the bounty of his pockets. They checked the insoles of his shoes – mobsters were notorious for keeping money there. They found a .38 snub-nosed pistol strapped to the ankle of his right leg. They also found five thousand in cash, a 2-carat diamond pinky ring, an 18K gold Longines watch, and a gold cross around his neck with a red gold crowned horn charm hanging next to it - this allegedly would protect him from the evil eye.

They packaged up Harry, searched the couch and vacuumed the rug, making sure that nothing of him was left behind.

When they completed their cleaning tasks, Concetta-Marie asked them if they wanted something to eat. They both answered in unison with a panicked look on their faces, "No, no thanks. We ate already."

Then they took Harry down the back stairwell, through the alley, and out to the station wagon. They slid the bag in, and secured the tailgate.

In the car, one whined to the other, "Somet'in' to eat? Gimme a break."

The other remarked, “You have to be out of your fucking mind to take any food from that broad.”

Fingers stayed behind to snack on the leftovers and congratulated Concetta-Marie on her first formally ordered hit.

“Baby, this really went smooth and the bosses will be happy.”

“Yeah, I guess you’re totally in now.” The words brought a proud smile to her lips.

6.

1955

Kevin Mandrell departed Huntington Station on the 6:25 a.m., bound for company business downtown. An ordinary stop for him, but one that could fray the nerves of formidable men. He did not know as he left his parents' house for the city that this stop to kick off his three-month leave with a visit to a mid-town music store would be sidetracked and he would be catapulted into another world.

Rumbling along that weekday spring morning in a worn carriage car he sat in buoyant contrast to the commuters making their routine trip on the vibrating Long Island Railroad commuter train. He was happy to be home. The morning sun streamed through the window glass streaked with grease from the foreheads of weary commuters.

The noisy diesel engine resonated with a whining hum. His mind drifted. He was reminiscing about how his parents took him on trips to the City as a kid. New York meant going to Radio City Music Hall, or the Museum of Natural History, or Madison Square Garden to see the Rangers or the Knicks. He played hockey and baseball himself then, but this day's jaunt had nothing to do with sporting events. His focus was on an assigned task, making a covert delivery that would serve to bolster national security.

At Pennsylvania Station, Kevin acknowledged its timelessness with the first tilt of his head. It was unchanged from years before. *It will last forever.*

His nose twitched at the pungent mix of aromas of soft-centered pretzels baking in a cart run by a New York-a-Rican man, and beyond that another man sporting a turban was barking out the deliciousness of his roasted nuts and Middle Eastern finger food. These were two were among a myriad of other vendors. The aromas of their offerings combined with the body odor of hurrying people bearing unseasonal heat in their business suits, all under a humid scent of spent engine oil that filled the main hall.

He melted into the rushing crowd whose force swept him through the terminal to the platform where he headed for a connecting downtown subway. He boarded a waiting train as though he did this every day.

The full car was littered with discarded newspapers and cellophane wrappers. He helped himself to a cast-off copy of the *Daily News* lying on an empty seat beside him, and read the screaming headline, "Mad Bomber Strikes Again." He mused to himself, *Home sweet home, nothing like New York with a wild man on the loose.* He shook his head. A recent bombing had occurred. He read the article with a sense of irony, in deference to the many unwritten stories that lay in his head, stories of those he pursued, and whose dark exploits would never see newsprint.

At his stop, he tried to ignore a rank odor of urine fused with cheap perfume and stale cigarette smoke, and held his breath while he climbed the steps two at a time to the freedom of open air.

Bursting onto the street, his lungs burning, he realized he wasn't in the right place. In fact, he no idea how far away from the right place he had wound up.

This is dumb, he admonished himself giving the air to a mock right hook. He further marked his unease as he felt his pants pocket to ensure his delivery remained secure.

Then he stopped a passerby who had broken from a parade of harried subway bound pedestrians, asking, "Excuse me. Do you know where I might find DiGiaccomo's Watch Shop?"

The man, who was clad in a gray Con-Ed service uniform, turned to face him, as he held on to a dangling large ring of keys from his belt that marked his importance in the City's sphere of commerce. He responded with hurried New York curtness, "Eh, you kiddin'? I used to work that district. Go one more stop, down Canal to Mulberry, right past Birdie's Drug Store."

The man started down the stairs, but turned again and shouted, "Hey man! Catch a bus at the next corner and it'll take you right there, the watch shop is a few doors down." He rushed on.

He followed the man's advice and made his way down the narrow street scanning the mix of urban tenement housing and small retail shops. He mused on the neighborhood's architecture and other contrasts to his current quarters in Zurich, Switzerland, a bustling city, but one marked by clean streets and manicured views surrounded by majestic Alpine grandeur.

Kevin crossed the busy intersection, and the street became starkly less appealing. It seemed eerily quiet for a workday in New York City. Many of its old brownstone buildings were in disrepair, evident by gaping windows. Stained and cracked concrete stoops uninvitingly led up to their entrances. The sidewalk was strewn with the decaying contents of overflowing garbage cans. Kevin imagined it provided meals the night before for resident alley cats and worse.

His home, Huntington, Long Island, just 35 miles away, stood in awesome contrast. He had been shielded from this part of New York as a kid. This neighborhood was not the city of Central Park, Carnegie Hall, and parades on Fifth Avenue that he planned to enjoy after completing the day's assignment.

His pace quickened. His six-foot stature, pale skin, and tailored suit marked him as a stranger. His eyes widened as he caught a side glimpse of a shadow, quickly followed by the full-on reality of a young thug wearing a bandana about his head, and brandishing a stiletto in his hand.

In a second the knife found Kevin's throat and the predator was in his face, shouting, "What the fuck you doin' here, man?"

Kevin found his words unintelligible, probably because of the man's missing two front teeth and raw Puerto Rican accent.

The attacker continued, with a sleazy grin. "You lookin' for some shit? You huntin' for little white bags?"

What scared Kevin most was the man's drugged, lifeless, cold black eyes. Kevin tensed, his adrenalin pushed him to go, to get free and run. But he forced himself to hold back when out of the corner of his eye he saw two more young thugs swiftly approaching. His training cautioned him to hold off. He needed the three up close to him and to each other for what he planned to do.

He couldn't lose sight of his mission. He needed to get the job done, to get the watch to his contact in one piece. It must not fall from his possession, even at the risk of endangering himself.

The knife wielder menaced Kevin, pressing the razor sharp blade into his skin. Then as his partners closed in from behind, Kevin erupted, addressing first the blade at his throat by clamping down on his assailant's wrist while at the same time wrenching the thug's elbow with his other hand. He slammed his elbow into the attacker's throat and plunged his knee into his groin. This last thrust finally sent bandana boy careening into the remaining two, which caused all three to lose balance and fall one over the other.

While they were still dazed, Kevin retrieved the knife from the ground. As he did, he realized that the blade dripped blood and that his wrist has been cut; however, he kept his eyes on the three young rogues as they untangled themselves and rose with a slow rock to their feet.

They seem stunned, unaccustomed to the velocity and accuracy of this counter-attack. They regrouped. Their faces indicated far less arrogance as they positioned themselves to take off, if need be, while they tried to read any further aggression from the man they initially thought a pushover.

"Okay, man, everything's cool," said one.

"Yeah, man," another said. He peered down at their knifeless leader, the last to rise from the pavement. He gasped for breath then barked out the hollow orders, "Ice, Ice him, man."

"Huh, man? This is one mean *pendejo*."

Kevin felt for the timepiece, relieved that it remained undisturbed tucked in his watch pocket. He caught his breath, and remained vigilant.

"Listen, Paco, let's split." Still searching for breath, their leader snapped back, "No, man. Not until I do this guy."

"Hey! Come on man, stop the bullshit and let's get out of here. We don't need no more fuckin' heat."

A young voice shouted from the other side of the street. "Hey, Paco, lay off him! He's family. Works for "Fingers."

Paco yelled back, "Get the fuck out of here before you get cut, too."

Frenzied with pain and unaccustomed to defeat, the punk's eyes flickered back and forth between the caller and Kevin.

"No, come on Paco, let's go," his accomplices tried to convince him once more. "Yeah man, let's split now, we don't need this shit. Listen to Billy-Boy. Let's go. Fingers is already pissed at us. Remember what he did to Pepe! His family got him back in pieces."

The other squirmed and supported him. "Yeah, shit, man, we don't need any more fucking heat from them guys either."

Apparently, Paco did not like to lose but this comment stopped him. Wary, he stepped back, raising his hands into the air. As the threesome moved off, they gave Billy-Boy the finger in defiance, and Paco gave Kevin a vengeful look while he continued to shout obscenities at Billy-Boy, with a warning, "Hey, motherfucker, you better stay out of my shit, or someday I'm gonna cut you too." The trio took off.

Billy-Boy waited a distance away and then dashed across the street to Kevin. "Are you all right man? Where did you learn to fight like that? Are you a commando?"

"I'm fine, thanks to you," Kevin replied, with a smile at the bravado of this young rescuer. The youngster focused on the bloodstains that painted Kevin and his clothing.

Billy-Boy took a deep breath and blew it out, regained his composure, and boasted about how lucky Kevin had been that he had come along.

"Listen, man, you can't stay here. These guys are crazy. They ice people for kicks, man. They might even come back. So let's go. My place, it's just across the street. You can rest there and get a drink." *Katie will know what to do,* he thought.

Kevin was grateful to this boy – perhaps fourteen or fifteen – for his kindness and his courage. Yet he saw worry and discomfort in the boy's eyes.

Kevin put his hand up to wipe the perspiration off his neck. The moisture did not have the feel of sweat and he noticed that a quantity of blood had oozed onto his clothes. Still, he felt he had to see the boy home safe before seeking first aid.

"Well, I think a glass of water and a towel would do me some good."

7.

In the early morning light, Kevin could see the outline of a three-story tenement building, resting in the dwindling shadow of the fading night. His rescuer, Billy, steered him toward the stone steps of a weathered Brownstone. He led Kevin into a dark recess of a basement apartment. Billy without being asked supported Kevin as they negotiated the steps and came to an ornate wrought-iron outer door. The youngster pressed a finger to his lips, as a signal to be quiet, and eased the door open.

Devoid of windows, the only illumination was a faint light from the crack of a closet door at the rear of the tiny space. Billy guided Kevin to an armchair near the center of the room. The spiking pain in Kevin's shoulder and neck reminded him of his injuries as he let go and, even in the subdued light, he could see the blood stains on his clothes.

Billy bent close then pressed his finger to his lips once again. Kevin nodded understanding. The boy mimed drinking and pointed behind him. Kevin nodded again.

"Yes," he whispered, "anything would be good."

Billy moved away, his eyes on the bedroom door, thinking on how to awaken Katie.

Even with everything else that spun through his head, and not knowing how badly he'd been hurt, Kevin wondered why the need for quiet. *Is this his place or not?* Billy had offered sanctuary with bravado, but now Kevin wondered if he'd found himself in another tight spot. *Had this been a bad decision?*

Something exploded behind him. He jumped forward and cried out in pain. He froze and listened if anyone had heard, though he didn't know who.

"Damn!" Billy bayed hoarsely, as he brushed aside pieces of the fallen vase with his foot. He whispered in Kevin's ear, "Here's some water." Billy put the glass on a small table at his elbow.

"Who the hell are you? What are you doing in my apartment?" a piercing female voice came out of the darkness, startling Kevin.

Great, he thought, *the kid has brought me to some woman's place – not his.* He rolled his eyes. Then he saw a young woman who charged out of the bedroom holding her robe closed with one hand in defense, reaching for the phone on the table next to his chair with the other hand.

"Not good, not good at all," He said under his breath. Still feeling dazed, Kevin stuttered a reply, "I'm sorry. Billy said–"

Billy interrupted in defense and shot to block her from the phone. "Katie! Wait! He's okay. He's okay. He's hurt. I rescued him! I helped him escape."

Billy jumped between Kevin and the girl, waved his arms, and took to a knee in front of her in a melodramatic pleading stance. He threw Kevin a conspiratorial look, accompanied by more theatrical words.

"Women. They're scared of everything." He shook his head, as he got up and sat on the arm of Kevin's chair.

Katie dropped the phone into its cradle and demanded, "Billy, I want you to explain what's going on. Right now!" She turned to Kevin, "Can you please tell me who you are? And what are you doing here?"

Before her uninvited guest could explain, her eyes widened in horror at the sight of the blood on his tailored jacket and shirt.

Kevin's eyes followed hers and he muttered, "Oh, damn."

Kevin tried to pull himself forward, to keep from staining the chair. He reached for his neck. Billy made an attempt at black comedy. "Take it easy, man. With a cut throat you wouldn't be able to talk," he said with a laugh at his own words.

Katie's anger turned to panic. "What's going on here?" she cried. "What happened to him?" she said, tightening the belt of her robe and paced back and forth in front of Billy and Kevin. Billy grinned like a Cheshire cat.

"Well, he really got his tits in a ringer."

"Watch that mouth of yours," Katie snapped.

"Hey, dig it. I'm telling ya. He was up to his ass in alligators and I drained the swamp. If I didn't tell Paco and his gang that he worked for Fingers, they woulda knifed him."

"Are you crazy?" Katie stepped up nose-to-nose with Billy. "Just who did you bring home?"

Billy threw both hands up, palms out, and took a step back.

"No, no, no, you got it wrong. He isn't a wise-guy. They were tryin' to rob him." Billy flashed a huge grin again. "But I gave them the story that he worked for the *Man*." The grin got wider, and turned into a proud smirk over his tough-guy description of events.

Katie softened her stance and turned to Kevin, beginning to be resigned to the situation.

"My God, sit back."

She studied him closely and gazed into his eyes. His handsome face melted her fears. Her hand trembled as she nudged his head back to examine the extent of his wound.

"So, what's your name?"

"Kevin, Kevin Mandrell."

"Okay, Kevin Mandrell. Let's take a look at you."

She inspected another cut on his wrist, turned to Billy, and ordered, "Bring me soap, a clean hand towel, and a bowl of warm water. And try not to knock anything else over."

Kevin explained the bizarre events that had brought him to her home, but Katie shushed him and handed him the glass of water.

"Careful, sip it slowly. No talking just yet."

Kevin took the glass with both hands, and sipped, trying not to let on to how much pain he felt.

Katie sat back on the edge of the sofa and stared at him.

"It's a small slice but you may need stitches." She paused to consider her words, "Or maybe you could get by with a tight bandage." She hesitated, made a decision. "Let me clean you up and I'll take you over to my father's drug store. He's an expert with small wounds."

Billy returned with a basin of warm water, an armful of towels, and a bar of soap. Katie came to her feet with a mother's authority.

"Let's clean you up before we go." She soaped a towel in the basin, and wrung it out. "We could go to Beekman General, but you'd be there all day. Don't worry. My Dad's had a lot of experience with wounds of this kind." She frowned as she mentioned her father's skill.

Kevin nodded, knowing that if he went to the hospital, the police might be involved and questions asked. He still had his meeting, and needed to see DiGiaccomo with as little delay as possible. He decided to go along with Katie's suggestion. "Sure," he said.

"Katie," Billy broke in, "you had to see this guy. He wrecked them. Unbelievable. Three to one!"

Katie shook her head, raised an eyebrow. She felt Kevin's body wince from the sting of the soapy liquid, and reassured him as a nurse would a patient, "I know. Almost done."

She folded several towels into compresses, and instructed him to apply pressure to the wounds while she called her father and got dressed. Kevin watched her move to a curtain covered alcove that served as a walk-in closet. As she drew the fabric behind her, she took a quick sneak peak at him. His mind and body were registering the loss of blood and the slump that followed his adrenalin rush, and drowsiness slipped in.

He thought of his alluring nurse. She was a classic Italian beauty. Slim framed with radiant light olive skin, and smoky gray eyes that spoke of the Mediterranean. He thought about her deep black, glistening hair that danced as she moved. *Wow,* he sighed, *she's something.*

Still adrift, he wondered why this stunning, well-spoken young woman became a finished diamond in a timeworn cave of a building sharing a two-room basement apartment with an adolescent street kid.

How are these two connected?

As Katie dressed, she found it odd that it did not worry her having this stranger in her house. One, apparently, who was no stranger to violence.

She emerged from the make-shift closet.

"How're you doing? Kevin the alligator slayer," she teased.

She glanced at Billy who hadn't left his side. Kevin drank in the image of her adjusting her NYU sweatshirt over a pair of worn jeans. She bent to roll up the cuffs.

Kevin smiled, even more struck by her, as she tightened the ring on her ponytail. He studied her. She caught him as his eyes followed the outline of her well-formed breasts as she bent to fold up the sofa bed. She tidied the room, and tried to hide the flattered curl of her lip.

Maybe a few years younger than me? Early thirties? It didn't feel like the usual manly stir he received when meeting a hot woman. *Why am I so taken by her?* He shook himself mentally back to the now as they prepared to head with her to her father's pharmacy.

"Your father's drug store, would it be called 'Birdie's' by any chance?"

"Yes, I'm Katherine Burdino. Do you know my father's store?"

"No, the guy I asked for directions at the subway exit sent me up this street to the bus stop. He gave it as a landmark."

"Oh."

"Actually, I was trying to find a watch shop."

"DiGiaccomo 's?"

"Yes."

"Well, then, what were you doing all the way up here?"

"I had gotten off at the wrong stop and the guy told me that taking the bus would make it easier to find." She nodded in agreement.

"Okay, Billy, let's get your friend to the car. Then you get your butt to school. You're late for class."

"Do I have to go? The Dragon Lady is going to be there today." Katie threw him a look and handed him lunch money.

"The last time I saw Mrs. Carmichael, she wasn't breathing fire. She's just your music teacher. Now, get going. Besides, you have just a few more weeks to the term, so don't blow it."

At the car, before closing the door, Kevin asked, "By the way Billy, who's Fingers?"

"Oh, he's my old man he–"

"Billy." Katie scowled. "You say you don't like him, you refuse to live with him, but at every opportunity you tout... Oh, never mind, get going, now!"

Kevin gave Billy a manly handshake, thanked him for risking his neck, and promised to see him again with a gift in gratitude.

The promise brought a swagger out of Billy. "Nah, no sweat man, Paco's just a faggot."

"Never mind about that. Billy, just stay away from them. They're bad news."

Billy bobbed his head at her and turned to Kevin in a whisper, "Don't worry, she's cool."

With a wink at Kevin, Billy slammed the car door shut. He stepped away, announced with false bravado, "He doesn't scare me, that punk."

"As you can see," Katie remarked with a smile, "Billy is his own man." She started the engine and pulled into the street just as Kevin lost his battle with curiosity.

"Are you his sister... his mother? I can't resist asking."

"Mother?" she laughed and feigned indignation, "Do you think I look old enough to be his mother?"

Shit, no, of course not. His foot in his mouth, he tried to recover, "But he looks a lot like you."

"I'm kind of like his guardian. Well, perhaps you're not used to meeting Italians. You probably believe we all look alike."

"I'm sorry, I wasn't thinking, it just came out."

Changing the subject as they rode on, he asked, "So tell me what you do."

I figured we'd get to this, she said to herself before responding, "I'm the Program Director for the St. Francis Mission Shelter. Since being a little girl, I have always felt that God wanted me to help people. I guess that's what led me to Social Work."

"It shows a warm heart," Kevin said. "A noble profession, to say the least, and in good company with the saints."

"Wow, thank you, I have never heard it described that way." Katie paused taking a swallow of air at his compliment, then spoke more of Billy.

"Billy sought me out one evening. He stayed on at the center for short time as we tried to mediate his family issues. A short time later, I took him in at the promptings of both our fathers. My father is Billie's godfather."

Kevin said, "Wasn't that a lot to take on as a single woman with heavy work responsibilities?"

"Well yeah, it started out as a temporary arrangement. To my amazement, Billy just stayed."

"Do you feel obligated in some way?"

"No, I don't think obligation is the thing. You may think I'm bonkers but it's more like spiritual. I feel an extraordinary bond between us and have questioned it many times in an attempt to get a handle on it."

Kevin noticed her protectiveness for Billy, and thought, *There's a lot more to this story.*

She smoothly changed the subject. Katie led him into an easy conversation. Both were surprised that they shared similar interests about lots of things. He relaxed, until the pain in his neck returned full force. He moaned and put his hand to his neck.

Katie understood his discomfort. She tried to distract him and gave him more background about Billy, their common denominator at that point.

"It's so sad. Billy's mother became the victim of a hold-up and was killed by thieves."

Kevin sighed, "That's a bad break, the poor kid."

What she did not tell him was that Concetta-Marie's bullet-ridden body turned up in a dumpster, on the Lower East Side.

"Yes," she continued, "tragic. I'm surprised at how well he copes with it. He just sometimes comes and holds me. I know he's thinking about her."

"Anyone would be traumatized, particularly a young boy."

"The cops called it a robbery since her pocket book, wallet, and all her jewelry were gone."

Katie left out other details. The word on the street pointed to Claudia, an uptown Madame who supposedly worked for Concetta-Marie and was believed to be the last person to see her alive.

"After her death, Billy refused to live with his father, who he blamed for not protecting his mother. Billy began getting into trouble, and skipping school. Truant officers were always looking for him.

"He had worn out his welcome with friends. With nowhere else to go, he wound up at the Mission. I'll never forget that night."

She slowed the car to make a turn.

"I happened to be at the front desk the first time Billy wandered into the Center. The cold was brutal that night. He had asked me permission to wait inside for his friends. I asked him why he wasn't at home. He gave me an annoyed look then said that he didn't live there anymore."

Kevin asked, "Did he say why?"

"I didn't pry because I knew Billy had recently lost his mother and was having problems. My Mom and Dad were concerned about him."

"I get it now. He knew you," Kevin assumed with a smile, "and I guess he knew he'd be safe with you."

"Maybe, though I hadn't interacted with him very much prior to that night." She paused in thought. "I remember how he waited for some time, peering out the window, still shivering he was so cold, looking for friends that never came. Well, maybe that's true. Maybe he did feel safe with me.

There were no friends. I knew that. All he wanted was out of the cold or maybe to stay with me, but he was too proud to ask."

"Well, he has good taste. I think I have encountered a family of rescuers," Kevin said with a grin.

Katie returned his smile and paused in her story once more, maneuvering in traffic. Recounting that she had brought Billy a cup of cocoa and a sandwich, she remembered that as he ate, he had continued to justify his presence, pretending anger at how late his friends were, and seeding doubt that they would even show up.

He told her, "I think I'm getting screwed."

Still part of the act? Or his outlook on life? She had thought.

Billy had devoured the food, all the while giving her an elaborate routine about how you can't count on anybody and how much he had done for friends in the past.

Katie flashed a grin at Kevin, "You may also have noticed his flair for the dramatic."

Kevin nodded, gritting his teeth against the pain.

Katie rambled on through her account, saying that she had finally asked Billy if he had any place to stay.

"I can stay lots of places," he had told her. "I'm not homeless like the people at the shelter. Everybody knows my family. We're *people*," meaning they were connected.

She had expressed surprise that he had not called her parents - his Godparents - but all she got in reply was the look of a caught sparrow.

"I suggested that he might like to stay the night, and offered to settle him into a nice warm bed. He made a face.

"Look," I told him, "you're shivering. It's just too cold and late to be walking around."

Reality sank in. He dropped his guard. "Do you sleep here at the Mission?" he asked.

"No, I live a few blocks away, but I will return early in the morning and we can talk over breakfast. How's that sound?"

Billy had stuck in her mind. She left for home that night with a sense of worry and a strange feeling he would remain a part of her life. Once at home, she called her father and asked that he tell Uncle Tommaso, Billy's father, that Billy was out of harm's way and staying at the Mission. Not long after, Billy moved in with her.

"I still can't explain it, but I believe Billy feels the same way about me as I do about him, even though he tries not to show it. It's odd how patient I am with him even when he's annoying, which is much of the time." She laughed.

Kevin listened, allowing Katie to distract him from his pain.

"He reminds me of my father," she said, "as far as how much power he seems to have over me." She giggled and Kevin smiled at her. In his mind, she was a woman with a magical, healing laugh.

"I'm sorry, I'm talking too much. How are you feeling? You must be hurting."

"Kate, I'm fine ..." Kevin winced as he tried to straighten up in the seat to show just how fine he was. "I think I spoke to soon. I'm starting to feel some pain now." He rubbed his shoulder with his free hand. "I guess my adrenalin pumped so hard, I didn't feel much before."

"Well, we're almost there. I just need to find a parking space." She threw him a shy smile. "You know, it's funny that you called me Kate!"

"Oops."

"No, that's okay, I like it. My mother sometimes calls me Kate. She thinks it is more sophisticated, *a la* Kate Hepburn. You know I was even into the debutante thing for a while, but it's just not my style."

Katie spun the steering wheel to negotiate a parking spot, but did not miss a beat. "Our family home is in Scarsdale, but I keep the apartment here in the city because of my work schedule. Most of my friends and people here in this neighborhood call me Katie, because they know me from childhood."

She made one more spin of the steering wheel, turned off to park, and gave Kevin a big smile. He acknowledged with one back as he caught movement out of the corner of his eye.

"Watch out, Kate! There's an old guy walking straight out in front of your car!"

"Don't worry, that's only Anthony ... Anthony 'Rest in Peace,'" she said with a grin. "He knows my car and lets me park in front of the funeral home here.

"Oh."

"Yea, he does odd jobs, answers the phone and watches the place for my godfather, Giuseppe, who owns the funeral parlor."

Kevin asked, "Is that how he got the nickname Anthony 'Rest in Peace', because he works at a funeral home?"

Katie laughed back an answer, "You'll find out soon enough." As they get out of the car, Anthony greeted her in a classic Italian manner, by taking both her hands in his, and acknowledged her with an affectionate pinch of her cheek.

"Katie, my little birdie. *Quanta si Bella. Dio di Benadiga*–You're so beautiful. May God bless you. Birdie is so proud of you. He still keeps your communion picture in the store window." As the gentle old man went on, Katie's face turned a bright crimson.

"Don't worry. Stay as long as you like. I'll move the car into the parking lot if your Godfather, Don Peppino, comes back early."

"Anthony, this is Kevin. We're going over to Dad's now."

Holding out his hand, the older man introduced himself to Kevin, "A pleasure. Stampadello, Anthony."

Then he noticed Kevin's blood-soaked towel and jacket, and became alarmed. "Poor thing, poor thing. Don't worry. You're in good hands —don't worry—Birdie fixed me up, too. He will take care of you." He rambled, "Once my grandmother, rest in peace, that crazy woman, threw a saucepan at me just because I put my dirty underwear in the refrigerator.

So, I ... I ... make a mistake," he said, gesturing with his hands cupping the air, then continued with a puff, "I mean, please. The washing machine was right next to it! Oh, my goodness. Oh, my goodness, she gives me six stitches, that *credina*! –fool. But, Birdie fixed me up! Look." He pointed to his temple and lifted his graying hair.

"You can hardly see the scar. Anyway...ah...yeah...well, she didn't mean it. She was just crazy. Everybody knew it. You ask anybody around here about Antoinette Buffa, rest in peace, my grandmother, rest in peace, they'll tell you she was crazy."

"Anthony," Katie said holding back laughter, "I have to get Kevin to my father now."

"Okay, go, go, Katie-doll, don't worry," he said, but continued to amble along with them. He motioned to Kevin.

"You, know, I used to rock this one in her baby carriage and I wouldn't let anybody make noise or bother her while she was sleeping. By the way, Katie, you know who just died. Rest in peace, Angelo Buccasano. Yeah, Buccasano, the fish man, rest in peace. We have him inside, nice, nice job they did on him. He looks good. But, you know, he used to sell bad fish sometimes, Buccasano, rest in peace!" He turned to Katie. "Remember when Senora Pizzano got so sick after she ate his baccala? She went to his store and threw up out his window! She hated Buccasano, rest in peace. He deserved it ... he did, rest in peace."

Breaking in with a caring smile, Katie patiently answered, "Oh, that's too bad, Anthony. See you when we come back, okay?"

At that, Katie urged Kevin forward with long strides toward the pharmacy, both trying to remain straight-faced as Anthony drifted back.

Their eyes matched and they broke out in laughter as she answered Kevin's unspoken curiosity, "He may seem older, he's only late fifties, I believe."

"He's a character," Kevin quipped trying to bring his laughter under control.

"Some think he was born a little slow. Others think it came from the clobbering he received from his grandmother. His mother was unstable herself, so she left him with her aged mother and returned to Italy when he was very young. Sad, isn't it?"

"Yeah, it is, but it seems he has had support."

"He needed it. His grandma was like most of her generation and background, marginally educated and very superstitious. She believed in the evil eye. You know what that is?"

"I take it is something like black magic."

"Yeah, pretty much so, she imbued those arcane beliefs in her simple-minded grandson as a result of her strong hand over him. People in the neighborhood, those who knew him, trusted that if told to keep what he heard in confidence, he would never utter a word because of those instilled superstitious fears."

Katie laughed, "From what my parents told me, his grandmother was quite a character. She was a lonely widow with a compulsion for gambling, and was as much compulsive with rearing him. She made him her companion. He placed her bets and she shared intimate stories with him about her early days in Italy, and gossip about her friends, who, for the most part, lived close by in the neighborhood as he grew up.

"The information included intimate details of their private lives, the secrets of many who had died but were kept alive in her memories that she passed on to Anthony, who, in spite of his mental deficits, remembered everything. It was through her, he adopted the expression of 'rest in peace' after the mention of a deceased person, as an Old World sign of respect."

Katie continued as Kevin listened with the interest of an explorer who had landed in the midst of an alien culture. Kevin believed that Katie retained a childlike fondness for Anthony as she expounded how lucky he was to grow up in the neighborhood, closely tied to her father who was called Birdie, and to her Godfather, Don Peppino, the funeral director, and their wider group of childhood intimates. Billy's parents, Concetta Marie and Tommaso, "Fingers," and Aunt Carmella, who owned a local Italian restaurant, which she pointed to across the street, were all close to him.

As children, they shared hardships, forming an unbreakable bond, one that lived on to this day.

"They have all cared for Anthony since the time his grandmother passed. But when they were kids together, the *gang* really earned a reputation for mischief. At that time, everyone in the neighborhood referred to them as, 'the wild kids from Hester Street.'"

Katie added with affection, "It might be hard for you to believe, but this has always been a good neighborhood full of basically honest people who have always cared for one another. It's real life, with a strong pulse and big hearts. Usually, what you see is what you get. I hope you won't remember it or mark us as bad because of what you went through earlier."

Why did I say that? To defend the neighborhood? she thought. *For heaven's sake, this is the city.*

The day's events caught up to Kevin who was tired and dragging. Unexpected emotion swung him between laughter and tearfulness, and hearing the voice of Katie's heart throughout the morning together. The underlying story she told was unfamiliar, though it intrigued him. He had never before felt, nor witnessed, such words and animated emotion in such a short timeframe. All this emotion triggered thoughts of his mentor's words. *Is this the passion he wishes me to seek and embrace, for creative growth?*

8.

When they got to the drugstore entrance, he admired the hominess of its window treatment, which displayed old-fashioned, decorative glass apothecary jars, each filled with colored water along with some leafy plants in need of some water. A taped poster for the Knights of Columbus dinner dance was prominently placed, and as Anthony had told them, the treasured photo of Katie's first Communion was displayed front and center. A true old neighborhood shop.

Kevin opened the door for her, as if to win her with gallantry, and fumbled with the towel compressed upon his wound. "Oh, a gentlemen," she said, and reached to help him with the makeshift bandage.

As they proceeded in, the aroma of vitamins combined with the scents of cosmetics shelved within aged wood cabinetry filled his nostrils. The vintage wood-planked floors squeaked under their feet, orchestrated by its many years of patron wear.

Starting down the main aisle, they overheard the voice of a woman in a tone of annoyance, from the next.

"Why do I keep coming here? Take an enema. That's all he ever says. Take an enema. For twenty years that's all he says."

So unexpected was the voice, the words ringing with a New York accent, Kevin's knees buckled trying to stifle a burst of laughter. Katie bent down to help him up, lost her balance, and went down with him. Kevin pointed toward the next aisle and Katie apparently caught on. He whispered, "Maybe it's because she's been constipated for the last twenty years?"

His words triggered Katie's laughter, and now they were both struggling to subdue their giggles and snorts of mirth.

Regaining their composure, they heard another customer call out, "Dr. Birdie, I think someone collapsed in the main aisle!"

"Oh God," they said in unison as their eyes locked on each other and they continued to laugh.

Birdie ran down the long aisle to their rescue, and reached Kevin and Katie just as they rose from the floor. Seeing the amount of blood on Kevin, Birdie asked, "What happened? Did he fall? Are you all right, Katie?" He was concerned that Kevin had injured himself there in the store.

Katie assured him that they were fine and related what they heard, and he managed a laugh himself as he reached to Kevin for a handshake.

"Those two," he said, shaking his head, "they're something, aren't they?" He ushered them down the aisle, past the nosey eyes of patrons, into the back room.

Kevin hadn't eaten, and felt unsteady as they made their way through boxes and worktables to an alcove at the rear and into a tight room that contained a surgical table and a hospital style medicine cabinet. Birdie asked Kevin to sit down while he examined his wounds.

"I see that the bleeding has stopped, but the wounds were deep. What's your name, son?" he probed as if he had paid no attention to his daughter's introduction.

"Kevin Mandrell."

"Well, from what I see here, Kevin, we have two choices. We can take you down to Beekman for some stitches, or we can try butterfly bandages. But stitches might leave larger scars. I believe butterflies will work fine."

Kevin glanced over toward Katie. She reassured him and offered, "Dad's famous for his butterflies, so you probability won't have much of a scar at all."

Kevin winked back. Birdie, smiling with confidence, went to the medicine cabinet for his first aid supplies. As he rummaged through the drawers, Kevin flashed a peek at Katie, and caught a returned smile. Her eyes expressed her shared interest. Birdie, with the eyes of a hawk, observed the exchange and rolled his eyes.

"Daughter, this will take a few minutes. Why don't you go and get us some coffee, and maybe some orange juice to perk up this young man?"

"That's a great idea. I'd like one myself. You're in good hands," she said to Kevin. "I'll be back in a few minutes."

As Katie exited the rear door, she overheard her father asking him if he was married. *Oh my, poor Kevin*, she thought.

"So tell me, Kevin, do you live here in the neighborhood?"

"No, sir. I took the subway and got off at the wrong stop. Searching for DiGiaccomo's Watch Shop."

"Well then, you were certainly in the wrong neighborhood. I guess in more ways than one. Hah! Myself, I don't like Katherine living on that block. Believe me we have had many arguments about that. She claims that it's fine. Because of the late hours she puts in at the Center, she says it's convenient. She believes that all people are good. It's true that down here, we all know one another, look out for each other. The street element knows that, if you catch my drift."

"Well, I guess they found an unfamiliar face," Kevin said.

"Nevertheless, the punks that mugged you have been told in no uncertain terms that *we* will not put up with their nonsense down here. But sometimes, I guess, they're so drugged-up it doesn't sink in." Birdie stopped preparing the butterflies and raised his eyes at him, "Why didn't you call the police?"

Kevin hesitated as he searched for a credible excuse.

But Birdie continued. "From what my daughter heard from Billy earlier today, I guess you're quite capable of taking care of business yourself. I like that."

"Dr. Burdino," Kevin asked, "Do you think I should file a report with the police?"

After a short pause, the pharmacist responded.

"You can if you'd like, but I believe we will get the message to the powers-that-be without putting you through any more hardship."

Once more without waiting for a response, he asked where Kevin lived.

"I'm visiting with my parents on Long Island for the summer. I grew grown up there, but have been living for some time now in Zurich."

Birdie asked, with a puzzled look on his face, "Switzerland?"

"Yes, I'm a member of the Zurich Philharmonic Orchestra."

Birdie's eyes opened, "Oh! That's really interesting. What do you do for the Philharmonic?"

"I'm a pianist and arranger. I also serve as the cultural attaché at the US Embassy in Bern and manage our Cultural Exchange Program there for the government."

"That sounds exciting." Adding cryptically, "A musician that can strike more than the keys, and a swashbuckling diplomat to boot. Have you mentioned to my daughter what you do? She's very interested in the arts, especially classical music."

"Well, we haven't had enough of a chance to talk about much else with all that happened."

"I'm sorry. I've been asking too many questions. How are you feeling now? Do you have much pain?"

"Some. Mostly in my shoulder and fingers."

"Well, I'm going to give you a pain killer, a little something to help you relax." Birdie took his hand to examine his fingers.

"Have you eaten anything today?"

"Just a cup of coffee early this morning. I was going to visit the Automat. I haven't been there in years." Kevin felt better.

"You do amazing work, Dr. Birdie. Thank you very— "How are you guys getting along?" Katie asked as she returned juggling cups of coffee and juice. "Did my father ask you a million questions?" Kevin just smiled.

"Katherine, we've got quite an interesting fellow here. Kevin tells me that he performs with the Zurich Philharmonic. Evidently, he's an accomplished piano virtuoso. He lives there and works there. He's here visiting with his parents for the summer."

"Did you interrogate the poor man?" She winked at Kevin.

"That has to be an exciting life."

"That's what I told him! Kevin hasn't had anything to eat yet today, and he'll need to take something for the pain, but not on an empty stomach. If he likes, take him across the street to Carmella's for something. I believe she makes minestrone today. Something like that will calm his stomach and be easy to eat, even with these tight bandages. How does that sound?"

Kevin nodded in the affirmative.

"Just give me a couple of minutes to prepare a prescription. You may have some pain for a few days."

Kevin felt better after drinking the orange juice. It seemed to recharge him. He thanked Birdie when he returned with the medicine, and reached for his wallet, but Birdie refused payment for his care. With a firm hand gesture, he dismissed the topic.

As one accustomed to having his way, the subject was dropped.

Birdie escorted them down the aisle to the wood-framed glass front door, turned to Kevin and extended his hand. Kevin took it, and thanked him again, appreciative both his skills and his welcoming treatment of him. Birdie kissed his daughter and told her to have Carmella put their lunch on his tab.

9.

As they left the store, Katie suggested that he might want stop at the watch shop before they headed to the restaurant. He thought it a good idea. He was overdue.

"Won't you be late to the Shelter?"

"No, it's fine. I'm not scheduled to go in until later in the afternoon. My only plan for this morning was to do some laundry, and almost anything can take precedence over that chore."

After a short stroll to DiGiaccomo's watch shop, they entered the long, narrow store. The door chimed their presence amid a mix of tones from the dozens of clocks that lined the walls. They were mechanisms of time that represented almost every era, style, and detail. Still, it was not a chaotic noise. The disparate ticking created a harmonic repertoire that lent an appealing ambiance to the shop.

As they approached the rear of the store, the top of a balding head appeared above the clutter. The old watchmaker sat engrossed in detailed work. He peeked over his glasses. Recognizing Katie, his face lit up as he greeted her in English laden with the old country.

"Katie, what a nice-sa, soo-priz-a!"

"Hello, Uncle Jocko, *como sta?*"

"Very good, very good. Whos's-a? Someone special?" he asked.

"No, *Ziu,* Kevin is a new friend, who had quite an experience trying to find you this morning."

Kevin extended his hand and slipped the watchmaker a disguised signal revealing his identity.

"It's a pleasure to meet you, Mr. DiGiaccomo. I've heard a lot about you and your work."

"Thank-a you, thank-a you. And, how can I help-a you, my son?" DiGiaccomo asked.

Kevin gave him a quiet stare, pulled the watch from his pocket and handed it to him.

"Santa Maria!" the old man gasped in disbelief. He placed the timepiece on the velour jeweler's pad resting on the glass counter. He handed Katie a ring of keys, "Please lock-a the door."

Katie did not question nor hesitate and turned toward the door. Katie knew Uncle Jocko as a mild mannered man who was not easily impressed. *Umm, Jocko doesn't usually get that excited. This must be ringing his bell.* She heard him whisper "Mamma Mia," creating more drama. It may have been for her sake, but he eyeballed Kevin in confirmation of their mutual secret.

He appeared reluctant to take his eyes off the timepiece, aware of what it contained. But for Katie's benefit, he studied it with the aid of a jewelers' loop–a magnifying glass–placed over his right eye.

Adding to the theatrics, his demeanor elevated, like one who had just won the Irish Sweepstakes and was now viewing his winning ticket number in disbelief.

Katie locked the door and returned to the counter. "*Ziu,* is something wrong?"

"No, no, *Bella.* This watch is very old and may be quite rare, with a lot of history behind it. I have seen only one other in such good condition and that was many years ago."

His shrewd explanation concealed their agenda. Kevin followed the man's lead, gratefully, and in awe of his mastery in the deceptive trade. He tied up the cover story.

"If this is an original, it is a priceless family heirloom, originally owned by Victorian royalty, handed down through generations."

Unaware of their well-executed subterfuge, Katie accepted what they told her at face value. She explained to the old man that Kevin had suffered through an ordeal, and needed to get something to eat before taking his medication.

"We're going to Carmella's for some soup. Maybe we can return after lunch, if that's okay."

"Sure. Sure. I'm so sorry I didn't even think to ask you if you wanted anything."

Kevin said, "Thank you, but we're fine. We'll come back later. That will give you a chance to spend some time with the watch."

The old man reacted to his words with another deep look, and led them back to the door. He waved, and then secured the door after them.

Relieved that he had completed that part of this business, Kevin took Katie's arm and spirited her across the busy street. She smiled and put her free hand on his arm.

10.

As Katie and Kevin entered the restaurant, a large bald man at a corner table complained about the quality of the fish.

"They call this flounder filet. Give me a break. Even Americanos won't eat this." He feigned spitting on the floor.

The sound of the front door caught the attention of Carmella's son, Dominick. At the sight of Katie, his frown transformed into a broad smile.

"Cousin Katie, what a nice surprise," he greeted her. "Sit over here, by the window. It won't get too sunny until later."

Tying on a fresh apron, he made his way to the table and embraced Katie, then turned and gave Kevin the once-over. "And who's this?" he asked with a wink to Katie. "Did you catch a live one?"

"Dominick, behave yourself. This is Kevin Mandrell. He—"

"Oh, I know. I know what happened. Everyone knows. So this is the guy. Hi, Kevin, how are you? Please, sit, relax." Then he shouted over his shoulder, toward the kitchen, "Mimi! Mimi. Bring a bottle of the homemade and a basket of bread."

"What-a-you-want-a?" a woman's voice called from the back.

"Oh, give me a break, Mimi. Are you just taking up space in that school? This is two years of English classes. Give me a break, Mimi," he repeated. A young waitress with large almond-shaped eyes and deep Mediterranean skin emerged, and approached the table. She put her arm around Dominick.

"Give-a-you-a-break, I break-a-your head, Domi?" she shot back with a cracked smile, "Ah, Signorina Caterina, *come sta*?"

"*Bene, Bene,* and how are you, Mimi?"

"Imma-fine-a, let me bring-a you-a some-a bread and wine."

Dominick raised his arms toward heaven, "Aha, there is a God."

"Oh, you shut-up," Mimi snapped, gesturing with the back of her hand. She did an about face and disappeared into the kitchen.

"So Kevin, how are you feeling? You hurting?" asked Dominick.

"No, I'm okay, thanks."

"Dominick, who told you what happened?"

"Oh, Don Tommaso sent one of his Neanderthals over a little while ago to ask Jose our Puerto Rican dishwasher for the whereabouts of those idiots. You know, only they are allowed to rob people, or worse."

"Sure, but how did they know so soon?"

"Come on Katie, they know if someone farts in Palermo. I didn't have time to get the whole scoop. Carmella caught him dipping a piece of bread in her tomato sauce and chased him out with the broom."

"And how is your mother?"

"Who, Lucretia Borgia? She's making rice balls in the kitchen. She can't stand that I'm still single. She's already invited everyone in the neighborhood with an unmarried daughter or niece here for coffee. Now, she's on a Mimi kick. 'Dominick, help Mimi with her English, help Mimi with the soda, help Mimi carry that package home, Mimi doesn't have anybody to go to the movies with.' My mother should have been a madam." Katie and Kevin were laughing at Dominick's complaints.

"She thinks I have no life of my own. This is a crazy woman. Complains to everybody in the neighborhood. I don't work hard enough. I'm stupid. I'm here six days a week, ten hours a day and I can't walk down the street without meeting one of her black-dress widow friends who stop to tell me to respect my mother. You know, they give me the 'shame on you' finger. I'm thirty-two years old and I have to listen to that? Give me a break!

"Not to mention my sister, the saint. She mustn't even look at a man. If somebody shows the slightest bit of attention to her, especially *e malamente*, –gangsters–Momma sends her back into the kitchen. 'Angie,' she says, 'we need to make more ravioli.' Sometimes there are enough raviolis to have a ticker-tape parade with them."

Kevin and Katie were now laughing as if a stand-up comic entertained them.

"But, my sister is so good! She's so patient with her. It's a miracle how she does it." He raised his arms to heaven once again, "I wanna drown her in a pot of minestrone."

Dropping his arms, Dominick apologized.

"I'm sorry, you must be hungry. What do you feel like? We have fresh minestrone soup today and I can try to find an edible piece of flounder, something soothing for Kevin."

"Sure, that would be fine for me."

"How about you, Katie?"

"Yes, Dominick, that sounds good to me."

"Okay, let me go and tell vampire lady you're here."

"He's a trip, isn't he?" Katie said with a giggle as Dominick walked away.

They drifted, relaxing for a few moments alone with their thoughts, and gazed out the window at the noonday traffic passing by. There they sat, captives of circumstance, enjoying a few moments of silence waiting for the next page to turn.

Kevin focused on Katie, amazed that she appeared so familiar to him. He wondered if she shared his sense that they already knew each other.

"You know, Katie, as I look around this little restaurant with its murals and checkered tablecloths, I think it's a perfect place for a 'getting to know you' first date."

"Yes, I guess for someone seeing it for the first time," Katie laughed. "Maybe the dusty leaves and clumps of imitation grapes lend as much romantic ambiance as is available in this part of the city. Perhaps, like lonely widows, it needs the help of creative, romantic dialog to keep the ambiance glowing, no?"

"Touché. My thought exactly," Kevin said. "You're amazing. Despite the circumstances of our meeting, I honestly can say that since we met I haven't smiled or laughed so much in years."

Katie was still talking about the restaurant. "Seriously, this is a nice place, and it's like a second home to me. Carmella is my second mother." Then his words caught up in her mind, and it hit her.

Wow, I think he's interested.

Kevin broke into her thoughts, "Who is that man in the picture hanging over the bar? The one with the horse?"

"Oh, that's Aunt Carmella's late husband, Paolo. He made that brightly painted Sicilian horse and cart by hand."

"Hold on, I'm trying again. You know I've been to many similar little restaurants in Italy but this place already seems special to me. How am I doing now?"

"Let me see. Are you trying to say that you see me as a stunning, intelligent woman, rooted in her culture, open to new life experiences and full of life? That also embellishes the ambiance of this place?"

At her perfect summation, Kevin laughed so hard, that the Butterfly stitches threatened to open up. "Yes, those are exactly my thoughts. Exactly."

"Then, I think you're doing very well. So far."

It was obvious now that he wanted his life to include more of her. Uncanny as it seemed, he'd never before felt this intensity of emotion for a woman he'd only just met. A new passion stirred within him. He pondered the possibility of God having permitted the morning's violence to jar his waning emotions alive.

He pondered, *Zeigfried, is this not exactly what you as my musical mentor had in mind when you recommended a break to jostle me beyond my musical plateau.*

His recent playing had lacked the deeper emotional component that would elicit a brilliant performance. Kevin had to search for that within himself. He had come to accept that his music needed to embrace an inner fount of feeling. Showing emotion did not come easily for him. His nature was one of reason and logic. Tapping into his feelings risked compromising the performance of his sworn clandestine duties, an aspect of his life that his mentor was not privileged to know.

He flashed back to the morning's encounter. His ability to act swiftly had saved his skin. Any hesitation born of dipping too much into the emotion pool may have caused serious-trouble, even death. He had long held that success came by maintaining a strong body and performing under cool, intelligent control.

Meeting Kate had tapped into a well of feeling he did not know he had. Events this day had placed him in situations not within his control. His trip that morning enveloped him in a group of unique strangers who expressed every emotion, every time. He'd surprised himself, by submitting to the guidance of a young boy.

Just hours later, he sat enjoying the mere sight of Katie's face opposite him.

Choked with surprising emotion, eyes watering, the debris of a peculiar day full of early frustration, fear, and tension caught up to him. Above it all, he felt happy. The tears he held back were tears of joy.

"Kevin. Kevin. You okay?" Katie reached across the table, placed her hand over his. Startled, he looked up at her, grasped her hand tightly in return and tried to thank her for being there for him.

"Katie, you don't yet know me well but I can tell you that, normally, it's not easy for me to reveal my feelings. I'm afraid that I can't express adequately how grateful I am to you, Billy, and all these other people of yours. Even though we came together under ugly circumstances, everyone's been kind to me. It's been such a total pleasure meeting you all. Especially you. My only fear is that this day might end without your promise that we will see each other again, and very soon."

"Oh, listen to this. You want to see plain, unworldly me?"

"Plain, are you kidding? You have a perfect nose."

Perfect nose? This guy's got moves. Next, he'll tell me he likes my shoes.

"I think that pain medicine is going to your head, but tell me more. I'll take it. Oh, Kevin, it's been a most wild day. We met under incredible circumstances. You've been through a lot and I've been happy to do whatever I could. But, even more pleasing to me, I feel as though we have known each other for a long time. It's been a welcome reawakening for me. I believe we've shared something important today, that we're already good friends. Let's start there."

Beaming at her words, he tightened his grip on her hand and thanked her again.

Dominick was watching them. He retreated to the kitchen. They laughed, both embarrassed, as they heard Dominick speaking to his mother:

"Eh, Carmella, where's Katie's soup?"

"Do not call me Carmella. I'm your mother!"

"Don't remind me."

"I'm heating it. You left it on the counter. Why didn't you serve it, there's no one else in the place?" Carmella complained.

"Well, Katie and her new friend seemed to be having a serious conversation. I saw heavy faces."

"Here! Bring them the soup. Maybe that will make them feel better. Sure, you worry about other people's tears, but what about the insults, the tears you put in my eyes?"

"Here, let me hug that chubby belly."

"Stop, get away from me, you have no respect."

"Ah, let me sing to you. I hate you, and you know I hate you. I love to make you cry, oh. Give me a break, la, la, la."

"Shut up and go. Here's the minestrone. Go!"

As Dominick served the soup, Katie saw her Godfather, the undertaker Don Peppino, on the street approaching the restaurant with two business associates. As he entered the restaurant, he caught her eye. She began to stand but he motioned to her to stay seated, and leaned over and kissed her, while taking her hands in his.

"Hi, *Cumpari*–Godfather–how are you?" she asked. "I'm fine. Your Godmother and I were just talking about you last night. As always, she has a surprise prepared for you. She'll call to ask you and Billy-Boy to join us for dinner next week."

"Okay, that sounds good. And how is my *Gummatta*?"

"Oh, she's fine. A little arthritis here and there. What can you do? Old age."

He turned as Dominick arrived and took his hand, "How are you today, Dominick?"

"I'm good, Don Peppino," and leaned forward, kissing his cheek as a sign of respect.

Don Peppino pointed to his colleagues. "Dominick, we have some business to discuss, can we..."

Dominick responded the unspoken question, "I'll set up the back dining room right away."

Dominick excused himself and greeted the two guests waiting by the door. He escorted them to the private dining room. They passed the photo of his humble father. He squinted his eyes as he did.

Kevin rose and extended his hand to the man.

"This must be Katie's friend, that Anthony couldn't stop talking about," he announced, winking at Katie.

"It's nice to meet you Mr. Cortese, I'm Kevin Mandrell."

No, please call me Peppino. I heard you had a little problem this morning?"

"Yes. But, I'm okay, now."

"And where are you from?" Peppino asked.

"I'm visiting with my parents out in Huntington, Long Island."

"Oh, that's nice. Hey, I just thought of it, my driver has to run an errand for me out on Long Island later today. I'll have him take you home."

He spoke as if it would be unacceptable to refuse this kindness.

"Thank you, Peppino, but I wouldn't feel comfortable imposing."

"Nonsense, it's no imposition." His words were firm. "He has to pass by there, anyway."

Kevin accepted. Don Peppino kissed Katie and asked her to let Anthony know when Kevin was ready to return home.

"Cumpari, that's so nice of you."

"Katie, any friend of yours is also a friend of ours. We love you."

He extended his hand to Kevin again, "A pleasure meeting you, young man, and I hope we meet again. If you like, please join us for dinner when Katie and Billy come over next."

Kevin flashed him a shy grin, "Thank you."

Katie shook her head and blushed again. After her Godfather left, Katie explained, "You know, Kevin, the neighborhood people who watched me grow up are very protective of me. But they have no concept of me as being an independent adult woman, content with living a single life. They feel sorry for me because I'm not yet married. They hold to an *old-world* mentality that identifies a woman's possibility for happiness based solely on whether or not she's married and has children."

In fact, in their minds, Katie's education and self-sufficiency paled when compared to what they were sure she needed - a man to take care of her and with whom to raise a family.

She appreciated and shared many of the values and customs of her heritage. She tolerated their concern, although frustrated by their attitude, which didn't leave room for a woman's personal or professional growth.

It was a sticky point for her that he immediately picked up. She told him that her mother, a third generation Italian-American, also held onto those views of a woman's place, and although she had come from an educated family, she remained traditional and was determined to see her daughter married. The only difference being that her mother wanted her to marry into a prominent family, one that was well-educated and cultured.

Sensing her embarrassment on this issue, Kevin said, "Maybe I can help them in their quest. Let's exchange telephone numbers. I'd like to call you, and perhaps we can do something together this weekend."

Katie's eyes sparkled at the invitation, but she played hard to get. "Oh, I made plans to visit my parents in Westchester for the weekend. With a series of emergencies at the Center, I haven't spent time with my mother for a while. But, I'll have a better idea tomorrow after I speak with Mom."

Kevin felt encouraged at this sign of interest.

A woman approached their table. She was full-bodied, in her late fifties, with graying hair pulled up in a bun, not beautiful, yet with a sensual appeal common to Mediterranean women. She carried a steaming platter, with a wonderful aroma.

Katie followed his eyes. "Hi, Aunt Carmella."

"Katie, so nice to see you. Here, let me put these plates down." Carmella embraced Katie, and welcomed Kevin with a robust, "Hello."

"Katie," she said, "I'm getting busy in the kitchen just now and Peppino thinks this is his private dining room." She lifted her eyes toward the ceiling. "But I do want to talk to you. Can you come to dinner Monday night? Angela goes to the movie with her friends and Dominick play poker thank God, so we can talk.."

"Sure, Aunt Carmella, I'd like that."

Carmella turned to Kevin with the customary good-bye, adding that she hoped to see him again soon and with Katie. Kevin smiled, knowing that this no doubt embarrassed Katie anew.

Carmella had prepared stuffed fresh flounder with crabmeat and tiny bay scallops, prepared *a la bianco*–in a creamy scampi sauce–plus a side dish of fresh baby spinach, moistened with olive oil. The room filled with the aroma of lemon and garlic. They dove into the two beautifully presented classic dishes. They were both ravenous.

After they devoured every morsel, using the warm crusty bread to wipe up the remaining juices, Dominick cleared the table, returning with a small pot of espresso, a bottle of anisette, and freshly stuffed cannoli.

Satisfied, Kevin asked Dominick for the check

"Kevin, you're kidding. There are five people fighting over this check. Birdie called earlier and told us to put it on his tab. Don Peppino also wanted to pay, my mother said to forget about it, and I had no intention of charging you to begin with."

They laughed and thanked him, somewhat bewildered but appreciative. Dominick hugged them both as they left to return to the watch shop.

11.

Crossing the street, Kevin took Katie's hand, this time with more confidence. She said nothing but didn't pull back. She wrapped her fingers around his.

They rang the bell of the shop and waited for DiGiaccomo. He greeted them warmly, and led them to the rear of the shop.

"Did you enjoy your lunch, Kevin?"

"Yes, very much so. Carmella is a fantastic cook."

Well, I found a gear had dislodged in the watch, which I can easily repair. Would you object to my showing the piece to my friend Julio? He's a master watchmaker in his own right. He has had much experience with similar timepiece mechanisms."

"That would be fine."

"The watch appears genuine, but it might be a very good copy. Nevertheless," he cautioned Kevin, "it has value, and upon its return it should be insured and kept in a safe place."

Boy, DiGiaccomo can act, Kevin thought.

The watchmaker informed them that he expected Julio to visit at the end of the month to attend the Feast of St. Rocco, and asked Kevin if he planned to return for the Feast. If so, he'd arrange for the three of them to meet at that time, adding that Julio, knowing its history, had a keen interest in seeing the piece.

He slid the watch into the small velour pouch, and locked it in the safe. Kevin thanked him and asked how much he owed him at this point, at which the older man merely waved him away.

"Thank you. I look forward to meeting soon again."

Katie and he hugged fondly as they parted.

Making their way to the funeral parlor so that Kevin could be driven to his parents' home on Long Island by Don Peppino's driver, they were silent. Reality sank in. Their time together was ending, but as they approached the elaborate parlor awning, Kevin stopped and took her hand.

"Thanks for this memorable day. I will call you tomorrow night."

Katie clutched his hand and whispered, "I'm looking forward to hearing your voice. I mean, I would like to know how you're doing."

As they were about to embrace, they heard Anthony call out, "I'll tell Mario you're here." Waiting, eyes glued to each other, Kevin spotted a burly, six-foot-two, curly-headed, dark skinned bruiser of a man in his late thirties come out the front door. He was dressed in funeral garb, a dark blue suit, a white button-down, custom-made shirt, and a black silk tie. He greeted Katie in Italian, "*Signorina Caterina, come sta?*"

"Hi, Mario. It's been a long time."

He responded in English with a tinge of an accent. "Your Godfather keeps me busy."

Katie introduced Kevin to Mario. While shaking his hand, Kevin took in the large diamond pinky ring, the expensive suit and shoes, and the strength of his grip.

Mario spoke. "Heard what happened to you. How you feeling?" pointing to the bandages.

"Okay, thank you."

"Anthony went to bring the car around. I should have you home in less than an hour at this time of day."

Moments later Anthony pulled up to the curb in a polished black Cadillac Limo. As Mario opened the rear door for him, Kevin reached for Katie's hand to say a reluctant goodbye. She, in turn cupped his hand, leaned forward and kissed him on the cheek just missing his lips. She reminded him not to remove the bandages.

With a final wave, he was able to whisper to her, "We'll talk soon."

As Mario drove them away, Katie and Anthony waved. Anthony rambled on, "*Nice-a. Nice-a guy.*"

Mario made his way through the thick traffic with confidence, weaving around cars and pedestrians who darted across gridlocked streets in typical New York fashion, ignoring both sidewalks and lights. Mario asked Kevin if he wanted a drink, indicating a bar console in a rear compartment.

"Don Peppino likes to keep a bottle or two of brandy for his ride home at night. You might as well rest until we get to the Route 25 in Syosset. Then, I'll need directions to your place in Huntington."

"Thank you, Mario. I think I'm less overwhelmed by being mugged than by the hospitable way I've been treated by everyone."

"Kevin, you've gotta understand. We love Caterina here in this neighborhood. All the work she does for the poor, for one thing, and her parents are very close to Don Peppino and his wife. They grew up together. Besides Don Peppino and his wife never had children, so Caterina is like a daughter to them, too. They would do anything for her."

Mario paused, then spat out with a twinge of anger, "Just the fact that those punks who jumped you were on her block upsets her godfather."

"Mario, maybe I shouldn't ask. What's going to happen to them?"

Mario laughed, "Forget about it, don't trouble yourself. They're not going to get whacked."

Mario turned on the radio. He hummed to Puccini as he drove. Kevin's eyes got heavy. He drifted into a half-sleep, musing on the terminology. *Whacked. Definitely mob vernacular.*

How properly courteous this Mario cast himself and yet, he radiated an aura of restrained anger and darkness.

Soothed by the cushioned roll of the limo, Kevin let himself wander to more pleasant isles: Katie's face and the pleasures of the day.

He awoke with a start at Mario's announcement.

"We're almost at Woodbury."

"I think we go just head straight up Route 25, then left on 110 then north on 25A, into the Village of Huntington. Do you know the area?" Kevin asked.

"Sure, friends of ours live nearby."

He directed Mario along winding country roads onto a private road. The house was at the end of a long driveway, a hundred and fifty feet off the street. Its setting was a delight to Kevin's eye. A postcard of neatly clipped hedges, lined with solid old trees, blanketed with multicolored leaves, and highlighted by shimmering streams of light breaking through the canopy.

He told Mario to turn into the carport, marked by two stone pillars. As he did, Mario saw the home, a large, classically styled New England Colonial saltbox, complete with weathered Cape Cod shingles, atop of which sat a green copper cupola crowned with a seagull weather vane.

"This is really nice. The house is beautiful and the landscaping is like a park, with room to breathe. My mother would love it. If your family wishes to sell someday, let me know."

"We love it too, Mario. This was a great place to grow up."

As Mario opened the car door, Kevin asked him to thank Don Peppino again. "It was good of both of you."

"No trouble," Mario replied. "I hope you heal quickly. You shouldn't have much of a scar. Birdie is the master when it comes to these things. Maybe we'll see each other again in the neighborhood, now that you've met Caterina. She's a nice girl, the best. You follow me?"

Kevin nodded, acknowledging Mario's subtext. Mario drove back out.

Kevin unlocked the front door, and called out a hello but got no response. He picked up mail on the hallway table and climbed the stairs to his old room. Leafing through envelopes, he found a welcome note. It was from his childhood best friend, Timmy Cavallero, who had stopped by earlier that day. Happy that he was close by, but too tired to call, Kevin collapsed on the bed, and slid into deep sleep.

12.

God, I'm overdue for some girl talk. Wow, I lucked out. A spot in front.

Katie parked in front of her Aunt Carmella's restaurant. She locked the car just as the skies opened up. She dashed up the steps to the door Carmella held open. They glanced out to the street arm and arm in the foyer watching the falling raindrops. There was little street traffic. The neon lights of the deserted storefronts glistened through the rain, and reflected on the wet pavement.. The cascade hitting the old cobblestone street and uneven slate sidewalks brought out the old, familiar scent of the neighborhood, a scent that spoke of long-ago memories for each of them.

Carmella broke the moment of reflection. "I made gnocchi for you today. And beef brasciole."

"I can smell it. It calls to me. I've given up trying to make gnocchi myself. Mine come out like lead and never tastes as good as yours."

"I set the table in the kitchen. Is that okay?"

"I wouldn't have it any other way. This is home for me."

They made their way through the darkened restaurant into the kitchen, where Katie grabbed a breadstick. "I think you have special air in here, Aunt Carmella. Or Italian cherubs or something," she said, crunching. "Everything tastes better here. It's always felt cozy and secure."

"Good. I always loved having you. You were so bright for your age. Picked up Sicilian like a native. *Una bedduzza ... una principessa*– a cute princess–" she said while leaning her head on Katie's shoulder.

Her face changed. "Katie, I want to talk to you about an idea I have. Maybe you can help." She placed the bowls of pasta and sautéed meat on the table, served Katie and sat.

"Sure, Aunt Carmella. Is anything wrong?"

They made the sign of the cross. Carmella paused. Distracted in thought, she wiped sweat from her brow.

Katie took a fork full of gnocchi and rolled her eyes in pleasure as the matriarch continued.

"I'm thinking about selling the restaurant and moving away from the neighborhood."

Katie stopped chewing. "Oh my God!" she murmured, waiting for an explanation.

"I knew it would trouble you. I'm sorry."

"It's just the shock. I don't even like to think of your not being here."

Carmella motioned to her to continue eating. "I know, honey, but when I explain, I think you will understand. It's a long story." She picked at her pasta.

"You're aware that my Paolo worked as a longshoreman on the Brooklyn docks. What you don't know is that he was a first cousin of Jimmy Urbano, a connected union boss, who they called 'Iron Man.' Paolo, being a cousin of his, never lost a day of work throughout the Depression and World War II. You know, Paolo radiated goodness. He was such a fine man. The best. Friends and family knew to call upon him for a bag of groceries if they were short of funds.

"It angered Paolo to know that his friends had to pay ten cents of every dollar they earned to his cousin and his mob cronies. He compensated as much as he could for his special standing by using his position to help the other workers, most of whom were illiterate. He was the only one in his work-gang that could read, so he helped them to write letters and he read the replies for people in the neighborhood."

"I know my parents had many good things to say about him," Katie said with a crinkled brow, not sure where Carmella was headed with this.

"My Paolo, my sweet humble man, valued them as they did him. They were bonded together by the shared adventure of settling in a new land. They had no choice and they knew it. They were trapped by the dark hands that held our lives. Puppeteers that pulled all the strings, they controlled our lives and our future."

The matriarch sucked in a breath, "And there were the Americans. All of us here in the neighborhood endured the prejudices and lack of opportunities which blocked Italian immigrants back then. The Irish were dominant and controlled all the civil service jobs. To them, us and the Jews, *eravamo degli intrusi*– we were intruders."

Carmella swallowed hard, as she visited the past, remembering her husband and how he had to pay as his friends did. He shared their lack of personal freedom.

"Fortunately for Paolo, his suffering didn't include the poverty that came from lack of a job. But if he had chosen to refuse his favored status, his powerful cousin would have suffered a serious loss of face, not just on the New York waterfront, but back in their home village of Milazzo, in Sicily.

"Katie, such embarrassment in the old country would have placed Urbano in an untenable position, and it would have resulted in violent repercussions for our family. Jimmy resented

Paolo because of his honesty. My Paolo rejected the life of a wise-guy and he paid the price in hard work and sacrifice."

She described, with a stinging memory that brought tears to her eyes, Paolo's failing health, compromised by too many long nights on the docks. He succumbed to pneumonia, dying at the unforgiveable age of thirty-two.

His premature death left her with just enough money to bury him. However, out of deep respect for his generosity and his good works, his co-workers collected a fair sum of money for her and the kids. When his cousin Jimmy became aware of how Paolo's death affected the people around him, he decided to cash in on her husband's good name, with a big gesture. He paid for Paolo's funeral.

Carmella wiped her tears, and Katie took her hand. "That's so sad, Aunt Carmella. You have been through so much."

"Katie, I'm telling you all this because I want you to know how they think and what they are capable of. The day after Paolo died, I was getting ready to go to the funeral parlor to make the arrangements. Jimmy came to my door. I was in the bathroom.

"Angie was five then. She opened the door at his knock, and took him by the hand and led him to me in the bathroom. I had left the door partially open, so I could hear my children. Before I could react to their footsteps, Angie pushed open the door. I'm standing there naked, toweling myself dry. I tried to hide behind the door while I grabbed for my housecoat.

"It sickened me that he had seen me naked. I wrapped my robe around me, stormed out to the hallway, grabbed Angie's hand, and screamed at him. I said, '*What are you doing here?*'

"He stood there with no shame. He was dressed in a dark-blue suit complete with white silk shirt and diamond stickpin in his tie as if he was going to a wedding.

"He said, 'Please, please, Carmella, I'm sorry I surprised you. I just wanted to give you my condolences and tell you that I have taken care of all the arrangements for Paolo's funeral.'

"He was trying to charm me, telling me how kind he was being, pledging his deep sorrow over Paolo's death. But he spoke with the split tongue of a snake, that one.

"'Ah,' he said, 'Paolo, may he rest in peace, was my dearest cousin, and a loyal worker. When I heard of his death, I thought of his hard work for us. I fear I failed him. I should have paid more attention to his poor health and given him more help. I have disgraced myself. Such a young man. What a tragedy. Why didn't you tell me of my cousin's condition?'

"I was no fool. I responded with the feigned humility I'd seen Paolo use when dealing with that ilk. Him standing there giving me this crap. I gave it right back to him."

'Oh, Jimmy,' I said. 'You know Paolo loved his work. He knew only how to work hard and he would have continued for a long time had he lived.'"

"Then he came forward, and pulled me to him, "Ah, cousin, if you need anything for yourself or for the children, you call upon me. Okay?"

"I felt as if *essere in preda* –I was prey–caught in the grip of a vulture. I backed away as he placed a card with his private number in my robe pocket."

Carmella paused. "Then he says, 'I ask the privilege of leading Paolo's funeral procession,' and tells me that Monsignor Scalvo, then Father Scalvo, has already agreed to give Paolo his best eulogy."

"As he spoke, I tried to avoid his hands, which he moved from my waist onto my buttocks. I pulled firmly away from him with my Angie in tow, and darted to the door. I could barely conceal disgust as I opened it.

"'Please give your wife my warmest regards,'" I told him.

"He left with the false smile of a caught street dog. He saluted like a cavalier as he retreated down the stairs. I bolted the door behind him, and then watched through a crack in the window blinds as he got into his car with two of his henchmen. I had a shudder of relief as they pulled away."

Katie raised her fist, "What a miserable... "

Carmella turned from the vision of her memory and looked straight at Katie. "Katie, it was so sad, they turned Paolo's funeral into a complete farce. A Radio City floorshow. It had a level of grandeur as if he was a politician or a big name racketeer."

"What sneaks," Katie said.

"Would you believe that Jimmy helped carry the coffin through the neighborhood streets, accompanied by my husband's true friends?"

Katie shook her head, "I guess they had no choice. Grieving at the same time they had to be play actors."

"Then it was a flower show. Three flower cars. For a humble man who used to pick wild flowers in the empty lots for me."

"Aw, what a sweet man," Katie said with a sad smile.

"The nerve of them. They had gangs of dockworkers in their work clothes marching like soldiers with their cargo hooks in their back pockets following behind the hearse. Their faces were somber. Not one of them spoke. The so called *men of respect* had made their orders clear. It was a show and a message sent to the neighborhood that it paid to be favored by the local boss."

"Jimmy had even convinced Monsignor Scalvo to lead the procession with him. I found out years later that for this honor Urbano had promised Monsignor the names of a couple of winning horses when they next met at the track."

Carmella rode back in time. Present in her mind's eye was the ending of an elaborate procession that culminated with a High Requiem Mass, celebrated by three priests, with an eloquent eulogy by Scalvo. Adding to the snap shot was Jimmy Urbano nodding his approval to the priest as he completed his homily with flowery words.

Pictures flashed of lines of people who waited outside the church to pay their last respects, many of whom Paolo did not know. She heard the distant voices of friends that told her then of puzzled locals making comments like, "He must have been a big shot." More than a few others gestured with a bent finger to the side of a nose, the familiar "crooked nose" symbol of a Mafioso, labeling him so.

Others asked whom they were burying, and were amazed on hearing that it was Paolo. Embarrassed by their innocence, they remarked how they had always thought him an honest man. Complimenting their misguided assumptions were the natural cynics whom were saying things like, "Well, it just goes to show; you never know! He appeared to be such a gentle soul, above suspicion."

She could still see plainclothes police everywhere, taking photos, and asking people how they had known Paolo. A detective was heard to comment, "Looks like one must have gotten away from us."

Then the touch of Katie's sympathetic hand jolted her from that painful recollection.

"Oh, Katie, it was a tragic comedy. I'm glad my children weren't old enough to understand what was going on."

She paused, and bit her lip, "Katie, I found myself alone with two children to raise. I didn't know how we would survive. If it were not for the kind-heartedness of Paolo's friends, I do not know what would have happened to us.

"They gave me a gift of two hundred dollars they had collected and suggested a solution to the future survival of my children and me."

"So nice," Katie mirrored, "I guess a fortune for that time."

"Yes, they suggested that I could earn a good living by preparing lunches and late night dinners for the dockworkers working ships in the area."

Many of the men had eaten at her home as guests of Paolo, especially when things were tough. They knew of her cooking skills. She had converted her living room into a dining room, put a small sign in the window and proceeded as they proposed. The word soon spread. She gained a reputation for preparing quality homemade Italian food.

Even the union bosses became customers. They called days in advance to make reservations for dinner. Within a few years, she worked herself out of a hole. She had saved enough money for a down payment on the Mulberry Street property across the street from Peppino's Funeral Home. She remodeled the house and made the lower level a restaurant and the upstairs became their home.

"In Paolo's memory, I continue to serve free meals for those in need in what we call Paolo's dining room in the back. But too often, the room is used for private lunch and dinner parties by the so-called 'men of respect.'"

"This is so sad," Katie said. "It must have been so hard for you. You did not mention my father or uncles. Didn't they offer to help you?"

"Yes, they did, but I was angry. I didn't want anything to do with them at that time."

"I don't understand."

"Katie, I'm exhausted reliving this and I'm neglecting you. Let's speak of something happier for a little while. Tell me about this young man, Kevin."

"Oh! Aunt Carmella, I don't know where it will go but he's unlike any man I've met for years now. He's so centered, just the way he handled what happened to him that day. It had to be draining, not to mention the cultural shock. We're talking about a white bread and mashed potato American here. Yet, his demeanor remained pleasant and courteous. He's fit, intelligent, and humorous. For the first time in a long time, I'm attracted to a man."

Carmella perked-up at her words, "It's a miracle," she said. Carmella smoothed Katie's hair, "That's what you need, a good man and to look forward to a new life. You're smart and educated. The world can be larger for you. You need to leave this place." She sighed, her face darker. "Katie, do I have to tell you how much I love you? I know that what I'm about to say will have hurt for you, but I must. The time has come for you to know. I'm so worried for you and Billy and for my children."

"Please, Aunt Carmella, tell me what this is all about."

"I know how very much in love you were with Carmine, and how shocked you were when he died. Your first love and High School sweetheart, I was so happy for you, being in love with this nice young man. Both of you so full of life, you glowed when you were with him. It has been a long time since I've seen such joy in you."

Katie sat rattled by the mention of Carmine's name. It had taken years for her to be able not to think of him every day. They had grown up together, had similar storybook backgrounds. She, the only child of the neighborhood pharmacist, and he, the only child of the neighborhood florist. Each worked in their father's store. They would often manage to steal time together, meeting on the street as they made deliveries. They loved listening to their favorite rock n' roll tunes on the jukebox, and sharing slices of pizza.

"You have never spoken to me about this before. Why are you bringing this up after so many years?"

"Katie, I know this will be hard for you to hear but I have always believed that *e malamente* –the mob– murdered that boy."

"Aunt Carmella, how can you say such a thing? It was an accident. The brakes on his truck failed. The police investigated."

"Katie, I know this is difficult for you but the time has come. It must be said once again, I'm worried about you and my children"

Katie, dumbfounded, took a breath, and tried to regain composure. She demanded an explanation. "Why do you believe someone did this? Who are they? And why? Why are we in danger?"

"Katie, that day, you and Carmine left school early to be together for a while because you were going away for the weekend with your parents, and you wanted to have some time together before you left. Remember?"

"Yes. But how do you know that?"

"Because Carmine had my table-flower order along with the funeral parlor flowers in his truck when he went to meet you. After you two parted, he first drove to the funeral parlor to deliver their flowers. There, the front door was locked. Anthony wasn't around either. So, Carmine went around the back, to the garage, thinking to leave the flowers there for a wake that evening.

"He unloaded the flowers and put them in the garage. As he brought in the last arrangement, he heard voices coming from the basement, so he started down the stairs to let whoever was down there know that he had delivered the flowers. As he got closer, he stopped short. He heard a man's voice screaming for his life, choking and gasping for breath. In the background, he heard loud voices shouting back, cursing and calling names in Italian, *'Vigliaccu, Bastardo,'*–jackal, bastard–and he recognized a voice shouting, 'Die, you bastard. We're going to cut you in pieces.'

"When I asked him who it was, he just shook his head but the expression on his face was terrified. He was crying and rocking back and forth, and he told me that he panicked and ran back to the truck. But as he pulled away, he thought he saw the shadow of someone inside the garage from his truck window. He was afraid someone saw him.

"I know all of this because he showed up here with my flowers. He was shaking. He couldn't even speak. He was so pale I thought he would collapse. It was as if he had seen a ghost.

"I gave him a glass of Marsala to calm him, but he could hardly hold the glass. He couldn't speak. When he finally could, he told me what he'd heard. Oh, my God, it scares me as if it were yesterday. I'll never forget what he said - 'Carmella, they were killing somebody.'"

"No, no, Aunt Carmella, this can't be true, no!" Katie shouted, "Take it back. Oh, God, take it back!"

Carmella lifted her apron and wiped tears from her cheeks. "I know, honey. I asked him to calm down and to think hard. Did he think someone had seen him there? He repeated he was afraid.

"I told him not to say a word to anybody. This I have regretted every day of my life since."

Whimpering, Katie asked, "Which funeral parlor?"

She whispered, "Your Godfather's. Peppino's."

Katie moved to the other side of the kitchen and buried her head in her arms on the counter top. She wept, once more for Carmine whom she had loved, and for the shock of this terrible story.

Carmella, overcome with the weight of the grief she had just laid upon her niece, waited a few moments, but felt compelled to continue. She needed to purge it all.

"Don Peppino is not only a powerful man, Katie, but a cold smooth snake." She moved close to Katie, placed her hands on her shoulders, and whispered, "We're always pretending. We don't allow ourselves to think about what they do. It's easier and safer to deny the truth. They pretend also. That they're gentlemen. They treat their wives like queens. But they are not gentlemen; they are dangerous men who are killers without conscience. Katie, I've known them my whole life. Back in the old country as a young girl, and here in America."

Katie tried to absorb Carmella's words as her mind repeated in a daze, *they murdered my Carmine.*

Katie's mind swam, but Carmella continued. "Many of them came as I did, as children from the same town in Sicily. We grew up together here on Hester Street. They were my playmates. Some were even related to Paolo in one way or another. But I've always known how ruthless they are, capable of anything, hiding behind their businesses and making friends with innocent, honest people in order to maintain faces of respectability."

Trying to absorb this revelation, to make sense of it, and trying, above all, to find a way to deny it, Katie was near collapse. But she knew Carmella.

Carmella had never been fanciful. She was not a woman who makes up stories.

Katie lifted her head from the counter, stared at Carmella, and tried again. "But the police investigated the crash. They concluded that it was the brakes."

"Oh, Katie, Katie, the police are here all the time. The sergeants, the captains, even the inspectors. They eat in the backroom with all the *malamente*–the wise guys–and then they leave with bulging envelopes in their pockets. You can't trust them, these police, and these politicians. Not a single one of them."

"But the voice, the voice Carmine recognized. Whose was it?"

Carmella repeated that he had not given her the name, but, as she spoke, Katie noticed that her facial expression subtly altered. Katie didn't push, almost relieved. She was afraid to have her worst fears confirmed.

"The only other thing Carmine mentioned was that he had seen a white Cadillac with Nevada plates parked in the driveway. He almost backed into it as he drove away."

Carmella got up to clear the cold and uneaten food from the table – neither she nor Katie had an appetite at this point. Carmella poured coffee and said, "I've told you all of this not to hurt you, but because it's time for you to know. Not everything you see and hear in the neighborhood is what it appears to be. We're not free. We're under their thumbs, and they take from everyone. They control our lives and the lives of our children. When they do you a favor, you can be sure they will take what they want in return."

Katie felt dazed by the information Carmella had given her. "Aunt Carmella, is it okay if I stay here with you tonight? I feel paralyzed. I can call Sister Regina and ask her to pick up Billy and keep him with her for the night."

"Of course, you'll sleep with me. Call the Sister. I'll go upstairs and get you something to wear."

"Don't fuss. I would be happy to have one of Dominick's old sweatshirts to sleep in."

Katie called Reggie–sister Regina's neighborhood name–and asked her if she would pick up Billy. Without a question, Reggie consented. Katie and Regina, though very different personalities, were as close as twins. Their friendship had been secured by many years of proven trust and faith in God. They accepted one another with no explanation needed.

Katie reflected on how Billy also loved Reggie and was always happy to be with her, although he would never admit it. Katie knew that he thought she was hip. She played poker with him, could talk like a longshoreman, and, occasionally, even allowed him a puff on her cigarette. When she spoke to him of Jesus, she used cool analogies. Once, she had likened the long hair worn by Jesus and his disciples to that of a motorcycle gang leader and his followers. He'd told Katie that she likened St. Michael, the Archangel, to a modern day gang warlord.

Katie would just shake her head when she heard statements like these, agreeing "Reggie is a rip." But, she knew that underlying every joke Reggie made, was the truth of her deep love and unshakeable belief in Jesus and his Church.

Although her faith underscored Reggie's commitment to serving those in need, she was sure that Reggie spoke to God in the same streetwise manner she spoke to everyone else. Katie asked herself, *has Reggie seen through my denial?*

She needed to continue this conversation with her Aunt, knowing how difficult it must have been for Carmella to make these revelations. She knew Carmella as a proud woman, one of calm strength. She had always colored the world in roses for young Katie, and contributed toward her secure childhood. She was a peacemaker, known for listening to her friends with patience, and was trusted to keep their confidences, all the while offering emotional release and support.

Admitting her hidden fears and anger was profound, and had profound meaning.

Katie was aware that Carmella had acknowledged her maturity that night. Her Aunt believed that Katie was wise enough to learn about ugly secrets of the past. *Why now? Was it simply because these were events too momentous and too terrible to hold within her heart forever?*

Denial, Katie knew, can conceal such things for only so long before they destroy a person. They must be released if one is to survive.

Katie identified with Carmella. She had long felt her bond with her closer than that with her own mother. Although she loved her mother, there was an emotional gap between them. Katie often saw her mother as a spectator who, while keenly interested in her, and loving her, somehow lacked a visceral maternal attachment to her, and was unable to have a true intimate relationship with her daughter.

Her father had sometimes alluded to his reaction to this aspect of her mother's personality. He would joke and attribute it to the fact that as a third generation Italian-American, she had been *Anglicized*. He intimated that she had lost the connection to an earthier old world heritage. Sometimes, when angry, he referred to her as the "Queen Mother."

Carmella returned to the kitchen, saying that she had laid out a few things on the bed to choose from, and she suggested that Katie take a soothing bath to help her sleep. Katie, still agitated, hugged her and made her way to the stairs, fearing it would be a long night.

13.

Carmella secured the restaurant and cleaned up the kitchen. It's been years since Katie mounted those stairs. How small they must appear now. She remembered Katie sliding down the banister as a kid, Dominick and Angie cheering her from below. It seemed all much longer and larger then. She recalled that time of innocence and shook her head.

Carmella's bedroom was ornate with Italian Provincial furniture. Katie saw the bed turned down as usual on her side. She inhaled the familiar scent of Aqualina bleach that emanated from the freshly laundered sheets. On the cluttered dresser were baby pictures of Dominick and Angie, and one photograph of her own First Holy Communion, all surrounding a lighted statue of the Blessed Virgin Mary. The light was reflected in a large, gilt-edged mirror, replete with pictures of saints and pieces of Palm Sunday palm fronds wedged into frames, hanging above the dresser.

Over the bed hung a hand-carved cross given to Carmella and Paolo by Paolo's parents on their wedding day. Katie found comfort in the fact that this room and its contents had not changed since her youth. It gave her a sense of returning to her childhood home. Carmella had left a nightgown, a robe, and one of Dominick's sweatshirts on the bed, as always, respecting Katie's wishes, and giving her the opportunity to choose.

Katie folded the nightgown and robe, placed them on the chair, picked up the sweatshirt and got ready for bed. Returning to the bedroom, she found Carmella sitting on the window box sill of the tall French windows that opened to a deck over the dining room extension on the floor below.

An awning above the deck sheltered a floral patterned wrought iron outdoor table and chairs, and a statue of the Madonna with a bouquet of artificial flowers placed in a glass jar before it. Katie remembered this roof garden as Carmella's private oasis, where she escaped often to pray or to think. She also remembered how, on hot summer nights, her Aunt would often let the children sleep outside there in the cooler air.

The rain had stopped and the air was still. Katie sat beside Carmella. She was calmer, more austere, almost trance-like, showing her usual resolve as a woman who had survived hardship and achieved wisdom by calling on a foundation comprised of her Sicilian culture, her unbending faith, and her life experiences that no amount of formal education could rival.

"Katie, I had to tell you what happened so long ago. I know you're strong. Telling you more about what I know could put you and those you love in danger. You and I have been close, very close. You're special to me, like a daughter, and you're, how do you say it, my confidante."

Carmella smoothed Katie's hair as she gazed into Katie's wide, moist eyes.

"You're intelligent and have the capacity to see more clearly than the average person. However, you've remained tied to this neighborhood. It holds you, and you've never tried to leave. Think about it. When your parents moved to the house in Westchester, even when you went away to college, you were still here."

Katie had never heard Carmella talk this way before. The intensity of her tone emphasized the truth of what she was saying.

Carmella was affirming Katie's private thoughts. Katie couldn't understand why, unlike most of her youthful friends, she had never wanted to move away.

She was well educated, and she had some money stashed away, saved from an assortment of insurance annuities her parents and grandparents had provided. Nevertheless, there was something—indistinct up until now—holding her there in spite of her having the means to leave at any time.

Carmella continued, "Katie, I fear for Dominick and Angie. Your godfather is encouraging Mario to pursue my Angie, and I don't trust Mario, despite his respectful behavior toward me. I know that he's already a Mafioso on the way up to a Capo Regime. I know that people fear him."

She stopped, bit her lip, and peered out to the dark night sky. When she spoke again, her voice was lower, just a whisper, and tears ran down her cheeks.

She revealed to Katie that Paolo's cousin, Jimmy "Iron Man" Urbano, the union delegate, had pursued her for many years after Paolo's death. For years she rebuffed his advances.

"Katie, one night about ten years ago, Jimmy was having dinner at the restaurant with Tommaso, your Cumpari, Peppino, and a few others. He had drunk a lot of wine. He followed me to the kitchen and moved behind me. Then, he grabbed my waist with one hand and forcibly covered my mouth with his other."

Katie said, "What? That bastard," in angry disbelief.

Carmella's jaw tightened, as the memories began flooding back to her. "Jimmy pushed my face down hard on the table. I was paralyzed with fear. He raised my skirt and ripped down my panties. He was so powerful, I couldn't stop him or scream. He threatened that he would kill me if I made a sound. Then, he forced himself on me from behind."

"He defiled you!" Katie cried.

Visibly shaken by what she was relating, Carmella paused to catch her breath.

"Luckily, your godfather heard something and rushed into the kitchen. He pulled Jimmy off me. He threw him back hard, then crashed his head and face repeatedly against the stainless steel refrigerator door. The blows knocked Jimmy unconscious, and he slid to the floor.

"I was frozen with shock and fear. I tried and failed to lift myself off the table. Peppino, who was Jimmy's Capo at the time, eased me to my feet, and helped me pull myself together, much as a father might. He asked if I was all right, and if I needed a doctor. I was in shock and unable to speak. It was a vision of horror. Jimmy was lying there exposed and bloodied. He was absolutely helpless, unconscious, a pathetic sight."

"Animal, animal," Katie muttered in response.

"I remember that Peppino grabbed a tablecloth and covered him. Then, he lifted me to his chest, and cradled me while he dialed the phone. I heard him speak with quietly in Italian, but I could not make out his words."

"Oh, Aunt Carmella, you poor woman, my stomach is in knots."

"It felt like hours but probably within minutes Mario came in with two other men. They lifted Jimmy's body from the floor and took him out through the back. As they left, I believe I heard Peppino instructing them to take him to his embalming room and to call your father immediately. He said to them, 'No one is ever to know about this, you hear?'

"Peppino helped me upstairs, and left me to rest on my bed and returned downstairs to wait for Dr. Amato. I was in a fog, but I believe the doctor came quickly. He cleaned me up and treated me for cuts and bruises, and gave me a sedative.

"When Amato left, Peppino came back in and patted me on the head, leaned over, kissed me on the forehead, and reassured me that he would have the restaurant closed and cleaned."

Katie cried out with choked words, "Oh, Aunt Carmella, I am so sorry, so sorry."

Both crying heavy tears now, Carmella patted Katie and went on, "As he was about to leave, he turned back to me and promised that nobody would ever know what had happened that night, that I would not lose face or suffer any more indignation."

"Lose face? That is what he cared about? What barbarians," Katie spat.

"Just before he left, Peppino told me that from that point on I was under his protection and that Jimmy Urbano would never bother me again. He left after apologizing profusely for what I had suffered.

"When I awoke the next morning I was still drowsy and had pain and was unable to get my thoughts together, and a panic took hold of me. After a long shower, I dressed and made my way down to the restaurant. I found it cleaned, all the dining tables were set, and resting on the kitchen counter were five one-hundred-dollar bills." Carmella paused for a breath. Her face tightened as she went on.

"They think they can buy everything with money. Money is their cure-all, their god. Peppino never spoke of it again. Dominick and Angie never learned what had happened to me. They were visiting with their cousins in Brooklyn that night."

Carmella went on to relate that six months later the Daily News reported that the Police had discovered a man body, with his throat cut and his genitals removed, concealed by tall weeds in an empty lot on Cropsie Avenue in Brooklyn. It was Jimmy. The newspaper article suggested that the killing had the Mafia earmark of revenge for a sexual infidelity.

"Good," Katie said with anger, "God forgive me for saying it." Carmella paused with a sigh. "Katie, my son Dominick is very sensitive. He takes after his father, bon anima. He is not as strong as you are. These men all make a fuss over him. They give him big tips, and they invite him to the racetrack. He doesn't accept only because he knows I don't want him to. He thinks that I'm worried that he will become a gambler. That isn't the main reason. I'm worried that one way or the other, they will attract him to that life, then use him and kill him in the end as they have done to so many others."

"You think he would have the heart for that?" Katie asked. "He's such a gentle soul."

"No, but he thinks he knows everything. I know I treat Dominick cruelly. I ridicule him so people will not know how smart he is. That way, I hope they will never consider him a threat or someone who could make money for them. I know what I really need to do is get my children out of this place, but I'm afraid I know too much. And you need to get out, as well. We need to accomplish this thing without giving them concern, though, so they won't try to stop us."

Frozen in thought and fear, Katie did not answer.

"Katie, the Mayor and the Governor have had private dinners here in the backroom with these men. It has been a life sentence for me, but I do not want it for my children, or for you. You must not tell any of this to your father, not one word. Everyone respects him. We were all kids together. Hopefully we can present it to him in an innocent manner, in a way that will convince him to plead my cause without bringing suspicion on me or you however that may be accomplished."

Katie took a depth breath. "Zia–Aunt– I've known this in my heart. What they are. This is difficult to accept. I know I have been fooling myself. But what's more important to me is to know what is my father's connection to the rest of them? He is an educated man, smarter than any of them. So why is he so close to them? What attracts him to them and vice versa? I know they make him feel special. They seem to listen to his every word with never any disagreement. They treat me like a princess. Why is that? Is it only to flatter us?"

On my father's part, is it the security of knowing that we have powerful friends and it gives us all a sense of power?

"Even Billy is attracted to them. I see it in him. He mimics them, Aunt Carmella. Sometimes he even talks like them. I try to remind him of his talents, and that he does not need role models like that. I tell him he must be his own man but–"

"Katie, we have all been taken in by their power. They fix many problems but there is always a cost, and make no mistake, nothing happens here unless they want it to. They are evil, and evil can have the taste of the sweetest fruit when it suits the purpose. Even Jesus was tempted."

"I still don't understand my father," Katie said. "It's as if we have this unwritten pact between us regarding this subject. We never speak of it. Even when we read in the newspapers that one of his friends was arrested or killed."

"My old age tells me that everything in life shouldn't be known or brought to one's lips. The answers we seek are often too painful to live with, if we hear them. Your father had his childhood with them. They go back a long time together to what they call the Hester Street Days."

The weight of the night fell upon them. They were both drained and exhausted.

Carmella hugged Katie. "More has to be said, but for now, let us just say our prayers and put ourselves in the arms of Jesus and his Mother as we sleep. Pray for me, pray for a safe way out."

She kissed Katie on the forehead. "I do not want to spend even one more year here. As much as I love the neighborhood and my friends, my children's future must be protected before something bad happens."

They retired. Katie lay next to Carmella and placed one arm over her mid-section as she had done as a child. Carmella covered Katie's hand with hers. They drifted off into the healing escape of deep sleep.

14.

Katie heard the hi-fi blasting as she turned the key to the apartment door. The Everly Brothers song, Bye-Bye Love.

"Billy, hello?" she called. Entering, she knocked on Billy's door, calling again, "Billy, I'm home."

Finally, she heard the music stop. Billy stormed into the living room with a complaint replacing any greeting. "There's no food!"

"I know I haven't had a chance to go to the grocery with so much going on. Why don't you go down to Felix's and pick up a pizza for us?"

"Can I get it with extra cheese?"

"Fine, but skip the anchovies this time. Come here, little monster, I need a long hug." Billy shook his head, sighed, and embraced her.

We need each other more now than ever, Katie thought. She ruffled his hair and went for her purse.

Billy nodded as she gave him a five-dollar bill and instructed,

"Make sure you give me the change."

He started for the door. "Wait a minute." Reading a scribbled phone number stuck to the refrigerator, she asked, "When did he call?"

"I don't know. Yesterday, I think."

"No, Billy, this wasn't here yesterday, or the day before."

"Hey, I'm not a secretary. I forgot to write it down."

"Well, what did he say?"

"He thanked me for helping him," he told her, moving again toward the door.

"Just a minute, buster. What else did he say?"

"I don't remember. Oh, yeah, something about getting together, and that he has a present for me."

"Ah hah, and what did you say to him?"

"That's good."

She shook her head in frustration. "Go, go and get the pizza. I need to get our clothes ready. We're going to Nana's in the morning."

"Do I have to go?"

"Yes, she's making lasagna for you. She said that your little girl friend, Geraldine, was asking about you."

Billy blushed. "She's not my girlfriend." He huffed and left for the pizza.

Katie could not help herself. She did a little skip into the air, happy Kevin had called. As she heard Billy's footsteps climb the outside steps, she dialed Kevin's number. A woman's voice answered, and Katie said, "Mrs. Mandrell? This is Katherine Burdino." She felt her face warm. "I'm returning Kevin's call."

"Oh, sure, Katherine, I'll get him for you."

Somewhat relieved by the welcoming tone, Katie hoped it meant that Kevin had described her as more than just a kind person he'd met.

"Kev... Kev... you have a telephone call, dear," Katie heard Mrs. Mandrell call out.

A distant reply, "Okay, Mom, who is it?"

"It's Katherine."

"Okay, please ask her to hold on. I'll take it in Dad's study." Katie listened, glad to connect with Kevin's world, enjoying the tone of his voice as he answered his mother. He sounded loving and happy as he spoke.

"Katherine? Still there?"

"Yes, I'm here, Mrs. Mandrell."

"Kevin will be right with you but, first, I need to thank you for all the help that you and your father gave him."

"Oh, I'm just glad that we were able to be there. What happened to him was terrible enough and–"

Kevin picked up the extension. "Okay, Mom. I've got it."

"Goodbye dear," he heard is mother say to Katie before hanging up.

"Hi, Katie."

"Hi, Kevin, how are you doing? Recovering well? Still in pain?"

"No, not much, I feel fine. Our family doctor checked me out yesterday. He didn't remove the butterflies, and said he admired your dad's expert work. He advised not to remove the bandages too soon as that might open the cuts.

"And you. How's my rescuer?"

"Fine, thank you." She apologized for not calling him sooner, explaining that she had just gotten his message, but he had been on her mind and she was planning to call him to see how he was doing.

Kevin told her that he knew she was okay since he and Billy had spoken for almost an hour, adding how easy it was to get along with Billy. That miserable kid, she thought, not saying a word.

"Ah, so, what did you two guys talk about for so long?"

"Mostly you."

"Me? Billy doesn't even know that I'm alive most of the time."

"Oh, he knows. From what I heard, he knows exactly where you are, what you're doing, who you're with, and so on, all the way to the flavor of Italian ice you like. Pineapple, isn't it?"

"That little stinker. He's always so cool, and doesn't give me the time of day, yet he blabs to complete strangers."

"Well, perhaps he doesn't believe I'm such a complete stranger. In any case, I can tell you this, he gave me the impression that he's deeply devoted to you. He wants you to be happy. I asked him what he liked, for a reward for helping me, but he said whatever you'd like."

"Ah, Kevin, you don't have to bring us anything. We'd just enjoy seeing you again."

"I know, but it will give me pleasure to do something for you guys. You can't deny me that."

"You have no idea how pleasant it is to hear a happy voice. I've had a trying couple of days and I'm not looking forward to a weekend with my parents in Westchester. But then I am, too. It's been a while since my mother and I spent some girl time together."

"What's troubling you?"

"Troubling me? That's a mild way of putting it. I received some unsettling information that I need time to sort out."

Kevin's voice dropped in timber. "You've been on my mind," he said. "You were the more memorable part of our day together. The mugging was nothing."

She responded in barely more than a whisper. "Really?"

"It was like a melody playing over and over in my head. I'd really like to see you again."

"I'd like that, too. Saturday after next is the big Italian Feast here. Would you like to come into the city? We could spend the day together uptown, and then you can enjoy an authentic Italian Festival here in Little Italy."

"Perfect, I'll call you Monday to firm up the details. And Katie, I'm really happy...you know."

"Me, too."

When Billy returned with the pizza, Katie hugged him.

"What's that for?" he yelled.

"You don't have to know."

He shrugged. "Women!"

When the phone rang again, Billy answered with, "It's your dime."

Katie heard a familiar female voice speaking loudly to him. It had to be Reggie. She heard Billy say, "Well, how do I do that?" A pause. "Okay, I get it. I listen to her, ask her what she wants to do, act like a gentleman and don't talk about sex. Okay," and then handed the phone over to Katie.

"Hi, Reggie, I knew it was you."

Reggie told her that she had been in a "Self-Sufficiency" meeting when Billy left the Center earlier. She called to wish him a good weekend and to support him because she knew he was anxious about what to say to Geraldine, on whom he had a crush.

Katie pulled the phone from her mouth and said to Billy, "Aha, Geraldine! And you were complaining about coming with me. What a phony."

Billy fumbled his pizza onto a plate.

Reggie asked if Kevin had called. She happy that they had spoken. With Billy eavesdropping, all Katie felt free to say was that they had a date to meet for the Feast.

Reggie knew that Katie was unable to speak openly but it didn't matter. Billy had caught on and began mooing Kevin's name in between bites of pizza. Reggie laughed when she heard him in the background.

Katie reminded her of their plans to visit the New York Cares facility the following week. They could continue their conversation then.

15.

Kevin heard the doorbell and went downstairs.

"I'll get it, Mom," he called. "It's most likely Timmy."
He opened the door, happy to greet his childhood friend, Timmy Cavallero. They gave each other a manly hug, and slapped their hands down on each other's shoulders as if wearing shoulder pads, reminiscent of their high school football years.
Timmy was taking the day off to catch up with his old friend on each other's lives.

Kevin led Timmy into the kitchen where he greeted Kevin's Mom. Like all Kevin's friends, Timmy loved her as a second mother. She had always been supportive and hospitable while they were growing up. Lunch at Kevin's had always been a treat for them. She made man-size hero sandwiches, piled high with cold cuts. This day was no exception. She had prepared lunch for them.

She was always willing to lend a sympathetic ear when they were upset over what they believed was an unfair parental decision. Timmy had fond memories of those times. He kissed her warmly on the cheek as they left the house. Kevin thanked her for the small cooler containing lunch and they were off to spend the day fishing at the beach.

Timmy spotted Kevin's bandages, and asked him if he had undergone surgery.

"Kind of," he said, and told him the story.

Timmy was one of a very few people to whom Kevin would ever open up. They were close friends, but more significant, Kevin knew that if he told Timmy something in confidence, you could take it to the bank, an expression that meant for them that the information shared was as safe as if placed in a bank vault. In turn, Timmy knew that Kevin would do the same for him.

Their backgrounds and childhood paths had been very similar. Both men's parents were educated professionals. Timmy's father had served in World War II field hospitals as an Army dentist, specializing in reconstructive dental surgery. Returning home after the war, he became a partner in a prominent Upper East Side dental practice.

His mother Margaret was the daughter of a retired New York City Internal Affairs Police Captain, who had spearheaded the effort for revolutionizing the department with state-of-the-art intelligence procedures.

Kevin's mother was a professional paleontologist and the recently retired Curator of a well-known Long Island Museum. His father Peter, a civil engineer, had served in the Navy as a Seabee officer. After leaving the service, he had continued his engineering career with the New York City Bridge and Tunnel Authority.

As boys growing up from similar backgrounds and living in a small upscale community, the two friends enjoyed happy lives, having more advantages than many children of their generation did. Active youngsters, like most boys, they got into trouble from time to time. Their antics included pranks on friends and teachers, and drinking. In their teen years, make-out sessions with girls was their specialty.

They were raised with a strong moral footing, enhanced by a good education and traditional values that included love of family and country–attributes that served well as the foundation for their respective adult lives.

The two men shared intelligence, and a keen curiosity for life. They achieved honors academically, and participated in after-school activities, music, and sports. Both had earned top of the class rankings, enhanced by a good-natured competitiveness. Whatever they undertook, they made it a goal to do it well.

After high school, they enrolled at different universities, yet their developmental paths remained similar. Both played in their college orchestra, and both joined the Reserve Officers' Training Corps, or ROTC.

Upon graduation, each served in the Korean War, although stationed in different divisions. Timmy served as a Second Lieutenant in the Military Police while Kevin served in the U.S Army Field Band, due to his unique status as a concert-level pianist, writer and arranger. He was called upon to perform at diplomatic functions throughout Asia and Europe.

After completing his military service, Timmy returned home and joined the FBI. From Quantico, he was assigned to the Chicago field office in the Criminal Division, specializing in kidnappings and capital murder cases. He earned a reputation for tackling complicated cases.

Later, he was promoted to the New York field office. There, he partnered with Colleen Murphy, a fellow Special Agent. Murphy had been a Supervisor in the FBI's Washington, DC, crime lab, also transferred to New York where they often worked cases together. It wasn't long before their relationship became the talk of the 23rd floor.

17.

Saturday morning. Kevin drew up in front of the famed Sherry Netherland Hotel, opposite Central Park. The uniformed doorman pointed him to a parking space a few car lengths ahead. His mother's Karmann Ghia, perfect for weaving through city traffic, easily negotiated the tight parking spot. He made haste toward the hotel, his stomach stirring with anticipation.

The sky was clear. The early morning sun brightened the tops of the American elms circling the Park. New York's most resented residents, throngs of pigeons, were busy foraging the remains of bread crusts and peanut shells left by visitors.

Uptown Fifth Avenue was as elegant as he remembered, though it was unusually quiet for a Saturday. The tranquility, Kevin noted, would be short-lived as the stir of tourists and resident dwellers seeking relaxation was already in the air.

As he approached the regal awning of the hotel, the doorman saluted him with a cheerful, "Good morning," and opened the door. Kevin motioned that he wouldn't be going in. The doorman took a few steps to join him. He folded his white gloved hands under the brass buttons of his gold-braided, military-style red coat and began searching for incoming taxicabs.

Turning to Kevin, a congenial smile on his face, he remarked, "Even after twenty-six years of tending the door I never get bored with the view."

Kevin nodded in agreement, glancing toward the majestic Plaza Hotel and the entrance to the Park across the way. All he could say was, "New York!"

Katie's arrival was signaled by the trumpeting horns of passing taxis. Her Checker Cab came to an abrupt stop directly before them. The doorman opened the rear door as Kevin paid the driver. They locked eyes for a moment gazing at each other, Katie fumbling as she juggled purse, sweater and a paper bag. Kevin took the bag and inhaled a fresh pastry aroma.

"I passed Ferrara's Pastry Shop, and just couldn't resist the aromas so I brought us some coffee and my favorite pastries."

Kevin said, "Let me see... chocolate-covered horns?"

Katie laughed. "Well, it's clear that Billy covered everything."

He took her arm and guided her across the street heading toward the Park. He acknowledged the doorman with a nod and a wave. The man responded with a thumbs up.

They circled around a street musician who was surrounded by a flock of variegated pigeons competing for space as he wrestled his violin from its case. They entered through the arches into the heart of the famous City landmark. Central Park, a sprawling green oasis, unfolded before them.

It was a special place where New Yorkers and tourists alike refreshed themselves within a haven of bucolic beauty amid the towering skyscrapers. The city could be forgotten as they strolled under a canopy of trees lining the myriad of small, quiet paths.

The noise of the city dropped away, becoming a distant drone fostering peace of mind. Sounds of children playing, skaters whizzing by, and musicians entertaining added to the ambiance.

They looked for an unoccupied bench on which to enjoy their goodies.

Kevin pointed to one in the distance. As he did, a straggly-haired vagrant seated nearby mistook his hand gesture as a command and gave up his bench, ranting in protest as he angrily scurried off grumbling.

They laughed and sat to enjoy Katie's breakfast of sweets. As Kevin lifted the lid of the coffee, he thanked her for her thoughtfulness and added, "This is probably not cool but I have not been able to get you out of my mind all week. I'm very happy to be with you again."

His words stunned her, and her eyes sparkled. "Well, is that all? No sleepless nights, tossing and turning with my image before your eyes?"

"You're brutal. Okay, how about this? Butterflies in my stomach and tingling all over my body at the thought of you."

"Well, that's somewhat better, but no cigar," she said with a mischievous laugh.

Katie felt herself welling up with happy relief. She reached toward him and caressed his face without a word. With her fingertip, she loosened a crumb of pastry from his lip.

Silently, exchanging glances, they devoured the delicious chocolate treats. Kevin told Katie that he had a surprise that might alter their plans for the day.

She raised her eyebrows, sipped her coffee and waited for his explanation.

"Well, I know you wanted to spend most of the morning in the Park and it's something that I really want to do, too, but we've just been invited to lunch with some great people in an extraordinary setting."

"What people, what place?" Her eyes grew wide, "Oh, gosh, whatever it is, I'm not dressed for it."

"You're perfect. That blue dress is stunning and you're altogether beautiful!"

Katie was thrown off-balance. This sweet, reserved man is a little unpredictable. It was a new, though welcome dimension to him. She noted that his demeanor that day was self-confident, charming, and romantic.

Look at him, Katie thought, a cowboy shirt, pale dungarees. So casual. Let's go with this. Let it unfold.

"This is my idea," he said, "what say we take a carriage ride after we finish our coffee? That way we can circle the park and have plenty of energy for a lunch and then the feast later on."

"Sounds like a plan to me."

They approached a Hansom carriage with a plumed white horse. The driver was dressed in ragged tails and a misshapen top hat. The carriage, lined in tufted leather and decorated at the seams with brass fasteners, made its way leisurely round and about as they chatted. The conversation turned to their personal histories.

"I had a high school sweetheart, Carmine. When we were kids, we talked about taking a coach ride together when we were adults."

"Yeah, my friend Timmy and I fantasized about taking girls for a ride to soften them for a make-out session amidst the trees in the park."

"I guess I'll have to keep my eye on you."

Katie spoke of her childhood, her relationship with Carmine and her friendship with the nun, Reggie.

"Reggie's parents were both alcoholics. I can tell you this because she has made her story public to witness the destructive effect that alcohol can have on one's life. She started to drink heavily in high school. She was underage of course, so she sought the help of an older family friend who would provide the booze for her.

"When she was drunk he took sexual advantage of her. She was eventually rescued by a nun who found her practically unconscious, lying in a doorway in close proximately to the convent house. The nuns took her in and through their charity and example she realized she was called to their life. Reggie was already at the mission when I was hired. That's how we became close."

Kevin spoke about his boyhood chums, women he had dated in college and his relationships and activities throughout the world.

"The Army recruited me to serve in their intelligence corps. I was promoted to First Lieutenant, and posted to work as Military Cultural Attaché at the US Embassy in Zurich, under the auspices of my musical ability."

Katie stared at him. She thought, I'm way out of my league here.

"At the completion of my tour of duty, they offered me a job with the State Department as a Foreign Service Cultural Attaché, and I remained in Switzerland, encouraged by my mentor, Professor Otto Siegfried, a great human being whom you will get to meet.

I also accepted a contract to perform with the Zurich Philharmonic Orchestra to do occasional concerts. Soon after my State Department superiors broadened my duties to assume the function of Cultural Liaison with the US Embassy in Bern, Switzerland."

"Looks like a lot of people have great regard for you."

Kevin said, "I guess I've been blessed."

"You're amazing. I've only heard or read about people like you in movies and books. A world traveler with a mission. Wow."

Kevin smiled shyly, moved by her generous comments.

"My position required extensive travel for the US State Department as part of the Diplomatic Corps, which allows me to perform with the Philharmonic throughout Europe, Russia and the Far East. I return to the States from time to time for briefings and R&R with my folks."

"That must be hard for them with you being away from home so much."

"Yes it has been, but for me, after seeing the carnage and devastation wrought by the Nazis and Imperial Japan, not mention the new threat from the Soviets, we can't allow it to happen again."

Katie was impressed as he shared his story. She learned that he was an intelligent, exciting, and complex man of many dimensions. She sensed that the down-to-earth demeanor he presented barely scratched the surface of who he was.

How can anybody bat against a pitcher like him? she wondered.

More and more as she listened, she saw that he was a big picture kind of person, a man with a deep sense of patriotism, family values, and moral fortitude. He wasn't a square or a musical egghead, but a vibrant man of action in every sense of the word. Balanced, she summed up.

This is too good to be true. Pinch me, I must be dreaming.

She was falling for him in a big way. He was someone that she could talk to. He listened to her and respected her opinions. She sensed that he was emotionally reserved, and could be shy. It might be hard at times for him to share his feelings. She appreciated the effort he was making to gain her trust about his intentions. She felt comfortable with him and believed that what she did not know about him would not turn out to be sinister or, worse–commonplace.

Kevin shared, as he had never been able to in his life. It amazed him how he could open up with Katie. They harmonized like the tones of a beautiful well-played chord. He knew that their lifestyles were different, but she was a joyful woman, strong-minded, imaginative and intelligent. He knew that she could be comfortable in his world, and up for any challenge she faced.

18.

Stepping from the carriage, they had bonded in a loving way that neither of them could have predicted. They walked to his car.

"Is this the best you can do? A kiddy-car?"

He laughed and opened the door for her. She slipped in. He winked as he closed it.

"Prepare for the ride of your life," he said.

Kevin wove through traffic, and in a few short minutes they were in front of the US Mission to the UN on First Avenue. As they exited the car, Kevin grabbed a leather briefcase that had been wedged behind his seat. A security guard approached them and asked Kevin's name as he checked a clipboard to confirm Kevin's appointment.

"This must be Miss Burdino," the officer said, welcoming Katie.

Surprised that he knew her name, Katie nodded in agreement. The guard asked Kevin for the car keys and assured him that he would take care of it while looking at it as if it were a toy.

"Come on, it has a Porsche engine," Kevin told him with a salute.

As they entered the building, a Marine sergeant in full regalia greeted them, asked for identification, and escorted them to a large foyer. Katie was overwhelmed with anticipation. Gripping Kevin's hand, she asked him in some disbelief, "We're having lunch at the US Mission to the UN?"

Kevin smiled, "Oh, there's more, Katie."

The Marine guard invited them to be seated and advised that the Ambassador's executive assistant would be out to collect them shortly. Katie's eyes rolled up in disbelief. She whispered to Kevin, "My friend Reggie is just going to flip out over this." He tightened his grip on her hand.

A tall, well-dressed man in his late forties came down the winding marble staircase.

"I don't know if you remember me. I'm Jack Osborne," He said as he extended his hand to Kevin. "We met at the South African Embassy in London a couple of years ago, and I truly enjoyed your music."

"Yes, I remember." Kevin smiled. "Didn't you almost spill a glass of champagne on the piano keyboard?"

"One and the same, one and the same, that's me! I'm notorious for it," Osborne said.

He turned his attention to Katie. "You must be Miss Burdino. It's a pleasure to meet you."

He said to Kevin, "There's an old friend upstairs who wants to say hello." Shifting his attention to Katie, he said, "If you can spare Kevin for just a little while, I'll give you a personal tour of our facility. There's a lot of history here, and some of the artwork is priceless. We'll meet up with Kevin in the salon, say, in about twenty-minutes."

Katie nodded agreement. Osborne asked the Marine guard to escort Kevin to suite Two East.

Kevin squeezed her hand before letting it go, and then followed the Marine up the stairs. He glanced back to her over the carved mahogany banister and could see that she was aglow and looking beautiful.

He entered the room to which the Marine had escorted him and caught sight of a tall, lanky figure in a black suit, facing the window. He called out, "Malcolm, is that you?" as the older man turned to greet him. The two men moved forward to embrace.

"Kevin, my boy, it's been years, hasn't it? How's the young man who saved my life?" Malcolm asked warmly.

"I'm fine. It's good to be home," Kevin answered.

Malcolm led Kevin toward a bookcase on the far wall. He reached up to the third shelf and pulled out a leather-bound copy of Machiavelli's, The Prince about two inches wide.

"My favorite," the older man said.

As the book slid out, there was a click as the door to the room locked shut. The bookshelf swung wide, revealing a lead-lined steel door and a mechanical keypad. Malcolm pushed a series of numbers and the vault opened.

"Technology," he whispered.

They entered a large windowless room furnished with a row of wood filing cabinets, a large antique conference table, and high back, thickly tufted leather chairs. At the back wall of the room were two large, richly upholstered leather chairs, between which rested a small, decoratively hand-carved cherry wood bar. Malcolm invited Kevin to sit, and asked him if he would like a drink.

"Yes, thank you."

"Is it still Campari and soda?"

"Yes. You've got some memory, Malcolm."

"Just part of the job, my boy."

"Am I right in thinking that part of the job tomorrow will include Agency business? I thought I might have some time off while I was home."

"Well, yes, Kevin, I understand, but I'm actually going to ask you for a favor. I know you're on leave and I don't like to interfere with that. If anyone deserves time off, it's you."

Malcolm reached into his pocket and pulled out a small brown envelope. "This is from the Director. A kind of bonus. We just did your performance evaluation together. He considers your background as a successful Army Intelligence officer, concert pianist, and arranger impressive, and he noted your reputation for self-discipline.

"But what really rings his bell is your affinity for calculated risk-taking and the cool demeanor you exhibit in dangerous situations. You should be aware that he considers you one of our most valuable covert operatives. I get the feeling you're on the short list for a Deputy Station Chief spot."

"Thanks, Malcolm," Kevin said. He moved in his seat, uncomfortable with the praise. "I'm sure you had a lot to do with the evaluation, but I wasn't angling for a reward."

"Well, sure, but he was really pleased with the job you did in Damascus. The information has proven invaluable."

"Yes, everything seemed to fall into place on that one," Kevin agreed.

"Actually, the Damascus information led us to the delivery which we need you to accept for us tomorrow. The Algerian attaché is a known aficionado of the concert piano. He will bring a piece of music to discuss with you after your performance tomorrow, which I understand is Rachmaninoff's Second Concerto. You will invite him to sit with you at the piano, offering to help him with difficulties he has had with this piece. After you have done so, you will make the switch."

"Who dreams up these scenarios?" Kevin asked stroking his brow.

"Our creative analysts, of course. Having acknowledged his thanks, you will pack up your music, positioning the transferred material as the third piece from the top and taking care not to crease it. The Marine Guard will approach you as you lift your rather bulky music bag and ask if he can help by putting it in the car for you. Grateful for his help, you will hand the bag over to him and proceed to mingle with the guests."

Kevin nodded his understanding.

"Stay and chat as long as you like, but for no less than ten minutes. At the same time as you're mingling, the attaché will be setting the stage for an invitation for you to play at a festival in Algiers sometime in the spring, got it?"

"Ten-four."

"Also, if the Algerian Ambassador bites, you will tell him that you would be honored but that you will need to wire the Philharmonic's scheduling secretary to confirm your availability with a firm date. Note that this assignment is not related to your project with the watchmaker. And, by the way, the abort code is 'quarter-note by two.'"

Kevin stored the instructions into memory. Malcolm added, "Another thing, you're going to be assigned to a new handler on the continent. I will arrange a meeting for you before your return to Zurich. In the meantime, I will remain your person here in the States. Your contact code for me on the Algerian matter is: 'Johnny One-Note.'"

With that, Malcolm indicated that this briefing was over by closing his notebook.

Reverting to his former stance as cordial colleague and friend, Malcolm complimented Kevin on his choice of female companion, commenting on how attractive she was, admitting he had viewed her on the security screen as they entered the building.

He asked Kevin if this was a serious relationship. Kevin nodded, sharing with Malcolm that they had only recently met but that he had serious feelings for her and that she had confirmed a serious interest as well. Malcolm announced delight for this development, exhibiting fatherly approval as he hugged Kevin.

"I apologize that I'm unable to join you for lunch, I'm off to DC for a briefing at the White House and then on to New Mexico."

Kevin said, "It must be lonely at the top."

"You have that right, my boy."

Malcolm told Kevin he planned to meet with him upon his return sometime the following month, and asked Kevin if he needed anything else. He made it clear also that he was aware of the incident during Kevin's foray into lower Manhattan and that Katie had been vetted, though her father's background was questionable. He ended by telling Kevin that he was relieved that Kevin had not been badly injured.

Kevin admitted to Malcolm that he never ceased to amaze him. Malcolm smiled, hugged him again and told him that he watched out for his people, appreciative of their dedication, patriotism, and courage.

As they left, locking the secure room behind them, Malcolm turned down the hall in the direction of the fire exit. Kevin was escorted back down the stairway to the main salon, there finding Katie seated at a table in the grand room conversing with the Ambassador and his secretary. As he approached, he heard them speaking about NYU.

The Ambassador rose to greet Kevin, complimenting him on his charming companion. Kevin was happy that Katie was enjoying herself. It confirmed his previous belief that she was not intimidated at all by mixing with powerful people.

Kevin's music bag was placed across the room at the feet of a Steinway piano. He excused himself, touching Katie's shoulder as he passed.

At the piano, He opened the music bag, pulled out his portfolio and found his copy of the Rachmaninoff piece. He checked that it was in order.

This would be the first time Katie would hear him play. He was surprised to feel a twinge of the old anxiety. This first exposure of his skill must be made special for her.

He began to warm up, testing the tone and resonance of the piano, with Gershwin's Rhapsody in Blue. As he played, he saw Katie's attention turn to him. She sat absorbed. As he closed, she hurried across the room, and threw her arms around him with a hug of delight.

They sauntered back to the table, hand in hand. Osborne and the Ambassador rose to applaud him. Osborne raised his wine glass, "Bravo, Kevin."

They sat and settled in for lunch.

"I was particularly pleased to hear Miss Burdino's keen perspective on Andrew Wyeth, his life and his art, particularly some lesser known works that I esteem dearly," Osborne said.

The Ambassador turned to Katie, tipped his glass and commended her intelligent insights regarding current world events and situations, diplomatic and political, which were much enjoyed during their short conversation.

It was Kevin's turn to be gratified as sincere accolades were visited upon her.

Rising from the table, the Ambassador invited Katie to join him and his entourage for Kevin's performance and the banquet the following day. Katie accepted with a broad smile and mild palpitations. Kevin thanked the Ambassador and Osborne both. Katie was overwhelmed.

As the Marine Guard helped them into the car, she nearly mistook the helping hand he offered for a handshake, pulling away just in time. When they pushed off, she exploded with nervous laughter, exhaling a whole day's bounty of pent-up anxiety mixed with glee. As they drove, Katie sat back reliving the afternoon and winding down from the excitement, and thinking about Kevin.

This is too good to be true. He seems to be everything a woman could want. He's sweet, unpredictable in a good way, bright, talented, more than a little mysterious, and good looking to boot.

Kevin broke into her thoughts. "I hope that was fun for you. Tomorrow will be more formal but we'll have an opportunity to goof on the rich and powerful."

"Kevin Mandrell. You're a madman. It was a wonderful day, but, one big but. How could you not say anything? Look at the way I've dressed. I was going to a picnic and wound up..."

"Ah, but you're so beautiful and smart. You disarmed premier diplomats. Had them eating out of your hand, and you know it!"

Katie blushed and took his hand.

"Kevin, I will never forget this day. Thank you."

"Hey! The day's not over. Now it's your turn to introduce me to the royalty of Little Italy."

"Yeah, and all the premier gangsters," she responded with a hint of dark comedy.

Kevin drove for a few blocks and pulled to the curb in front of Lord and Taylor.

"I have another surprise for you."

"What?" Katie asked.

"My mother wants to buy you a dress for tomorrow. She–"

"What? I can't accept that. You are a madman, aren't you? I can't accept a dress."

"My mother thought you might react this way so she sent this note."

He reached into his breast pocket, and removed a cream-colored envelope.

"For you," he said.

Katie opened the envelope with her fingertips as if it were a document of great financial worth. She read his mother's words, written in a perfect Anglo calligraphy.

Katie,

Please accept this gift. I want this day to be perfect for both you and Kevin. I'm so very grateful for the care you gave him. Moreover, just between us women, I know he is crazy about you and I'm looking forward to meeting you soon.

Enjoy, Lillian.

P.S. I know Kevin will ask you what I wrote. Tell him to bug off.

Katie just sighed with happiness as Kevin gently reached his hand out toher with a grateful smile.

19.

The Feast of St. Rocco honored a man of God born into French nobility in 1340 A.D. Upon his birth, it was noted that baby Rocco had a red cross-shaped birthmark on the left side of his chest. He displayed from a young age an inborn natural devotion to God and the Blessed Mother. Orphaned at an early age, he was left in the care of his uncle, the Duke of Montpellier.

While still a young man, he took a vow of poverty and distributed his inheritance to the poor. He divested himself of the clothes of a nobleman, donning the rough garments of a pilgrim for his journey to Rome.

This took place in a time of pestilence. Italy was besieged by the black plague. One out of three people died, many too poor to escape in any way. Rocco worked tirelessly on their behalf and he soon became known for curing victims of the disease. He sought healing on their behalf from God. He prayed and blessed them with the sign of the Cross. Healings–miracles–resulting from his care were attributed to God's intervention at Rocco's request.

Rocco contracted the plague. An open sore on his leg revealed his infection and he was expelled from Rome. To survive, he took shelter in a cave. His bed was made of leaves. He drank water from a small stream nearby. He was faithfully visited by a dog that continued to bring him bread as a means of sustenance. The dog always refused to eat any of the food himself.

The dog lived in a nearby castle and attracted the curiosity of the noble Lord of that castle, who spied the animal loping off as if he were going on a mission. His curiosity aroused, the Lord followed his dog into the woods, where he found Rocco near death. Taking pity on him, the nobleman brought Rocco to his castle where he recovered.

Rocco traveled through northern Italy for several years before returning to his birthplace in France. He arrived, suffering, weak, and so unfamiliar that the townspeople did not recognize him. He was thrown into jail accused of being a spy, although there was no evidence of his committing the crime.

He spent five years in prison. Then, on August 16, 1378, a guard entering Rocco's cell found Rocco near death. His cell was illuminated by a strange blue light that radiated from his body. Learning of this phenomenon, the town noble questioned Rocco as to his identity. He faintly replied, "I'm your nephew, Rocco."

His uncle knew that only one thing could prove this assertion. He had Rocco disrobed. There, on the left side of his chest was the red cross-like mark. The noble was convinced of his identity, but it was too late. Very soon thereafter, Rocco died.

Many miracles were reported and acknowledged after his death. He is commemorated every year in the month of August. On that day, many Italian American communities–Little Italy's–bustle with parades that wind through the Italian neighborhoods.

The festivities usually commence with a procession of parish priests, local officials and the leadership of many church and civic organizations. Supported by the harmonious sounds of brass instruments and the street beat of a skilled drum line setting the cadence, the procession is long and joyous.

In Manhattan, the Drum & Bugle Corp contingency for many years came from a namesake parish in Brooklyn, St. Rocco's Church. The marchers called themselves the Golden Aces. They were noted for their renditions of Christ the King and Lady of Spain, with overtones from a row of melodic glockenspiels complemented by the expert twirling of drumsticks and batons.

Church groups and Italian-American Club members proudly marched under their banners, following The Holy Name Society, Legion of Mary, and The Sons of Italy. They waved enthusiastically to familiar faces, to onlookers and passersby.

A large antique statue of Saint Rocco, borne on the shoulders of ten pallbearers, was a prominent feature of the parade. The statue was adorned with a satin robe on which donations of paper money are pinned by enthusiastic attendants. Volunteers circulated through the crowds seeking further cash donations in the Saint's honor to support the Church and local hospitals that served the area.

The procession made scheduled stops in front of Social Clubs, where refreshments were provided to the marchers, and club members proudly contributed donations. The money was ceremoniously pinned to the Saint's robe, invoking the applause of neighborhood well-wishers who lined the sidewalks.

There was, however, a dark side to the celebration that was unknown to most visitors. They were not aware that some of the clubs were notorious mob hangouts disguised as legitimate meeting places and used to plan illegal activities from prostitution to gambling and loan sharking to murder.

Some were headquarters of extortion rackets that controlled the neighborhood merchants. Their infamous practices took place under the shadow of the holy statue resting at their doorsteps.

This festival, and those honoring other saints, provided the opportunity for mobsters to cast themselves publically in the benevolent light of good citizenship. Their facade of generosity and love for the community helped them propagate the myth that the residents of this community were safe and secure only due to Mafia protection.

The statue continued to move through the crowded, festively decorated streets, led by a traditional Italian street band. The musicians' attire, faded white shirts hanging over black trousers, and worn narrow black ties draping short of their collars, all added to the small town ambiance.

They were followed by straggling members and friends marching behind. The band often stopped to play a special Italian song for a powerful mob captain and his cohort in appreciation for a large donation. The captain, in turn, rewarded the band with glasses of homemade red wine before they marched on. The ritual added to the revelry.

After making a complete circle of the community, the procession returned to the Church. The statue was placed upon its steps under a tassel-fringed canvas, an embroidered gold canopy, where it stayed for the length of the feast. Church volunteers, also in white shirts with ribbons and pictures of the saint attached, positioned themselves nearby to continue to accept and pin on donations.

20.

The crowd waited patiently for their Pastor, Monsignor Scalvo, who in his official function marked the opening of the Feast with great fanfare, welcoming the gathered visitors, and turning on the festival lights. Each night, a new Italian band provided entertainment, accompanied by robust, operatic singers and others whose voices resonated through the neighborhood streets well into the wee hours of the morning.

As the last opening words ended, the air was filled with the aroma of grilled Italian sausages, onions and peppers, the calling sounds of roulette wheels spinning, and the barking of vendors trying to attract people to their amusement tents that filled the streets.

Since the influx of Italian immigrants in the late nineteenth and early twentieth century, people had been coming from all the five boroughs, New Jersey, Long Island, and the entire metropolitan area to relive an old world tradition and to give their children a glimpse of their old cultural roots in the largest Italian community outside the home country.

Katie felt she might be viewing this traditional celebration with a more complicated, perhaps bittersweet, memory. One of wonderful joy for the promise of a new life with a much loved man, but her joy was clouded by her keen awareness of the impending darkness threatening to permeate the homes and hearts of those most close to her.

"Hi, Katie doll. Hi, Kevin."

"Hi, Anthony."

Anthony helped them out of their car, and said, "Katie, your Momma and Papa are at Carmella's with your Godparents."

Without waiting for a response, Anthony slipped behind the wheel of their car. Pointing to the crowded street, he shouted through the window, "This is gonna be-a the best festa of all."

He wished them a nice time and drove Kevin's car into the jammed parking lot of the funeral parlor.

Katie braced Kevin's arm in preparation of what was to come.

"I have a surprise for you," she said. "I hope you won't mind. My father wants me to introduce you to my mother. They always start the first night of the Feast at Carmella's with my Godparents and all their childhood friends. Carmella makes them traditional Sicilian dishes and joins them for dinner."

"That's okay with me. I'm having the best day of my life."

"We'll see if you feel the same way after the third degree."

They laughed as Kevin put his arm around her and turned them toward the restaurant. Katie was overtaken with a joy that reflected in the bounce of her step and the beam in her smile.

Katie spotted her Godmother with her nose pressed to the restaurant window watching them with her mouth chattering away. *I know what she's telling them,* Katie mused to herself, *He's very handsome. If only he were Italiano.*

As they stepped inside the restaurant, Don Peppino said, "I think he has his arm around her."

Katie's mother stared at her husband, Birdie. "Don't ask him a lot of questions. Don't pry. You better not," Katie's mother admonished Birdie. "Remember, they're not kids. Be nice to him. He's a man, not a teenage boy taking her to a church dance."

Then she turned to Don Peppino's wife, "Birdie's terrible. He torments her. She has a right to her own life."

"Of course she does," the woman agreed with a cross look at Birdie.

Birdie and Don Peppino sat smug, shaking their heads and grinning. "Typical women."

The couple entered the crowded restaurant, weaving their way between tables crowded with diners who laughed and talked. The diners' hands became animated as conversations became intense, and at every table there was the flash of forks shoveling Carmella's delectables into anxiously awaiting mouths.

When Katie and Kevin arrived at their table, the men there rose. Katie's father shook Kevin's hand and introduced him to his wife and the others at the table. Birdie proudly remarked, "Kevin, your wounds seem to be healing well."

"Yes," Kevin answered, "thanks to you." Kevin thanked him again, reporting that his family doctor had also complimented Birdie's work.

Birdie invited Katie and Kevin to take chairs between himself and Katie's mom. Before sitting, Katie left for ladies room. This apparently was the cue for all the matriarchs at the table to join her, and Don Peppino joked to the men, "It's an odd phenomenon that women love peeing together."

Even before Katie made it to the Ladies Room, the interrogation began. Carmella emerged from the kitchen upon hearing their chatter. But they were so hungry for details they went right past her without seeing her standing there, drying off a large zucchini. Carmella followed the line into the restroom, the squash upright in her hand. Katie was backed into a stall, captive to the women's insistence for details of her date.

Carmella shouted, "So, what happened?"

Katie's mother, trying to rescue her daughter, derailed the inquisition, and answered for her, "They had a date. They spent the day uptown. Oh, he's such a handsome boy."

Katie exited the stall, smiling, understanding their ways and having prepared herself. She had resolved not to spoil their fun.

"It's okay, Mom. Cool your pits, but I will tell you this much. First, we meandered through Central Park, followed by a ride around the Park in a romantic horse-drawn carriage. Then off to the US Mission to the UN where I had an escorted tour, followed by a magnificent lunch. Imagine me sitting at the table with the Ambassador, his Aide and their special guests. During lunch Kevin performed a beautiful piano Concerto by Rachmaninoff for an important group of officials and some society types."

The women had stopped dead, staring at her with their mouths open, locked in shock, as Katie continued.

"The applause for Kevin's performance was overwhelming, and after we left, we did a little shopping. All I can say about my date is it was a perfect day with a perfect man and that's going to have to do for now."

Smiling at her silent and awed audience, she added, "So, let's get a grip, go back to our table, and talk about other things."

As the group returned to their table, an elderly woman entered the Ladies Room and saw Carmella standing there still clutching the zucchini. She just shook her head and muttered "Ma, tutti pazzi!"–they're all crazy–and turned around and left straightaway.

Carmella laughed and followed the other women out to the table. She said, "I'm sure everybody's hungry. Go. Sit. Have some vino. I'll bring everything out in a few minutes." As they moved away, Carmella kissed Katie, telling her how happy she was for her.

As Katie got back to the table with her entourage in tow, they heard Don Peppino telling Kevin how taken Mario was with his family's house. Moreover, he repeated that if he ever wanted to sell it, he would buy it for his mother. Katie sat down next to Kevin, touching the back of his neck with affection. Kevin sighed with relief.

Carmella arrived at the table with her son Dominick and Mimi. They all carried large trays overflowing with aromatic Sicilian fare. Carmella presented a selection of fresh antipasti and rice balls, Dominick held a giant bowl of angel hair pasta dressed with garlic and oil, and Mimi followed with a platter of seafood Fra Diavalo over linguine. Katie cautioned Kevin not to overeat as he would want to sample food from the street vendors later on.

The women shared the titillating tidbits they had heard from Katie in the ladies room with their husbands. The men were duly impressed about her welcome at the US Mission. But despite their happiness for Katie, they were naturally suspicious and less than thrilled to hear of Kevin's close ties to government officials. Who might he tell if he got a glimpse of how they ran the neighborhood? Nevertheless, dinner proceeded in familial conviviality, culminating with Italian desserts and espresso, and soothing after-dinner cordials.

When dinner was over, Dominick, Mimi, and Angie joined Kevin and Katie for a stroll to the Feast. They agreed to meet their parents later at the bandstand to hear the traditional Italian musicians and operatic singers.

21.

The lighthearted group made their way through the decorated, well-lit streets. Encouraged by the barkers, they stopped to try their hands at various games of chance. Katie noticed how playful and affectionate Dominick behaved toward Mimi, letting down his guard to insure that she had a pleasant evening. He even let her take his arm. When she joked with him, asking if he would allow it, he patted her hand without uttering a word. Mimi beamed.

Katie greeted people she knew and introduced Kevin as her friend, blushing as she did. The responses were classic: "It's about time you had some happiness," and "God bless the both of you," and "Remember, time doesn't wait for anyone."

Kevin laughed, understanding that "my friend," carried a deeper meaning in this neighborhood.

On the way to the bandstand, Kevin found himself as determined as any adolescent to win a stuffed animal for Katie. Spotting a shooting game, he paid for all of his companions to try their luck. All failed to win a prize. He, however, shot the "Star off the Page" with a BB gun every time, quitting only after complaints of what to do with the many stuffed animals. He had won two each for Katie and Mimi. Dominick expressed awe with a puff of his rounded cheeks, repeating, "I don't believe this."

Katie, thrilled at Kevin's skill, wondered what else about him she had yet to learn. Who are you, Kevin Mandrell?

At the bandstand, they scanned the crowd for Katie's parents. Katie heard an elderly woman calling to her in Italian. Turning, she saw Carmine's Aunt Paulina. She stopped and greeted her and introduced Kevin.

"So, how are you?"

"Oh, please," the old woman, sighed. "How could I be? I'm full of pains from old age, sad memories. I was just thinking of how much Carmine loved the Fiesta. I used to take him every year when he was a little boy. I miss him so much."

"Aunt Paulina, I miss him too."

"I don't know what's going on, Katie. All my friends are dying. One right after the other. They find them in their beds all dressed up, their hair combed like for a wake."

Kevin listened, jolted by the woman's words, remembering the conversation at the beach with Timmy. Katie tried to console the old woman, pained by her sadness. As they began to move on, Kevin turned to the sweet old woman, clasped her hands and cautioned her to take care of herself and to be sure not to let strangers into her home. Katie wondered, why did he caution someone he'd just met like that?

Katie spotted her father and godfather engrossed in a heated conversation. The aged Chairman of the Feast, Marco Colombo, was red faced and gesturing with his hands in typical dramatic Italian style.

Birdie greeted them and asked if they were having fun. Dominick jested, "Cumpari Birdie, we're having fun, but it doesn't look like you guys are!"

"Well, we're a little upset. Marco just received a call from the band leader. Their bus broke down and they're going to be at least an hour late. Maybe more," Birdie said. "Monsignor is ready to give the Blessing, the Mayor is supposed to give a short speech about Italian culture, but he can't stay too long, he's scheduled at another engagement. So, it looks like when they're finished there will be no music. And, there's no one to accompany the singer, so she's very upset, too."

Katie turned to Kevin. She tightened the grip on his hand. He understood her plea. "I don't mind," he whispered to her.

"Mr. Burdino," he said, "I'll be glad to help. I can accompany your vocalist on the piano."

Katie's father took Kevin's hand. "Thank you, thank you," he repeated. With a broad smile, he said to the festival chairman, "Marco, why am I always the one to pull you out of the fire?"

Within minutes, the chairman escorted Kevin up the wooden steps to the ornate, lighted bandstand and introduced him to the robust, Italian operatic singer, Maria Vitale. As she spoke no English, the chairman translated for her. During the conversation, her eyes, starting at Kevin's hairline, scanned him down to his shoes. She traced him back up to his hands and stared at them. Her brow was scrunched and she looked down her nose at him, even though he stood a full head taller.

Handing Kevin the music, her face was marked with a tinge of worry. Crossing her fingers, she took position beside him as he sat at the piano. He reviewed the music. When she heard his warm up, her countenance relaxed.

The dignitaries sat. Monsignor welcomed the crowd reminding them of the importance of their financial support, heaping guilt upon them so they would want to mimic the generosity of Saint Rocco.

The crowd applauded the Mayor's flowery words about the Italian immigrant population and its contribution to Little Italy, the city, and to American society overall.

Monsignor Scalvo returned to the microphone and read from notes. He introduced Maria Vitale. She was known in the Italian community and opera circles, but had never achieved the international career for which she had hoped, and had retired early to teach in the US. She rose to jubilant applause. Monsignor also introduced Kevin as a world renowned pianist who would accompany Maria until the band arrived. On the final words the Monsignor lifted his eyes to God and crossed himself.

The Soprano spat air at his words "world renowned," and tightened her lips with a hint of jealousy. Scalvo motioned to Kevin to stand while eyeballing bio notes provided hastily by Birdie. He introduced him as a member of the Zurich Symphony Orchestra, and said that he had played for Heads of State.

The Monsignor took the prima donna by the hand and escorted her with great pride to the microphone. She turned to Kevin and signaled her readiness by waving a silk handkerchief which she then draped it from the lace cuff of her sleeve. The crowd fell silent as Kevin began the introduction to Una Voce Poca Fa– "A voice has just echoed here into my heart."

Vitale's eyes widened as she heard him play. Katie beamed with pride, admiration, and gratitude, knowing how taken her parents and their friends must be by the beauty of his music. Just as Kevin and Maria finished her final piece, O Solo Mio, the musicians arrived.

The crowd applauded with fervor. Kevin followed Maria down the steps, where she drowned him with a juicy kiss to his lips in appreciation. He turned beet red. Katie waited as the singer embraced Kevin with a bounce of her chest in another gesture of appreciation. Katie choked with laughter. Poor Kevin, what have you gotten yourself into?

Mario stood next to Katie and also had a hearty laugh at the scene. When Kevin was able to disentangle himself from the vocalist, Mario took his hands with respect, complimented him, and escorted him to the officials assembled in front of the Social Club. Mario thought, *this mayonnaise American has wound up in a pot of tomato sauce.*

Don Peppino embraced him and handed him a glass of Strega, a traditional Sicilian cordial. He introduced Kevin to the club members who were seated at card tables. As they made their way through the maze of chairs, the men came to their feet, bowing their heads and kissing Don Peppino as a sign of respect.

Don Peppino took Kevin's hand and led him toward a metal barbeque pit constructed from oil drums cut in half lengthwise, welded together and filled with hot flaming charcoal. Large strips of steak sizzled as they were dressed in olive oil and aromatic Italian spices.

Joined by Birdie, they introduced Kevin to the cook. "Kevin, I'd like you to meet our childhood friend, Tomasso Fingarro."

Tomasso raised his hands, motioning them to wait as he wiped them on a towel and handed the fork to a huge man, posted directly behind. Kevin noticed that he responded without hesitation, taking the utensil from him, while Fingers came around to the front of the barbeque and took Kevin's hand.

"Nice to meet you," Fingarro said. "This is our ritual each year. My job is to grill the horse-meat steaks."

Birdie chimed in, "We've been doing this for over thirty years. Sometimes under difficult conditions."

Fingarro asked Don Peppino, "Where's Anthony? He likes to get the first piece."

"He'll be here in few minutes. He's getting the parking lot organized."

"A few minutes? He should have been here an hour ago!"

Looking at his watch, Birdie explained to Kevin that Fingarro, his late wife Concetta-Marie, Carmella, Don Peppino and Anthony grew up together on Hester Street and that the feast was an annual reunion. No one was ever late.

Fingarro–Fingers, in neighborhood parlance–moved next to Kevin as if waiting for an opportune moment to chat. He took Kevin's arm, motioning him toward the doorway of the club. Kevin followed him in, noting that the men seated inside bowed their heads, then vacated the room as the two entered.

The older man gave Kevin the history of the social club, telling him that his father and the fathers of his friends, whom he called "old timers," used it as a meeting place. It was their center of entertainment. A sanctuary of where they played cards, and held dances, christenings, weddings, and parties.

Pointing to an old picture of St. Francis begging for alms, mounted on the wall behind the bar, he told Kevin that they named it after the saint because he and his group all came from poor family backgrounds and St. Francis was the patron saint of the poor.

Kevin sensed that Fingers wanted to share something more with him. As they reached the bar, he invited Kevin to sit, looking toward the front door with a smile, as if he had pulled off a caper on his friends by taking Kevin from them. He reached for an antique crystal decanter that sat on a silver tray, and poured two shots of clear liqueur. He handed one to Kevin, and spoke in a low tone.

"Homemade grappa. From wine grapes, but not wine. It's very strong, and symbolizes the strength of the Italian people."

He lifted his glass. Kevin did the same as Fingers toasted "salute," and they emptied their glasses.

Fingers, his tone serious, said, "I'm sorry for that problem you had. I can assure you it won't happen again. How are you doing? You're lucky they didn't hurt your hands."

Kevin assured him that he was fine and that if hadn't happened he wouldn't have met Katie and Billy.

"Oh, Billy, he's a piece of work. You know he's my son?" Kevin was startled at this. Fingers continued, explaining that Billy had come to see him after the incident. "He was very impressed by the number you did on those punks but he insisted that something had to be done about those thugs.

"Billy must like you a lot to come and talk to me. He's got it in for me since his mother died. He refuses to live with me, talk to me, or take any money from me. Luckily, Caterina and her mother do a good job taking care of him. But what a mouth on him! He's somethin', isn't he?"

Fingers led Kevin to the door where Kevin expressed his thanks for the special honor of having a drink with him. Kevin thought, *this guy is eerie. On the surface, a gentleman, cordial, making me feel welcome. But underneath, I can feel he's as dark as the devil.*

Kevin studied the old man. Slight build, neatly dressed, soft spoken and slow paced, but his eyes remained cold and piercing, with no hint of emotion.

As they ambled back to the street, Kevin spotted Katie with her parents. He read a mixture of concern and protectiveness on her face. She placed her arm under his as they said their good-byes.

Kevin said, "I have an appointment to meet with the watch-maker DiGiaccomo."

Birdie questioned his wife, "What was that about? Watch-maker. Where they are going? Why?"

"Oh, come on honey," she replied. "Don't you remember when we were young?"

He smiled and shook his head, still uneasy, and unconvinced.

22.

Katie led Kevin through the festival streets at a brisk pace. He stopped her and studied her face for meaning before asking about her haste. She told him that she didn't want him to miss seeing the watchmaker. He knew there had to be something else going on, as if she was trying to shield him from something. As they got closer to the watch shop, she seemed to relax. She loosened her grip on his hand to one more tender while slowing her stride.

People were standing in front of the shop, smiling and telling stories, holding glasses of red wine and enjoying the festive evening. At their approach, Katie was greeted warmly in Italian and directed inside to DiGiaccomo. They found him pouring wine for a crowd gathered around him.

He took their hands and insisted that they have some wine as he introduced them to his friends. One of the women recognized Katie. Her deceased daughter had been a schoolmate of Katie. The woman took her aside to speak with her.

DiGiaccomo used the moment to excuse himself with Kevin to the back office. Privacy assured, the old man addressed Kevin in a more professional tone and asked why spy handlers had contacted him at this time.

"They need to activate you for a short period" Kevin said. "Only you can do this work. They're asking you for a special favor."

The watchmaker argued, "Come on, I'm an old man. I gave them the best part of my life, and I'm done. I don't have it in me. I'm over the hill and I fear for myself and my family. My cover will not hold with all these Mafiosi around here."

"The work will not be here and it will be short-lived. What do I tell them?"

"Tell them I'll accept only technical, no physical stuff. And something for my grandson's future."

"Okay. Got it. I don't know who will handle you. Bosco will meet you himself at your next doctor's appointment and give you the package. He really wants to see you again, he sent his regards."

"Yeah," the old man responded, "we did a lot together."

"Do you need tools?"

The old man nodded in the affirmative and said, "I will prepare a list and give it to Bosco. There are some new things I could use." Then he asked, "Is Katie involved in this?"

"No, definitely not. We just met. She's special to me on a personal level."

The old man's eyes rolled up in a hopeful gesture and said, "She is special to me, too. I have developed a fondness for her. She has the spirit of an angel."

He stared hard at Kevin, who realized he was being cautioned to keep Katie out of harm's way.

After a moment DiGiaccomo said, "Okay, let me get Julio. He'll give you the rundown on the film you brought us."

While he waited, Kevin saw an engraved wooden plaque, "Jocko's Place," on the wall. He presumed the moniker was the old man's nickname.

Jocko's workspace was well organized for easy access to his tools and clock parts. A picture of his daughter cradling his grandson also hung on the wall just above the arm of an extended magnification light. The room had a life to it, Kevin mused, *it's as if it had taken the occupant's personality into its turn of the century presentation. A comfortable place for a man alone with tragic memories of loss and horrific battles.*

Kevin was aware of the inner strength of this man, Jocko, who had accepted his fate and remained dedicated to fighting injustice with a reservoir of fortitude that would carry him through the reflections and regrets of his later years. Malcolm, Kevin's agency mentor, had shared stories of the watchmaker over the years. He regarded him as a man with great faith in God who had suffered the sorrows of Job.

A man who had suffered the loss of his wife and son in an allied bombing, and the subsequent rescue of his infant daughter from the rubble having suffered second degree burns across her little body.

After she had spent many months of healing in an Italian hospital, he was able to bring her to neutral Switzerland with the help of the resistance. There, she was placed in the care of the Sisters of Charity. They cared for her until the war ended and then the two of them emigrated to America.

Jocko could have remained with his daughter in Switzerland and earned a good living. He was an experienced watchmaker, highly valued for his creative design talents. Nevertheless, he had chosen during the war to return to Italy to fight with the Resistance against fascism.

Jocko wore many hats in the resistance. He accepted assignments that required him to defy death crossing through enemy lines many times both to acquire information as well as to perform acts of sabotage.

The code name that identified him was "21." It was the day of the month his family was killed, and a name that reverberated in the agency with accolades for integrity, perseverance, and patriotism.

He also was a master bomb builder. He had the ability to build a reliable timepiece that enabled the exact timing of detonations. This allowed allied forces safe corridors for movement for brief windows in time, after which many strategic bridges met their demise through the work of his expert hands. Because of this experience, after the war the US Government recruited him to join a newly established covert intelligence agency dedicated to thwarting the spread of Russian communism. His hands-on knowledge of timing mechanisms proved priceless for the budding defense industry for which he worked.

Julio, his friend and technical collaborator, was also an explosives expert. He was a mechanical engineer with small mechanism design experience, who also specialized in timing devices. He had suffered a similar fate, losing his home in France to the Germans, interrogated regularly by the SS while held in prison for months until they verified his Italian citizenship.

He had been working with a French partner developing small mechanical components for manufacturing equipment. Upon his release, he returned to Italy.

Incensed by the German occupation, he too joined the resistance, where he met Jocko. They developed a reputation among their foes that referred to them as "ghosts from hell" for their ability to cause complete destruction, and then disappear. Both received the highest honors for their service, albeit bestowed in secrecy.

Jocko returned with Julio, who greeted Kevin, kissing him on both cheeks and extending his hand. Kevin noticed that this medium-built unassuming man had three fingers missing from his left hand.

"Hello, Kevin, I have heard a lot about you."

"And I about you, Julio."

"I know that you're pressed for time, with your charming friend waiting. But, I can tell you that the film they provided lacks enough detail in a critical section. It's not possible for us to discern the extent of their capability. Given what we have, I placed instructions as to what we need in the watch for you to return."

"I read you. I will get that done."

"When do you expect to meet with them? And, how long do you think it would take for them to provide the additional information?"

"Not soon. I'll call when I'm in Europe at the end of the month when the mole comes out of his hole."

"We scientists are always anxious to find answers, but safety first."

Julio smiled and gave him a double handshake before leaving to join the others. Jocko gave the watch to Kevin. He whispered, "Be safe," as he shuttled him to the front of the store.

Kevin found Katie leaning on a car just outside. She was drying her eyes.

"Are you alright?"

"I'm fine, I guess it was just remnants of all the emotional excitement today, meeting old friends and revisiting memories. Everything is fine. Just dealing with some things right now."

Kevin nodded without pushing to know more.

As they said good-bye to Jocko and the others, Jocko reinforced Kevin's cover story for Katie's ears, stating that the watch was not the original piece they had hoped it might be but that it did have great value as an antique.

Katie and Kevin headed in the direction of their car.

When they reached the corner, she stopped him, encircling him with her arms, and placed her head upon his chest.

In an unfamiliar, more vulnerable voice, she asked, "This may sound bizarre or premature, but I was wondering if you'd spend the night with me. I just don't want to be alone."

Kevin held her and whispered, "I want nothing more than spend the night. I know something is weighing hard on you. And it will be fun."

"Wait a minute, you're not thinking –"

"No," he interrupted. "Cool your pits. Clean fun, okay?"

23.

The Three Feather Bar and Grill, a local landmark with an infamous past, was a meeting place for colorful underworld figures. It was a nefarious establishment cloaked as a legitimate business. But on the street it was also known as a watering hole for embryonic members of the Sicilian-American Black Hand, a secret organization that darkened the lives of the humble Italian immigrants of New York City at the beginning of the twentieth century.

At one time, ninety percent of New York City's Italian population had received blackmail letters marked with a black hand, threatening death. The Black Hand was the precursor to the modern Mafia.

As time went on, the bar evolved into a gambling parlor, then a house of prostitution, and later, during Prohibition, a speakeasy behind a façade of a laundry and tailor shop. After repeal, it adopted the guise of a neighborhood bar and grill, one passed down through generations of dubious owners who were Mafiosi who gained their titles by assassination.

Behind the bar's glass-etched, monogrammed doors, creaking floors, tarnished bar rails and speckled ornate mirrors, descendants of the original Black Hand pursued their criminal tradition. The bar now served as the headquarters of a prominent Italian mob family, though it masqueraded as an Irish Bar. Its décor was one of a traditional establishment, complete with rows of tables covered by starched white tablecloths, and a classic oak bar, the back of which was lined with posters listing prices of drinks by the shot.

At the rear was a steam table stocked with slabs of corned beef, pastrami and brisket, surrounded with mounds of seeded rolls and French fries, all offered at a reasonable price to encourage drinking. It was a place where legitimate patrons could enjoy a beer and man-sized sandwich. Nevertheless, for those in the know, one could consult with a shylock for a loan, or place a bet with a bookie on the numbers or a horserace.

Mario parked the sleek black Caddy and proceeded across the street to the Bar. Dressed befitting a mob Captain, Mario was elegant in his long black coat and silk scarf. As he approached the painted wood storefront, Cosmo, the bartender, wearing a clean white apron, was sweeping the entry way with a tall wire-banded straw bristle broom. He turned as Mario stopped to greet him.

"Aye, Cosmo, come sta?" Mario said in greeting, receiving a warm handshake from the large, quiet man.

"Buon giorno," was the response. Cosmo opened the door, pointing him to the back office. "I just made a fresh pot of espresso and there are fresh biscotti, still warm from the bakery."

Mario thanked Cosmo, smiled, and made for the rear of the establishment. He was greeted by two men dressed in dark suits with the physiques of wrestlers who sat in front of the mirrored door to the private room. When Mario approached, they arose, nodded acknowledgment, and allowed him through.

"Fingers" Fingarro was seated at a back corner table, set with a white tablecloth, a large pot of espresso, two cups, two plates, and a large platter of biscotti. He motioned to Mario to join him. Voices in the room were lowered as Fingers and Mario embraced, kissed each other on both cheeks, and settled into their seats.

"Your mother?" Fingers asked.

"Bene. Good," Mario said. "And Billie, Mathilda? I trust everyone is in good health."

"Yes. We are all very well."

They sat sipping their coffees for a few moments without speaking, each waiting for the other to begin. Their Code insisted that business was important but respect must be shown one for the other, between Under Boss and Capo Regime. Mario waited for the older man to speak.

"So," Fingers began, "you want to talk about how we handle the spic kids?"

"Don Peppino and some others think these kids have overstayed their welcome. They do too many drugs and anyone who crosses their path becomes fair game. We have told them, and our cops have told them, but they don't seem to get the message. I know that they've done some work for us in the past but they have no concept of rules. I don't know if they are arrogant or just stupid."

"Sons of bitches," Fingers seethed, "I can't be happy if punks like them get close to my son or to Caterina. But, you know they live on the edge of the neighborhood and can't resist. We warned them the last time, you know, when they grabbed Angelina's pocketbook. Stealing from a ninety-year-old woman. Bastardos. We told them to keep away from here. And still, our people gave them some muscle work to do for us."

The slim, wiry mobster took a sip of coffee. "This is what I propose. I can have the cops pick them up, put them on ice at the meat plant and see to it that they get a good education. Then, Frankie's crew can use them again for a couple of things that they got going and later we will clean them or, who knows, maybe the cops will do them first.

"I hear the cops are looking for a nut job in the neighborhood, maybe they could tie them in. Ask Peppino if this is okay with him. If not, we'll just clean them right away."

Mario asked, "If it's okay with you and Peppino, I would like to do the class with young Mateo, who's showing some promise."

"Sure, his father was a good friend of ours."

With that, the two men finished their coffee, stood, and embraced.

"Please give my regards to your mother," Fingers said.

Mario nodded. "She'll really appreciate that."

The old card players heard Fingers' comment and nodded their approval of his sign of respect.

The guards rose as the bosses approached, saluting Mario once more. Fingers gave orders, "Tell Cosmo that when the Sergeant comes in for lunch, I want to see him."

Waiting for Don Fingers to be out of hearing distance, one commented, "I told you somethin's comin' down. Why else does a Capo pay a daytime visit? I'll bet you this is about Don Peppino's goddaughter and her piano player."

"Yeah, those Spics have really got their tits in a ringer this time. Let's see who he gives the job to," his counterpart said. "Probably the cops. They've got it in for them, too."

* * *

Mario returned to the funeral parlor and was about to knock when the door opened and a collegiate-looking young man in a seersucker suit exited. He acknowledged Mario as he left. Don Peppino waved Mario into the room and closed the door behind him.

"Mario. That was a messenger from 69th Street, giving us a heads-up that Feds have been assigned to the neighborhood to search for that psycho killer."

"He reassured me that they were here for that and that alone. They are asking for cooperation from us, and neighborhood people, too. Nevertheless, it would be prudent to keep the blinds drawn, so to speak, in the event that law enforcement not known to us are in the area."

Mario nodded.

"So, let the crews know about this," Peppino continued, "and arrange to have pickups and drops done outside the neighborhood. Maybe this would be a good time to do some public relations work with the local Feds. Have somebody with a little finesse take 'em to the game, or something. We need to assure them that we're earnestly looking for that maniac, too.

"I'm going to take a break and have something with Birdie at Mela's. What else you got going?"

Mario related what Fingers and he had discussed and Peppino agreed with the strategy that he'd do the tune-up on the Puerto Ricans.

"I got young Mateo under my wing for the next two weeks while Bundles is away. He's coming along good. He's alert and it looks like he has potential for earning. This will give him an opportunity to learn how to use some muscle. Right now he's running numbers, and he's had a couple of successful heists out of Idlewild with Bundles' crew. And, what I also like about him is that he respects his mother. He's taken good care of her since his father bought it. I'm thinking about proposing him for promotion in time."

Don Peppino nodded affirmatively. "His father was a stand-up guy, a high earner and very respectful."

"Boss, I just wanted to mention there are a lot of guys at the Three Feathers and if we need to take a low profile, that ain't gonna be too good."

"I know, but these are tough times, and we've got things going on with the other families right now. We're trying to stay out of it but we may be on the brink of a war. Fingers wants to keep his men close. But I'll talk to him about it."

Breaking the business focus, Don Peppino needled Mario, "My wife keeps asking me when you're going to get married? What's it all about anyway? There are plenty of nice Sicilian girls in the neighborhood. What are you waiting for?"

"Peppino, please, I got enough trouble trying to keep my mother and you happy. I'll get around to it."

The older man laughed. "I hope I won't need crutches to stand up for you."

* * *

Mateo's mother Maria Patrino heard the phone ring and scurried to answer it.

"Hello, Senora Patrino, this is Mario, come sta?"

"Bene e lei?–I'm fine and you?—Is your mother's arthritis giving her a lot of pain?"

"No. She's been doing pretty good this week. She even did some work in the garden, planting tomatoes and peppers."

"That's good. Hold on, I will get my son for you."

Mario could hear her calling out the window, "Mateo. It's Mario for you."

Mateo made it to the phone out of breath. "Hey, Mario, I was painting the bench in the yard."

"Good," Mario replied, "but you're working with me for the next couple of weeks. Meet me at the corner of Mulberry and Mott at 2 p.m. Wear a suit and bring an extra shirt. Tell your Mom you'll be working late."

"Great. Okay." The young man ended the call with anticipation.

"Mom," he called into the next room urgently. "I need two white shirts and my suit ironed. I'll probably be home late."

He didn't hear her answer so he went to see where she was. He saw her standing by the closet door, crying.

"Mom, what's the matter?"

She turned to him and cried. "Son, you're a man now, but still only twenty-seven. I can't tell you what to do. But remember what happened to your father? They used him and then they killed him. Think of your soul. Don't be tempted by money, Jesus preached, 'What you sow, you will reap.'"

"Mom, give it a break. It was a construction accident. The scaffolding broke and he fell."

She stared at him with stone eyes. "Watch out for yourself," she said. Don't believe anybody is your friend there. Mario is high up, and once they get you they never let you go. You make money for them, you go to jail for them like your father did, and then you die for them. Your wife, your family, they're second to them." She lifted her finger, pointing at him and cautioned again, darkly serious, "Think what you're doing."

He embraced her. "Mom, don't worry. I'm careful. I just want us to have a good life. I don't want to eat pasta fagoli every night and I don't want my mother slaving at a sewing machine in a dress factory."

She stared at him with sad eyes, then turned without another word to go to get his suit for ironing. Mateo went to bathe and shave. Soon the young buck was dressed and he blithely kissed his mother goodbye. Her face was a map of despair as he did so, but he was too excited to see.

He made his way on foot through the crowded streets of Little Italy with the extra shirt folded under his arm. He had the feeling he'd just been given ownership of the neighborhood.

When he turned onto Mott Street, Mario was leaning on his Caddy talking to two members of his crew, both dressed as if they were going to attend a matinee at the Paramount. Mateo approached, but then stopped and waited a few yards away. He knew enough not to get too near made men while they were in the middle of a conversation.

This impressed Mario. *This kid knows what the word respect means.* He waved him in and introduced him.

"You guys know Mateo."

"No," one replied, "but we heard about his work from Bundles."

"Ok, listen, I gotta go. Take care of what I asked you to do. We'll meet again at the end of the week, uptown. Again, listen to me. Make yourselves scarce in the neighborhood for a while. Whatever work you got here, do it and do it quick. In and out. Don't hang around. Play someplace else, too, for now."

"Why? What's going down?"

"There's nothin' goin' down, but we just may have some visitors around here. Make sure you call in regular, too. There may be some news coming. Also, try to avoid the other families for now, make some money, and if you need somethin' call the booth. Ciao."

They tapped Mateo on the shoulder goodbye and made their way down the street. Mario gave Mateo the keys to his car and directed him to drive to the Downtown Athletic Club by the Battery. Driving the boss, Mateo felt like a million dollars.

As they made their way through bustling lower Manhattan, Mario told stories about Mateo's father, how well liked he was and how people felt he could be counted on to do the right thing, encouraging the young hopeful to follow his example.

"If you listen to me and Bundles, who's putting a lot of faith in you, you might get in and then you'll really make some money and be protected."

They pulled up in front of the Club and waited for the attendant. Mario began his first lesson of the day.

"To do the kind of business we do, you need to be in shape, physically and mentally fit. I work out three or four times a week. I see you look like you're in pretty good shape."

Mateo assured him that he had weights at home and he played softball with his friends on Saturday mornings.

"That's good, but as we get older we have to be more disciplined to stay in shape. That's why I joined the club. It also gives me some time by myself and time to mingle with straight people.

"It's important to make friends with people that are not in the life, and besides, you do not have the pressure of watching your back with them. It gives you a perspective of what those people want and need and maybe an alibi now and then." He grinned.

An attendant approached the car and saluted Mario with familiarity as he opened his door. In the gym, Mario asked a trainer to provide his guest with workout clothes, and show him to the track and weight room. They would meet in the steam room an hour later.

When Mateo finished his workout, another attendant escorted him to the steam room, which was crowded with business executives and their customers sitting on concrete benches with their faces masked by a hot steam veil.

Mateo searched around through the mist of heavy air, spotting Mario. He sat down next to him and noticed how muscular and powerful he was. Being somewhat smaller himself, he vowed to work out more. Mario rested with his eyes closed for a while.

Mateo was careful not to disturb him, but then realized that he wasn't asleep when he began to comment on the conversations they could hear around the steam room.

"See, kid," he whispered, "those guys," pointing to a group of men at the far corner of the room, "they're in the oil tanker business, ship brokers. These others," pointing to another group, "they're in the grain and feed racket." His eyes half-closed, circling the room with his finger, "Those over there, those're stock brokers."

Mario laughed. "What's funny to me when I sit here listening to them, is that we control it all. Their ships, their trucks, their buildings. They don't move without us. In a way we're their silent partners." He howled with laughter, breaking the quiet calm of the room. All the other men turned to look at him, startled. Mateo smiled, understanding the irony.

24.

Uptown at the Casa Filipo Italian restaurant, Mario told Mateo to park right in front. Mateo did as instructed and shut down the engine.

"Let me have the keys," Mario said, and as he took them he looked around the car. Then he unlocked the glove compartment, reached in, and took out two snub-nosed revolvers, handing one to Mateo.

"No safety. Do you know how to handle it?"

"I'm cool."

Like a pro, Mateo placed the piece under his jacket, wedging it in his belt. He reached for the door handle.

"Wait, this is what you do when you exit a car. Take a quick look all round from left to right, see if you notice anyone who looks interested in you or if you see any strange movements by anybody nearby. It don't matter who. Women, kids, anybody. Then, clock the other side until I get out. Get in the habit of doing that. It could save your life someday."

Mateo exited the car doing exactly what he'd been told.

In the restaurant, a waiter greeted Mario with his eyes and showed him and Mateo to a table at the back of the room. "Mr. Mario," he asked, "the usual?"

"Yes, Aldo. Thanks." Mario sat with his back toward the wall, at a table in the far corner of the room. Mateo attempted to sit opposite him, with his back toward the door, but Mario pointed to a chair on his right.

Aldo came back with two glasses and a bottle of Chianti. As he placed the wine on the table. Another waiter came with an appetizer dish of fresh bruscetta.

Mario helped himself.

"Have some," he told Mateo. "Just about the best anywhere, outside Sicily. They use the ripest, perfect tomatoes, basil they grow out in the back, and the most expensive extra virgin olive oil. I have it flown in from Palermo for them." The waiter poured their wine.

Mario put his hand on Mateo's arm and scanned the room so the younger man could see. "It's important to sit in a place that allows you to see anyone who comes toward you from a distance."

Then he pointed to an exit sign over the kitchen door, and told him that it was also important to know how to get out quickly.

Mateo registered the lesson with a nod.

Aldo returned and read the specials from a list written on the back of his order pad, naming the fresh fish of the day.

"What the fuck is a Mahi Mahi?" Mario laughed. "Hey, kid. Is there anything you don't like?"

"I like everything," Mateo answered.

"Okay, Aldo. "Let's leave it up to Philly."

The waiter smiled. "Good choice, Mr. Mario. I think he's already started."

Italian bread, bread sticks and a hot antipasto with stuffed eggplant, mushrooms, baked clams and mussels marinara were served moments later.

While they ate, the two men spoke about their mothers' recipes, how they made their homemade pasta, tomato sauce and, of course, their meatballs. It was a classic conversation, and one which Italians usually indulge in when bonding in friendship. For those of Italian descent the discussion of food and its preparation is a sacrament. In their minds, Americans had no sense of taste.

"Americanos eat to live," Mario said. "We live to eat. Jarred tomato sauce and canned vegetables are a sacrilege."

Aldo brought veal piccata with side dishes of angel hair spaghetti topped with garden-fresh tomato sauce.

"Mr. Philly's finest," Aldo exclaimed as he placed the platters in front of them.

As he finished his meal, Mario wiped his mouth and asked Mateo to have his coffee at the bar, saying that he needed to conduct some business for an hour or two. As he rose from his seat, Mario introduced him to Filipo–Philly– the Chef, who was about to sit.

Filipo Calabria was the legal owner of the Casa Filipo. After a few pleasantries were exchanged, Mateo made his way to the small bar where the waiter brought him a pot of freshly brewed espresso and a family sized slice of Italian cheesecake.

The young man glanced toward Mario and Philly, noticing the chef sliding an envelope to Mario under his napkin while continuing an animated conversation accentuated with hand gestures and bursts of laughter.

Mateo felt he was really on his way to being considered for membership in la famiglia. This is how unschooled twenty-seven year olds were recruited, with the promise of mentoring, wining, and dining.

Puffed-up by the unaccustomed attention he was receiving, he felt proud. The excitement of the heists, holdups and hijackings in which he had already participated paled in comparison to what he envisioned ahead.

He'd turned a page and was now a believer. It was obvious that men of honor know how to live. He acknowledged that he wanted in, he deserved it, and would do whatever was necessary to get a piece of this life for himself.

Mateo's bright new future was interrupted by a female voice jarring him back to reality.

"Why are you sitting here at the bar all by yourself?"

He turned to see a stunning young woman. He glanced to Mario.

"Ah. You're with him."

Startled by her, Mateo tried to concentrate, but all he could register was, *She's beautiful.*

Her shining auburn hair crowned a face accented by large dark blue eyes, enhanced by classically chiseled features sprinkled lightly with freckles. Her cheeks had a subtle blush of rose. She had a sleek young body.

His heart pounded, trying to find the right words, Mateo could only come up with, "You work here?"

"Oh, God, another mental giant," she said. "What does it look like?"

"Hey, take it easy. I'm just trying to make conversation here. Are you married, uh, goin' with somebody?"

"Unbelievable, you don't talk about the weather. You don't introduce yourself or even ask my name. Are you married, you ask. Like that means anything to you people, with your five cummaris and your flashy women?"

Mateo marshaled his best defense. "Hey, I didn't mean anything by it. I'm just trying to make conversation. I'm sorry if I offended you. And no, I don't have a wife, or a girlfriend or, cummaris, if you need to know."

They continued verbally fencing until Mario called.

"Hey, Mary Patricia! Bring some Sambuca, the black one."

"So, that's your name? Mary Patricia?"

"No, not for you. Neanderthals call me Marypat."

"Okay, now that I know your name, you can call me Mateo, the Caveman."

At this, Marypat had to restrain herself. She smiled and thought, *Well, at least he knows what a Neanderthal is.*

Marypat delivered the cordial to the table. She felt Mateo's eyes steady on her.

"Hey, Marypat, how are you?" Mario asked.

"I'm fine."

"I see you met young Mateo."

"Yeah, I'm really thrilled, Mr. Mario. In fact, I'm going to write to all my relatives in Italy."

Philly admonished, "Mary Patricia. Please. For once, can't you be nice for five minutes?"

She put her hand on his shoulder and whispered, "Come on, Dad, don't worry, you know you're the only man for me."

"Yeah, but I can't afford you."

Turning back to Mario Philly said, "This girl is drunk with buying clothes and knick-knacks like porcelain figures. Every day, she's got something new, she needs–"

"Dad, I'm going to the market now."

"Okay honey. I left the list by the phone in the kitchen."

Marypat called out, "Ciao," as she headed for the kitchen. She did not look in Mateo's direction.

Mario continued to receive a steady stream of visitors. Some stayed for a while, and others were in and out in minutes. The exchange of envelopes and pieces of paper was routine. The restaurant was filled. Most tables were taken by office workers from local businesses in the neighborhood.

Mateo could see why Mario had asked him to wait at the bar. From this vantage point he had a protective view of all the tables, the front of the restaurant and the kitchen doors. His eyes continuously clocked the entire space as he hoped Marypat would return.

Giuseppe "JoJo" Marino and Vincenzo "Little Vinny" De Marco, two well-dressed, veteran mob soldiers came in. Mario nodded and they sat at his table. Mario waived for Mateo to join them, too.

He introduced Mateo as a friend. Mateo knew that Mario must have mentioned him because they had both looked in his direction at the bar.

"Mateo, you'll be working with JoJo and Little Vinny for a couple of hours. We'll all meet again, later." Capo Mario turned to JoJo. "Did we get the delivery at the meat factory?"

"Yeah," JoJo answered, smiling. "I heard that the meat was a little bruised."

Mario said in a quiet but heated tone, "Call over there and tell them to keep the meat on ice. We will all meet there at six. We don't want any more bruising, got it? Take Mateo with you."

Mario counseled Mateo. "Observe what they say and do, keep quiet and listen! See you later, kid."

Mateo noticed how JoJo and Little Vinny surveyed the street as they exited the restaurant. When they reached the car, Little Vinny motioned Mateo to the front, next to JoJo, while he entered the back of the late model white Chrysler Imperial. Little Vinny saw Mateo's reluctance to take what he assumed to be the prized front seat.

He asked, "Mateo, did you never hear the expression 'Watch my back?'"

"Yeah."

"Well, whenever you can, you cover your partner and he covers you."

After hearing that, Mateo sat in silence, not thrilled with his special place in the seating arrangement, a spot customarily reserved for those about to be hit from the rear. They drove uptown, pulled into a used car dealership, and parked next to the sales trailer. Peering in the window, they saw that the sales manager was selling to a customer so they decided to have a smoke and look at cars while they waited. JoJo asked Mateo what he drove. Mateo turned red with embarrassment, and admitted that he didn't have a car, explaining that someone had totaled his modest sedan and that he didn't have insurance coverage.

"I'm looking for one now."

"What are you looking for?" Little Vinny asked.

"I'd like to get a '51 or '52 Chevy, and soup it up."

"Well, look around here. We'll see what we can do."

"You can drive, right?" JoJo asked.

Little Vinny said, "I heard he's a good wheel man."

"That true, kid?" JoJo asked.

Mateo just smiled.

They could hear a voice coming from the direction of the trailer office as Herbie Cole, owner of the Save-More lot, concluded with the customer.

"The credit should take no more than three days. The car will be serviced and cleaned for pick–up."

Herbie, a five–foot-six, pot-bellied, haggard-looking auto salesman recognized JoJo and Little Vinny. His smile turned to an expression of panic as he spotted them.

JoJo needled, "Making money, Herbie?"

"I told you guys over the phone that I didn't have anything this week. I'm waiting for a few deals to come through."

"Look, let's go inside and talk about it," Little Vinny said.

JoJo grabbed Herbie's arm and ushered him through the trailer door with some force. Little Vinny whispered to Mateo, "Stand inside the door as a lookout and keep your hands in your pockets."

Little Vinny took a quick look around to see if anyone else was still in the office, checking the toilet and the walk-in supply closet.

Herbie said, "I told you I couldn't come up with it this week." His voice cracked before he could finish the sentence. Sweat beaded on his brow.

"Look," JoJo roared, "you gotta accept that you have a problem here. You're not making steady payments for a long time now, you're into us for fifteen G's, the vig's goin' up every week and you're gettin' deeper and deeper in the hole with no end in sight."

Herbie pleaded, "Yeah, I know, I know. I've had some hard times lately, but you guys, you guys, you know me. I have always met my responsibilities."

JoJo continued, "Yeah, we know you a long time, and we like you. But business is business."

Then the mobster let him have it. "But, we also know that instead of paying us, you're gambling, and you're now gambling with our money! Can't you see that?" he shouted. "With what you owe us, the bookmaker and your other debts you don't have a business anymore." He took a few breaths and lowered his voice. "However, you do have a couple of, what they say, um, options. You could say a prayer and then goodbye, or," offering the solution, "you take us in as partners and let us help you, and then we all make a little money together."

Herbie's face flushed to beet red. He began to rant while pacing back and forth in the small trailer office. "You can't do this to me. I built this business from scratch, working seven days a week, for over twenty years. Who do you think you are, God?"

Little Vinnie lunged, and grabbed Herbie by the throat in a chokehold.

"I don't think you're listening. Yeah, God is talking to you. He's asking you if you want to live or die."

Herbie gurgled, and stared at the two men goggle-eyed. JoJo picked up a picture of Herbie's children from the desk.

"Do you want to take these fucking kids with you?" he threatened. Little Vinny relaxed his grip on Herbie just enough to allow thought processing to take place. Herbie stared at Jo Jo, terror on his face.

"Alright, now, let's just sit down like gentlemen and discuss your situation."

As Herbie sat, Little Vinny spoke in a calm tone. "Herbie, we've been friends for many years. We buy cars from you, we give you deals on parts, and we've made money available to you when you needed it."

Herbie nodded weakly. "Yeah and I've paid you good money for all of it."

"Herbie, shut up and listen to me. When things got tight, we gave you loans and we lowered the payments. Come on, nobody in our business does that. We've never laid a hand on you or muscled you in any way. But, now things have gone too far. You're gambling too fucking much, and with our money. You're not paying attention to business anymore and you can't pay us back. We need to make this right. So, we're going to be fair with you and take a partnership for the money you owe us."

Herbie stared at him as reality set in. He knew it was all over. He was fried. He struggled to get a grip on his head.

Through the fog, he heard JoJo. "We'll even pick-up the three G's you owe the bookmaker. Our lawyer will give you the split when he comes with the papers for you to sign after our accountant reviews your books tomorrow."

In a firmer tone JoJo said, "But here's the deal, Herbie. No more betting. You've been cut off. Nobody will take your bet. Herbie, believe me.

This is the best thing for you and your family. You will now have protection and suppliers at the best rates."

As JoJo finished, Little Vinny stepped over to Mateo and told him quietly to give Herbie a couple of body shots in the gut as a reminder. Mateo, eyes open wide in surprise, nodded as he acknowledged the order. His face took on a sinister stare. Little Vinny, as if nothing significant had taken place, spoke once more to Herbie, "Hey, Herbie, do me a favor. I need a Chevy, low mileage and big engine for Mateo here. Give me a call when you get one in, okay? We got to go now. Your troubles are over. Take the family out to dinner and celebrate."

He and JoJo shook hands with Herbie, and made their way to the door.

Mateo closed the door as they stepped out, and without hesitation grabbed Herbie by his tie and gave him two hard blows to the stomach. The punches left Herbie gasping for air, on his knees. Mateo left the trailer without a word and strode to the car.

As they pulled out of the lot, the three men began to laugh, making fun of Herbie's ineffective responses to their performance. Little Vinny, sitting in the back seat, said, "That circus guy, Barnum, was right. Did you hear what he said? There's that sucker born every day."

"Well, now let's see if he signs," JoJo said. "He could try to bring it to the cops or skip."

"I don't think he's that stupid. He's been around us a long time, he knows how it works."

"This could turn out good for him if he's smart. The boss wants to keep this place going. It's got a lot of potential for our thing, good place to move money through, and it's in a prime area, too. Hey Mateo, what do you say, we take a break for a couple of hours."

"Sure,"

"JoJo, what do you think we take him up to meet Claudia?"

"Oh, yeah. Well, that's part of the job and we're due for a pick-up."

They rolled through midday traffic on the badly aging, winding cobble-stone West Side Highway to the upper West Side, pulling up to a classic, four-story brownstone in a prime area of the city just around the corner from Grant's Tomb.

JoJo found a space, put the car in Park, and reached under the visor for a placard that read "Diplomat," and placed it in the front window.

Mateo shook his head, "You guys are wild," as they laughed and proceeded up to the front door.

A dark skinned, elderly Latino man, dressed in a butler's jacket, white shirt, and black bow tie, answered the door.

"Senor JoJo, buenvenuto."

"Hi, Ricardo, this is Mateo, an associate of ours."

"Welcome," the old man answered in accented English. Ricardo showed them into a front parlor. Pointing to a decanter of liquor and cordial glasses resting on a mahogany coffee table, he poured each of them a shot as they waited.

"Ah, Benedictine this time. That Claudia sure has class."

Claudia Gutierrez de Maria, born into a Cuban peasant family, was sold by her father into prostitution at age fourteen. She was the oldest child of nine whom her father could not feed. During her first month of captivity, Claudia had been raped repeatedly by her owners and kept locked away in a dirty, rodent infested attic. She understood she'd have to comply with their orders, but she was not broken.

Strong willed and smart, she learned the art of survival under the new rules of her position. Someday, men like these will live in fear of me and they will do my bidding, was the mantra she repeated to herself.

Two years later her pimp wound up on the coroner's slab after a knife fight over a gambling debt. A housekeeper friend at one of the hotels in Havana took her in. She learned the trade and got a job as a housekeeper for a widower, a retired Army Colonel and wealthy tobacco farmer, many years her senior. Her new employer fell in love with her and she became his mistress. He provided an apartment for her in an exclusive section of the Cuban Capital.

Claudia could ask for anything she wanted, and he was delighted to provide it for her. For the first time in her life, she felt secure. Men found her to be a captivating young woman. She dressed in expensive garb and men would often stop in their tracks to watch as she swayed by them on the upscale shopping boulevards of old Havana.

Her long jet-black hair reached to her waist, contrasted against golden brown eyes that sparkled like highly polished jewels. Her full lips led the eye to a long slender neck and down to the perfectly shaped breasts on her slim well-balanced body.

But above all, Claudia possessed a warm, alluring smile that could disarm even the most treacherous of men. Although Cuban by birth, her skin tone and features were Mediterranean, further adding to her mystique.

Claudia's presence oozed sensuality. It was her tool. Her provider had not only introduced her to the finer things of life, but because of his military standing, he taught her how to use firearms, and the art of self-defense.

With her disarming beauty, the people skills of a diplomat, and a knowledge of firearms and hand-to-hand combat taught to her by the Colonel, she became an effective assassin at her keeper's bidding.

The colonel, a member of Batista's inner circle, gave her intimate exposure to high-ranking members of Cuba's organized crime family, as well as Cuban and American politicians with interests in Havana's gambling establishments. Because of the Colonel's relationship with them, Claudia worked as a courier from time to time, travelling often to major cities in the United States. She learned English and the American way.

Some years later, Claudia bought a house in New York. She loved New York and she had been seeding money away in different banks for some time. She recognized that Cuba was politically volatile and on the brink revolution. Through her own and the Colonel's connections, she obtained US Citizenship.

She swore to herself she would not lose the life she had gained. No man would ever dominate or exploit her again.

When the Colonel, her protector, was executed in a failed coup attempt, she left Cuba for New York, and made it her new home. Her contacts in the criminal underground in Havana had close ties to those in Little Italy. Through new alliances with the mob, Claudia turned her house into an upscale brothel, frequented by powerful Italian-American friends, politicians and a growing list of corporate executives.

Mateo's eyes perked as Claudia entered the room. There is something about her for a woman her age, he thought.

"Hi, boys," she greeted them with a tinge of accent. "What brings you here so early today?"

Both men rose and gave her a hug and a kiss.

"And, who's this young stud?" she asked.

"Mateo. He's working with us."

"Come over here and let me take a good look at you."

Pulling him close, she kissed Mateo squarely on the lips. He shivered with her heat. She turned to JoJo, "I didn't expect you so early today. Can you kill an hour or two, while I put it together?"

"Oh sure, that's fine, we wanted to relax a little and have a few drinks anyway. We want Mateo to get to know you and the girls."

"Ok, good, I'll send them in. Mateo, you wait about fifteen minutes, I have someone special for a macho hombre like you," she teased.

When Claudia left the room, JoJo whispered to Mateo. "Don't let her looks fool you. She's not just a madam. She does work, too. You follow me."

Shit. He's not telling me she's a hitter, is he?

A few minutes later four young women stepped into the room, each seemingly more attractive than the last. All were dressed in expensive silk lounging pajamas. JoJo and Little Vinny made their selections and wandered off with them up the stairs. The two remaining girls made a fuss over Mateo.

He fidgeted, nervous with the forwardness of these women who pinched his cheeks, then his nipples through his shirt. They taunted him by saying that Michaela would be with him in a little while. One said she was jealous because of his looks. The other grabbed him through his pants and said she was doubly jealous.

Mateo felt more than a little guilty, remembering his conversation with Marypat, whom he had met at the restaurant just hours earlier. He knew he wanted to see her again, recalling her fiery personality as they traded words. He knew that his mother would like Marypat, too. He read her as a down to earth and unpretentious, yet smart girl. He smiled as he thought of her.

"What's so funny?" A tall Italian-looking woman approached him.

He looked to her as she descended the stares and had no words.

"I'm Michaela. You're Mateo, right?"

Her eyes registered surprise at his good looks. Her persona seemed one of classic Italian birth, with strong, chiseled features, not unlike Sophia Loren. Her hair, a mix of reddish blonde complimented a stylish black business suit with a ruffled white silk blouse and a black ribbon tie.

"Follow me," she said.

She took him by the hand and led him up the stairs to her room. The rival of any hotel suite, Michaela's quarters had a separate sitting area, a formal Victorian look with a metal-framed, four-poster bed at its center, covered with lavish bedding, and matching embroidered draperies. Antique French doors opened onto a balcony that overlooked a large garden with a trellis and stone railing, which provided privacy from the adjoining houses.

Am I to suppose she's not just a hooker?

"Make yourself at home. Help yourself to a drink."

She pointed to a small marble-topped bar in a corner of the room.

"I'm going to change into something more comfortable. While you're at it, I'll have a Bourbon straight."

Mateo poured the drinks, brought them out to the balcony, and dropped onto a chaise longue. The events of the day bewitched him. He felt as if he were on top of the world. Michaela came out and lifted her drink from the wrought iron patio table.

"Mmm...that's good," she said at the first sip. He saw that she was surer of herself than the other women were. She had changed into a starched white cotton men's shirt, which came down to her smooth olive thighs. Unbuttoned on top, the shirt exposed her breasts, well-shaped and firm, her erect nipples pressing through the material as she moved.

She smelled fresh and clean, with a slight air of a floral perfume. The light contrasted her hair and her green eyes. She sat down next to him on the edge of the lounge seat. She asked him questions about himself. He evaded answering directly.

As they conversed, she moved closer. She picked up one of his hands and placed it on her bare thigh, and he began to stroke her smooth skin. His heart was pounding. He reached up to caress her breasts at intervals, and she did not stop him, only said, "Mmm," as if his touch pleased her. He teased her nipple between a thumb and forefinger and she smiled and laughed a little as she arched her back. He felt himself swelling with excitement and all the while she continued the conversation as if her only purpose was his amusement, occasionally touching his face or running her hand down the back of his neck.

She asked if he would be coming to visit on a regular basis, as JoJo did. He told her that he did not know, and that he was new and they were showing him the ropes.

She stopped a moment then, sat back a little, and studied him with her eyes.

"You're different from the others. You have smoother moves. Classy."

"I bet you say that a lot."

"Likely I do, but this time I think I mean it."

She touched him.

"This one is on the house," she said.

As they spoke, Michaela massaged him through his pants. Mateo gasped with a sharp intake of breath. She could feel he was ready. She tantalized him with practiced moves, and then pulled his zipper down.

"Let's get you comfortable."

Mateo, more than pleased, unable to speak now, groaned with pleasure as she found and finished him with her lips. It had been a while for him, three months since his split with his ex-girlfriend.

Afterward Mateo whispered, "You're so beautiful and so sexy. I'd like to spend more time with you. Maybe we could do something later in the week?"

"It's been a while since I just had fun. Are you asking me out on a date?"

"Sure. Why not?"

"Do you know where you are, and who you're with?"

"Yes."

"Well, if it's really a date, it would have to be on my day off. Would you like to spend the day with me? Go to the beach, or do some shopping?"

"Yeah, I'd like that. I'll give you my number. I'll be free all this weekend. Call me and we'll set something up."

"I'll call you tomorrow after I find out what I've got going."

They returned to the main parlor.

Mateo had thoroughly enjoyed her company, but not just for the sex. He believed that their conversation indicated that they enjoyed many of the same things, and he suspected that her world contained another mysterious dimension of which he knew nothing as yet, and he wanted to learn. There was so much he wanted to learn.

25.

JoJo turned the corner. A large, red brick building, time-worn and crowned with a sign covering the entire side of its large exterior loomed up before him.

"Imperial Meat Packers. Wholesale Meat and Meat Product Distributors since 1909."

JoJo honked twice and the garage door opened. Once inside, the door closed tight as a jail cell behind them. Men in long white butchers' coats were busily working. Without a word, JoJo led Little Vinny and Mateo to the rear corner of the building and into a back office.

An unshaven, six foot five bruiser of a man with a ski hat and a blood stained white coat greeted them.

"Hey Sparky," Little Vinny said. "How's it hanging?"

"Better than yours," Sparky ripped back. "The spics are in the fridge. They started mouthing off so I decided to cool them down."

"Shit," JoJo erupted. "You were told, no more body work."

"We didn't touch them. They're just hangin' on hooks, and they only been in there about ten minutes. One of 'em has been bawling the whole time."

"Shit. Mario will be here any minute. Cut 'em down and take 'em over to the sausage room," JoJo ordered. "And have somebody bring in some hot coffee, too."

As the big guy left through a set of swinging doors, Little Vinny turned to Mateo. "The guy has no sense of humor. You know why we they call him Sparky? The guy's a torch. He loves fire and blowing things up. His whole personality changes when he does a job. He can't stop talking about it. We worry about him sometimes."

Mario arrived. Vito Imperiale, the brawny owner of the meat plant greeted him. His graying head accentuated by his cold stark eyes revealed he had arrived at mid-life. His appearance though was comically dimmed by his custom made shirt and diamond studded tie that protruded from his blood stained butchers coat. Vito told Mario he'd have someone put some meat packages for everyone on the ramp by his car. Mario kissed the man on both cheeks in appreciation. He left the room.

"Okay, how you guys doing?" Mario turned to Mateo. "How you holdin' up, kid? Aren't these guys a pieces of work?" Mateo laughed, nodding in agreement.

"Vinny," Mario asked, "how did Herbie take it?"

"Well, I think it's gonna be okay, once he rethinks this day through. The lawyer will be there in the morning with the accountant. Mateo gave him a small reminder as we left. He did okay, too."

Mario scrutinized Mateo, searching for a reaction, maybe some hint of dissatisfaction about his role but Mateo showed no emotion.

"All right, then. Where are these idiots?" Mario sneered.

"They're in the sausage packing room."

JoJo showed him to the door and led them through a damp, poorly lit hallway. Entering the icebox, they saw Sparky had them sitting on the floor in the center of the room. They were close to frozen.

"They are pretty banged-up," Sparky admitted.

"The cops did this?" Mario demanded.

"I guess so," answered Sparky, "that's how I got 'em, boss. Their faces were like this, swollen, bruised, bloody."

Blood had already frozen on the floor during their stay in the freezer.

"Now, you see what happens when you don't listen?" Mario said to the Puerto Rican boys in a reasonable tone. "You were told to stay out of the neighborhood." Mario motioned to Little Vinny who, as if they had rehearsed, lifted Paco to his feet, holding him up against a stainless steel worktable.

As Mario moved closer toward him, the boy, frozen and in fear, tried to slide down to avoid his approach. Just then, a worker came in with a carton full of coffee containers. Mario barked at him, "Put that down and get out!" The man did as he was told.

Mario turned to JoJo, who as if on cue, grabbed Paco by the throat. Lifting his head to the side, he pointed to an electric meat saw and calmly told him, "We can have all of you guys cut in pieces and packed for shipping in less than an hour."

Little Vinny turned the meat saw on. Paco struggled in fear. Mateo could smell urine.

The ominous sound of the machine gave away its age by a menacing screech of the motor. The piercing noise made another of the Puerto Rican boys, hunched on his knees, cry and beg. Little Vinny kicked him in the side to shut him up, but the petrified kid couldn't stop.

JoJo asked, "Maybe you're not as tough as you thought, huh?" All three nodded and babbled that no, they weren't.

Mario chided, "So, you get yourselves all drugged up and then you don't see or listen but, mark my words – and here he leaned in toward them and pointed a finger at them one at a time as he spoke - "If I see or hear about you being in that neighborhood again, unless we told you to come in, you will be hamburger meat for pigs. Or maybe worse than that. We'll turn you over to the Irish cops so they can finish the job they started. So, if you clean your act up, we give you work, but you will follow the rules.

"Stay out of the neighborhood and, especially, stay away from Billy-Boy and Caterina. Wait until we contact you. Got it?"

They responded like a church choir, singing out as one voice a "Yeah" in staccato. Mario approached Mateo, who had remained by the door.

"Give them a couple of slaps, just to underscore the drill." Showing him an open hand but cautioned, "Not too heavy, the cops have already done a job on them." Then he handed Mateo a twenty and told him to get them a cab when he finished.

"I don't want them around here, either," he roared loudly to be sure they had heard.

JoJo dispensed the coffee. He followed Mario out of the room, leaving Mateo and Sparky to give the punks a final lesson.

They had them get up on their feet and without compunction, backhanded each of them with just enough force to jar their heads.

Sparky motioned them to a street exit and held Paco by the shoulder until he flagged down a taxi. Mateo handed the driver the twenty, instructing him to take them where they wanted to go.

When they got into the back of the cab, Sparky asked them, "Is everything cool?"

They couldn't answer any quicker. "No problem, man. We're cool."

Mateo made his way back to the truck ramps where workers were putting boxes of meat into Mario's and JoJo's cars. JoJo and Little Vinny gave Mateo a convivial pat on the back.

Mateo got behind the wheel of the car. Mario sat shotgun. He opened the glove compartment and asked Mateo for his gun.

Mateo removed the revolver from his belt and handed it to Mario, who placed it next to his own, locking the compartment door. He handed the keys to Mateo. Mateo felt that his performance this day had pleased Mario.

Mario said, "Okay, let's go home."

Mateo headed for Little Italy and the parking lot of the funeral parlor. Neither of them spoke as they drove downtown. Mario had closed his eyes and rested. Mateo took advantage of the quiet time to replay the exciting moments of his day with Michaela. His mind drifted back to her. She had excited him as he had never been excited before.

He thought Michaela was much like him, rationalizing that she did what she had to do to survive. Like him, she just wanted a piece of the good life. But his mind went to Marypat, who also lived her own way, though he considered her way as the right way. She was a woman with whom a good life could be built. They could raise a family together. She was a person who would show him love, and give his mother respect.

The argument raged on in his head.

The funeral parlor parking lot was filled, but Mario directed him to a reserved spot around the back of the building. A large group of people stood and talked, mostly in Italian, at the entrance to the building. Anthony was at his post opening and closing the monogrammed glass doors for mourners. He greeted Mario without his usual fanfare.

"Who do you have here tonight, Anthony? The place is packed."

"My goodness," Anthony said, "Its Senora Pellegrino, rest in peace. I didn't know she was so loved."

"Anthony, we've got some meat in the car trunk. Some's for you, too. It's separated by name. Please do me a favor and put ours in the cooler. We'll pick it up later. Is Don Peppino inside?"

"Yeah, he's in the office, talking on the phone."

Mario and Mateo made their way through the room. The fragrance of fresh-cut flowers, mixed with the scent of too many perfumes filled the room. Monsignor Scalvo's voice could be heard settling down the mourners that had crowded him for attention and directed them with impatient hand gestures to sit for evening prayer.

Mario knocked on the office door and was surprised when Birdie opened it. Don Peppino, with a phone to his ear, signaled for them to come in and sit. Birdie greeted Mateo, asked him how his mother was and if the medication he had given her provided some relief. Don Peppino finished his call, something about roof repair, and greeted them.

Mario went to a file cabinet, took out a few envelopes from his jacket pocket and placed them in the top drawer.

"Unless you have something else," directing his words to Don Peppino, "I was thinking of having dinner with Mateo at Mela's."

"Fine, I had dinner earlier. With this crowd, we're a little short of staff here tonight, and I wanted to spend a little time with Birdie, too. We'll stay until about ten. Call your mother so she won't worry, and please bring me an espresso when you come back."

Don Peppino got up and showed them to the door, giving Mateo a warm pat on the back.

The restaurant was crowded with mourners from across the street. After paying their respects, most stopped at Carmella's for a bite to eat or for an espresso with dessert.

Dominick greeted them as they came in and gave Mateo a hug. They had gone to school together, playing on the same softball team.

"Hey, Mateo, how you doin'? Dropping any grounders lately?"

"The only way you can stop a ground ball is with that big belly of yours," Mateo laughed.

Dominick led them to a table in the back. Mateo remembered to sit facing the door.

"Going with Mama's suggestions, or you wanna order from the menu?" Dominick asked.

"I can go for linguini with white clam sauce. The rest I'll leave up to you."

"And you Mateo. What would you like?"

"That sounds good to me, too."

"Oh, Come on, don't be such a diplomat, I could make you a nice steak."

He laughed. "No, no, I'll stick with the clam sauce but I'll have it with angel hair instead."

"How about a little homemade white to go with it?"

"Is it from the same barrel we had last week?"

Dominick smiled, "Yeah, good stuff, eh?"

Angie came out of the kitchen with a basket of Italian bread and bread sticks, placed it on the table and greeted them.

"How are your mothers?" she asked them. She did not wait for an answer. She turned back to the kitchen.

Mario told Mateo how much he liked Carmella's family and that Dominick, her son, was funny but also respectful, adding that Don Peppino considered Dominick and sweet Angie as his Godchildren.

He explained to Mateo that Dominick's mother Carmella, Don Peppino, Birdie, Anthony, Fingers and his late wife, Maria-Concetta, had all grown up together on Hester Street. He related how close they'd remained, never saying a cross word to one another, and always there for each another.

"Your Father hung out with them too. They liked him a lot. Don Peppino is looking at you closely right now."

Mario pushed a chunk of bread into his mouth and began speaking as he chewed.

"They may be opening up the books soon. There's so much stuff going on, that they'll want to add men of respect to the family. You haven't been around very long. Guys sometimes wait their whole lives to be so honored. Your father paid his dues and you get some credit for that, too. With your talent, we might be able to open a window.

"The way you handled yourself today proves your value. I'm going to give you a little incentive. I want you to take over my vending machine route. I will get you stickers for five machines of your own from Don Pedro.

I'll lay out the money for the new units, you'll pay me back when you're on your feet and, later, you may be asked to do the Don a little favor."

Mateo beamed. He knew nobody could get machines without permission from Don Pedro, but with his stickers, there would be protection. He could make a few hundred a week, plus a cut from Mario for covering his machines.

Dominick brought a platter of baked clams and two bowls of Manhattan clam chowder to the table. His sister, Angie, followed with homemade white wine and glasses. When they were alone again, Mario told Mateo to stay close to Bundles, his assigned lieutenant. Then he reached into his pocket and gave him an envelope.

"A little something," Mario whispered. Mateo discretely slipped it into his vest pocket.

The young man thanked Mario as they continued to speak in between bites of food. The conversation was largely about Mateo. Mario asked him about his childhood, his friends and his interests.

In return, the seasoned gangster told Mateo stories of how he grew up in Sicily and the circumstances of how he found himself in America. How he was distantly related to Don Peppino through his mother's side of the family and that Don Peppino had helped him arrange to come to New York after his father died. He explained that his parents had a small bread bakery in Palermo in a working class neighborhood.

"So, what do you think about Marypat?" Mario asked.

"The girl is on fire, tough as nails. She was making sausage out of me with her mouth," Mateo said. "She's something."

"That she is. Drives Philly crazy, but she's sharp. Runs the place, and she's good at it. But she doesn't like us goodfellas.

She thinks we're all womanizers and she believes we stole the place from her father. But he was into the sharks big time, and I cleared that all up for him and he's doing pretty well now.

"A lot of guys would have raped the place and left him with nothing but now his business is stronger than ever. He makes more money and he has friends. She can't seem to get that into her head. I think she needs a man in her life."

Mateo asked, "Yeah, but would she let one in?"

Mario sensed that Mateo had more than a curious interest in her.

"You, kid," he advised, "why don't you take your Mom there for dinner on a Wednesday night. I'll let Philly know. Who knows what could happen. Maybe you're the cowboy who can break the mare. And if she sees you respecting your mother, she'll soften up."

Mario sipped his wine. "Listen, kid, I'm not one to talk. I have not gotten married myself yet, but I know it is a better life if you do. It's nice to have a home and a family. Our life is exciting but, it can get a little too wild, too much vino, too many cummaris, late nights. Catch my drift? It can get you off the track and damage your earnings. The guys at the top are all family men. They respect guys more when they are family men, too. Catch my drift?"

Mateo, like a school kid, tried to soak it all in. He put his thoughts together while they ate, and reviewed what he learned that day. He had flashes of the day: sitting with his back toward the wall, covering your partner while he drove and, giving reminders. He realized that there are tried and true operating procedures to follow, as in any business. Rules of thumb designed to keep you and yours from harm. The idea is, if you work the system, the system works and protects you.

Mateo knew things would be asked of him. He would be asked to do brutal things that would test his conscience and his faith in God. Things he really didn't want to do. However, there was a greater purpose. The purpose that would support his ability to earn for himself and his loved ones. It would mean the power and respect of la famiglia.

Mateo was filled with a skewed youthful idealism. He felt he was becoming part of a powerful world, a secret world. He was amazed at what just one day had brought. The best food he had ever eaten, athletic clubs, women, cash and slot machines, not to mention the promise of a car. This beat working in a retail shop or lugging cargo from the bowels of ships on the waterfront for fifty bucks a week. Being a 'made' man would give him life. It would make him a man of respect.

Carmella observed Dominick preparing a tray, with a small pot of espresso and miniature cannoli. "That going to Mario?" she asked.

"Yeah."

"Let me take it," she said.

"Why?"

"They're getting a little too friendly with you lately."

He barked, "Look, Mela, don't you ever stop? Don't you think I know what I'm doing?"

"Yes, but they're too interested. Look who he's got out there now. It wasn't enough that the kid's father lost his life with them."

Dominick just shook his head, "Do what you want."

She ripped back, "Think. Those free baseball tickets he gives you. They don't have a cost?"

As Carmella approached the table, Mateo noticed that she had a surprised expression, and maybe a bit of disappointment seeing him with Mario. Mateo greeted her with a kiss. He remembered how Carmella had always treated the kids in the neighborhood. Dominick and Angie could always bring their friends in for a free pizza or hero sandwich. Mateo had fond memories of her generosity.

She motioned him to sit. She placed cups before them, and she rested her hand on Mateo's shoulder and asked about his mother. As she spoke, she bathed him with the wise eyes of a mother. He definitely knew she wasn't pleased at the company he was keeping.

"Mario, let the coffee rest in the pot for a minute or two to cool it down and to enhance its flavor."

"I know, I know, grazie." Mario thanked her in Sicilian dialect, addressing her as Donna, Carmella, a sign of respect.

Nevertheless, Carmella didn't trust their smooth ways. They rarely did something for nothing. Associating with them always had a cost. A price had to be paid someday, somehow. Mario asked Carmella for a container of espresso for Don Peppino to take along on the ride home and placed a hundred dollar bill in her hand for the dinner. She thanked him and returned to the kitchen thinking, the day must have been prosperous for him, but a great loss for someone else.

* * *

Mateo woke up with his mother beating him on the chest. Screaming and crying, she was calling him a bum and a disgrace. Startled, he grabbed her hands and held them firmly.

"Mom, what's happened? Why are you acting crazy?"

"Crazy?" she screamed. "You! Hurting people!"

"How did you get this blood on your shirt? Whose blood is it, some poor working slob?"

Mateo was foggy but he knew he had to think fast.

"Mom, calm down, it's most likely from the meat."

"What meat?"

"I was at the wholesale meat warehouse and they gave us some meat. I was standing right there when they cut it. It's in the refrigerator. You were sleeping when I came in so I just put in the fridge."

"You better not be lying to me," she growled as she went into the kitchen. Mateo waited a few minutes then followed her in. He saw that his mother had opened the large bag of meat.

Mateo wiped his brow, relieved to see that the steaks were still oozing blood. He wrapped his arm affectionately around his mother's waist and soothed her.

"See, it's loaded with blood."

She wanted to believe him but, without looking up, she protested to him, "I'm telling you right now. I'm not living another life like this. I will kill you and myself before they kill you."

She told him to sit down and she would give him coffee. They sat together, he mentioned the dinner at Carmella's, adding that he talked with Dominick and that Carmella sent her regards.

His account made her think about how Carmella must be in a panic also about her son. Mateo interrupted her thoughts.

"Mom, I had lunch at a great restaurant uptown. I met the owner and his daughter who runs the place. She's kinda cute, red hair, freckles and tough, a lot like you. The food was great. I'd like to take you there for dinner one night this week. Would you like that?"

"Come on," the shrewd mother answered. "You want to take me to dinner, or do you want to see this girl again?"

"Mom, why do you always do that? Why does there always have to be a motive? Can't I do something special for my mother?"

"You can charm these girls, but your mother, how do they say, she can catch-a you'r-a moves."

With a smile and a hug, he corrected her, "Mom, I think you want to say, you clock my moves."

"That's right, I clock-a all your moves."

Hester Street – 1900's - 1

Typical Italian feast, Little Italy - 1950's -2

PART TWO

Many Jewish and Italian immigrants settled in the Lower East Side at the end of the 19th century and into the beginning of the 20th.The influx of Italian immigrants began in the late 1800s when unemployment and poverty in their home country forced the move. The Italians living in New York numbered close to 400,000. By the Roaring 20s, Little Italy subdivided into enclaves of immigrants from specific hometown areas in Italy, settling with their landsmen and reunited by their culture and dialects. Northern Italians settled in Greenwich Village. Southern Italians: Neapolitans, Sicilians and Calabrians, claimed Little Italy. Mulberry Street housed a number of immigrants from Napoli, and Sicilians preferred Elizabeth Street. The first pizzeria in New York opened on Spring Street in 1905. Immigrants from southern Italy started celebrating street festivals–feasts–along Mulberry Street in the mid-1920s.

26.

As they drove to her apartment after the feast, Katie rested her head on Kevin's shoulder. They parked in a space in front of her gateway. He turned off the ignition and leaned to kiss her, lingering to breath in the aroma of her hair. She looked at him with adoration.

Kevin held Katie's arm as they got out of the car. He opened the trunk to retrieve the Lord and Taylor dress and accessory boxes.

"It is so sweet of your mother to have done this," she told him.

"I guess she knows I need all the help I can get to land a sweet babe like you," he quipped.

"Come on, you charmer, I think all the food you ate has made you delirious. I think we can both use a Brioschi."

"If that's an antacid then you read my mind. Or, maybe it was my stomach?"

As they entered the apartment, Kevin had a flashback to what had brought him there the day they met. He was happy to be in her life.

"This is where it all started," he said.

"Yeah, it wasn't the classic prince on the shining white horse scenario, but I'll take it. How about you?"

He laughed. "Well, you could say I shed blood for you."

"Shush, here. Let me take your clothes and hang them. I have a sweat shirt for you if you want to take a shower. I always buy extra-extra-large because they are so nice to lounge in."

"No that's okay, I have stuff in my bag. Always prepared," he said with a smile."

She pointed him to Billy's bedroom door to change and cautioned, "Don't trip over the electric trains on the floor. One of Anthony's birthday gifts to him." She promised that she would have the famous bubbling antacids ready for him when he returned.

"Italians love to eat, and Brioschi is a must to have in any medicine cabinet."

He turned to her with schoolboy admiration.

"You Italians even make antacids a cultural experience."

He smiled and left for the shower. When he emerged from the bathroom, he found Katie in the kitchen unfolding her new dress.

"Did you have enough hot water?"

Without speaking, he drew her close. Taking her into his arms, he kissed her with passion and she responded with abandon. As their kiss broke, her head nestled in his shoulder, holding him tightly. She felt secure in his arms. Then she realized she was on the brink of losing control. She slid from their embrace.

"Be a good boy. Have your Brioschi, and let me go and freshen up. Turn on the TV if you'd like."

Kevin lay down atop the couch. He could smell the fresh scent of the apartment. *Italian girls,* he mused. He remembered how she sparkled when they first met. The cute surprised expression of shock she had on her face was embedded in his memory. He laughed and thought how fate had brought them together and how much he wanted everything to be special for her.

He sensed something, though. What's troubling her? He cautioned himself not to pry, to allow her more time to work things out in her mind.

He switched the lights off. Only the glow of a night light in the kitchen provided illumination. Kevin waited. He saw her silhouette glide toward him. His heart raced.

She crawled onto the couch and slid into his arms. They kissed and let their hands explore each other. She trembled when he touched her breasts and responded with a tighter and closer embrace.

"Kevin," she whispered, "I want you, but I don't..."

He stopped her. "Don't worry, sweet heart. We have plenty of time. We'll know when it's right. I'm happy just being here with you. I'll sleep in Billy's bed."

She sighed at his tenderness and understanding. She hugged him, acknowledging that fate had bestowed her with a good man.

Still in her arms, Kevin broke the silence.

"Anyway, I need all my strength to play tomorrow."

She pinched him and moaned at his joke. He went to Billy's bed and they drifted off to sleep.

The next morning they awoke to the sound of an alley cat rummaging through trashcans in the gateway. They both came out of their rooms at the same time and they discovered each other once more in a morning embrace. They both felt refreshed and energized with the joy of awakening together.

"I need a cup of coffee desperately," she said to Kevin adding, "but first... and bolted for the bathroom. When she came out, she made her way to the kitchen, filled the coffee pot and placed it on the burner.

"Who's that?" she questioned seeing a shadow through the below street level blind kitchen window followed by a gentle knock at the door.

She tightened her robe and slid the chain latch to open the door a crack.

"Hi. What are you doing here?"

"Oh, Miss Katherine," one of her father's employees said, "your father asked me to pick up the order from the bakery and bring it here to you."

Katie shook her head in disbelief. "I can't believe that man," she said, frowning at her father's tenacity.

"I think the cats got to your pails, I will clean up for you." She took the boxes from the elderly man and thanked him sweetly.

"Tibi, you're a doll. Please give my regards to your wife."

Kevin laughed, now stretched on her bed waiting for her. "I wish I had a camera, the look on your face, standing there with those big boxes in your hands." He laughed again.

"Really? How do I look? You want to fight?" She charged the couch, bouncing the boxes and all atop of him.

"So you think, that's funny, ha," she said.

"I guess your dad will do anything to marry you off," he ribbed.

"That's it. You're dead." She pounced upon his stomach.

He could feel her strength. Wiry too, he thought as she tickled him with her fingernail and then squashed a jelly donut into his mouth.

"No, now and then he'll stop here on a weekend morning before he opens the store. He brings rolls and buns. Usually when he knows I'm annoyed with him."

Then the sound of the coffee pot boiling over interrupted their playfulness.

"I'll get it," he insisted and flipped her off to the side onto a cake box.

"Caveman" she screeched, rubbing her posterior and rolling aside to move the cake box.

Katie joined him in the kitchen with the crushed pastry boxes.

"Nice, real buns," she said as she jabbed the box into his rump with a coy smile.

He laughed and filled their cups with the fresh brew as she opened the first box of pastry.

"Let me guess. Chocolate."

"Shush, you. I don't know what's wrong with my father. He is obsessed with my love life. Poor Tibi, he made that poor guy get up early on a Sunday morning. It's not enough that he has him working at the store sixty hours a week."

"I guess our parents just want us to settle down. I guess they look forward to grandkids."

"You know, I think your parents are obsessed with marriage, too," she laughed. "That's normal, I guess, if you could ever accuse my father of being normal. But he can get compulsive about it. Sometimes I think that me not being married is an embarrassment him."

Then she giggled out, "Who knows maybe he just wants to get rid of me. I wonder if he believed you'd sleep over and if so why the pastry? Normally if that's what he thought, he would have been enraged by it. Instead of Tibi, he'd be at the door himself with a shotgun and a priest. I do have a reputation for challenging the system."

They laughed together. Katie sighed and went on. "I know I don't follow the norm for my culture. Usually, girls are encouraged to marry early, say between the ages of twenty to twenty–three. Twenty-five is considered a late starter and only acceptable if you're homely." She giggled. "They like them married off early, with short engagements so they'll not be tempted to have pre-marital sex and cause dishonor to the family."

"Yeah , it's the same in the Irish culture. But maybe your parents are still concerned about the effects of your loosing Carmine? Believing you may be in fear of investing your feelings into someone again."

Katie crinkled her brow, "Maybe so."

The mention of Carmine brought back thoughts of his early death and the conversations she had with Carmella and Carmine's Aunt at the feast. She slipped into her thoughts and said nothing for a few moments.

"Hello," Kevin whispered, breaking her silence. Maybe I shouldn't have mentioned Carmine.

"Oh, I'm sorry. I got lost thinking for a moment. Come on, let's enjoy our surprise breakfast. Do you want me to scramble some eggs?"

"No thanks, honey. Not for me. The pastries and rolls are more than enough."

"Honey. Wow. Nobody has called me honey for a long time." She tried to hide her smile. "It sounds good coming from you."

"Well, be prepared for more to come. I don't know if it's too soon for you, but I would like you to meet my parents."

"I'd love to. I'd like to thank your mother personally for the dress and her note. It was so sweet."

"What about next weekend?"

"Oh, I'm sorry, my dear. I told Father Tony that I would spend the weekend with him and Reggie, helping them straighten out his house upstate. He just inherited it from his grandmother. I was hoping you'd come with us."

"Hey, 'my dear.' That's a first, too. But it makes you sound like my mother."

"Your mother! You're cruisin' for a bruisin', buddy boy."

"A trip upstate sounds like a lot of fun. I would love to meet your friends, too. We can do something with my parents after that. And I'd like you to meet my friend Timmy. We grew up together. He has a new girlfriend whom I haven't met, and maybe we can spend a day together and then have dinner with my parents."

"I would like that, too. I'm so happy." She paused, and then looked dismayed. "You're not going to break my heart, are you?"

Extending his arms, he reassured her. "If I broke your heart, I would break my own. I can't believe how much I feel for you. This has never happened to me before. I feel good about us."

After breakfast, Kevin dressed awaited for her in the living room. When she entered the room, her beauty dazzled him as if it were the first time he saw her. Her hair was styled in a French twist and fastened with a jeweled hairpin that accentuated her black velvet ruffled dress. Her soft olive skin contrasted boldly against the dark colored dress. Kevin felt captivated.

She is breathtaking.

As he opened the door of the small car he asked, "Do you think your dress will wrinkle sitting in such tight quarters?"

"No, my dear. I had the kiddy-car in mind when I selected the dress. Velvet doesn't crease easily."

"You are absolutely beautiful."

"Eat your heart out," she giggled.

27.

The ride uptown was a storybook fantasy. Kate felt like Cinderella, beaming with beauty, youth, and excitement. When they arrived at the US Mission to the UN, Marine guards greeted them again. One of them, as if programmed, took possession of Kevin's music bag as before, and told him that he would place it by the piano. The other asked for the keys for his car glancing at Kate with an appreciative raised eyebrow.

As they entered the building, a Marine sergeant asked them to wait as he called for Jack Osborne. Jack came rolling down the stairway with a bounce to his step, and greeted them.

"Katherine, you look absolutely stunning. You will be the belle of the ball."

Katie blushed and Kevin grinned with pride.

"Okay, let's see now. Kevin, how does this sound? The orchestra is setting up. Maybe you would like to do some preparation, too. In the meantime, I will introduce Katherine to the women. The bulk of the other guests should be arriving in about forty-five minutes. After you're settled please join us in the Ambassador's suite for a cocktail and then we can all parade in together."

Without waiting for Kevin to answer, Osborne offered Katie his arm and led her toward the stairwell. He told her about the latest Wyeth painting, recently donated to the Mission. Kevin hesitated a moment as they parted, and smiled. *She amazes me, how wonderful she is. People immediately take to her. She is so well received into their confidence.* He followed the sergeant to the banquet salon.

When Kevin arrived at the Ambassador's suite he spied Katie talking to the Ambassador's wife, Cornelia, and the wives of the Algerian ambassador and his attaché. The Ambassador's wife had locked her arm around Kate. Kevin approached the women, and greeted them formally. The Ambassador's wife complimented him on his choice of companion.

"Kevin, it has been awhile and I do not have to ask if everything is going well for you. It seems you have been cavorting with angels."

The others smiled and shook their heads in agreement. Then the older woman introduced him to the others boasting that they were in for a treat with his musical talent. The Algerian Ambassador's mesmerized wife, Marisha, openly gazed at him with adoration. Katie took notice.

The Ambassadors joined them and they made their way in pairs to the main salon. Following protocol, the dignitaries and their wives were announced and greeted with applause as they entered. The band played Where or When. They made their rounds from table to table welcoming the other guests. Kevin and Katie sat at the Ambassador's table waiting their hosts' return.

"You having a good time so far?" he asked her.

"The greatest, honey. Everyone is treating me as if I'm royalty. You don't look like you are wanting for attention either. The Algerian Ambassador's wife, what's her name again?"

"Marisha."

"Well, she seems to have taken a shine to you."

"Do I detect a shade of jealously?"

"You just behave yourself, Kevin Mandrel, or I'll tell your mother."

The Ambassador and his party returned to the table. His wife, saying she felt as if they had abandoned Kevin and Katie, encouraged her husband to dance the first dance with Katie. Katie accepted and made her way to the dance floor with the ambassador. Kevin, in kind, invited his wife to dance.

Marisha flirted with him as he rose. "I hope I will also have an opportunity to dance with you."

He smiled with diplomatic finesse and nodded.

Time raced by. Katie had made such a splash that all the men at the table had asked her to the floor. Kevin returned the compliment by asking their respective spouses. Marisha mellowed after a few glasses of champagne and tapped Kevin on his butt after their dance had ended. The provocative gesture was caught by the band's vocalist who glanced at her with a naughty smile.

With sculptured Middle Eastern features, Marisha exhibited sensual charm in her own right. She was a leading lady of sorts in the diplomatic arena and though no longer young she was yet well proportioned and carried herself with the vitality of a younger woman. Her reputation preceded her. She was internationally known for seeking and holding the attention of powerful men because of her striking features and her beckoning black eyes that had disarmed and drawn so many into seduction.

After dessert, the bandleader introduced Kevin as the US Cultural Attaché stationed in Zurich and noted his affiliation with the Zurich Philharmonic. "By request of our ambassador's wife, he will be playing Gershwin's Rhapsody in Blue."

Kevin sat at the piano, opened his music bag, and placed the score on the music rack. The vocalist winked at him. He returned a smile.

He massaged his hands briefly and began to play with a deep passion showing his profound love for music, a love that competed with his patriotic love of country. The guests were speechless, uttering not a word or a sound while he performed. When he ended the classic piece, the guests rose to their feet applauding in a show of great appreciation. Kevin bowed and returned to the table. Katie beamed with pride and joy for his success.

The others at the table complimented him, and as guests settled down into discussion, the Algerian attaché asked Kevin, "If you would be so kind, I can use a few pointers on the Rachmaninov II piece I have been suffering with as an amateur." Kevin nodded with a smile. The attaché asked the waiter to call his aide who returned with a large envelope containing the sheet music.

The others at the table were engrossed in conversation. Katie had gone to the powder room with the wives. Moments later Kevin and the attaché went to the piano where Kevin shuffled through his music and exchanged the music scores by placing the transferred piece, as previously instructed, third from the top. He then gently gathered his sheets of music together and placed them in the black Bag.

They spent ten minutes discussing the score and the attaché's true comprehension of the music surprised Kevin. As they finished, a Marine approached and asked Kevin if he would like him to place his bag in his car. Kevin accepted, feigning surprise and gratitude.

At the table, the other guests complimented him again and the Algerian ambassador's wife suggested that Kevin come and play at their Embassy in Algeria.

The attaché used that as a perfect intro and suggested that maybe Kevin could play at their winter music festival in Algiers. The Algerian Ambassador formalized it into a verbal invitation. Kevin accepted but as instructed by his agency handlers, expressed his need for a wire to be sent to the scheduling secretary at the Philharmonic to coordinate the dates.

The Ambassador invited Katie to the festival as well.

"Thank you, I'm speechless. What an honor." Katie thanked him again and graciously and accepted, noting that she and Kevin would need separate bedrooms.

Cornelia told Katie she would be calling her for lunch and a shopping date as they had discussed in the powder room. Jack also mentioned he would be calling her in a few days, too." Kevin was surprised by the exchanges and curious about their interaction. She's incredible. Amazing.

On the drive downtown, Katie was still excited by it all.

"I'm completely overwhelmed by how kind and generous everyone has been." She beamed like a teenager.

"Jack is going to call about joining a committee for a charity fundraiser and Wyeth Art Exhibit. He believes my non-profit background might aide the committee to secure community-based outreaches that are worthy of receiving donations."

"Sound like you and Jack are instant old friends."

"Why? Does that make you feel insecure?" she asked. She tried to suppress her smile as she waited for his answer.

"Astonish me, why don't you? Lunch with the ambassador's wife, and an invitation to Algeria. You're an ambassador yourself. You seem to be highly skilled at developing relationships at lightning speed."

"Well, I got you under my spell, didn't I?"

They both laughed again as she said, "My family is going to go nuts over all this."

They both felt as if they were on a magic carpet and did not want to get off. When they got to her apartment, Billy and Reggie were playing Parcheesi. Katie introduced Kevin to Reggie.

"My God! He's a hunk!" Reggie exclaimed.

"Pay her no mind," Katie said. "She is still recovering from alcohol addiction."

"That's one to the mid-section. How do you know that statement wouldn't attract him even more? After all, he's got Irish blood."

Kevin laughed and blushed. He deflected the comment by asking Billy to come out to the car as he had something in the trunk for him. Embarrassed by Reggie's comment, Katie followed out to the car. When he opened the trunk, Billy recognized the distinctive box of the AC Gilbert Erector Set. He found it impossible to keep his streetwise persona. He whisked past Katie to take the toy into the house.

They enjoyed his boyish exuberance and settled in to discuss travel arrangements for the trip upstate.

Katie walked Kevin to his car where he gave her a full kiss on the mouth goodbye. He saw Reggie peeking through the kitchen window and gave her a boyish wave.

When Katie returned inside Sr. Regina gave her a hug, sharing her happiness.

"Wow, he's so nice. With a great butt to boot. Looks like you caught a live one."

"Reggie, your mouth. He does have nice buns, but act your age. Need I remind you that you're a nun?"

* * *

The week went briskly for them. Kevin made the rounds visiting relatives with his parents and catching up with his old friends. Katie had an emergency with Billy to deal with, and had to meet with his father regarding the trouble Billy got into. Father Tony asked Katie and Reggie to do some shopping for the coming weekend.

Katie answered the phone.

"Hey, Madame Diplomat. How's it going?

"Just great, my musical government friend. Glad you called. I spoke with Tony and he's looking forward to meeting you. He also extended an invitation to your friends to join us upstate. I think he needs all the help he can get."

"Terrific. This will be a fun way for all of us to get to know each other."

She chuckled. "I don't know how much fun it's going to be. Tony invited his best friend Joey, 'Lungs,' the singer. The combination of him, Reggie, and Dominick will put us on a trip for sure."

"Sounds like we're traveling with a comical team."

Kevin was excited as he had missed having outings in America. He felt isolated from American culture working in Europe. He would call Timmy and see if he and Colleen were free.

Katie asked him if they could meet at her parents' house in Scarsdale. She needed to drop Billy there to spend the weekend with her parents so they could keep an eye on him. Kevin took her directions to the house.

28.

Westchester County, just north of New York City, had its own renaissance after World War I. Builders and developers of the time chose a medieval style of architecture known as Tudor and adopted it for homes and business centers alike. Even automobile service stations were modeled in the so-called Tudor "look" that embodied Westchester's construction industry of the 1920s.

Birdie's home sat grandly on a large wooded lot, substantial in size and landscaped with a slate stone path edged with evergreen hedges. A carved circular oak front door took light from a wrought iron framed stain glassed window.

In his youth, Maryann Burdino's grandfather, a well-known medieval architect in southern Italy, had specialized in restorations. His work required international travel and one that eventually brought him to America. He worked as a consultant joining artisans in the Westchester building revival. Maryann inherited the house shortly after her marriage to Katie's father in 1921. Birdie and his wife rode the crest of an unprecedented wave of prosperity, part of a generation that spurred the growth of the 1950s.

Most middle class women at that time did not work. They married after finishing their education – high school or college – and spent their time caring for their homes and children.

Scarsdale became an affluent bedroom community for the corporate executives of New York City who left their wives to the task of assimilation into finer society, a membership marked by their grandiose homes and the weight of their assets.

Because of the late hours her husband spent working in Little Italy, Katie's mother became engrossed in social and cultural events and service clubs that filled her need for companionship when she wasn't mothering her only child through her primary education and high school.

Kevin arrived at the Scarsdale Parkway exit at 3:00 p.m. Following the directions, he found himself passing through beautiful tree lined streets with large ornate stone and brick homes. As Kevin negotiated the long winding driveway, he found himself in front of a spacious aged fieldstone Tudor home. Kevin parked beside a black and gray late model Chrysler Town and Country station wagon classically adorned with decorative wood body molding. Billy came out through the side door to greet him, followed by Katie and her mother.

"Hi, Billy. How're things going?" Kevin asked.

"Not good," he answered.

He shook Kevin's hand and shot an angry stare at Katie as he rapidly scooted down the driveway.

Kevin gave Katie a hug and a kiss and acknowledged her mother.

"Hi, Mrs. Burdino. It's so nice to see you again."

"Welcome to our home." She gave him her hand and a polite kiss on his cheek.

"My mother prepared brewed English tea and finger sandwiches."

"Yes, I guess that's right." He consulted his watch. "It's almost four. Time for high tea."

"My goodness, you're a sophisticated man, aren't you?" Mrs. Burdino said. She was thrilled that he knew about the tradition of high tea.

Kevin turned to Katie and said, "The English tradition of high tea is credited to Anna, 7th Duchess of Bedford, in the early 1800s. The Duchess got hungry between her early luncheon and her late dinner, and got the idea of a small separate meal in between, one that consisted of tea, of course, plus sandwiches, pastries, and teacakes." He bowed as if finishing a performance.

"You never cease to amaze me," Katie said, laughing.

"Katie, why don't you and Kevin have a seat in the parlor while I attend to our high tea?"

The parlor had a classic French décor with a Louis the XIV flair, its wood painted a cream color and burnished with gold leaf. The artwork throughout the room complimented the décor and, reminiscent of the era, was further augmented by large sculptured brace lamps.

As they sat, Kevin noticed how much care Katie's mom had given to impressing him. He did not know how much he fit into the woman's fantasy of a prince charming for her daughter.

As far as Mrs. Burdino was concerned, he was well educated, world traveled, and ran in the circles of world leaders. He was an accomplished artist to boot. To her mind, he, and people like him, were true society. While she felt she had fallen short of attaining that rank, Mrs. Burdino wanted it for her daughter.

Kevin and Katie sat close to each other on the couch.

"My would-be debutante mother lit up when I told her about the luncheon at Mission. When she heard that I received an invitation to Algeria, she almost fainted."

Katie put her hand on Kevin's knee.

"You're very high on her list. My father, too, and he's not easily impressed. He can't stop talking about it. He makes excuses to call me three or four times a day."

"Princess Katherine," he said, "when one has it, one should flaunt it. Listen to this, Princess. I'm glad there are high ceilings in this room."

She kissed him and took his hand firmly in hers.

The doorbell rang. Katie jumped to answer it. Two friends of her mother's from the local civic association came barreling in.

"Hi. Hope we're not late."

Katie stood, open mouthed, and tried to force a smile for the unexpected guests and escorted them to the parlor. Kevin rose to his feet and she introduced him as her friend.

"A pleasure," one chirped. "We've heard a lot about you."

Katie invited them to sit and excused herself, rolling her eyes to Kevin as she left the room to inform her mother of their arrival. She entered the kitchen irate.

"Mom, why did you do that? Can't I have a life of my own? Do you have any idea what pressure you and Dad put on me? You treat me like a puppet, and this has got to stop."

"Katherine, please calm down. They called just after you told me about the luncheon. I just told them how happy you were."

"Mom, I will help you out with the tea tray and then we're leaving. We have a long trip up to Tony's cabin and I don't like driving up there after dark."

"Okay, but just let Kevin have a little something to eat. To hold you on the trip."

Katie picked up the tray. In a huff, she made her way back to the parlor. As she approached, she heard one of the women asking Kevin to play for them at an upcoming fundraiser.

That's it, she said to herself. She signaled to Kevin to get up and they excused themselves, explaining to the women that they were late and had people waiting for them. They both pecked her mother on her cheek, and made their way to the door.

Katie's car had been already loaded with her clothes and food. Kevin retrieved his luggage from the Karmann Ghia and placed it in the rear of the spacious Chrysler Wagon. He opened the passenger door for her. As he circled around making his way to the driver's seat, he saw Katie's mother and her two friends at the door, watching his every move. He waved goodbye, and turned the key with haste.

Tears flowed down Katie's cheeks as they made their way through the suburban neighborhood in the direction of the highway. Road surveyors were laying the ground work for the construction of the new interstate.

The air had started to cool. Fall was approaching. Changes that would collide with those in the wind for Katie.

She finally cried out to Kevin, "I feel like my life is a joke."

"Come on. We have a wonderful weekend ahead of us. We're making history together."

"Funny man. You're so good."

29.

They drove for a while. Kevin remarked about the aroma of food coming from the rear of the wagon.

"I'm sorry. Between Billy, his antics, and all that confusion my mother caused, I didn't have a chance to tell you what I brought. If Italians are going to be away from the house for more than three hours, they prepare a stash of food. What we have is a feast to last three days for ten people. Other people, those we call the Americans, could gorge themselves on it for three weeks."

Kevin grinned. "Tell me more."

"We have fresh sausage and steaks for the barbeque and my mother made two pans of manicotti, plus an assortment of cold cuts, dried salami and imported cheeses."

"I hope you brought the Brioschi, too," he said.

"Yes, I did, in fact, two bottles. We're going to need it. I'm sure Aunt Carmella will load Dominick up with a couple of trays, too."

"I guess we all follow our own traditions, I packed bottles of vodka, gin, rye, and scotch, plus a bunch of mixers. My mother sent along a five pound box of Barricini chocolates."

"Your Mom has a sweet tooth?" she asked.

"Yep. Which means she's dying to meet you."

Katie sighed. "I'm really looking forward to meeting her, too."

"Don't worry. She won't invite her friends until something formal happens. However, knowing her, she will show you all of my baby pictures. And, who knows, if she likes you she may even give you one of her petrified bones."

Katie's brows crinkled and he added with a smile, "She's an anthropologist." She laughed.

Kevin stopped for a moment to study her, wanting to know more about her life. Katie read his thoughts. She revealed that information surfaced from the past and that she expected to learn more. Then she confided that something already had deeply troubled her.

"As soon as I have some more pieces of the puzzle I'd like to talk to you about it," she said.

"Okay, I'm here."

"In the meantime, I have to deal with Billy, that little stinker." She paused for a breath. "He caused a great deal of trouble this past week. I'm shocked about what he did. He cut school to hook-up with a couple of older boys to steal hubcaps."

"Why would he do a dumb thing like that?"

"God knows, Kevin. I give him money and he doesn't want for anything. I think he's just hanging with the wrong kids."

"Are the police going to pursue it?"

"I don't think so. The police sergeant who caught them recognized him as Tommaso's son and brought him to the Three Feathers. Uncle Tommaso reprimanded him. He made it worse by disrespecting him with bad language and he gave him a hard slap. He had him sit in the corner until he spoke with me."

Kevin patted her hand. "He's safe for now. Relax and enjoy trip."

30.

Although embarrassed and miffed with what Billy had done, Katie recognized his anger at Fingers for the loss of his mother. Billy looked at the world differently than she did. After she assumed care for him from Fingers, she had brought him to her workplace at the St. Francis Center.

Katie received a call from her father at that time. He accused her of being too lenient with the boy. Infuriated by his comments she decided to bring things to a head, and made an appointment to meet at Carmella's the following day with Fingers and her father to devise a better strategy.

When Katie arrived at the restaurant, Carmella understood a pow-wow was to be held. Katie's father had picked Billy up from school. When Katie approached the table, she overheard Fingers and her father pampering him, suggesting he order a steak with vegetables. Katie flipped out.

"What's wrong with you two? He steals and is rewarded with a steak dinner?" She waved her fist in his face. "I'm not going to let him turn into a street thug. He has to know that his behavior cannot continue and that I'm not going to spend my life bailing him out of jail."

"Calm down, honey," Birdie cautioned.

"Please, Katie, don't get upset," Fingers said. Ripping Billy a bad look, he went on, "Do you see what you did? Do you know how much she has done for us? She loves and cares for you like a mother."

Katie was still furious.

"Calm down. He's not turning into a gangster," Birdie said.

It took a long minute, but Katie marshaled her composure.

"I have been giving this some thought," she said. "We have to get Billy out of the neighborhood. First, I thought about having him move in with my father and mother and enroll him in Scarsdale High. But that would put a burden on my mother and I don't think she could handle it. She loves him and they have a good relationship, but it would be confining for both of them. So I did a little research and found a private Catholic military school on Long Island."

"No way!" Billy yelped. "No way, forget about it. I'm not going to wear no uniform and march around like an idiot."

Billy got up and tried to leave the table. Fingers grabbed his arm.

"A gray uniform with numbers and stripes would suit your better?"

Katie's eyes welled up. "Let's face it, Billy. You're out of control. You have been this way since your mom died. I have tried to fill the gap and I love you deeply. But you're not getting the message."

Katie paused, took a breath and reached for his hand.

"Billy, you're special to me and it will be difficult for me to be without you. I'm trying to save your life. The things you're doing are not just the antics of a teenager. These things are criminal, and if they continue, they will lead you deeper into a life of trouble and danger. I'm not your parent, and I have no authority to tell you where to go."

Fingers interrupted, reacting to Billy's facial expression. "Listen to her."

Birdie waved to let her continue.

Katie said, "I know you trust me and you love me, too. So believe me. This is the best course for you. You can't con me, so don't even try. I know the street. Think about it. There will be much more to learn at the academy. It will help you develop confidence in yourself. I will come out to see you on a regular basis and take you with me on free weekends and summer vacations."

Fingers reached to his son. "Look, this is the chance I never had as a kid. I had no family. Only your mother. I grew up in a cold-water flat. We used a wood stove to cook food. You froze to go to the toilet in the back yard. At your age, I had to work so I would have a place to live. I only had seven years of school."

Billy whimpered. He tried to force back the tears, as he spoke. "You did all right for yourself. You own the bar and people respect you."

"Wake up, son. They don't respect me. They fear me. They respect Uncle Birdie and Katie for their education. That's real respect. Look, I'll make a deal with you. Complete this school and I will buy you any car you want. You complete college and I will buy you any house you want."

Not waiting for Billy to reply he asked, "Caterina, what do we have to do?"

Katie was surprised by Fingers' willingness to get his son out of the neighborhood. She was gratified that he did not want Billy to be part of the life that had been forced upon him.

"I'm going to make the interview appointment at the school. It's La Salle Military Academy. We need to get references."

Birdie volunteered, "I will speak with Monsignor Scalvo and a couple of political friends I have. Just let me know who to direct the letters to."

Dominick served lunch. The conversation changed. Katie's father asked her about her luncheon at the US Mission.

Carmella came to the table, hugged Billy, and invited him to the kitchen to help her stuff cannoli for their dessert. Billy, who was sitting silently, got up and trod off following Carmella, who had heard bits and pieces of the conversation. She told Billy to wash his hands and showed him how to use the pastry bag to fill the pastry.

"Billy, be smart. Build a life for you. Your mother and I grew up together and we had tough lives. She always wanted to have a child of her own, one that she'd give everything to. You were a dream come true for her. I never saw a mother so loving and caring. Her only worry was that you wouldn't stay out of trouble. She wanted you to have the best of everything, including the best education.

"I believe that people who go to heaven are still involved in our lives, I'm sure your mother is. I'm sure she is watching out for you through other people in your life like Katie. She is guiding you to do the right thing. Make her proud."

Carmella hugged him again. His spirits lifted and his sullenness evaporated. He took one of the freshly filled cannoli broke it in half, and shared it with Carmella with an appreciative smile.

After they left, Carmella sat at a back table of the restaurant with a cup of tea. The conversation about Billy's welfare brought her fears for her own children to a higher level. She knew the neighborhood family and believed that when Billy came of age they would try to recruit him into their world.

It's in their blood. They can't be trusted. Their minds and hearts are fixed, and they know no other way.

Carmella gasped, thinking of what she would tell Katie the next time they met privately.

31.

The ride to the cabin in Windham took two hours, yet it flew by for Katie and Kevin. They were engrossed in each other, enjoying the breathtaking views of the mountains and valleys. They stopped at the famous Five State lookout to see the panorama in the waning light of late day. They were unable to resist picking at the cold cuts and cheeses whose aroma filled the cab of the wagon.

"Does the view before you pale compared to that of the Alps?"

"The Alps are magnificent, but nothing could thrill me more that the beauty of America, my home. It has the woman of my dreams."

Katie blushed. In an instant her mood changed and panic came over her. She remembered that he had to return to Europe.

"Oh my God," she muttered.

"What?"

"You're going to leave."

He sighed. "Yeah. When you mentioned the Alps, I was reminded, too. But don't worry. I know in my heart that everything will work out. God would not play a trick on us. We're right for each other."

Hearing his words – his commitment to her – she cried with tears of relief. He hoped to lighten the moment.

"Who knows, maybe we'll get married at the Sultan's Castle in Algiers.

"You dog. My mother would have a heart attack."

They drove through the quaint mountain towns of Windham and Hunter, in an area known for its scenic beauty, woodworking artisans, antique shopping, and home cooked food eateries.

Father Tony's house sat on twenty acres recessed a thousand feet back from the road. Hiking paths made mountain peaks accessible along with winding waterways, meadowlands and dense forest. Surrounding the house were stands of majestic spruce and balsam fir that spread out to acres of a nature preserve encircling the home. It was secluded serene, and in harmony with its wild life neighbors.

When they arrived at the property, they made their way up the dirt drive, which opened to a clearing where the cottage was nestled. It had a worn, aged look but appeared structurally sound.

Kevin honked the horn. No one came. They parked by the side door, which, Katie was told, led to the kitchen. On it, they found a note.

Yes, Katherine my love, you're at the right house. The door is unlocked. Reggie and I had a couple of errands and needed to go to the hardware store. You and Reggie get the large room with the bay window overlooking the pond. Thought Kevin would be comfortable with the room at the end of the hall with the double bed. The water is on and the plumbing is working, I will be back soon. Relax! Tony

The house was spacious with four large bedrooms. It was styled as farmhouse, circa 1900, still with its original windows and shutters. The interior was accented with a handcrafted staircase that had its original newel posts intact. It complimented the wide planked floorboards and two stone fireplaces, one in the living room with a hand-hewn mantle. Deer antlers hung in the large dining room with matching rustic furniture, heavy and made to last a lifetime.

They threaded their way up the stairway to the second floor and found Katie's room. Its large window overlooked a kidney-shaped pond with floating lily pads and circled with cattails.

The room was rustic, simply furnished with a triple dresser, and had twin beds adorned with multi-colored, hand-crocheted bedspreads. Kevin placed Katie's suitcase on the bed. He joined her gazing out the window admiring the delightful view. They embraced. They savored the moment and the magic of their budding love but both were trying to be patient, holding back their physical impulses. They were cautious and taking no chance of losing one another.

After unpacking, they made their way to the living room.

"It's chilly in here," she said. "Think we should light a fire?"

"I saw a pile of logs on the back porch. See if you can find some matches."

Kevin brought the wood in, opened the damper, and prepared the hearth. Katie found stick matches in the kitchen next to the gas stove. Working side by side, they put down a layer of kindling and loaded wood on top, two small logs on bottom with two larger ones crisscrossed on top. The wood was dry and the fire began to warm the room in minutes.

"I'm impressed. You remembered to open the damper, something my father never did. At home, he usually fills the house with smoke and cinders."

Kevin retrieved a bottle of wine from one of his cartons, and pulled the cork with finesse. He never took his eyes off of Katie. He poured a splash into one glass and sipped it.

"You're going to like this," he said.

He filled his glass and then one for Katie. They relaxed on the couch and waited for the others. The flickering of the flames and the warmth of the fire warmed their outside, the wine warmed them inside. Their love warmed their hearts.

They relaxed until their reverie was broken by Father Tony's excited voice directing Reggie where to place the groceries. His footsteps drummed on the hardwood floors as he entered the living room.

"I thought that was the aroma of a fire. How are you two? How was your drive up? Did you find the place okay?"

A sleepy-eyed Katie embraced him and wished him good luck on his home, adding that the place was adorable and cozy. Kevin shook his hand and congratulated him. Introductions were unnecessary.

"Did you find your bedrooms?"

"Yes, the names on the doors gave us good clues," She giggled. "We're all settled in, and we also loaded the refrigerator with goodies."

Reggie came in, greeted everyone with kisses, and flirted with Kevin. "Hey, Nordic idol. I could give up my vocation for a hunk like you."

He blushed and laughed. Father Tony peered at her with a taunting look and threatened, "Good Sister, you had better behave yourself, or I will inform Mother Superior."

"Who knows? She might even get a spark or two."

"Well, I guess I'm jealous. Wait, I hear a car pulling in."

Katie peeked out the window. "I think it's Kevin's friend Timmy with his girlfriend Colleen."

Kevin and Katie went to meet them and made introductions. Kevin joked with Colleen about Timmy's driving skills. The four of them hit it off well from the first moment.

The arriving young couple also brought bags of groceries and sweets. Tony and Reggie joined in the welcome and helped with their luggage. After adding their groceries to the already overcrowded kitchen table, Father Tony poured wine for everyone.

Katie and Reggie showed Colleen to her room. Kevin and Timmy volunteered to help, and were given the task of taking food to the basement while Father Tony prepared the barbeque grill. They were charged-up with the excitement, anticipating a great weekend.

"Look, Kev," Timmy said. "A full basement with another full kitchen and all."

"Yeah, a great hideaway. Spacious. The furniture gets lost in it. Whoa, a pizza oven!"

"What man could ask for more? I understand it was originally built as a hunting lodge. Kevin, can you see us here on weekends sitting at this oak bar throwing down a few after a day in the field?"

"I can't believe the workmanship. Couldn't afford to do this today," Kevin said. He knelt down and ran his fingers over the multi-colored flagstone. He noted the fresh scent of disinfectant.

They headed for the stairs. Timmy pointed to a small hallway.

"What's down there?" he asked. Kevin looked at him and shrugged to indicate he didn't know. Reliving boyhood mischievousness, they sneaked down the hallway together. They found a bathroom with two shower stalls, and a bedroom with what were apparently Father Tony's belongings.

"More rooms. This is a complete apartment."

At the end of the hall, they entered the small room adjacent to an outdoor staircase with steps leading up to outside doors. Kevin turned on the light.

"Armory?" Timmy said.

There were gun and bow racks, and a large cabinet with a wide assortment of vintage firearms.

"I'll be dammed," Kevin said. "Look at this stuff. It even has a rubber-padded worktable. A gunsmith."

"Shotgun shell reloading equipment with boxes of shot and ammunition. A nice place to clean guns."

"Or start a war," Kevin said.

They were laughing as Father Tony came down to open the cellar doors. He found them admiring the firearms.

"Oh, good, you found the artillery. With your military experience, I was hoping you could help me evaluate this stuff. I would like to sell most of it. Maybe keep a couple of shotguns for target shooting."

"Sure, we'd love to," Kevin said. "It appears you have a bunch of quality pieces here. A collector will have interest. We'll give them some care. See if we can clean things up if we have the time, and prepare them to show."

"That sounds great. Thanks. I think we should eat down here in the kitchen as the table is large enough to accommodate all of us."

The women joined them and set the table. Kevin and Timmy kept the wine flowing. Platters of Italian sausage, hot dogs, and burgers for barbeque were carried up the narrow staircase to the outside deck.

The men tended the grill while the women prepared the room for the feast. Mellowed by the quantity of homemade wine they had consumed, Father Tony, with Kevin and Timmy in tow, bounded down the stairs, the aroma of the sausages preceding them.

Their personalities blended well. Kevin, Timmy and Colleen felt comfortable and at home. Amazed by the banquet before them, they toasted the cooks. Father Tony raised his hand while whistling for attention.

"Let's settle down for grace."

Their attention was drawn to the slam of the screen door upstairs. Footsteps and a voice singing I've Got the World on a String announced a new arrival. Father Tony rose and called up the stairwell.

"We're down here, you guys. You're just in time to pray."

Joey, known as "Lungs," sang out as they descended, "Pray? We're here to eat, drink and who knows? Some of us might have other things on our minds."

He winked at his girlfriend who returned his smile with an enthusiastic one of her own. The others came to their feet, and Katie made introductions all around.

"This is the Lungs, our neighborhood crooner and childhood friend and his hopefully soon to be Mrs. Lungs, Millie. She's a high school classmate of ours and a woman of great fortitude and patience as you will appreciate more as the weekend unfolds."

When they settled down, Father Tony led them with the sign of the cross. They followed in kind and bowed their heads. He clasped the hands of Reggie and Katie who were seated at his sides and began to pray aloud.

"Heavenly father, we give you thanks for all that we have, the wonderful banquet laid out before us. This beautiful house and the fond loving memory of my grandparents, with gratitude for their many gifts to me. I also thank you for the friendship and love of those present. We ask you to bless this food, to keep us close and safe as you guide us on our life's journeys. In the name of the Father, Son, and Holy Ghost. Amen."

"Tony," Lungs said, "I thought you were reciting the Gettysburg Address."

"Shut up and eat, before I have you excommunicated."

32.

They ate, consumed bottles of wine and reminisced about the antics of their childhood. They laughed and told tales from summers and Christmases past. They were brought to tears at the memory of beloved high school friends who hadn't survived the war.

After dinner, they all pitched in to clean the table and wrap the leftover food.

"Everyone want coffee? We'll get the pastries out in a few minutes," Reggie announced.

There was a collective groan, but no one told her not to bother.

After stretching their legs out on the deck, they returned to the table for dessert. Timmy expressed how invigorating the night air of the mountains was, and how it refreshed him. He loved the property.

Lungs agreed, and told him that he had been there before.

Father Tony said, "You were here? When was that?"

"While you were away at college, your father had called me and asked me to bring up Chinese food for their Friday night poker game. He and his friends were up here for the opening of hunting season."

"You drove all the way up here just for Chinese food?"

"Yeah. They let me use one of Don Peppino's limos."

Katie quizzed, "That's long drive just to deliver take out."

"Hey I know, but you couldn't beat the tip. I also sang a couple of Old Italian songs for them. They were having a ball."

"How did they know how to contact you?" Father Tony asked.

"I was singing at the 900 a couple of times a month. Fingers has an interest in the club. Odds-on they got my number from the bartender. Them? They can find anybody. I still sing there when they need someone to fill in."

"I didn't know that Uncle Tommaso had ownership in the club."

"He comes in once in a while with Mario. They'd have an espresso with anisette, and listen to me belt out a few. I like it when he comes in. He good. He's trying to help me connect with a good manager to put a demo together."

"I'm impressed," Reggie said. "A great voice and personality to boot."

"Personality?" Father Tony said. "He's got personality alright."

They all laughed.

Lungs laughed along and remained convivial. But his mood had changed. I'd be in a pool of shit if they knew what went down that night.

The Chinese food was only part of the delivery. His instructions were to pick up a limo at Don Peppino's funeral home. When he arrived, Anthony had readied the car. The trunk was loaded with securely covered pans of Chinese food, cases of Manhattan Special Espresso Soda, and boxes of Italian cookies from the pastry shop.

As Anthony escorted him to the driver's door, Lungs heard conversation and laughter coming from the rear seats. He opened the back door and was greeted by three hookers laughing and drinking champagne.

He laughed when he peered in. "Hey, I know you guys. I remember those private parties at the 900. You upstaged me all the time."

One licked her lips and winked at him. Hearing what Lungs had said Anthony shook his head in disapproval. "Shame on them. No nice."

Lungs smiled to himself. This is going to be a trip and a half.

The trip was uneventful. The girls giggled, playing among themselves, passing a bottle of champagne back and forth, and finally abandoning glasses in favor of drinking directly from the bottle. They heard Lungs humming and encouraged him to sing a few songs a cappella. One flashed her breasts in the rearview mirror.

Upon arrival, the three party girls were poured out of the back seat and sent upstairs to freshen up.

Lungs realized now that Reggie the nun and Katie were to sleep in that same room. The room where it happened. The memory continued to unfold in his mind.

"Hey, kid, the boss is hungry. Help me bring the food into the kitchen and heat things up."

"Sure, Mario. Be glad too."

"Did the girls give you any trouble?"

"No, No, they were cool, we had fun talking and I sung a couple of songs for them."

"Good," the older man replied, "Mr. Pena and Mr. Fingarro are grateful to you for doing this favor on such short notice, and would appreciate you not mentioning anything to anybody about the girls."

"What girls?"

"Good boy," Mario said. "I'm not crazy about the idea myself but it's a special occasion for one of the guys."

Lungs squeezed his lips shut, "Forget about it. I had a singing gig and picked up some food as a favor if someone should ask."

Mario thanked him and reminded him of his efforts in pursuing an audition for him in Las Vegas. The young man got the message. Keep your mouth shut and you will have friends.

Mario and Lungs heated the food and placed it on the table for the men who unsteadily descended the stairs to the lower kitchen. When they greeted and thanked Lungs, he noticed they had red cheeks, and breaths reeking of wine. He recognized four of the eight men. Besides Mario, there was Pena, Father Tony's father, who was the host, and there were Don Fingarro, Don Peppino, Bundles, a mob associate he knew from the club, and three well-dressed older men. They dove into the food.

They ate ravenously.

"Great food needs great song," Don Peppino said.

Lungs didn't need a second invitation. He sang every current hit of Frank Sinatra and Dean Martin he knew.

"Ya know," one of the older gentlemen said, "I banged Dino's girlfriend in Atlantic City while he waited out in the hall."

Another said, "You, too?"

The all laughed.

They returned to the living room upstairs. Lungs helped clean the table and brewed three large pots of espresso. When ready, they brought the pots up on silver serving platters resting them on a table set with cups, liquor, and cookies.

The girls came down clad in black mesh hose, fringed garter belts and pointed lace bras. Their brightly colored short silk unbuttoned robes were just garnish. They greeted each of the guests with hugs and kisses, rubbing their breasts across the men's faces and allowing themselves to be groped.

Lungs smiled at them when they started to do their thing. Professionals, he thought.

Mario signaled for Lungs to follow him downstairs. When they got there, he asked Lungs if he would take food and coffee out to the man guarding the road. "Stay there. Keep him company until I call you," Mario said.

Lungs found the car, a late model black Olds parked at the head of the driveway. The light shown inside with a man reading the Il Progresso, an Italian newspaper. The man greeted him in broken English, thanked him for the food and invited him to join him to eat in the rear of the car. He introduced himself as Gaetano. Lungs conversed with him comfortably in Sicilian.

Gaetano told him that he was feeling nostalgic, that he had only been in America for two years and missed Milazzo, his small hometown in Sicily. He reminisced about the mountains and farms surrounding the village.

The two men kept themselves occupied talking about Italian singers, the differences in regional Italian food, the quality of gelato, and culture – or the lack thereof – in their newly adopted home.

Gaetano asked Lungs to join him to return the platter and dishes and check around the property. When they returned to the car, Mario was waiting, biting his lip.

"Gaetano, follow me. I need you at the house. We have a heavy package to carry." Gaetano frowned as if there was a subtext that Lungs didn't understand. It became clear to him when Gaetano mumbled, "Questo Americano non può avere anche una festa senza un corpo che gira su."

These Americans can't even have a party without a body turning up.

Mario said to Lungs, "Pull the car around to the side door and wait at the wheel for the girls."

Lungs returned to his car, checked the time on his wristwatch, Geez, I thought I'd catch a nap before the drive back. Something's up.

Two of the girls were ushered into the car by Mario. He handed each five crisp one-hundred-dollar bills.

"You were never here," he said to them.

"Yeah. Sure," one answered sarcastically, cracking her gum.

Mario reached out, grabbed her cheek and squeezed. She shrieked.

"What did you say?" he hissed through his teeth.

"Never here. Never here," she yelled in pain.

He looked to the other. "You?"

She reflexively covered her face with her hands. "Never here," she whispered in fear.

He closed the door and told Lungs that the third woman would be staying.

"Here," he said, handing Lungs a roll of money, "for your music lessons."

Mario watched as they drove off. As the car rolled down the driveway, the girls remained silent until they reached the main road a few minutes later. Only then, one dared speak a few slurred words.

"They really rushed us out of there, didn't they? I still taste them." She giggled. As if someone threw a switch, the girls were back to giggling and playing undisturbed by the absence of their friend. They uncorked a new bottle of Champagne.

"Wash them out with this," one said.

The laughter continued until they were on the highway, then the girls focused their attention on Lungs.

"He's so cute, not like those old farts. I'd rather wash it down with him."

"Hey," she called to him. "Want a freebie?"

He answered, "Thanks for the offer, but I'm working."

"Yeah, sure," the other one said, drunk and half asleep. "You're probably in love."

The rest of the ride was in silence. Lungs made good time with no traffic at that time of the morning. The espresso he shared with Gaetano kept him perky. They made a quick pit stop at the Red Apple Rest where they used the toilets and bought containers of fresh brewed.

The coffee sobered the girls. They expressed concern for their compatriot who had remained behind.

"I wonder what happened to her?" one asked.

Lungs was cavalier. "They told me she had too much and passed out, that one of them would take her back in the morning."

"That's not like her. She's the one that can drink us under the table. I've seen her polish off a bottle of bubbly in no time at all."

Lungs would learn later that during the party, Bundles had gotten rough, and not for the first time. He had tied the girl, gagged her, flipped her over, raised her on her knees, and was violently pounding her from behind. She struggled, twisting and writhing, and shaking, increasing his satisfaction. Then she stopped and remained motionless. Bundles interpreted her lack of movement as complete submission, driving his egotistical arousal even higher.

After he was done, she did not move when he slapped her buttocks. Then he slapped her again, and still no movement. When she fell over on her side, motionless, he smelled it. She had brought up food. Hands bound behind her, mouth gagged, she had drowned in her own vomit. He dressed and made his way down the stairs to Mario.

The sight of the young woman's limp body lying on the bed when they entered the room infuriated Mario and he lunged for Bundles, grabbing him by the lapels of his unbuttoned shirt.

"Can you believe, she croaked on her own puke?" Bundles said with a smirk.

His words angered Mario even more. He slapped Bundles across the face.

"That's a wasted human life. You snuffed this beautiful young thing and you make jokes? You're supposed to be a responsible leader. This is how you lead? Bringing heat down on the bosses?"

Bundles' face registered panic as he considered the weight of the possible repercussions.

"I didn't realize she was choking. It was an accident, I thought she was gettin' off."

"Gettin' off? She's a whore!" Mario fumed. "What's wrong with you?" he said. "Ropes. Gags. That's sick. You know who's here, and you bring this down on them?"

"Mario, what do we do?"

The veteran mobster thought for a moment. "She can't stay here, that's for sure. Fingers is sleeping in this room. Okay, this is what we do. Stay here and put her clothes on. I'll get the boys down to the basement to play cards, and I'll send the other two broads home. Gaetano will help you wrap her up and put her in the trunk of your car."

Mario returned to the living room with the serenity of a saint and addressed the girls, "Collect your stuff, it's late and you have a long trip ahead of you. Your driver is waiting for you out front."

One of the older men, filled with wine and exhausted from lust, said, "Hey, Mario, you sending them home? How do you know we had our fill? Do you think we need to save some energy for playing cards?"

"Come on, you want to get a heart attack?" Mario replied. "The table downstairs is set up with cigars just off the plane from Havana. Shuffle up the cards. I'll be with you in a few minutes."

Fingers, the seasoned street-wise boss, knew that something had happened and ushered the group down the steps to the card table. As Mario waited for the girls by the door, Fingers whispered, "What happened? Is Bundles in this?"

Mario coolly reassured his Capo, "Boss. I have it under control."

Fingers nodded. "I guess you want me to keep them occupied."

"Yeah, please, for half an hour."

Lungs remembered hearing that her body turned up in an alley behind a Latin bar a few days later. A dead whore was not a priority for the police or the newspapers. The coroner set the cause of death as asphyxiation without foul play, so even other street walkers weren't alarmed. No one claimed her body, and she was sent to potter's field. The young woman simply ceased to exist.

Hearing the sound of his name ended Lung's recollections.

"Lungs," Father Tony said, "Now that you have filled your belly and dazzled us with your charm, how about finishing that song you came in singing?"

He forced a smile, shook it off with a large swallow of coffee and a quick peck on Millie's lips, and said, "Okay, I guess you people know talent when you see it."

They clapped hands as he pulled the chair out and placed his foot upon it. He turned to face Millie who blushed. She loved when he sang directly to her. Lungs began to sing I've Got the World on a String mimicking Frank Sinatra's arrangement, and went on to sing others. He moved about the table, singing verses with a finale that embarrassed Father Tony, by sitting on his lap as he ended with a grand finale, holding the final note for a minute.

Impressed by his talent, the group gave him a standing ovation. When they quieted down Father Tony invited them to make themselves comfortable, enjoy the house and relax until bedtime.

Father Tony needed a short nap. At 10 p.m. he would be praying the "office of the hours" in his room at the end of the hall. He invited those who wished to join him.

They cleared the table and left to freshen up. Katie, Kevin, Timmy, and Colleen opted to take a walk. Sister Regina helped Millie and her singing beau with their belongings and showed them to their rooms.

The couples held hands as they strolled up the road under the summer sky that held shadows of light. The pastel colors of orange, pink, and yellow that welcomed them earlier were part of memory. A full moon about to take its place was rising above the ridges to the east and preparing to re-ignite the sky. The pure mountain air invigorated them.

They stopped at a ball field used year-round by residents and faintly noticed a small bevy of deer foraging at the edge of the clearing. The reflection of light on their eyes from a passing car gave them away.

"Shall we sit for a while here to enjoy the moonlit sky?" Kevin said.

Kevin dusted the roughhewn benches for them, but Timmy and Colleen, flashlights in hand, continued their stroll, reveling in the chance to experience each other as a civilian couple for the first time in a truly relaxed setting. The FBI would survive this evening without them.

Timmy said, "This is the first time you've held my hand."

"Just shut up and walk."

"I like it. I like being with you. I think about you a lot, especially when I'm alone at night."

Colleen stopped in her tracks, and then twisted his arm as if he were a perpetrator.

"Don't you ever stop with your bull? We're having a nice time and I'm enjoying it. But you're not man enough or mature enough to have one special person in your life. I have seen your eyes ogle every female badge you meet. I'm not going to be another conquest for you or anyone. Don't try to fool me or you with the effects of a romantic country night."

Colleen continued to walk ahead. Timmy was left to stand in amazement.

Wow, I have hurt her. Maybe because she digs me?

"Wait!" He caught up to her. "You're right. I can be an immature fool at times."

"You see? You're doing it again."

"Doing what?"

"You're trying to sell me so you can get me into bed."

He playfully grabbed her arms in a lock,

"You...Colleen...maybe you don't like yourself, maybe you cannot believe that someone could be interested in you...more than interested in you. That someone could think about you all day and long to be with you."

"Well just listen to Dr. Freud. Maybe if that someone appeared, I could believe it."

"Well believe it. I'm here."

He took a few steps ahead then turned to face her.

"I was trying to tell you what I learned about myself, and how I thought of you when Kevin told me how much he loved Katie. I teased him but I knew then that I felt the same feelings for you."

"You're serious? I can't believe this."

She came to him. This time she put her hands on the sides of his neck and lifted his head. She had tears in her eyes.

"What are you saying?" she asked.

He placed his hands gently on her hips and drew her closer. "What I'm saying is that... I think I'm falling for you."

Softened by his words, she folded her arms around his neck. They held each other under an umbrella of stars and kissed for the first time.

Her eyes fluttered as their lips parted, "You have to promise to be a good boy."

"I will. I would never do–"

Before he could finish, her lips were on his again for a long moment.

He whispered, "This is the happiest night of my life.

"Mine, too," she whispered back.

33.

The sky totally darkened but the full moon guided their steps back to house. Kevin and Katie found their friends snuggled together on the couch by the fireplace. Kevin mused, Boy, he fell pretty quick.

After evening prayer, the group succumbed to the demands of the exhausting day and retired to their rooms. As she closed her eyes, Katie longed to be in Kevin's arms. She recalled the way she felt when they tenderly caressed each other, and how they were inching closer to consummating their love. She was morally conflicted and unable to abandon her faith in God. She could not negotiate with the morals she had been taught. Although she was tempted, after learning of the moral hypocrisy of her parents.

Kevin knew Katie had unresolved feelings. Something had cut to her core. He would not press her. For him it was an opportunity to prove his love. Their abstinence served as a reassurance to her. He wanted her to trust and count on him. To be her special someone, who would sacrifice for her and the future family they'd build together.

Katie dozed for a while. Her thoughts rustled her from a restful sleep. Not to wake Reggie, sleeping on the adjacent twin bed, she quietly slid out, put on her robe, and went to the kitchen. She boiled water for tea, and sat in the living room staring at the last embers still glowing in the fireplace.

She sat for a good while trying to organize her thoughts, and doing an inventory of her life starting from childhood. She remembered the observations she made in the past and realized that there were a number of questions and doubts that remained unanswered. What a damned fool I've been.

As she sat, the sound of the side door closing broke her focus. Father Tony stood there, wearing a red hunter's jacket over his pajamas. He had a flashlight in his hand.

"Where were you?" she asked. "Do you have any idea how you look? You're a combination of Elmer Fudd and Tweetie Bird."

"Stop, please. I wrestled awhile trying to sleep. Then I remembered I had forgotten to change the light bulbs for the driveway lights. Dominick and Mimi were supposed to head up after closing the restaurant and are likely arrive to before sunrise. It's easy to miss a house set-back so far from the road in this area."

He turned off the flashlight and removed his coat.

"What about you?" he asked. "I thought you would be in the grip of romantic dreams."

"I wish. Sometimes doing the right thing really stinks."

Father Tony lay down on the couch with his head resting upon her lap, a position they had assumed many times growing up together. "Reggie's lap is more comfortable. She's not as boney."

She reacted by pinching his cheek. "Shush, you. What do you know, preacher boy?"

They sat that way for a while, looking at the fireplace, their spirits recharged just by being together with the memories they shared. Although they never spoke at length about their feelings and their families, a quiet understanding existed between them.

"I can count on you," she whispered.

"And I, you."

They both felt that their parents' world was a narrow one, concerned only with what they saw as material success. Kathy and Tony were both singletons of first generation Italian-Americans with parents who had businesses and roots in Little Italy's culture. They held many of the same opinions and felt the same pressures imposed on them by their families.

"We were both reared to be perfect little people, proper miniature adults, groomed for presentation like royal heirs."

"Yeah. Manufactured roles. Those hypocrites. So tell me what's going on. You seemed to be very happy with Kevin. I can see that he adores you."

"I can't begin to describe the depth of love I feel for him. He is the warmest, kindest, most thoughtful and loving man I have ever known. I love him so much and I know that he will always be there for me. He is bright, strong and honest, a true prince. I don't know if I'm worthy of him."

Father Tony bolted upright. "What are you talking about? Worthy! You are you! And on top of that you're an educated successful empathetic woman. What is really going on? Come on, out with it."

"I don't know, I have been questioning my life lately. I feel like I have been in denial for most of it. Terrible things have been flashing in my head since I spoke with Aunt Carmella a couple of weeks ago. She confirmed some things I've suppressed that still haunt me. I search my reason and understanding for answers, but these are dark questions, and I fear the answers."

She paused as a single tear traced down her cheek.

"Ah," Tony said, shaking his head. "I've had the same questions taunting me since the evening of my ordination," he said. He took a deep breath and expelled it.

He turned to Katie and asked, "What did Carmella tell you? I have been trying to console myself. I've been trying to explain it away with the impact of the permanent life changes I've made.

Accepting celibacy, obedience, and the loss of my personal freedom. As I work through those changes, I have resolved to affirm them. Funny though, that you mentioned denial. Early this morning, while scrubbing the basement floor, I came to see it in myself."

Katie stirred and said, "It's frightening, isn't it?"

"Yes, and talking about it now, I can admit to myself that there have been many things troubling me about my family and their values. I think what motivated me to evaluate my life has been the intimacy I have with Monsignor. I have discovered he has a similar pompous, self-serving approach to life, like so many of that generation."

Triggered by his words Katie burst with emotion. "Oh, my God!" she cried. "I don't know if I can tell you this."

"Katie, please let me help," Father Tony insisted.

"Tony, you must promise to keep what I say under bond of confession. You can't slip. Someone could get hurt."

"Get hurt?" he asked. "You mean physically hurt?"

She answered with an affirmative nod.

After composing herself, she told him of her visit with Carmella, explaining that since her childhood it was a ritual for them to spend special girl-time with each other.

"I found Carmella frightened, nervous and concerned about the well-being of her children." Katie went on in detail, speaking in a way in which she could self-analyze the words she spoke out loud. She told him that after dinner, they sat by the window in Carmella's bedroom peering out at the rain and that Carmella spoke reluctantly, and couched her words in a shroud of mystery.

"She told me that while delivering flowers to the funeral home, Carmine stumbled upon a murder."

Father Tony blanched. "Who?"

"When Carmine got there, he found the front door locked and Anthony wasn't around. He went to the back of the building knowing that they usually left the garage unlocked for deliveries.

The garage door had been left wide open, so he unloaded the flowers. As he placed the last piece, he heard voices coming from the basement stairwell.

"He wanted to let them know that he delivered the flowers. As he got closer to the door to the basement, he heard a man screaming for his life, choking and grasping for breath, and heard voices taunting the man, calling him names in Italian."

Katie wiped tears from her eyes. "My poor Carmine."

Father Tony, in shock, his lip quivering, muttered, "But who was it?"

"He told her he heard a voice which he recognized shouting at the struggling man. When I asked Carmella whom she thought it was, she shook her head and her face turned to sadness. She told me that when Carmine came to her back door to bring her flower order his body trembled in fear. He was pale white, like he'd seen a ghost. She gave him a glass of Marsala, but he could hardly speak or hold the glass. Sitting on the back step with her he told her they killed somebody.

He got scared and ran to his truck. As he turned away from funeral home, he thought he saw a shadow of someone in the garage, but was not sure if they saw him."

Father Tony begged, "But who was it? Who was murdered? Who was the murderer?"

"It doesn't matter, Tony!" she shouted, then dropped her voice once more. "I don't know if Carmella knows, but if she does she hasn't told me. Not yet, at least. More important, Carmella asked Carmine to think back, and asked if he really thought that someone had seen him. He believed they did. Carmella told him not to say anything to anybody. She has regretted it ever since."

As she paused, Father Tony put his arms around her. "My dear Jesus," he said in a low voice. He let go and sat back, looking at her with compassion. Katie went on.

"She asked me if I felt that I could handle it. She said that I'm strong, but telling me more of what she knew could put my life, and the lives of those I love, in danger."

"Danger?"

"She said that she loved me as her eldest daughter, her confidant, and that I'm intelligent and had the capacity to see more than most people. Nevertheless, she believes that I am too emotionally tied to neighborhood. That it holds me."

Katie paused to wipe her face as Father Tony, entranced by her words said, "She's right."

"I believe Carmella's words are undeniable. She confirmed my suspicions and I understand her fear for her children, Dominick and Angie. She also mentioned that Don Peppino, my godfather, is encouraging Mario to pursue Angie."

Katie shook in her seat. Father Tony grabbed her by the shoulders to steady her. Katie cried, looked into Tony's eyes and whispered, "She told me that after her husband Paolo's death, one of them raped her."

The tears streamed down their faces as they steadied each other.

"Tony, Carmella is worried about Dominick, who she sees as susceptible. He could succumb to their soft talk and fast cash. In that life they would use him up and kill him as they did to his father and to so many other young men in the neighborhood.

"She wants my help to get Dominick and Angie away from there. She believes that she knows too much about them and that they will not let them go without good reason. She needs my help in devising a way, without raising any suspicion. She fears that I need to get out, too, and that this had been a life sentence for her. She does not want this for her children. Nor for me."

Katie voice was hoarse from crying. "She warned me not to tell my father or mother, not one word, and implied that they were closely tied in, having grown up together. The Hester Street Kids. We've all heard the stories.

"Tony, I know this in my heart, and I have known what my parents are for so long. I don't know if I denied it because I could not I accept it, or because I selfishly didn't want my tidy, secure life to tumble."

"Dear, Jesus," he consoled, gripping her hands tightly. His face grew pale as he internalized her sorrow.

"I'm baffled by my father's connection with them," she said. "He's an educated man and smarter than they are. What attracts him to them and them to him?"

Tony sat backed stunned. "I'm rocked to my soul, and I'm disappointed in myself because your words have convicted me too. We've had our heads in the sand."

"I want to meet with Carmella again but I'm afraid of what she's going to tell me. How do I tell Kevin? We're getting closer and closer. He's hinted at wanting to marry me. He knows that I've been troubled and he's been patient with me, but I'm afraid of losing him.

"Kevin is an all-American guy, a patriot, cleared by the government at the highest level, he's talented and cultured. How can I enter his world if my suspicions prove true? That my father is a mob associate, or worse, part of the gang. This could destroy any possibility of a future with this man I love. It works both ways. Kevin is respected not only for his music, but also as a young diplomat with promise. Our relationship could devastate his career."

"You need to hear Carmella out," Father Tony said, "and I know you want to help her. I will help, too. As far as Kevin goes, you need to trust in him. Do not think for him or underestimate him. He is very bright and well connected for a reason. Just think about how you met. I'm convinced divine intervention was at play.

"Think about it, he wound up hurt on your street and of all people a spoiled teenager shows sympathy for him and walks him into your life.

Maybe you and Kevin not only received the gift of each other but also an assignment.

"I'm in the same boat as you. I have many suspicions and am not looking forward to the answers to the questions I have posed to myself. Could this be merely a coincidence? I don't think so.

"We have to digest and work this through. I think we need a break. Let's try to have a good weekend. Enjoy this time with Kevin. A few more days living in denial isn't going to mean much. Speak to him. You have nothing to lose and all to gain. You deserve a life. Let's go to sleep and give it to Jesus in prayer."

She felt some relief in the confession. She knew she could trust him and that he would support and protect her. She made her way back to bed, and prayed to God that he keep her and Kevin together as she drifted into sleep.

34.

The next morning Kevin awoke early. Timmy had risen, but that most of the guests were still sound asleep. He dressed and made his way downstairs following the aroma of fresh coffee. He found Timmy, who poured cups for both of them.

Timmy pointed him to note on the fridge from Father Tony letting them know that he and Katie were up late talking, and most likely, she would sleep late. It added the suggestion: For those of you who arise early, enjoy the morning, make breakfast for yourselves and breathe in the morning air. Next to it was a note from Dominick: Hi guys, we got here at five will probably; sleep out the morning. Lungs- Do Not Disturb!

Timmy and Kevin decided to explore before breakfast. They followed a path behind the house leading into the forest.

"You can really breathe here. The air is fresh and clean," Timmy said.

Birds rustled about, and sang out warnings as they were startled by the two men making their trek along the trail. The path opened to a small apple orchard.

"Ahhh, one of upstate New York's famous apple farms," Kevin said. "Remember our school bus trip to see the foliage and pick apples?"

"Definitely. We had fun pitching apples to each other and shaking the girls' ladders. Remember Christine Polanski who wore a dress instead of pants?"

They laughed and continued their meander through the grove. Tiring after a while, they decided to stop and sit upon the remnants of a low stone wall to one side of the path. Kevin congratulated Timmy once more on his relationship with Colleen, and wished him the best.

"Yeah, Kev," he said, "maybe we can have a double wedding."

They sat thinking about that prospect. Then, the mood changed. They were on the same page, as they had been most of their lives.

"You think there're any connections there?" Timmy asked.

"You mean, connections, connections?" Kevin said as he pushed his nose to one side with his finger.

Timmy nodded.

"I've been thinking about that. I believe Katie is troubled by it, but has not broached the subject."

Timmy told Kevin about the briefings he has been receiving regarding the neighborhood and its major players. There was a lot of local mob heat. Informants had told them that a war might be imminent between rival mafia families, and that the mob bosses were concerned with increased law enforcement activity because of the murders.

"The local Goombas have pledged assistance in searching for the killer, however they're asking the department to discourage the news media referring to the neighborhood as being mob run."

Kevin laughed, "They really have balls, don't they?"

"Yeah, what troubles me is that our presence, Colleen and I, may be perceived as an infiltration. They are a paranoid lot.

They live with mistrust and suspicion, and are in all probability concerned about you, too."

"Me?"

"Yeah. I believe they see you as heavily connected to the government. Remember, their dealings are international and they know they're of interest to many law enforcement agencies in many countries."

As Timmy spoke, Kevin thought of the watchmaker, DiGiaccomo. Kevin wondered if Katie's father or Don Peppino might question his seeking information about him and his FBI friend. *This can't avoid spilling into our agency work and affecting our cover.*

Timmy posed the idea that he could ask to liaison with the mob. Informants had already made contact with law enforcement, allegedly to aid in the search effort. Hopefully he could convince them that he and Colleen had a specific task concerned only with the apprehension of the serial killer.

He needed to convince the mob bosses to accept Kevin's and Timmy's friendship, and that their arrival in the neighborhood was a coincidence.

"Yeah," Kevin said, "those are real concerns. Let me give it some thought." *This is getting complex, juggling the agency cover, Timmy, and Katie.*

"We can look at it from the other end," Timmy went on. "My guys might ask you for intelligence when they discover our friendship. This could turn into a tangled mess."

Kevin affirmed with a slow nod. He needed to seek Malcolm's counsel. His mission was too important. It had global cold war implications, and the possibility of compromising the safety of a fellow operative had to be taken into account.

He was torn. Will Katie think I got close to her just to spy on her family?

When they returned from their hike, they found Reggie, Lungs, and Millie making pancakes and eggs. The others were still sleeping. They joined the trio of cooks in preparing breakfast.

Reggie ordered Timmy to start squeezing oranges for juice and Kevin to set the table. Lungs led them in the song, Whistle While you Work.

Millie danced around him and touted, "He's the singer and I'm the dancer."

"Don't give up your day job," Lungs said. She gave him a love tap in response.

Timmy got a taste of Reggie's raunchy humor when she goosed him while reaching over him for a plate in the cupboard.

"Nice buns," she teased. Timmy was confused.

Lungs said, "What? Is this the first nun you have met with sexual compulsion? Don't let that cool sexy exterior of hers throw you, she's a cross-carrying religious fanatic. Just has a funny way of showing it."

Timmy laughed loudly. "I love you people."

Once they had eaten breakfast, Reggie, Lungs, and Millie went to the village ice skating rink. Kevin and Timmy chose to wait for their ladies to awaken. They occupied themselves by working on the guns. They took an inventory of the rifles, shotguns, and archery equipment, making a list with detailed descriptions.

When they examined the empty rifle cabinet, an antique of fine quality, they noticed a latch at the back of the enclosure. It opened a compartment in which were hidden eight pistols hanging on hooks. These were added to the inventory.

"Look at this," Timmy said. He held the pistols under the light. "Three have their serial numbers filed off. The pistol grips were taped."

They looked at each other and sighed, opting to return them to the cabinet.

"Gimme those a second," Timmy said. "Better to be safe than sorry."

He wiped the barrels with a rag.

Kevin and Timmy did not realize that Father Tony, whose room sat just across the hall, overheard them discuss the suspicious weapons.

"Do we tell him?" Timmy asked.

"No," Kevin answered, "This will upset him. He doesn't know much about guns to begin with, and if we tell him that the numbers were filed and the grips were taped to block finger print detection it will shock him."

"So what do we say?"

"Well, the guns are not saleable to legitimate sources, so we could tell him they are worn and worthless and can be disposed of. Hopefully, he will never need to know."

"But what if they were used in a crime?" Timmy asked.

"Do you really want to get in to this? Chances are they weren't, or they would have been dumped. No, I believe these were stolen some time ago and were hidden to cool. Good possibility that the men who used these weapons are already dead."

Across the hall color began to drain from Father Tony's face. *I guess God has confirmed our suspicions.* These are good men. Father Tony waited until Kevin and Timmy went upstairs before leaving his room. Hearing their words, he grew angry. How could I have been so blind?

Later in the afternoon, with everyone together, Father Tony decided to say Mass. The men moved some of the furniture and placed the high hat table from the entryway in the center of the room as an altar. Reggie found a bed sheet, folded it, and covered the table. Angie and Millie brought in a pitcher of water, a goblet of wine and a hand towel and placed them upon the makeshift Altar. Dominick, who had served as an altar boy in his youth, reverently stood behind Father Tony to assist.

He began the Mass in Latin with the sign of the cross. He did not read the scheduled gospel for that day, but substituted Matthew 13:13 in which Jesus' explains His use of parables as a metaphor for all God's work.

Father Tony's eyes went to the ceiling as he recited, "...eyes to see and ears to hear..." a teaching that talked to humanity's struggle with denial, and ultimately a denial of God.

After serving each one communion, he blessed them all and prayed for the poor and for the salvation of souls. Following the service, they processed with him throughout the house while he blessed all the rooms with holy water, stopping longer at the room that contained the firearms, making sure that each piece received a droplet of holy water. As he performed the blessing, with the curiosity of the others, he asked God to cleanse the house of any residue of sinfulness that may have occurred there.

Father Tony lingered, doing an extra special job in the room in which Colleen and Millie slept as if he sensed a dark presence. The curious guests did not ask for an explanation.

After dinner, they played bingo, conversed, and listened to records on the Hi-Fi, including songs from Glenn Miller, and Frank Sinatra, Tommy Dorsey, and other popular bands from the war era. Their peace was interrupted when Dominick mentioned that he received a job offer from Don Peppino. He kidded Angie about her spending some time with Mario at the restaurant. His words struck at the hearts of Father Tony and Katie. They eyed each other knowingly, taking it as another confirmation of Carmella's account. Timmy and Kevin's eyes also mirrored concern.

The weekend proved bittersweet. It was an eye opening experience for most of them. They bonded more strongly with each other. Their friendship became more than just a generational attachment. The acknowledgment of things they had previously denied would set their life trajectories on different paths.

Close to bedtime that last night, Katie held Kevin's hands and said, "Honey, I don't want to go home tomorrow as we had planned, and I don't want to stay here. But, I'd like to speak with you in a neutral place, one without memories attached to it."

"Sure. My parents would love to have you visit. We could stay at the house and I can show you a bit of my world. I'll let Mom know that we need some time alone."

"That would be wonderful."

35.

The day ended early for Don Peppino. He expected a restful ride home. Mario drove through the Midtown Tunnel heading for his Long Island home. Don Peppino was considerate of Mario and suggested he turn on the radio to occupy himself as he drove. Mario cued a station without static and waited for the Alka-Seltzer commercial to end. Then there was a news flash.

The reporter said, "Mob neighborhood taken over by a Serial Killer."

Don Peppino's mouth opened. "What's this now?" he yelled at Mario.

Mario turned up the volume. The broadcast continued.

"Good evening, Mike Corcoran here. The Daily News reported minutes ago that the police and FBI are conducting an ongoing investigation into six suspicious deaths of elderly women in Little Italy, an area of lower Manhattan called Mob Central by police.

"Michael Munson, our feature reporter, says the authorities are baffled. The bodies of the women were all found lying on top of their made beds, with their hands clasped together holding rosary beads.

"According to an un-named law enforcement source, most of the victims had illnesses normal for their ages but were not diagnosed as terminal. The FBI has assigned a task force to aid with the investigation at the request of NYPD. Reporters said the Mayor was furious when confronted by the press waiting for him when he left his office today. The Mayor said he'd investigate the reports, that he intended to meet with the police commissioner, and he would hold a press conference to answer questions as soon as he got the facts."

Don Peppino fumed. "Mario. Turn-off at the Flushing exit and go to the diner. I need to make a few calls."

Within minutes, Don Peppino was pushing dimes into a payphone.

"Birdie. Did you hear the radio broadcast?"

"Yeah, a few minutes ago. I went to the parlor and Anthony told me you had left. Where are you?"

"I'm on my way home but when I heard the news we stopped at the diner in Flushing."

"Call Fingers. Tell him to meet us at Mela's. I'll wait for you there."

"Okay. I'll have Mario call the crew chiefs, too. We'll meet with them later on tonight. I should be back there in under an hour."

After hanging up the phone, he beckoned Mario to him.

"Call the crew chiefs. Tell them to meet us at the meat warehouse at nine."

"I don't know if I can get all of them together, boss."

"Listen to me. I don't care what you gotta do. Get 'em there. Understand?"

Mario entered the adjacent booth and began making calls. Don Peppino called Fingers and then his wife to tell her he would be home late.

At Mela's Dominick answered the phone.

"Domi. Please ask your mother to prepare a light dinner for three and set a table in the back room. We'll be there in an hour."

"Sure."

Dominick entered the kitchen. "Mimi. Table for three in the back room. Now."

Carmella knew from Dominick's urgency what was happening and who would be arriving.

"When will they be here?" she asked.

"An hour." He turned to Angie. "Put out bottles of white and red wine and set a side table for espresso. Dress it with cookies, pastry, Anisette."

"Do they want anything special?" Carmella asked.

"I got the impression that it's business, not pleasure."

"Okay. I can do a cold antipasto, gnocchi a la vodka, and veal Milanese with the sautéed broccoli and you serve family style."

Dominick sidled up to his mother and whispered, "They're probably pissed at the radio announcement."

"You keep quiet and mind your business," she said. "Once the food is placed on the table, you leave them. When they're ready for coffee they will ask."

Dominick looked at Carmella with worried eyes. "Yeah, Mom."

She kissed her son on the cheek and they got busy with their assigned tasks.

An hour later Don Peppino, Birdie, and Fingers, arriving within minutes of each other, proceeded stone-faced and staring straight ahead through the crowded restaurant to the back dining room.

Carmella greeted them. "I prepared a simple family style meal."

Don Peppino took her hand, kissed it with appreciation, and said "You always know what we need."

Once the food was served and they were left alone, Don Peppino locked the door and joined the other two who sat silently.

Peppino said, "Eat first. Then we talk."

Midway through the meal, Birdie_broke the silence.

"This is what I think we have to do. We need to contact our friends in the police, the Mayor's office, and even in Albany. We get as much information as we can on this crazy guy they're looking for. We promise our help. Get some of our people involved with this, but no made men. We need to patrol this neighborhood and let everyone know we're watching and we want their help. It's a returnable favor. Maybe we should think about offering a reward. We could have it sponsored by the Chamber of Commerce."

He stopped, cleared his throat and took a sip of wine before going on.

"Make it clear that we're not to get in the way of the police, and we are to show them our cooperation. Let them also know that we realize that these victims are our family and that we're just as interested in finding this lunatic as they are."

Birdie looked at his compatriots. They nodded understanding and agreement.

"This situation is just adding to our problems," Birdie continued. "We're getting heat from all directions and we need to keep our crews out of the neighborhood for now."

They finished the meal. Peppino got up and unlocked the door. He opened it an inch. In a moment, Dominick entered, cleared the plates and redressed the table. Angie was right behind with the espresso. When they left, the conversation continued.

Birdie said that a mob war was inevitable. They had to prepare to go to the mattress. They needed to get their safe houses ready both there and in Vegas.

"Bundles is going to need a team with him to protect our interests at the casinos," Don Peppino added.

"You have the authority to make three men," Birdie said. "We need hitters. I know you have two people who have been working for us for years who are anxious to make their bones, men who have proven themselves with their work and loyalty.

"While we're on the subject, I discussed young Mateo with the Don. He's leaving it up to our judgment. He knew his father well and had a great deal of respect for him as we all did. From what I hear, he has been doing well working with Bundles' crew.

"Listen, be prepared. It looks like we're going to throw the first punch, so if you vouch for him, he could make his bones by working with the mechanics. A courier will bring you the details in the next few days. I think you should keep him on the home crew under Mario for the time being, and let's give him something to start. You can use the help.

"In addition, we need to do something about this reporter, Munson, too. See if he would be open to a deal. Say we'll give him information and an exclusive if we get this guy. As a favor to us, he is to ignore the silly rumors about mob influence in the neighborhood. Remind him that we are civic minded. We keep street crime down, and bad press is not good for tourism. Use diplomacy, but he has to know we're serious about this. We got people that want to blind him, but I'm not crazy about that idea."

Birdie took a sip of coffee and a bite of biscotti. He chewed slowly as he deliberated the next order of business.

"Tell the men that we need to be conservative in our efforts," Birdie continued. "Watch for new faces. And by new, I mean anyone that we know less than five years. Limit the risks, and look out for setups. This means limited contact with other family members. This is not the time to take any chances. Make sure they call in on a regular basis. We need to know if they're okay and their whereabouts."

"The feds are all over with the Kefauver Committee Hearings," Peppino said. "They're herding in large number of witnesses and Valachi is singing like fuckin' Caruso. By the way, there's 100K on him."

Birdie nodded. "Next, we can't use Pena's mother's house upstate."

The men shuffled.

"Damn shame," Peppino said. "I liked that place."

Birdie continued. "Yeah, me, too. But his son, the new priest, has it now. Also, there's another house in Staten Island that no one knows about. Fingers, you go to see Pena. Buy a car from him for God's sake. He sees that old car you're driving around and it drives him nuts."

"There's nothing wrong with my car. "Fingers said. "It works fine and can still carry a bag of blood and bones."

"Come on, I saw a moth fly from your wallet. I bet ya got the first fuckin' penny you copped on Hester Street. Let him sell you a car. We're all partners. He has to meet his quota with the auto company."

They laughed. Fingers' frugality had been the focus of jokes for years.

"Okay," Birdie said. "That's the general plan. Agreed? Is there anything you want me to tell the Boss?"

Don Peppino answered, "Just tell him that getting his split may be delayed at times. We're altering the system."

Fingers responded, "Oh, he knows. Delay is okay, but let's keep our record keeping tight for him."

Birdie smiled. It was his first smile of the evening. "He also wants me to thank you for your loyalty. He will have a few minutes to talk to you both, individually, here and there, at his daughter's wedding. Let me know how everything goes with the men tonight. I'm on my way for a meeting in Brooklyn."

"Are you going alone?"

"No, they're sending people to pick me up."

As he left, Birdie hugged and kissed both men as a sign of respect.

Don Peppino and Fingers remained alone in the room.

"He's always been there for us," Fingers said. "I think he's worried about the possibility of war."

"Yeah, I think we need all the help we can get. Do you have any problem with bringing in Mateo?"

"If he's half the man his father was," Fingers said, "he'll do fine. He's smart. He doesn't have a hair trigger, and listens with respect."

Peppino nodded.

"What Birdie said. About eying new people. That new friend of Caterina came to mind. What's his name again?"

"Kevin. He's a mick," Peppino answered. "I'll talk to him tomorrow about it, and see if he wants us to check him out."

Fingers said, "If I didn't know how dumb those spics are, I would be worried about a set-up. Let's go over to the funeral home. I want us to prepare Mario for the meeting."

They left the room and stopped to pay the bill. Carmella sat at small table having a cup of tea and reading the Italian newspaper. Peppino took out his billfold and peeled out five one-hundred-dollar bills. He folded them and placed them in Carmella's hand.

"Your tab is not that big."

"Mela, I could never pay what I really owe. You've been a sister and lifelong friend." He kissed her.

Fingers handed Angie, Mimi, and Dominick each a fifty-dollar bill.

When they left, Carmella cornered her son and Mimi and shook her finger at them.

This is money squeezed out of the blood and misfortune of poor hardworking people."

36.

Chief of Detectives Walter O'Shay entered the crowded briefing room followed by a string of police brass and FBI agents. O'Shay had a towering presence. He was six-foot-four, muscular, and filled the image of the head of law enforcement for the largest city in the country. A man of few words, his greeting was brief, and his introduction of those that stood beside him was briefer.

"Listen carefully. Take good notes. And ask as many questions you wish. The public is frightened and seeking our protection. I can't overstate the importance of apprehending this killer."

His remarks continued for exactly ninety seconds. When he finished, he introduced the FBI's Psych team.

"Please welcome Tim Calavarro and Colleen Murphy who have been assigned by the Bureau to this case because of the possibility of organized crime involvement. Hate to admit it, but this time we can use all the help we can get."

Special Agent Calavarro greeted the assembly, thanked Chief O'Shay, the Homicide District Commander and the others officials. The muscles in his neck tightened as he faced a sea of skeptical expressions. The street hardened homicide detectives were already shaking their heads. He knew he and Colleen were outsiders, and would remain so. At best, they could work together with the detectives to solve the crime, but he and Colleen would go back to their office at the Federal Building without ever being considered part of the team.

"One of the deceased was a CI – confidential informant – of ours. The US Attorney General's office has authorized us to investigate her murder. After contacting Chief O'Shay, he suggested that we pool our resources and work together to bring this killer to justice. It is important for me to find out the reason behind the demise of our informant. We have already spoken with some of you who were involved from the beginning, and who may have been privy to the crime scene analysis already done."

He had their attention, if not their willingness to work under his leadership.

"We're very appreciative of the cooperation you men have offered, which has helped us to formulate a preliminary profile of this mad man. I will turn the podium over to my partner, Special Agent Colleen Murphy, a forensic specialist, who has had a history of success with other cases of this kind."

Colleen provided her sketch of the killer. Her beauty charged the men in the room. She re-focused them with her sharp professional aura.

"Serial killers for the most part are white, heterosexual, males in their twenties and thirties. In this instance however, we tend to believe that the perpetrator is older, maybe fifty-five to sixty-five because he operates with formality, is extremely disciplined, neat, and clean. Usually, these individuals are sexually motivated with their killing generated from a complex sexual fantasy, one that builds up to a para-sexual climax at the moment of the death of their victim. In this case, we find no incident of sexual assault, mutilation, or peri- or post-mortem contact of any kind, other than the posing of the bodies.

Serial killers customarily kill strangers. Here we suspect that the victims knew the assailant and trusted them. In all six cases, there has been no sign of forced entry, and the absence of defensive wounds on the victim indicates there was no violent struggle or attempt to escape.

"The uniformity of the victims – all elderly women of Italian heritage who lived alone – and the way they were posed post mortem is what brings these murders together as a crime being committed by the same person.

"Most serial killers have lived in violent households, many tortured animals and were bed-wetters when they were young. As adults, most killers have some elements of brain damage and many have addictions.

"In this case, it looks like he renders his victims unconscious with little or no struggle and then suffocates them, possibly with a pillow or blanket. It seems that this person gets peaceful when he kills. He displays his victims serenely as if for a wake, a picture of peaceful finality. He assumes the role of the undertaker. The rosary beads are a common thread in all the cases. Most Italian funerals display the body with hands clasped in prayer draped with rosary beads, sometimes a prayer book.

"It is likely our perpetrator – whom we've dubbed the Rosary Killer – is Catholic, too.

"Though we currently have only six victims, homicide has reason to believe that as the investigation proceeds, we may discover other heretofore unrelated murders that have been committed by our guy.

"We are awaiting the completion of the coroner's analysis. So let's break this down."

Colleen lifted a piece of chalk and turned to the black board.

"This is what we have," she said as she wrote on the blackboard.

"1) Cause of death, asphyxiation, most likely by smothering

"2) Location: confined to the Little Italy neighborhood of lower Manhattan

"3) Vic last seen usually after a Sunday Mass or a weekday church service

"4) Ages of victims: 73 - 79"

She retired the chalk, brushed the dust from her hands and turned to her audience. She was gratified to see they were all copying the information she presented. As eyes came up from their pads, she continued.

"We believe that the assailant is likely to be Italian. It is likely that he is tall, and strong, with a pathological dislike of elderly women stemming from a childhood incident of some kind. He's suffering mental illness, possibly paranoid-schizophrenia. As is common in these cases, he has sustained physical and emotional abuse as a child. He is someone who developed social and psychological handicaps from a young age.

"We believe that the killer accompanies the victim to their home or pushes his way in as they enter their apartment. He likely acts alone.

"He may not have a criminal record, but will have been a victim himself, or have witnessed violence, including acts of violence against women which may have impacted his psychological balance in his earlier life. He also may be a sleepwalker or have blackouts or violent seizures."

Colleen ended with another promise of cooperation. Timmy handed out a package of confidential briefing information to the detectives and officers.

Colleen turned the presentation back to the District Detective Commander, Deputy Inspector Jack Haverty who thanked her and Agent Calavarro for their help thus far. He promised them the continued cooperation of the department.

He addressed the group with a hearty good morning. "I believe that with the profile Special Agent Murphy has provided, and the investigative inroads we have already made, it is more than possible for us to apprehend this nut-job in short order. I'm confident that we have the talent, so let's get it done."

Haverty paused while he reached for a handkerchief in his back pocket to wipe his brow.

"I have authorized overtime and have postponed all vacations, including my own, for now. Let me invite Detective Captain Dursi and Lt. Morgan to bring you up to speed on the progress of the preliminary investigation.

Remember, good detective work, and team cooperation will help us fulfill our goal to serve and protect this community. Be safe and thank you."

He turned extending his hand to Captain Dursi who approached the podium with a cigarette dangling from his lip.

The Captain thanked the D. I. and proceeded to disclose what the investigation had brought so far. "We were fortunate here," he began, "that a rookie patrolman, responded to a 419 on Mott Street. The body he found appeared as a display. Too neat, to have fallen in that position. The fact that rosary beads where also arranged in the joined hands of the deceased enhanced his suspicion. Because of his concern, he called us in.

His observations turned out to be the key that tied the homicide to others in the neighborhood and to our subsequent belief that all these murders were committed by a single killer."

As he handed out his own packet of reports, the Captain urged them to read the details outlined in the 61 prepared by the detectives first on the scene and the DD5s that were added as the cases evolved.

"We've established a special command post here at headquarters for this task force. There are forty of you. Please remain seated, and Detective Lt. Morgan will shortly divvy up responsibilities and assignments so we can avoid duplication of effort. You will find individual team member duties posted on the assignment sheet. Please sign in if you haven't already done so.

In addition, the station houses, the communications division, and the detective squads have received the direct phone numbers of the command post for effective communication. We will organize teams according to assigned tasks.

For now, this is your home away from home. To get the ball rolling, Lt. Morgan will pair a couple of guys up with our Bureau partners to begin canvassing Beekman-Downtown and other local hospitals and doctors.

Please provide for the dissemination of information to all units involved in the homicide investigation. All investigators should be aware of all aspects of the case, especially those officers who are assigned to conduct canvasses.

The uniform commanders will inform the patrolmen to notify the task force should they find any other vics that fit this MO. Keep in mind that the smart, careful and effective retrieval of evidence is paramount to prosecution of the case. I admonish you to do it right the first time. Please direct all press enquiries to my office, and please, no leaks.We have spoken about that before. We have a killer to catch. Stay safe, good luck and thank you."

37.

Mateo's chest puffed out as he opened the door of his new '55 Chevy Bel Air. His mother looked in.

"Wow, this is a nice car. Congratulations. Drive it in good health."

Mateo could see his mother was thinking hard as her eyes surveyed the interior of the automobile.

"How are you able to afford this?" she asked.

"It was repossession. I he got a great deal on it and the payments are tiny with nothing down."

She did not push it further, not wanting to take away from her son's excitement, and his anticipation of seeing Marypat. She knew that the restaurateur's daughter had sparked him, but without asking, she assumed he wanted help in wooing her. It was uncharacteristic of him. She knew he had no problem meeting girls. *This one must be something special,* she thought.

Marypat peered out the window while speaking to customers seated at a table and noticed the blue Chevy parked in a space in front of the building. She recognized Mateo as he opened the door for his Mother and observed how respectful he was to her.

Marypat knew why he had come. She had connected the references her father made about him earlier in the day and the way he had complimented her. Excusing herself, she made her way with haste to the kitchen. She did not want to encounter him until he and his mother were seated.

The waiter made a fast stride toward them, took Mateo's mother by the arm, and escorted her to their reserved table. He treated Mateo as if he had known him a long time.

"Thank you, Aldo," Mateo said.

"How beautiful your mother is," Aldo fawned. "Senora, how about a glass of Chianti and a hot antipasto for a start. Chef Filipo will come and make menu suggestions."

Mateo thanked him again with a double handshake, and tried to hide being flustered by the royal treatment.

Aldo returned with a bottle of Chianti adorned in its classic straw basket. He broke the lead seal. Removing the cork from the bottle prompted the expulsion of a light vapor of gas. The experienced waiter poured a shallow sample for Mateo's approval. Content, they sat for a few minutes letting the wine warm their stomachs. Maria glanced around.

"Mateo, this is an elegant place. The customers are very well dressed too!"

Aldo placed a linen covered basket of fresh baked bread and a dipping dish with seasoned virgin olive oil on the table. Chef Filipo delivered the hot antipasto personally.

Mateo introduced him to his mother who the Chef addressed in classic Sicilian dialect. "*Un piacere venirli a contatto Senora Patrino. Posso li denomino Maria?* –Nice of you to come. May I address you as Maria?"

Maria Patrino, a proud woman, humble of heart, was impressed by his savoir-faire. She encouraged him with a coy flirt.

"Yes. If I can call you Filipo."

They laughed. He wished them "*Buon appetito.*" Filipo turned to Mateo. "My daughter will be out shortly to take your order."

Connected people can connive so well together, Mateo mused. They were helping sell Marypat and his mother both. It made him feel special. *The rewards of my new life.*

When Filipo returned to the kitchen, his daughter was expediting food orders. He asked if she could help Mateo and his mother with suggestions for dinner, reminding her that this was the woman's first time there.

"Mateo? Mateo who?" she asked.

"Come on. Don't be a smart mouth. The young man that came in with Mario last week."

"I don't remember." She put garnish on a plate.

"Please. Go and be nice. He's with his mother."

"I treat all the customers nice." She checked the status of an order.

"Be extra nice."

She turned her back on him, waved her hand in the air in feigned annoyance, and tried to suppress a broad smile. *So, the little boy brought his mother for support. I'll fry him like zucchini cucuzza fritti.*

When she got to the table, Mateo got up.

"Why did you stand? Do you have go to the bathroom?"

She turned to address his Mother who admired her fire. She saw how it stewed her son.

"Hello, Senora, it's nice to meet you."

The young woman beheld her hands and commented how similar they were to her late mother's, with long yet delicate fingers.

"You know," she told her, "my mother modeled her hands for jewelry advertising in her youth."

Maria blushed. "These hands of mine show only wrinkles and swollen knuckles from keeping my son in line."

They laughed and Marypat asked what she was in the mood for and suggested her father's specialty *Zuppa Di Pesce,* adding that he seemed happy with the quality of the seafood he found at the Fulton Fish Market earlier that morning.

"Sure, that's sounds great," Mateo said.

Marypat, turned to him. "Was I talking to you?"

Maria told him not to interrupt, and winked at her. She enjoyed her son's reaction to the heat Marypat gave him. *This is what he needs. A strong woman.*

"What we had so far has been tasty and spicy," Maria said. "So we'll leave it up to you. The Zuppa sounds good."

Marypat checked on them from time to time throughout their meal. She never made eye contact with Mateo.

Mateo and his mother enjoyed the food and their time together. They reminisced. She spoke of how close she and his father were. They had a strong love for each other. She sighed when she described how his work had interfered with their freedom.

Maria raised him alone. His father was mostly inaccessible over the years, some of them spent in prison.

"In the beginning, before you were born, to fill my loneliness, I spent time at church with grandma. Then there were times I was preparing for the feast and things like that. But all the time, I worried and feared for your father's safety."

Mateo's eyes filled and he extended his hand to her.

"Mom, I didn't realize how hard it was for you, and how young you were when this all started."

She said with a smile, "I was frisky too. A lot like Marypat." Her eyes perked at her name. "And I had a mouth on me, too." She looked toward Marypat, who was tending to another table. "When I was her age, I had romantic view of life."

She pushed a lock of hair off Mateo's forehead. "Your father and I were ambitious when we came to this country. We wanted to realize the American dream. To find streets paved with gold. We were young and stupid. When we discovered this wasn't the land that was promised, we gave in to our fears and insecurities. We were gullible, and believed the Don's way promised wealth and position. We were foolishly impressed, and ended up on a dangerous path. That was a journey that ended in tragedy." She looked down and sighed.

Mateo listened intently and for the first time he felt her pain. He comforted her, "I feel sad. You deserved better."

The reference she made to power and the double-edged sides of it struck home. *She's warning me. What am I getting myself into?*

Aldo and Marypat cleared the table. Marypat tempted Maria with dessert.

"I feel full."

Marypat pointed to the glass case displaying Chef Filipo's finest pastries.

"Are you sure you don't want just a tiny something?" Marypat said.

"Well, the pastries are enticing me. They are so beautifully decorated."

"Our baker is decorating pastries for a party. Would you like to see his work first hand?" Marypat asked.

Aldo arrived with a coffee pot of demitasse.

Marypat told Mateo, "Have a coffee and wait. Your mommy and I will be back."

"Boy, you never stop. You're something," he said as she walked away.

I think she likes me.

Marypat introduced Maria to the master baker who was applying whipped cream flowers to a traditional Sicilian Cassata. It was made from an ancient recipe for sponge cake with ricotta cheese filling that originated from the Muslim Middle East.

The baker preferred to be called by the French title Garmaché, a term he thought added artistic value to his profession.

Mateo's mom marveled at the man's skill. How delicately he worked. *Truly an artist*, she thought.

Marypat led Maria into the wine cupboard and there, with the familiarity of a daughter speaking to her mother, she said, "Mrs. Patrino, I'm attracted to him." Her eyes sparkled as she spoke. "He is good-looking and intelligent. We just met for the first time last week and I've been thinking about him a lot. But I'm concerned about going further with him.

"My father has mentioned Mateo a few times, I presume at the encouragement of Mario. And I know why he brought you here today, and please make no mistake. I'm very happy to have made your acquaintance."

Maria stopped her with a hug, "You're so sweet and kind. Any mother-in-law would be thrilled to have a daughter–in-law like you."

"Senora, I want you to know if Mario had not introduced him to me, I would have had three dates with Mateo already." She took a breath. "My mother loved my father dearly but lived a tortured life. He is a good man, and never had eyes for another woman. But his weakness is gambling."

Maria sighed. "Men. If it's not one thing it's another."

"The great Chef Filipo fell under their heel, and he's trapped. My mother believed that his cooking skills saved him because of their obsession with food. He's been able to pacify them. Otherwise they would have made him one of them. A thief. Or worse, a murderer. I love my father and I know he suffers from the loss of my mother, but I need a life with a person that I can feel secure having a family with. Someone I could sleep soundly with at night. Someone not under the control of Mario and his kind."

The older woman was filled with disappointment. She did not fault the girl for speaking her mind at their first meeting. She knew from her experience that Marypat reacted so soon because she felt a deep attraction to her son. There could be a special something between them. Disclosing her innermost feelings convinced Maria of that.

"I very much respect and understand you," Maria said. "I wish I had that presence of mind at your age to fight for my ideals. He knows that I'm not happy with his affiliation with Mario, and I have been talking to him about it almost constantly. I caution him not to allow himself to become attracted to fast money. Maybe your example will give him brains. I'm sure a wonderful girl like you would make him very happy and help him channel his ambitions in a positive direction."

Feeling bad for the woman, Marypat started to say, "I'm sorry, you may think I'm–"

"No," Maria stopped her. "Stick to what you believe in, and tell him in no uncertain terms what you want in your life."

They hugged again and made their way back through the bustling kitchen, passing Filipo, who was happy that the women had spoken privately.

Mateo had just finished the last bite of a cannoli that Aldo had brought to kill time. At table, Maria had a cup of coffee waiting in anticipation for a special pastry that Marypat had suggested.

Mateo signaled for the check, but received a wave back. As they rose, Marypat came to see Maria off and embraced her with emotion.

"Please thank your father. He's a wonderful chef," Maria said. "I'm proud to have met you."

Mateo was stunned by how they had taken to each other. He placed a ten-dollar tip on the table for Aldo.

Mateo helped his mother into the car.

"Wait, I'll be right back," he told her and reentered the restaurant. He found Marypat at the bar with her back to the counter. The place of their original meeting.

"Hey, Bella. Remember? This is our spot."

"You back?" she said as she turned. "Some mosquitoes just won't quit buzzing around. What do you want?"

Mateo leaned toward her. "Just give me a chance. One date, that's all I ask. Saturday. Okay?"

She hesitated.

"Just one date. Please. I'm begging."

"Okay, wise guy. One date. But it's not going to be what you expect."

"How about a kiss goodbye?"

"Don't push your luck. Go. Don't leave your poor Mother sitting in the car alone."

"Saturday. Seven. Okay?"

She turned and nodded her head with a small smile that she could not help.

His mother was happy to hear that Marypat had accepted a date with him. *She will put him to the test. It won't be easy. He will have to change his life.*

Maria resigned herself to do a novena and pray the rosary every day for her son. She prayed harder after learning more how involved he was with Mario. She hoped he had not entered *la famiglia.* She begged God that he not be allowed to pass the point of no return.

38.

Mateo took his mother home and walked her up to the apartment.

"Mom. I gotta go for cigarettes, do you need anything?"

"You know you can use the phone here," she said with a smile, presuming he wanted to call Marypat.

"Mom, please, I'll be right back."

He drove up the block to the public phone at the corner to call Mario. Mario answered on the first ring, took his number, and told him to wait for a call back in about ten minutes.

He thought about Marypat. He knew he could fall in love with her. He thought about what he truly wanted out of life. The phone rang. He picked up the receiver and heard Mario's voice correcting one of his subordinates in the background.

"Hey kid, how did everything go at Casa Filipo?"

"Great, she accepted a date with me for Saturday night."

"Geez," he heard Mario say, then a momentary silence. "I'm sorry kid but you have a big thing going for Saturday night."

"Oh, man. Mario, I'm always there for you. But can someone else do the work? It was rough getting through. You know her. I'm afraid she'll get pissed and write me off."

"I know, I know, kid. But this is not work. It's a special celebration. A celebration for you. *Capiche?*"

"Come down and see me tomorrow around ten for a late breakfast. I have something for you to do."

Mateo puzzled. *A special celebration. For me?* Then it dawned on him, *Shit, they're going to make me. Holy Christ! They're going to make me!* He almost shouted it out. Shaking with excitement, he decided to go for a drink at the neighborhood bar. He needed time to relax and think.

The image of Marypat came into his mind. Her Mediterranean skin, and eyes the color of the sea. A panic came over him.

"Is this really what I want?" he whispered as he sat in the car.

* * *

Mateo did not sleep. Nightmarish thoughts whirled in his head. He heard his mother's voice and replays of conversations with Mario. He heard Marypat's words of disdain for the mob, and his head was filled with the smell of Michaela. All were interwoven with scenes of violence. Things he'd witnessed. Things he'd done. Things he'd be asked to do in the future.

Mateo awoke, irritated by the sound of the phone. He heard his mother in conversation with her friend.

"Gertrude, I was just going to call you."

"Yes, I met the girl. She's lovely, perfect for him. She has beautiful red hair with light freckles. So cute. He met his match with her. If he wants to keep her, he has to toe the line." Her voice became girlishly excited. "They really only just met but she told me that she was attracted to him, loves his looks, and knows that he is intelligent ... Oh, I think he is crazy about her. He takes me to meet her? Even before they had a date? She's a good family girl, so nice. I hope he doesn't mess up. I'll call you later. I'm pressing a shirt for the prince."

Mateo's heart grew heavier. How happy his mother was with the prospect of her son falling in love with a nice Italian girl. Knives of guilt stabbed through him. He had so much love for his mother, more so now that they had talked and he knew of how she suffered. How she had hidden her tears, and sheltered him from pain, raising him with so much love.

He ticked through his morning ritual. He showered. He took the freshly pressed shirt from the closet, still warm from the iron, as he did every day. Clean underwear and socks awaited him on the bed.

He joined his Mother in the kitchen, thanked her for laying-out his clothes. This time he lingered just a little longer when kissing her goodbye.

"I'm late," he said.

"Be careful and be a good boy."

Still glowing from the previous evening, she had not read the internal torment on her son's face.

Her voice echoed in his mind. *Be careful and be a good boy.* These were words which annoyed him in the past, but now registered with profound impact.

The luncheonette was unusually crowded with men shoulder to shoulder at the counter. Some he knew, others he did not. Mario, at a back table, lifted his hand gesturing. Mateo approached.

"Wait for me at the back door," Mario said.

A short time later, the capo joined him. Mateo opened the door, stepped outside and looked in both directions. He signaled Mario that it was clear and the two men got into the black Caddy parked a few feet away. Mario explained that he wanted to speak with him undisturbed.

As they drove, Mario asked him again, "How did things go with Marypat and your mother?"

"My Mother, forget about it. She's thrilled. We were treated as royalty, thanks to you."

"You're part of something much bigger than you think. We're a family and take care of our own. If you had been in China, you would have received the same treatment."

The car stopped in the parking lot of the funeral parlor. He followed Mario through the large garage passing a limo, two funeral cars, and a flower car. The concrete floor appeared freshly painted in Battleship gray. They made their way past the vehicles down a flight of cement stairs into the basement passing by a variety of caskets arrayed as showcases.

The office appeared unused. Two file cabinets sat against a far wall, a small desk in the center sat atop a blue-gray commercial carpet. The smell of the new flooring filled his head. The walls had been sealed with acoustical tile like a recording studio.

As he sat behind the desk, Mario asked Mateo, "Have you eaten?" Mario didn't wait for Mateo's answer. He picked up the phone and buzzed Anthony in the front office.

"Anthony, do me a favor. Get a box of buns, a few biscotti and two espressos from the bakery. And some of those special jelly donuts for yourself." "

"Yeah, yeah," Anthony responded. "No, thank you."

They made small talk, mostly about the meal at Casa Filipo, while waiting for Anthony. When he came down the steps, he called out to Mario.

"I'm-a here, Mario."

Mario answered, "Okay, Anthony. We're-a waiting for-a you."

"He always likes to announce himself," Mario said to Mateo. "I think he's afraid he going to find us with butana's down here."

Anthony entered the room and placed the opened box of pastries and coffee on the desk. Mario handed him a tissue.

"Here, you have sugar on your chin. Anthony, do you know Mateo?

"Yes, yes. You ... Patrino' s boy? I know-a your father, Martino, a long time, rest–in-peace, rest–in-peace. Your mother's very wonderful lady. Say hello for me. I bet she's-a proud of you."

Mateo swallowed hard. "Yeah. Thanks, Anthony. I'll say hello for you."

As he left the room, Anthony pondered Mateo's face again, and displayed displeasure in his eyes seeing him with Mario. Mateo recalled a similar cold stare from Carmella as he sat having dinner with Mario a few nights earlier.

Mateo took a container of espresso and a cheese bun, and waited for Mario to speak.

"Please close the door and lock it," Mario said.

Mateo did as requested. He returned to his seat, but did not touch his coffee or half-eaten pastry.

"You've got a serious decision to make," Mario began. "Soon. You know the meaning of the Omerta – the Oath? You take the Omerta and from that time on, people are going to depend on you to do the right thing. To do what you're told. To do it for *la famiglia*, for the brotherhood, and to do it without fail. I know you're young, this is very exciting, and it's happening fast for you, so I need you to think and assure me that this is really what you want." Mario stopped and shook his head in agreement with himself.

"Up to this point, you decided what risks you would take for yourself. You will have to raise the stakes and do things, well, things you might find distasteful. You must follow orders with a blind obedience no different than that Army soldiers swear to obey." Mario took a bite of his biscotti while Mateo took in a solid breath of air at the severity of Mario's words.

"The Omerta has the weight of priest's vow of allegiance to their Bishops and obedience to the Church. So talk to me. Tell me how you feel. Ask me any questions you may have. Some I may not answer until I feel sure you want the life."

The young man picked his words with care. He felt sweat on his brow, and a tremble in his legs.

"Mario. I want the life, and I believe I've proven myself. I know I'm suited for it. I have hoped for this moment and thought it would take many more years for this privilege and honor to be offered"

Mario raised his eyebrows as if he knew what's coming.

"What worries me, Mario, is how it would affect my mother who has been very unhappy since I have been working with you. She blames the life for the loss of my father and has fear for my survival if I enter the same life. I know I can't hide it from her. All I could hide from her are the details, but she knows them anyway. She knows because she's lived it."

Mario's eyes widened. Mateo saw a twinge of controlled anger.

"You," he growled. "You're well into this already, how could you turn back now? Could you give up the money? What would you do? Mothers and wives always show concern and suspicion. We are no different from firemen or cop families. They will always be concerned about the danger. Nevertheless, we assure them that we're smart and we know what we're doing. We spend family time with them so they feel secure.

"Many people put their family aside to hang out, drink and screw whores. They put themselves in harm's way because of it. I told you before that the bosses are family men. They go home at night and enjoy their families, taking risks only for business. Risks that are studied and planned. I see this in you. You're smart. You do not hang around, and you act professionally without emotion when called to do a job. These cool tempered talents will help you keep safe, help you earn more, and move up."

Mateo listened with trepidation to his every word and was about to speak when Mario went on.

"Kid, if you had told this to any other boss you would be in trouble. You're too far into this already, and this would signal weakness. They would look at you as a security risk, especially with all the heat coming down." Mario pointed to his head with his index finger.

"*Capiche*? Like your father, I know that you're a man of honor, loyal, and you mean what you say. He was a stand-up guy who sacrificed for the *la famiglia*, holding their respect and trust. So, in his memory, for now, and until you get things worked out, I want you to continue with the machines and some driving. I will hold back work that is more serious until I feel you're ready and hope that the window will stay open for you."

Mateo rose when Mario came around the desk and grasped the young man's shoulders.

"Please understand that I'm responsible for you and if you go further, what you do will affect my wellbeing. Chew that. *Vederla dopo, va.* – See you later, now go. This conversation never happened. *Capiche*?"

For the first time, Mateo felt fear. He trusted Mario, but others might not feel the same way about him. He knew that many of them were ruthless and tended to overreact when it came to guarding their own security. He needed to chill out. He decided to call Michaela to see if she could spend some time with him.

39.

Upon Mario's return to the luncheonette, he learned that Fingers had been looking for him. He had called three times. He returned the call from the payphone at the rear of the store.

A voice answered, "Three Feather."

"It's me. He wants to talk to me?"

"Yeah, he needs to see you right away."

Mario hung up, dashed for his car, and was there in minutes. JoJo and Little Vinny were seated at the bar, with looks of fear on their faces. One of Fingers' henchmen stood by them.

Fingers waved Don Peppino's Lieutenant Mario to a table in the back. There was no exchange of ceremonial kisses.

"We got a big problem."

Mario asked, "What's going on? Why is my crew here?"

"They're here because they're a couple of stupid fucks. I guess you didn't listen to the radio this morning."

"What happened now?

"They met that reporter, Munson, Michael Munson, and scared the shit out of him. He ran out in front of a car and got killed on the spot."

"Holy shit."

Fingers got up and led Mario to the back room. He signaled to his bodyguard to bring Mario's crew.

The door had just closed when Mario stepped up to JoJo and slapped him across the face. "What the fuck were you thinking? You got any idea what the fuck you did?"

"Boss, I know you're upset but we didn't do anything. The guy made a mistake, and got spooked."

"What did you say to him?"

"Everything was going fine." JoJo's voice was barely above a whisper. "He knew we have given information before, and asked his help. We explained that we needed him to turn the heat down with his articles referring to our thing. We mentioned that we were in the process of looking for the maniac ourselves and helping the police. And in return for this favor we would get an exclusive for him when we bagged the guy."

Fingers interjected, "What did he say?"

"Well, his eyes lit up when he heard exclusive. We thought everything was cool and handed him a couple of box seat tickets to the Yankee game. He started to take them with a smile until he saw, you know, that fat fuck Rosenthal the bail-bond who sat at the counter. When he finished his meal, he got up he turned around looking in our direction while stretching his arms and yawning."

"Get to the point," Mario said.

Little Vinny said, "He saw his piece. Rosenthal keeps a snub on his belt and Munson saw it."

"Munson probably figured Rosenthal was muscle for us," JoJo said. "When he saw the gun he panicked and ran out. We followed trying to tell him he misunderstood, but the jerk runs in front of a cab that sent him flying twenty feet. As we were trying to help loosen his tie, the police came."

Little Vinny's lips quivered as he explained. "They questioned us. We told them that he just ran out. Then another patrol car came with two more cops who questioned people in the restaurant. They must have told them that they saw the jerk running from us. That we ran out the door after him. The dumb cops, looking for a case, took us in."

"And what the fuck did you two shmucks say?"

"We dummied-up and called the mouthpiece, Kramer, who got us out of there fast. It was a freak thing."

Mario fell into a chair, stunned, and unable to speak. He turned to Fingers who sat deadpan and silent.

Mario sighed. "Go outside. Wait there." They were terrified of how *la famiglia* bosses were going to deal with them. They stumbled over each other as they pushed through the door.

They knew that a death of a reporter attributed to the family would bring tremendous heat on all the New York mob families.

Fingers spoke in a measured tone, laying out one word at a time.

"How do you send idiots like that to do a job like this?"

Mario felt trapped. "They've been working with that reporter a long time, giving him information when it suited us. I thought they had a rapport. This is a freak thing, a curse."

"Take a couple of people and visit the bondsman to see if their stories match," Fingers said. "If it does not, make sure it does. You can bet there is going to be a high-level table over this, and it may cost us blood, yours included."

"Shit. A sit down, does Birdie know?"

"He's at the doctor for a check-up. This will give him a heart attack. But I will talk to him and explain. After you speak to the *Schiavo* (bondsman) meet me at Don Peppino's."

Mario slapped the table with his hand. He stood and left without another word.

Mario entered Rosenthal's office accompanied by two second-string enforcers. They stared at the short, obese man who sat behind a large oak desk covered with paper and files. The man knew who they were and asked his secretary to leave.

"Mr. Mario. It's been a long time. To what do I owe the–"

"Did you finger our people in the dinner this morning?"

The man started to get up.

"Just sit your fat ass down. Keep your hands on the desk."

"Look, Mario. Your two guys were sittin' at a table in front of me with this other guy. I didn't know him. He looked familiar, so maybe I was starin' at him a little.

"When I gets up, the guy looks at me, turns white as sheet, and runs out the door. That's all I saw, and that's all I told the cops."

"Stand up," Mario said.

"Hey, Mario. Really. I didn't say anything else. I swear."

"Just stand the fuck up," Mario repeated.

He stood up.

"Raise your arms."

"Ah, come on. Mario. Please."

"Just raise your fuckin' arms."

The man was sweating. He quaked as he began to raise his arms. He didn't have to lift them far for Mario to see his jacket – two sizes too small for this fat stomach – rise and expose the snub .38 he had in a belt holster.

Mario had begun to lead his men out of the office, but stopped and turned.

"Hey, Rosenthal," l called after him. "We're good, right? Next time you need favor, it's on me."

Mario made his way back to the funeral parlor, feeling confident that his men had told the truth. *It was a fluke thing. Once the bosses know, they'll go easy on us.*

When he entered Don Peppino's office, Fingers was there. The two men sat, leaning back in their chairs. Both had their arms crossed, their faces as stern as Mario had ever seen.

"So?" Fingers mumbled.

"The bondsman confirmed their story. My guys may be stupid, but they know better than to lie to me."

Mario took a seat. "We should let Kramer know this was righteous. An accident. This would make whatever case the DA has against them weaker."

"You think that the press is going to buy that?" Don Peppino asked. "You think that they're going to believe that their star reporter, one known to have the balls of a bull dog panicked out? And what about the bosses? And the heat thrown on the other families? *Marone* – Holy Mary – they already called us for a table tomorrow morning in Brooklyn. Make sure JoJo and Little Vinny are there. Hold them tonight if you need to. I will call the lawyer myself to get the signed deposition from Rosenthal, and have him get it done fast so we can show the bosses."

Fingers said, "We gotta keep our movements covered. You know the drill. Switch cars, and all that. Call that little fuck Herbie with the car lot. Tell him we need to borrow a few low profile cars. Chevy's, Fords. There are reporters all over."

"Go," Peppino said. "We'll be at Carmella's, if you need us." The sky was dark and a light drizzle had dampened the streets as Mario made his way to his car.

He approached Sally, his new right hand man, got close and whispered, "Take these two morons," pointing to JoJo and Little Vinny, "to the hotel. Make sure they're not armed. Spend the night and watch 'em like a fuckin' hawk. I'm not taking any more chances." Mario walked down the dark, deserted street. He Turn -ed his collar to the rain. At the corner, he hailed a cab.

40.

Dominick saw the long faces of Mob brace, Peppino, Fingers, and Birdie as they entered the restaurant. He led them to the back dining room. He could see they were in no mood for idle chatter. He asked them what type of wine they wanted. Birdie told him that he would like to start with a scotch on the rocks. The others nodded.

"Chivas or Johnny Black?"

"We'll all have Chivas," Peppino said. "Tell your mother we'll eat whatever she's cooking. And the homemade red with the food."

In minutes, Dominick had a pitcher of ice, three rocks glasses, and a bottle of Chivas on the table and served. Angie followed him with a family-sized bowl of crisp mixed salad and a basket of hot Italian bread. They complimented her on how nice she looked, making her blush as she placed the salad plates before them and began serving. Anthony arrived and entered the room uninvited.

"Anthony," Don Peppino asked him with surprise, "What's the matter?"

"Nothin' wrong. Mario watches the telephone for me," he answered, not wanting Peppino to think he had abandoned his post. Then he took small stack of envelopes out of his pocket. He handed one to Don Peppino, and another to Fingers, and one to Birdie.

"What's this?" Fingers said with a curious grin.

Anthony did not answer instead he asked Angie to invite her mother to join them.

Don Peppino, already agitated by the earlier events showed his impatience by pounding a fist into the air but received a paternal pat from Birdie to let him continue. He opened his envelope first and found that it contained an invitation. Professionally printed with the formality of a wedding announcement. It read:

Mr. Anthony Stampadello Cordially invites you to attend his 66th Birthday Celebration Sunday, September 15, 1956 at 2:00 p.m. At the old house, 210 Hester Street New York 2, NY. On the second floor roof. Please bring your families and please no gifts thank you.

They each tried to restrain laughter as they read their invitations.

Carmella came to the table in her apron wiping her hands on a dishtowel. "Hi, what's going on?"

"Anthony has something for you," Birdie said.

Anthony handed her the envelope. Carmella opened it and read. Her eyes widened as she went down the card.

"Wow," she said. "A birthday party. How nice." She hesitated, then read the address a second time. "At the old house?"

The dynamics of the group were prominent as if a flashback to their interactions as children surfaced.Each displayed their past roles, playing their parts as if they were sitting under Birdie's makeshift table on the roof shielding them from the rain, discussing a problem. They reflexively looked to Birdie. He shook his head and invited Carmella and Anthony to sit.

"Anthony, my brother, I believe I can speak for all of us on how flattered we are at receiving this invitation. I would like to ask you how we can help. You know the old house is owned by other people and I don't even know if anyone lives there. What made you think that you could have a party there?"

"I bought the house."

"What?" Don Peppino said. "You bought the house? And how did you do that?"

"Peppino, remember when I asked you for my bank book last month. I forgot to give it back to you, I still had it in my pocket."

"Yes?"

"You see I'm standing there on line, in Melaina's Pork Store waiting to buy the sausage and mozzarella for you to take home, and I heard Carlo Zuppa tell Sam the butcher that he put the place up for sale. Then I heard Sam ask him how much he was asking. He told him that he wanted $5000 for it. I remembered I had the bankbook so I took it out and saw how much I had. There was $12,987."

Anthony snapped his fingers with a smile. "Zuppa sold it to you? You know, without suggesting you might want to speak to someone? To us?"

"I followed Mr. Zuppa out the door and told him that I would like to buy the house. First, he laughed at me as if I'm crazy. I said, as Mario tells me how, I say to him, 'you know who I am?' He stared at me and told me to go to Di Napoli the lawyer on Mulberry Street five o'clock the next day. That he would talk to me."

Carmella asked, "You went to the lawyer by yourself?"

"Yeah, so the next day I went and they asked me how I was going to get the money, I showed him the passbook. He asked me if Don Peppino knew about my intentions of buying the house. 'No,' I said, 'What's the matter? It's a surprise.'"

Peppino stroked his brow. Birdie sat in awe.

"Di Napoli told me to come back in a few days with a bank check and in the meantime he would prepare the papers. "

Peppino whispered to Birdie, "I got a telephone message from Di Napoli but haven't had the chance to call him back."

"The Old man Zuppa," Anthony continued, "took me to see the house. My God, it was almost like we left it."

As he spoke of it, tears fell as he experienced a flood of dark memories as he stepped up on the second floor roof. Anthony leaned forward to Birdie. His eyes sparkled as if a child revealing a great secret.

"Birdie. Your table. It's still there! It's covered with tarpaper, and there are lots of plants on it, but it's still there. Can you believe it? I think I scared poor Mr. Zuppa because in my head I was thinking about everything we did there in the old days and I started to cry. He took me downstairs and his wife Marcella made me, *una tazza de cafe niuru*-- a cup of black coffee."

Birdie saw the concerned look on the faces of the others and asked Anthony, "Did you tell Zuppa about your memories there?"

Anthony became uncharacteristically indignant. "I know how to hold secrets better than all of you, and I know what you're thinking."

Fingers said, "Okay, calm down. Do you intend to live there by yourself?"

"No, I just wanted to keep it out of the hands of other people. All of our lives are there, nobody should live there."

"So what are you going to do with it?" Peppino asked.

"I don't know, but I will start with the party."

His mood rose again. "I ordered food from Château Gianna, And I fixed the table and made some other repairs with the help of my friend Zito Bruni, my bocce partner."

"The Zuppa's," Carmella asked. "What are they going to do? Are they staying in the house?"

"I told them they could stay as long as they want to. They are going to retire in Palermo and are finding out how they can get their social security checks mailed to them."

Carmella was the first to give Anthony a hug and wish him well. "Of course I'll come to your party," she said.

"Our party," Anthony corrected.

He whistled. *They will find out soon what I will do with the house.*

His childhood friends shook their heads at one another. Fingers questioned with an agitated twitch, "What got into him? Peppino followed with raised brows, "I didn't know he had it in him," before they turned to the business that brought them there that night.

41.

Mario met Fingers the next morning at the Three Feather Bar and they drove to the St. George Hotel in Brooklyn Heights to accompany JoJo and Little Vinny to the Table. They called the room from the courtesy phone in the lobby to let them know that they had arrived. Fingers and Mario exited through the back door and got into a waiting large linen supply van. They nodded to the uniformed driver. JoJo and Little Vinny were escorted into the van. They proceeded through downtown Brooklyn's traffic. Angelica's Linen Supply was well known in the borough.

To insure they were not followed the truck made a couple of bogus stops. The first was on 4th Ave, then another a few blocks further south. They ended their trip at the rear of a kosher Matzah bakery in Boro Park. They were politely greeted by two men in suits who searched them. As they sat in the hall lined with boxes of Matzah, Mario warned them, "*Non una parola, tiene lei è delle bocche chiudono.*" – Don't say one word and speak only if asked a direct question.

They were escorted to a basement storage area, a prepared space cleared to accommodate a large table with chairs where members of the mob's hierarchy sat awaiting them. In ceremonial Sicilian style, the New York group kissed the ring of Don Pedro, the boss of *la famiglia*, and kissed the others in attendance on both cheeks. They sat and exchanged pleasantries. Under-boss Ettore Balsamo signaled *la famiglia*'s attorney Zachary Kramer to speak first.

Kramer said he had taken the deposition of the bondsman whose statement supported JoJo and Little Vinny's account, and that he provided the police investigator in charge with the information. "If it were any other circumstance, there would be no case. However, because this guy was a newsman, the DA and police are taking a lot of heat. Our people inside insist that they can't do much because of it and that some jail time has to be done."

JoJo and Little Vinny started to fidget in their chairs. Mario cautioned them with his eyes. "Look," Balsamo said, "we know that this was a fluke thing, and it is a lesson to us all. We gotta be aware of how people fear us. Looking back, maybe it would have been better to visit him at his office or have the meeting in surroundings that were more private."

In any case we a have a problem. The media is not going to let this go. The other families are pressuring us to resolve this because they are already feeling heat. The DA and the Mayor are getting national and international calls from news organizations. Everyone wants this settled quickly." He stopped.

Don Pedro nodded to the attorney.

"We worked out a deal. One of you will have to do three to five for reckless endangerment. With good behavior, you could be back in your own bed in six to eight months."

Balsamo added, "They will put you in a place that has our people, so you will have everything - food, wine and even broads. The free one will share half his earnings to support the incarcerated one's family." Don Pedro looked at Mario.

"Yeah, I'll come up with the fix money. How much?"

"Ten large," Balsamo said.

"Done," Mario said.

Don Pedro smiled and bowed his head with regal recognition. Then the under boss took a half dollar out of his pocket. "I going to flip this coin to see who does the bit. JoJo will be heads and Little Vinny tails." JoJo raised his hand. Fingers looked at him and turned to Don Pedro. "Don. Your permission, please. May I have a minute with JoJo?

"Sure, take your time," Balsamo agreed. Fingers led JoJo to a corner of the room "Why're you asking to speak? Didn't we tell you to dummy-up?"

"Boss," he answered, "I have no problem with the deal. What I was going to say was that because Little Vinny has small kids at home, that I would take the bit."

Fingers' demeanor softened. "You're a good boy.

You sure?"

"Yeah, boss. No problem."

"Okay, let me tell them. You dummy-up."

Fingers said, "Don. You know, we all get these problems. But I got to tell you how proud of my crew I am. Mario and his boys have been excellent earners and work together as brothers. I'm proud to say that JoJo is asking to take the bit for Little Vinny because Vinny has small children at home."

Balsamo turned to Little Vinny, "Is this okay with you?"

Vinny nodded, then turned to JoJo. "You sure?"

Vinny asked JoJo. "Hey, you're my brother, man. I do it for you. I do it for *nostra famiglia." I get to sit out a full scale mob war in a nice warm jail cell while everyone else gets slaughtered,* JoJo thought. *And I get half of the payoff on that big construction job Vinny did as my spiff for taking the bit. So who's the schmuck moron now?*

"Okay, that's done," Balsamo said. "JoJo, you stay behind to wait for Kramer. He will brief you and take you down for book-ing. He will have you out within an hour on bail. In the meantime, make yourself scarce and do not talk with anybody. Vinny, you need to take a low profile too. Mario, can you find something for him to do for a few weeks in Vegas?"

"Sure. He will be out of here tomorrow."

Mario felt relieved and grateful that the deal did not require someone's blood and that there would be no admonishment for his leadership skills. He felt that the trip to the bondsman paid off. With their business done, they made their way back to Brooklyn Heights, this time in a Matzah Bakery delivery truck.

42.

The late summer day broke with strands of light slivering through the blinds as Kevin woke. He dressed and wrote out a note for her. *I'm off to town to phone mom and then to the bakery for fresh rolls.* He placed it under her door and smiled recollecting how they sat in the moonlight and kissed the night before.

He felt the calm stillness of the house as he tiptoed down the creaking steps on his way to the car. He took a deep breath of fresh mountain air. It had the essence of evergreen with a cool clean morning weight to it. He thanked God for the new day and the joy he felt with having Katie part of his life. As he drove a short distance on the winding country road, he wondered if the year-rounder residents appreciated the views and the abundance of nature in front of their eyes.

When he arrived at the gas station, he asked the attendant to service the car for the trip home. He dashed to the telephone booth to call his mother.

"Hi, Mom. I hope I didn't wake you."

"No, Kev, we were up early, packing our overnights. We're on our way to your Uncle for a day or two. He's not been feeling well, so we thought a visit would cheer him up. How about you, what are you two up to? Are you having a good time?"

"Everything has been wonderful. Kate has great friends, the house and property are beautiful and we even had our own private mass."

Kevin appreciated his parents. He adored them and enjoyed a relationship of mutual respect. He felt he could always speak freely with them, even regarding his personal life.

"Mom, I would like to introduce Katie to our world. She is looking forward to meeting you and Dad."

"That would be wonderful," she said. "We can't wait to meet her either."

"If it's alright with you, we'd like to drive out this afternoon and spend the balance of the week at the house."

"Of course. Do you even have to ask? I will prepare the guest room for her."

Lillian Mandrell was bursting with anticipation knowing she'd be meeting Katie.

"There's plenty of meat in the freezer and you can take her to the farm stand for fresh vegetables. I'm so excited."

"Thanks. We'll see you in a couple of days. Say hello to Dad and give my best to Uncle Basil. Please tell him that I will try to take a run out there myself before I leave for Zurich. Have a great time."

Kevin reflected on how he could always count on his parents. He felt he owed a great part of his success in life to their support.

He placed more change in the pay phone and dialed. A female voice answered, "Good morning, Apex Manufacturing. How can I help you?"

"This is Johnny-one-note."

"Do you have a good connection?

"Yes," he said confirming and alerting her in code that he'd be able to speak freely.

"Hold, please. I'm connecting your call."

Kevin waited.

"Hi. Just speaking about you," Malcolm said.

"Hope it was all good."

"Yes, in fact, very good. Your compensation is about to escalate to a management tier."

"Thank you. It's always good to feel appreciated. Do you have a few minutes to lend some advice?"

"For you, I have all the time in the world."

Kevin brought Malcolm up to speed on his project with the watchmaker. He shared his concerns regarding Katie's family. He assured his superior his work remained uncompromised. Nevertheless, he shared his apprehension about the possibility that his presence in Katie's life might be misconstrued, and viewed as an infiltration by the mob leadership, especially those closely tied to her father.

"On the surface nothing appears to be a problem," Malcolm said. "However, Let me see what I can find out about these people. I'll get back to you within a day or two. In the meantime, enjoy your time with your new lady. She's wonderful you know. We'll speak soon."

* * *

When Kevin returned to the cottage, his housemates were fully engaged in conversation. Everyone appeared energized. They were moving about the cottage cleaning and chattering on a variety of topics. Dominick called out when he saw Kevin with the bags of rolls and pastries.

"Breakfast is here."

Katie greeted him with a kiss. "Speak to your Mom?"

"She's thrilled about meeting you. They're leaving this morning for a couple days to visit my uncle, which works well for us. More alone time." He smiled.

"Let's have breakfast with the gang, and catch lunch or dinner on the road to break up the drive. How does that sound?"

"Perfect." He whispered, "I'm hot for you."

She surprised him with her response. "Me, too."

They all gathered at the kitchen table. Father Tony said grace and blessed them with the sign of the cross.

After they ate, the men went off to target shoot with the bows, and the women lingered at the table. Reggie prompted them to speak about their guys, hoping to hear spicy details. They giggled as they took her encouragement, each sharing the idiosyncrasies of the men. Millie was quite graphic as she spoke of Dominick. They had fun together for a while, then decided to start getting their things in order for the trip back.

Reggie followed Katie upstairs to her room. She knew Katie well and sensed that she had a heavy heart.

"What's wrong?" she asked.

"Nothing." Katie pulled her suitcase out of the closet.

"Come on, out with it," Reggie snapped.

"Oh Regg, I love that man," Katie cried, her hand coming to her mouth as she stifled a sob.

"Well, that's good. Isn't it? Love is good."

Katie plopped down on the bed and hung her head. Reggie sidled up next to her, put her hand on Katie's shoulder and waited.

"I have been coming to terms with things," Katie said. "Things I have denied about my family and the world we live in."

Reggie understood immediately and offered an older sister's advice.

"Look, kid. You're you, and you're not responsible for anyone's soul but your own. Beating yourself up for things that were out of your control is not going to get you anywhere but into a mental hospital. I'm not discounting the pain you may feel, but you're not going to blow this relationship. You know I can read people well and I'm telling you, Kevin is special. Whatever concerns you have, you and he will deal with together."

Reggie put her fingers under Katie's chin and tilted her face up.

"Go forward with your life. You're not an actor in someone else's play. Follow your own script and don't look back. God will support you. My prayers are always with you."

Reggie's words touched Katie to the core. She was so grateful for the nun's friendship. Although Reggie did not know the details, she had an uncanny intuition borne of a rough start in life. She was a streetwise ex-drug addict who had turned her life to God. Evil had no hold on her, and she was not about to let it consume her friend's future.

Father Tony accompanied Katie and Kevin to their car. Katie embraced Tony.

"Thank you for a marvelous weekend. We're not going straight home. We're going to stop on Long Island to visit with Kevin's parents."

"Allow yourself the freedom to express your feelings and fears," Tony cautioned in a whisper as they embraced. "He's a good man. He'll understand."

Kevin approached them extended his hand. Father Tony pushed it aside.

"Brothers don't shake, they hug," he said as he wrapped his arms around him.

"Okay, bow your heads," Father Tony said as he let go and stood back. "Please Lord, guide and protect these wonderful people, your children, and keep them safe under your mantle of love." He squeezed Katie once again then shooed them toward the car with a hand gesture. "Go, have fun, be happy, and please, no juicy confessions."

43.

The late summer day broke with strands of light. They took their time driving back, making stops at a roadside antique shop and a farm stand for fresh produce. When Kevin crossed into Yonkers from Westchester, he asked her if she wanted to stop for an early dinner.

They said in unison, "Patricia Murphy's."

"How do you know Patricia Murphy's?" she asked, surprised at the coincidence.

"Oh, that's mom and dad's favorite place. They love the candlelight atmosphere, the grounds and the gift shop. We've been going there for special occasions for years."

"My family, too. When my parents wanted to fantasize how American they were and dress up for dinner, Murphy's sat at the top of their list. They love the colonial atmosphere and classic American menu. I love the popovers."

"Well, I need my strength for later this evening. A nice piece of prime rib would fortify me."

"Really? What are you expecting?"

He looked at her with a sly smile.

She slapped his arm. "Nice. Spend a weekend with a priest and a nun, be pious at mass and all the time sinful thoughts were spinning in the back of your Irish Catholic head."

Katie joked, but she felt she was at the breaking point of reason herself. She considered the risk. She wanted him, but ... *this is a gamble.*

"Okay, Prince Charming, what happened to the white horse, the swooping down retrieving the fair maiden with vows of eternal love and that happily ever after stuff?"

He laughed as they drove up the long climbing driveway and parked in the tiered plaza. He ran around the car, opened her door, and fell to one knee, "My Lady," he said with his hand extended, "your castle awaits."

"That's it. Now you're getting it."

She exited the car and took his extended arm like a Princess, then, in a second, found herself over his shoulder being carried into the sedate restaurant.

"Sorry to disappoint you, but this is Attila the Hun, not Prince Charming," she said.

When they entered, he slid her off his shoulder in front of the host as if she were a piece of furniture. Her face turned red with embarrassment while the waiting guests applauded. He laughed loudly and she hid her face into his chest. Adding to her embarrassment, the hostess played into their lightheartedness.

"I think we should sit the young lovers in a quiet corner." she said. "Isn't love great?" She led them into the dining room.

Kevin ordered a bottle of wine and they recalled the fun they had at Tony's house, chuckling as they remembered the antics of their friends, especially Dominick and Lungs with Reggie's mischievous prodding.

Katie spoke about her friendship with Reggie and Father Tony. She admired their love for Jesus and the special closeness they had with each other because of their vocations. She felt they were more than friends. To her they were supportive, caring and her family.

"Reggie and Tony adore you," she said to Kevin. "They pray that our relationship will flourish. They believe we complement each other."

As they spoke, the first glass of wine began to have an effect on Katie, who lacked tolerance for alcohol. "I want to tell you what I learned from Aunt Carmella," she said in an attempt to unburden her heavy heart, but Kevin spoke up.

"Honey, we don't have to talk about it right now."

"I know. There's a lot. It's knocked me off balance," she said while fumbling her glass of wine. "You see," she laughed.

"I see my little Italian dynamo is more than a little tipsy. You know the beast will want to capitalize on that."

"You know, Kevvie my boy," she said with a slight slur in an attempt to add more spice to the moment, "I'm not going to get into all that heavy stuff right now. Soon you will see, given the green light from God, the beast hiding within me, one that will not be stopped. However, you must know that for the rest of your natural life you will know no other in the carnal sense but me. Got that, Buster?"

Kevin began to feel his loins awakening and played along, "I don't know if I'll be able to handle that side of you."

"Well, you better. I have waited a long time repressing my desires. You had better be up for it. Oops," she giggled, "for the challenge that is."

"What happened to this nice sedate Catholic school girl? Well, maybe we should forego dinner and go right to the dessert."

"Oh no, buddy-boy, that's just it. Catholic school-girl. You got that right. The Catholic Church believes in redemption, and given license. I will help you seek it."

"You're so sexy and cute I'd like you to start the redemption process right as we speak," he said, moving to her and landing a big kiss. Katie's face flushed from the combination of his words and the buzzing effect of the wine.

The waitress appeared at their side. "Now, now, y'all," she said in a Texas accent. "This is a classy restaurant. Bubba's gotta keep the pig in the pokey."

They all laughed and she took their order. At the conclusion of their meal they topped off their good fare with Patricia Murphy's ritual complimentary Crème de Menthe cordial.

44.

While riding to Long Island Katie dozed. He woke her as they turned into the driveway. His parents had left the lights on. A string of coach lamps illuminated the property and guided them to the front door. Katie gazed up at the house.

"This is beautiful, very colonial. You can almost smell the cornbread baking. Where are the fifes and drums?" she asked with a rub marking their cultural differences.

"Yes. Paul Revere lit the lanterns."

He turned the key and opened the door then threw her over his back and carried her over the threshold.

"I guess Attila is back?" She quipped with a quick flush of passion as he placed her back down. *Now I know what it means to be truly tempted.*

"Look around, and make yourself at home. I'll get the stuff from the car."

Katie went from room to room admiring the décor. The house had an aura of refinement, with original paintings and signed lithographs. She saw a picture of Kevin with his parents upon the mantle. *He must be about twelve in his Sunday best. Bedu -- so cute.*

She climbed the stairs and found four bedrooms. The yellow guest room had the bed turned down with a small envelope propped against the pillow. Katie's name was written prominently in calligraphy. *How sweet and thoughtful his mother is. Maybe I am a princess.* The note read, "*We are so happy that you will be visiting with us and we will have the opportunity to get to know each other. Make yourself at home and enjoy. We will see you in a couple of days. Mom.*

Her world seemed to be changing fast. Katie's emotions were in flux. Her joy and pain, her family, his family, Kevin, and the confessions of Carmella swirled in her mind.

When Kevin came into the room, he saw the tear on her cheek.

"Anything the matter?"

"No, nothing. Your mom left me a sweet note. It touched me. I can't wait to meet her."

"If I know my mother, she's counting the time. Would you like to freshen up? There are towels in the guest bathroom. I'm taking a shower. Then we can have a night-cap."

He hugged her and left for his room.

Katie chose to bathe. She soaked in the warm bathwater anticipating their time alone there. As she cleansed herself with the soapy washcloth her body seemed to tingle. She was aroused. She played wondering what his touch would feel like.

She let herself soak, and let herself dream. Her desire was not new, but the imminent anticipation was. Ambivalence forced itself into her fantasy. She turned on the shower and let the cold water cool her libido, but the cold water on her skin had no effect. She toweled with haste, robed, and glided down the hall in her bare feet.

"Kevin," she called in a sultry tone. "Where are you?"

"I'm in here. My room."

She followed his voice and found him on his bed propped up on pillows. The plaid pajama bottoms were comical, but his bare chest enticed her. She stopped at the doorway and admired him and the light brown chest hair that emphasized his muscular physique.

Without speaking, she slid in bed beside of him, and they could feel the heat of each other's bodies. She kissed him, moving from his neck, to his arms and chest.

As Kevin's hands moved to caress her breasts she stopped, hearing Father Tony's words ringing in her head. She fell to his side. Still aching for him, she shook him with frustration.

"I can't do this. I want to. Oh, God I want to, but–"

"Easy honey, you're worth waiting for, and we have a lifetime together."

She turned and stroked his face. "Thank you," she whispered with the glow of passion in her eyes. "Do you love me, Kevin Mandrell?"

"Yes, I love you Katherine Burdino. More than words could ever express."

"Do you promise to love me as long as we shall live?"

"Yes, my love, and even past that."

"Ooh, you smell so nice."

"Nothing more than my father's Old Spice." Kevin inhaled, and let his breath out, "Mmm. Your aroma is titillating, too."

"Nothing more than your mom's bath beads."

They kissed. "I'm getting out of here," she said. She blew him a kiss over her shoulder, and left for her own bed.

* * *

The next morning Katie rose to music and the aroma of coffee mingled with that of waffles. She put on her robe and followed the sound down the stairs, through the hall, and into the sunroom that provided ample space for a concert Steinway. Kevin did not notice her arrival.

As he massaged the keys to *If I Loved You,* Katie circled behind him, placed her arms around his shoulders, and gave him an affectionate good morning kiss.

With her at his side, he began to sing the words. She joined him, surprised that he could also carry a tune. He encouraged her, and allowed her to solo. Kevin ended the song with an improvised cadenza.

He told her that he had made coffee and breakfast, adding that he had set a table on the patio. She helped him with the breakfast tray and they sat looking out over the acre property to the sound.

"It was wonderful growing up here," Kevin said. "Christmas was amazing, especially when it snowed. And at Easter, the egg hunts. It was storybook."

"It is lovely. A great place to raise a family. It's so Colonial. I can picture you out there with your musket shooting rabbits."

How can I fit into his world? Can he accept mine?

Later, after dressing, they met in the kitchen.

"I've been worried about talking to you about my family," she said.

"Yes?"

She looked at him.

"Never mind. Are we going into Huntington Village?"

45.

Katie loved the quaint seashore community. Kevin shared the local history explaining that the harbor was active in colonial times and bustled with commerce for the early colonial settlers.

"It grew into a port," he said. " It amazes me how Huntington Harbor not only accommodated vessels that traveled from other ports along Long Island Sound, but other countries from here to the exotic West Indies."

"God, you're so American," Katie giggled, "Where's the grog?"

"I think that Timmy and I polished off most of it. We spent many summer days fishing on a small boat that my father bought for me. It was a great getaway from the pressure of school."

"Releasing pressure, hah? I'm sure there were a couple, a few, Bobby soxers floating around here."

Kevin let loose with a belly laugh before saying, "I plead the fifth."

"Is this where the birth of Attila took place?"

"Yeah, this is it. Would you like to spend some time together sailing?"

"Sure, I'd love to. You have a boat now?"

"Let me see what I can do."

He led her by the hand toward the wharf.

As they approached, Kevin waved to the dock master who smiled and waved back. He led Katie down onto a floating dock past several small boats to a forty-foot hand-crafted wooden sailboat. The name *Maiasaura* was painted across the stern.

"This is my dad's boat. He named it for my mother."

"I thought your mother's name was Lillian."

Kevin tightened the hold on her hand.

"It's the name of an extinct dinosaur. It means, good mother. The scientist who found it and determined its species gave it this name because he saw evidence that it took good care of its babies."

"Oh, that's right. Your mother is a Paleontologist?"

"Yep. She's known as The Dinosaur Lady with the kids in town."

Kevin gazed wistfully at the boat, lost in thought for a moment, then said, "Yeah, a Huntington local who passed away had built it. His wife knew that my dad admired her husband's craftsmanship, and offered to sell it him at a more than reasonable price."

"How nice of her. I guess she wanted someone who she knew would love and care for it the way her husband did."

"Yeah. And my Dad does."

He helped her on board, unlocked the cabin, and escorted her inside. She admired the artistry of the workmanship.

"Look at the detail work and the luster of the teakwood. Beautiful. It feels rich, and...homey," she said, looking around the cabin. She could see his mother's touch with the curtains and bedding. Everywhere she turned there was a picture of Kevin.

He got a bottle of wine from the galley.

"I hope you don't mind. My Mom loves a light wine, so all I have is Zinfandel."

"Oh, honey, that's fine. Do you think we could sit on deck and look at the water for a while? I know if we stay down here for more than five minutes the beast will present itself."

They laughed as they sat at the bow enjoying the view of the bay. The sun played hide and seek through puffy clouds causing the water to shimmer in places with silver streaks.

"It's so beautiful," she sighed.

Katie drank half the bottle of wine. Courage came to her courtesy of sparkling wine.

"Kev. I am so much in love with you. I have to admit it." She gripped his hand.

"You are a gift from God." Kevin's wrapped his fingers around hers.

"What I have to say may affect you and your ability to continue with me."

Kevin remained silent.

"You have a good life. There's your career, and you enjoy the respect of many people in the world of classical music, and also in the inner circle of government. And you have an untarnished reputation.

"And then there's me. Yes, I have a good education. Yes, I hold a respectable job, but recently I've become aware, perhaps conscious is a better word, of something I have blocked since childhood."

She stopped, cleared her throat, and gazed straight ahead for a long moment. Kevin was wise enough to wait in silence until she began to speak again.

"My father," she began, and then put her shoulders back as if steeling herself and went ahead. "My father may be intimately associated with mobsters, and I don't want to lose you because of that.

I know now with certainty that my Godfather, Don Peppino, and Billy's father, Uncle Tommaso, are active gangsters. Besides Aunt Carmella, they are my father's closest friends."

Kevin put a reassuring arm around her, and said, "Nobody wants to see faults in themselves or their family. In any case, you're not involved, are you?"

"No, of course not. But what really turns my stomach is that my mother and I have benefited from the evil acts they've done to innocent hardworking people. My mother. It hurts me. My mother is the biggest hypocrite on the face of the earth. She plays the sophisticated suburban woman, married to a doctor, seeking a prince for her daughter. What crap. Talking about having blinders on. She wrote the book."

Katie's face reddened and her lips pursed.

"Looking back, I can vividly see those times she made excuses. How she engineered her words to deflect any suspicion about my father's secret life. My life has been a joke, a comic book filled with characters that are not who they say they are. Oh my God, I can't say it. Aunt Carmella. She told me that Carmine was murdered."

Katie collapsed into Kevin's arms.

Kevin knew that reassuring words would not suffice. Katie had had her epiphany and she realized what terrified her.

Kevin held her tightly and let her cry. After a time, she composed herself. He decided to take a firm approach and speak straight.

"Honey, you are a strong person and have had the skills to build a life for yourself. Nobody promised that life would be easy. Unfortunately, the world we live in has evil that will always challenge us and work to distract us from the good that exists in greater measure. I know reason is telling you that you have no control of what your parents did, or what others will, or will not do. The only one you can control is yourself and deep inside you know that you have given it, you are giving it, your moral best."

She looked at him, beginning to feel calmed by his words. He went on.

"I don't believe in the Sins of the Father crap. I believe we make our own life decisions with help and nudges from God. I also believe that God expects us to grow where he planted us. From where I stand, I can see a woman who has grown straight, who has a moral conscience, and who has done good things while surrounded by dark forces.

"You don't need to worry about me. Your background can't affect my career or standing among my peers, because having you at my side will put a beacon of light around me. It is I who may not be worthy of you."

She hugged him.

"I promise you," he said, "that I will do everything in my power to help you overcome things from the past that bind you, so we can continue our journey together."

Her eyes met his and she muttered softly, "You are my prince."

They sat together for hours that day on the salty deck of the *Maiasaura.*

The next day, at the beach, Katie was moved to tell Kevin everything Carmella had said. She spoke of Father Tony's reaction to her revelation.

Kevin counseled Katie, and they decided the next step was for Katie to learn more from Carmella when they returned to the city. Kevin assured her that he would stay close by when she met with her aunt. Then the subject was dropped.

Over the next couple of days, Kevin showed her the world of his youth. He took her to his favorite places. He knew that more than ever he needed to disclose the reality of the secret world he also lived in.

Kevin's dad called and left a message that he and Kevin's mother planned to return home by suppertime on Friday. Katie, in appreciation, decided to cook a traditional Italian dinner for them. They searched for and found an Italian market and they purchased authentic ingredients.

When they woke Friday morning, Kevin pursued her.

"Stop. Your parents are coming home and we need to clean the house and start to prepare supper." Then she playfully pinched his cheek, "What's this, pizza dough?"

He grabbed and kissed her, and broke away.

"Okay, let's get dressed."

He knew she was anxious about meeting his mother.

46.

Kevin and Katie worked together sprucing up the place and preparing the food. She had him cleaning and stuffing artichokes, rolling meatballs and frying eggplant.

"You're amazing. You don't even need a cookbook," Kevin said.

They had fun. She loved the freedom of cooking in a spacious kitchen. He was enjoying the long-missed family activity.

"Kevin, I know that you are really into those artichokes but we have to hurry up and leave."

"Leave?"

"Yes, I have to get a gift for your parents."

"You don't have to get them a gift."

"Oh, yes I do. Come on, clean up and let's get going," she ordered.

"Okay, general, I'll get your jeep ready."

They rode into town, stopped to look into a few stores, and came across an antique shop that had an oil painting of a wood crafted sailboat almost like the *Maiasaura.* They were stunned when they read the name *Katherina.*

Katie purchased it and immediately asked the proprietor where they could have it reframed. She wanted it to fit perfectly in his father's den. On the way to have the pictured framed they passed a shop that sold fine glass pieces. A hand blown glass dinosaur sat in the window. Katie took it as another sign.

The two coincidences rocked Kevin. Though he felt that she was spending too much, he didn't try to stop her.

She took his hand and placed it on her heart, "Do you feel that, my love? My heart is pounding with joy, grateful to your parents for bringing you in to this world." He stooped down and placed his head on her shoulder while wrapping his arms around her.

The shopkeeper returned interrupting their embrace, "I didn't know that glass dinosaurs evoked such romantic passion" he said jokingly and added,

"You would think that they would stimulate one's appetite for a steak. I thought causing fear stimulated the appetite."

They laughed as he handed them the wrapped package.

Katie discovered a perfect piece of framing wood at the town's little frame shop. The wood was carved with circular curls of wood in the shapes of waves. She asked the owner if he would mount it while they waited. The man started to shake his head.

"You know, Mr. Stanley," Kevin, said, "it's a present from my girlfriend to my parents. They'll be meeting for the first time this evening. It would be wonderful if she could give this to them then."

Mr. Stanley had lived in the town for years, knew Kevin's family well, and had watched Kevin grow up. He did not have the heart to resist Kevin's argument. He conceded. "Let me see what I can do." He took the painting to his workbench.

They waited, browsing about for twenty minutes. When the man finished, he casually showed it to them.

"This is unbelievable," Katie said. "What an incredible job. Thank you so much. How much do I owe you?"

"Let's say it's a gift for a future event. Say... an engagement or even a wedding? And, one without the slightest taint of money. How's that? You two remind me of me and my wife starting out to together many years ago. Good luck."

Wedding? Starting out? Is this a sign?

Katie protested, but he would not hear of it and she thanked him once more.

At the house, they put the final touches on the food preparation and had plenty of time to relax on the patio with a glass of wine. Kevin told Katie about his life in Switzerland.

He knew that she had many unanswered questions about his life, his friends in Europe, his lifestyle as a single man, and perhaps past relationships.

A voice called through the house, "We're home!"

Kevin jumped to help his parents with their luggage.

"Where is she?" Lillian called. "Oh, I can't wait."

Katie rose to meet her. Lillian rushed out onto the patio.

"Oh ... Oh ... my God, you're absolutely beautiful," she said as they embraced. "Did my son treat you well? Did you find everything you needed?"

"Oh, yes," Katie said, smiling joyfully at this greeting.

Kevin and his father joined them.

"Daddy," Lillian said, addressing her husband, "isn't she a princess?"

"Well, hello. We finally get to meet."

"Mom. Dad." Kevin said. "Why don't you freshen up, Katie has prepared us an Italian feast."

"I'm sure it will be wonderful," his mother said. "We'll be right back."

Kevin opened a bottle of wine to let it breathe until his parents' return.

The dinner went extremely well. Naturally, Kevin's parents were inquisitive about Katie's life and interests, but did not make her feel uncomfortable, or place her under a microscope.

She spoke freely, complimenting them on how wonderful their son was.

"You're a delight," Lillian said. "How thoughtful your gifts are."

Katie told them the story of how she had met Kevin. "Can you imagine how frightened I was when I woke to find a strange man in my living room?"

They listened, captivated by Katie's animation and sincerity as she related the experiences she and Kevin shared at the US Mission to the UN and later that day at the Italian feast.

"You know, Katherine, my husband and I have been waiting for my son to have someone special in his life. We're glad he held out for a gem."

Kevin raised his glass. "To Katherine."

Kevin and Katie relaxed at the house for several days. The women had time to get acquainted and bond. Peter and his dad took Katie for a tour of the property, which helped them get to know more of each other.

Kevin and his mom also had some private time to discuss his intentions. He admitted to considering an engagement and speedy marriage.

"Mom, I don't know if I could handle being away from her for a long period."

"You're not a child. You've done marvelous things, accomplished much, and done it all independently and with maturity. At thirty-four, I don't see the need of a long engagement, if you're certain that you love her, though Katie's Italian family is likely to want a massive Church service and a party that lasts half a week."

They laughed, and then Lillian became pensive. A tear came to her eye. "Wait here."

When she returned, she placed a small velvet pouch in his hand. He opened the drawstring, and a wedding ring slid out.

"It was Nanna's," Lillian said. "Before she passed, she asked me to give it to you when you decided to marry. I believe that Katie will appreciate its sentimental value. Family is important to her, as it is to us."

Kevin stared down at the two-karat, pear shaped, antique diamond ring overwhelmed that his Nanna had thought of him so many years in advance.

"Nanna was a wonderful woman. And you're a great Mom. Thank you."

* * *

Katie called Carmella and said she'd stop by Monday afternoon after an early day at work.

Katie and Kevin left for Westchester after an early breakfast, making a short side trip to the south shore of Long Island to attend Mass at St. Anthony's Shrine Church in Oceanside.

Katie wanted to make this pilgrimage to offer prayers of thanks for her relationship with Kevin and to ask for spiritual guidance regarding her family and what she might learn when she met with her Aunt to get the final parts of the story.

"Amazing," Katie said, looking around the church. "I feel like I'm in Roman catacombs. This Church is truly underground."

"I love it here. I used to come here as a kid. There's an interesting story behind it. The Pastor, Father Barrett, came from a wealthy family and donated his inheritance to purchase works of religious art to adorn his beloved shrine."

"I'm really surprised I never heard about this place. My mother would love it."

"It's famous. People travel hundreds of miles to visit and pray."

After Mass, they strolled the property viewing the precious art. They prayed before the likenesses of Saint Francis and Saint

Jude. Kevin knew that Katie was preparing herself, trying to gain the emotional strength to deal with Carmella's next disclosure.

47.

When they arrived at her parents' house, she found her father on the patio firing up the barbeque grill.

"How was your trip?" he asked as Katie gave him an obligatory kiss. "Your mom decided to grill some steak and sausage. She's in the kitchen preparing the salad."

Katie took Kevin's hand and led him to the kitchen.

Her mother welcomed each of them with a kiss.

"Did you have a good time?" she asked.

"The best," Katie said.

Kevin excused himself and joined Birdie at the grill. Billy came to the kitchen when he heard Katie's voice.

"Come to the den. I want to show you something." he said, and left the room.

"He didn't even say hello," Katie said to her mother. "What's this about?"

"Oh, I made the mistake of showing him family pictures the other day and now he's obsessed. He thinks he looks like your father when they were about the same age. He's been rummaging through all the pictures for days. It's funny though, there is a remarkable family likeness."

"Let me spend some time with him. It upsets him when I'm away."

The oak paneled den had floor to ceiling bookcases. Two high back leather chairs faced the shelves. Billy had the Persian rug covered with piles of photographs.

"Look at this," Billy said as she walked through the door. "Doesn't that look like me?" He handed her a photo of her father at seventeen.

"Sure does," she said handing back the picture. "Hey," she said pinching him on the cheek, "I haven't seen you for a week and I don't even get a kiss hello."

"Okay. Cool your pits." He gave her a peck on the cheek.

"Why don't you go out back and say hello to Kevin?"

"Oh yeah," he blurted and ran out of the room.

Katie scanned the photos. One after another, she saw the likeness. Then she perused other photos of her mom and dad with Billy's father and mother. She could not see the same resemblance in Tommaso.

An emptiness opened in the pit of her stomach. The room felt foreign. The house felt alien. She wanted to run away, but knew she could not. For Billy's sake, she'd have to tough it out.

She stood. Feeling her way along the walls with her hand, she wondered. Prayed. She went to Kevin's side and wrapped her arms around him and held herself close. Her legs were weak. She let him support her weight.

He looked at her and scrunched his brow silently asking "What's the matter?" He didn't want to interrupt Birdie's discourse on how Italian sausage should be turned for barbeque perfection.

"Nothing," she whispered to him.

They had their early dinner and related the events upstate with Tony and their visit to Kevin's parents. Katie spoke of how well she was treated and how interesting she found their professions. She also mentioned the boat. This prompted a conversation between Kevin and Birdie about the design and maintenance of boats made from wood.

After dessert, Birdie invited Kevin to join him for fresh air.

"Occasionally, I like smoking a cigar, especially after a heavy dinner. How about you?"

"No thanks, never smoked. Sports."

Katie and her mom attended to the dishes and Billy went next door to see a neighbor for a while before his return to the city with Katie.

The men strode down the driveway. Birdie gave Kevin some history of the neighborhood, pointing out the Tudor houses and saying that his wife's grandfather had been a major architect in the area.

Birdie asked, "Did Jocko repair that watch for you?"

"Yes, he serviced, cleaned, and evaluated it."

"Did he say it had value, I mean, antique value?"

"The piece itself has some value because it's an excellent copy, and still over a hundred years old. However, it's not an original."

"I'm curious why you had it evaluated here," Birdie said. "Switzerland is the premier place for watch manufacture, isn't it? Couldn't you have found someone there?"

"Yes, of course I could have, and may still have it re-evaluated when I return. You see the maestro, Siegfried, is my mentor and friend. He has no children of his own and we spend a lot of time together.

"He is a widower, and being single, I guess we created a little family. I respect him for his musical training and his paternal affection. He is getting on in years and his eyesight is not very good, so I take care of him as much as I can. He gave me the watch as a gift just as I left for the airport.

He said it had value but didn't work. He recommended Mr. Di Giaccomo on this side of the world, whose expertise is apparently well known even in the fatherland of watch manufacture. If I was impatient to wait until I got back to Zurich, he told me, DiGiacomo would be the only one he'd trust. I wasn't going to bother, but I had a day free in the city, and something made me go downtown.

That's why I think Katie and I are destined to be together. I really could have waited to get that old thing repaired back in Switzerland. But then we would never have met."

Damn, I'm good.

Birdie continued to make small talk about the watch, commenting on how important it was to keep things up. Particularly one-of-a-kind handcrafted things that had sentimental value.

Birdie's focus shifted to their weekend upstate with Father Tony.

"A great place, isn't it? I spent some time there over the years hunting and fishing with Father Tony's parents and mutual friends."

Yeah, I bet. Hunting and fishing.

"You met some of my hunting companions at the feast. We got quite a few big bucks."

Birdie paused. Took a puff on his Cohiba.

"My daughter told her mother that some of your friends joined you for the weekend."

"Yeah. My best buddy Timmy – I've known him since elementary school – and his girlfriend Colleen. Timmy and I hadn't seen each other for a couple of years with all the traveling I do."

Kevin planned and chose his next words carefully.

"Timmy's quite a guy. He a Special Agent for the FBI. Up until a few weeks ago, he was stationed in Chicago working on high profile cases. He met his girlfriend Colleen there. She works in the crime lab. In forensics, I believe.

"He's a fan of yours, Mr. Burdino. He came to visit me the week after the incident and saw your bandage. I told him what happened, how I met your daughter and how you patched me up. He liked your work, though would have preferred I didn't need it.

"When I mentioned where it happened and that Katie lived in Little Italy, he flipped out. He told me that he and Colleen were assigned to the task force working in that area to find this Rosary Bead murderer."

"So, he's on that case," Birdie said. "That has to be interesting work. I know the people in the neighborhood are frightened and are keeping their eyes open."

"Yeah, I guess the FBI is working night and day to solve this one. It's their only priority, and Timmy is pretty serious about it. Timmy's a minor cog. As the investigation heats up, he won't get any time off until they catch that guy. It was lucky he and Colleen were able to join us for a few days."

Time not to overdo it, Kevin thought as they arrived back at the patio.

"Mr. Burdino, I'm glad I have this opportunity to speak with you. I guess you know I'm very interested in your daughter. She's a special girl. You and Mrs. Burdino have done a wonderful job in raising her. We get along, are interested in many of the same things, and are both at an age–"

"Hold on," Birdie said, stopping Kevin. He was becoming uncomfortable with what he thought Kevin intended to say.

"You know my wife is thrilled with you and I think she would love to hear what you're saying, too. Have a seat at the picnic table and I will get something cool to drink."

He abruptly left Kevin standing there while he went to call his wife at the screen door. "Maryann, Kevin and I are having an interesting conversation and I thought you would like to be part of it. We'd also like something refreshing to drink."

Maryann acknowledged him with a questioning expression. She knew from years of marriage that something had come up with Kevin that Birdie didn't want to deal with alone.

"Sure, I'll be right out, honey."

A few minutes later, she came out to them with glasses of fresh lemonade and handed them each one while asking how they were getting along. Birdie introduced her to the conversation.

"I thought you'd like to hear about Kevin's feelings for Katie."

Kevin, embarrassed, was put on the spot. He decided to go for it, but then Katie came out to join them.

"What are they doing to you? Is my father giving you the third degree?"

"Actually, I think I got myself into this jam all on my own. We were conversing, and I was about to tell your dad how I felt about you and he invited your mom out to join us."

Katie realized that her father had put Kevin in a precarious position.

"Dear Lord. Dad, you have to stop this," she told her father.

"No, no. It's all right. What I wanted to share was that I very much care for you and how much my parents were taken with you and that I hoped you felt the same way."

Then Birdie apologized, "I'm sorry, I jumped the gun. I should not have put you in this uncomfortable position. You are a very nice young man, educated and respectful and I think I can speak for my wife and me. Whatever you two decide will be acceptable to us."

Kevin said, "Thank you."

Katie shook her head. She led Kevin by the hand to the gazebo in the garden.

"I think you can understand how controlling and invasive they are. This is how they drive me crazy. You don't know who you're messing with," she told him. "They now believe that you have proposed marriage."

He answered, "Would that be so bad?"

"What?" she nervously blurted.

Kevin did not want to dampen the moment, but had to alert her that things in his life needed disclosure before they ventured to the next step.

"I asked you to trust me and allow me some time before I can make everything known to you."

"I trust you, my love."

"So getting back to the perceived marriage proposal. Tell me, would that be so bad? What if I were to go to my knee right know, like this?" As he said it he dropped to his left knee. "And what if I took a ring out of my pocket like this?"

Katie covered her eyes in disbelief. She peeked through her fingers.

"Then I tell you how much I love you, that there will be no other for me, and that I want to take care of you, protect you, and build a family with you."

He took her hand. "Katherine Burdino, will you marry me?"

"Oh my God," she gasped. Her left hand flew to her chest, where her heart was picking up speed. *Is this happening*? Her eyes were fixed upon the ring.

"You are a madman. Are you really sure you want to do this? Isn't this too soon?"

"I am surer than I have ever been in my entire life."

He slipped the ring on her finger. She did not resist.

"My grandmother wore this ring for fifty-four years of happy marriage, but if you would prefer something more modern–"

"Are you kidding? This is magnificent. I will cherish it as long as I live. You are my prince, aren't you?"

"Well, come out with it already. Do you accept?

"Of course I accept, my love, with my whole heart and soul. God has sent you to me," she said and wrapped her arms around him. As they kissed her tears of joy dampened both their faces.

Katie, although ecstatic, did not want to tell her parents. "Do you mind if I hide the ring until we leave for the city? I just don't want to get into it with them."

Her joy dampened as the anger at her parents boiled inside. Even more, her thoughts were on Carmella. Concerned at what more she had to say. She made up her mind that she would find out, secure that Kevin's commitment could withstand whatever she would learn.

After they ate, she asked her father if he would take Billy to school the next morning and that she wanted to spend some time with her mother before she left for the City.

48.

Katie called her aunt early the next morning and told her that she had things to share with her and wanted to continue their conversation. They met later that Monday at the restaurant, the only day of the week that it was closed.

The day was balmy and clear, so they chose to sit in the back yard under a grape arbor that was heavy with clusters of grapes. They were surrounded by pots of herbs used to season the dishes prepared at the restaurant.

Carmella's coffee was mixed with half milk, known as a Sicilian, a traditional breakfast coffee.

Katie was bursting to tell Carmella of her engagement. She uncovered her hand and showed her the ring.

"Oh, my dear Jesus!" Carmella exclaimed, "I'm so happy for you. When did this happen?"

"Yesterday, at my parent's house, when we returned from the trip upstate."

"How did they react, your parents?"

"I didn't tell them but they have suspicions. I know they are happy with Kevin and probably for all the wrong reasons. You're the first one I have told. Frankly, I'm so angry with them and so very confused about who they truly are..."

She swallowed hard, took a breath, and presented her thoughts.

"Since we spoke," Katie said. "I have realized many things. I have been recalling snap shots of the past that have showed me how much I didn't allow myself to see.

I almost broke off the relationship with Kevin because I felt that my ties to this neighborhood might damage his career. He is so wonderful, intelligent and respected. I didn't want to tarnish his life."

"Did you tell him about our conversation?" Carmella asked.

"I told him that I had developed suspicions, and that many things have become obvious about my parents, their friends, and their activities.

"I also told him of my fears. He reassured me that he had confidence in who I am, and that we would deal with whatever eventually surfaces."

"Yes, yes. You must go forward and build a life for yourself. You must leave this place. These people will always keep you confined, under their thumb."

Dominick appeared at the screen door and joined them.

"Hey, cousin."

Katie's ring sparkled in the sun.

"Holy cannoli, is that an engagement ring? When did that happen? We were just with you."

"Yesterday, and you're not to tell anyone about it Dominick. Promise?"

"If you say so. I promise. Wow, that was fast."

He hugged Katie and then gave his mother a kiss.

"Have a good day, Lucretia."

"Go. Go be a bum on your day off."

He shook his head and left through the side gate. He saw that the kitchen help had left the garden hose uncoiled in the alley.

As he curled the hose behind a stand of hedges, he heard his mother speaking in a concerned voice.

"Katie, he thinks he fools me, but I know he is doing work for them. I found a lot of cash in his bureau draw. He's had a passbook since he made his Holy Communion when he was seven. He's always deposited a portion of his earnings in it. But this, nothing. This money has to be dirty." She slapped her knees with anger and disappointment.

"I also know that Angie has been flirting with Mario and that he spends time talking to her here in the restaurant when I'm not around. Last week he brought his mother for lunch. She comes in once a month with him to go to the beauty parlor then they have lunch here. When I went to say hello, Angie follows right behind me. His mother showered her with kisses and compliments. Then she asked me if I would let Angie marry Mario. That she would dress her in thousand dollar bills."

"It's always money, isn't it?" Katie said.

"I let her know that my daughter planned to go to college and was too young for marriage. You see, my suspicions were right. Their hooks are already into my children, but I will straighten all of them out soon."

Katie knew that Carmella's instincts were correct based on what they heard from Dominick at Father Tony's house.

Dominick left the alley for the street. He knew his mother was hurt and that he had betrayed her wishes. *I am an adult. I have the right to make my own decisions. The extra money I earn can buy a house for Millie and me when we marry.*

"Katie, come with me upstairs," Carmella said.

Katie followed her with trepidation. She felt that more darkness was about to reveal itself. Adding to the tension, Carmella locked the door behind her and closed the window shades when they entered. Her Aunt took the lampshade off the cherub-embossed lamp, unscrewed the fixture, reached in, and took out a folded tan envelope. Written upon it were the words, "Open after My Death."

She sat on the bed and patted the mattress with her hand inviting Katie to join her.

"Giving this to you will put you in danger if someone should ever know you have it."

Katie's heart pounded. Carmella instructed her to give the envelope to someone in law enforcement that was beyond reproach, or the newspapers if she knew someone who could be trusted.

"Mani del loro potere raggiungere ben al di là della polizia locale e i giudici," Carmella said. The hands of their power reach far beyond the local police and judges.

Carmella only spoke to her in Italian when the conversation was of the utmost importance.

"Open a safety deposit box in a bank outside the city. Caterina, it must be a place where you and your parents are not known."

Katie rose from the bed panicked. She walked across the room and back, wondering, *Why me?*

"Aunt Carmella," she said as she dropped to her knees in front of the older woman. "How can you put this trust in me? How do you know I won't crack?"

"Because," the older woman affirmed, "You are stronger than you think you are. You have believed in justice and truth since you were a little girl. What I'm giving you is what you will need to buy them out."

"Buy them out? What are you talking about?"

Katie jumped to her feet and paced again.

"Sit here and I will make you understand. You will buy your blood back from them."

"My blood?" she raged. "This is crazy!"

"I'm not going crazy. Sit back down. Muster your strength and listen."

Katie sat. Her shoulders slumped and her head fell into her hands.

"Concetta-Marie, Billy's mother, and I we were like sisters. Besides your father, I was the only one she could confide in, especially about woman things. I do not know if you understand the relationship we all had. We were more than just friends. We were all lost and broken in our own ways, damaged by our parents' way of life, and insecure about our survival. For the most part, we were left in the street to make our way.

"We found ourselves in a new country under prejudice from the Americans who held all the power. The Jews were treated the same way. We were the grease balls, and they were the kikes. They saw us all as an underclass, the way they did colored people before us, and still. But at least the colored people knew the language."

"Please," Katie said, "I know all this."

"I know you think I am rambling like an old woman, but I need for you to hear this as a foundation for what I am about to divulge.

"As youngsters, we were badly treated by our parents and the teachers. For them, we were considered inferior because we did not understand English. They would hit and humiliate us in front of the other children. The nuns, especially the Irish ones, were brutal.

"Once when Peppino around eight years old he was called to stand before his class for speaking out of turn. The nun slapped him so hard that she left the imprint of her hand on his face. When he cried, she further humiliated him in front of forty-two children by calling him a cream puff."

Carmella paused, taking in air, then added with pain in her voice, "Anthony suffered too, he was brutalized by his grandmother in the same way. Tommaso's parents either died or abandoned him, no one knows the truth, and he had to do the work of a grown man at nine years old. Your grandmother, your father's mother, wound up alone in a strange country with a young son who had to fend for himself.

And Concetta-Marie, she was the most tragic of us all. Her father used her in ways that a father should never touch a daughter. He would get drunk and force himself on her mother, not with the love of a husband but with the savagery of an animal."

"Aunt Carmella, this is horrendous and it makes me very sad, but why are you telling me this?" Katie was beginning to get impatient.

"Wait, Katie. Listen. This is hard for me, too. I've been holding this inside for so long. Secrets have held me hostage. I've been bearing the hurt alone my whole life, and know that its revelation would be life changing for those I love. That is hard."

Carmella dissolved in tears. Katie comforted her, apologizing for her impatience.

"I am afraid of the hurt my words will inflict upon you," Carmella's eyes, full of sadness met Katie's as she took another deep breath and continued.

"Katie, my daughter, I spoke of how we suffered. I guess I am still trying to find a justification for what we became. But it's impossible because none exists. We all have choices to do good or let evil invade our soles. Katie. You may have suspected your father was involved. But Birdie is not just one of them. He's a leader. He's a high level Mafioso."

"Dear Jesus, dear Jesus, don't tell me that."

"He is their planner. He masterminds their efforts and decides many times who lives and who dies. They have kept him a secret for many years, even from their own members, so their greedy, evil pursuits could continue uninterrupted."

Katie sat speechless. Her mouth was dry and her temples throbbed. Carmella brought her a glass of water.

"There's more," Carmella said.

"Oh, dear Jesus," Katie wailed again. She sobbed, staring into Carmella's tear-filled eyes.

"He's using their terms, an Under Boss, but actually the highest and the smartest of them. He holds a great deal of power. He is their architect."

Katie's head felt like it was spinning.

"I have already signed my own death certificate by telling you this and with what I am about to say. Concetta-Marie was in love with your father, but he passed her up for your mother, who represented a toehold into the legitimate world to him. She could help foster his appearance as a successful businessman with respectability. However, he is a man devoid of feelings. His love for you is the closest he ever came to loving anyone, but you also fit the legitimate image with your education and the way you spend your days working in the community."

Katie kneaded her fingers, her feelings torn between protective loyalty for her father and disgust and shame all at the same time. She tried to remain focused on Carmella's words.

"However, Caterina, that's what I do not foresee for his son."

Katie gasped. "Son, what son? He has no son."

"Katie, after your father married, Concetta-Marie married Tommaso, but she did not love him and her heart grew cold. About sixteen years ago, she approached your Father. She knew that he would not deny her anything. He was always her rescuer. She told him that she and Tommaso had been trying to have children but were unable to. She did not believe that he could father a child.

Then she asked him to father her baby. She shared with me that if she could not have your father, then she would have his child. He made her take an oath that it would never be made known, that it breached the Omerta he and Tommaso both vowed to keep. She took it to her violent death. She made me promise to watch him from afar and when you took interest in him–"

"Billy? My Billy?"

Carmella lowered her head. Katie broke down and fell onto the bed. A half hour passed before Katie was empty enough to refrain from uncontrolled weeping. Carmella also cried and apologized for the weight she had placed on her shoulders. Billy was Katie's brother, and it was now her responsibility to save him from losing his soul to the mob.

They both sat blindly staring at the walls, just holding each other's hand. Katie thought of Billy, how close she had always felt to him. She remembered the picture that Billy had found, and his likeness to Birdie. *I knew it,* she thought. *Even then I knew it.* But the strict morality to which she so clung didn't permit her to admit it. *How could he do such a thing? How could he do it to Uncle Tommaso, and how could he do it to Momma? How could he do it and still take Communion?*

She recalled incidences of her mother's unkind impatience with Birdie and his intent interest in Billy's progress.

What am I to do?

At the end of the tears, a driving force of strength welled up in her. She knew she had deal with it. She did not know how, but she knew Billy had to be protected.

She walked into the bathroom and stood looking at herself in the mirror. She washed her face, applied her makeup, and combed her hair.

"Aunt Carmella," she said as she returned to the bedroom. "You will be safe." She folded and tucked the envelope into her purse.

"I will take care of everything."

49.

The afternoon had turned cloudy with an intermittent drizzle. It added to the oppressive humidity and heat of the August day.

Mateo grew impatient waiting for Michaela in front of the Horn and Hardart Automat on 42nd at Third. He wanted to lose himself in the excitement she generated, and escape the hounding thoughts of indecision.

His eyes spied passing taxis. He waited for her. A man in ragged clothes approached him. At first, he thought him a vagrant. Believing he intended to beg for money, Mateo reacted by shaking his head, and then with reluctance searched in his pocket for loose change.

The man did not take his money. He stared into Mateo's eyes for a moment, and spoke a warning: "What you sow you shall reap."

The vagabond continued on his way. Then Mateo remembered that his mother had made the same comment to him: "*What you sow you reap.*" The recollection sent a chill up his spine.

Mateo chucked it off as a New York moment and continued to search for Michaela. A few minutes later he felt a tap on his shoulder, turned, and received a full kiss on his lips.

"Hi, you gorgeous man," she said straightening her long red skirt and ruffled blouse as if she had just concluded a run.

"Hi," he replied, feeling the energy of her sensual gesture.

They made their way down Broadway, stopping to window shop along the way. They spoke of things they liked. Michaela told him about her coursework in school and the history of her relationship with Claudia. She wanted him to know that her call girl work was limited to just a few high-paying and politically powerful clients. She did other work for Claudia, outside the bedroom, and she earned more than enough for school and to live comfortably.

Mateo asked, "Do you enjoy what you do?"

"I like sex, and believe I need it more than most women do. I couldn't do it if I didn't like it. If I got married my husband would have to be able to accept my need for sexual variety. I also like being in a position to choose my clients... " She paused to flash Mateo a coy grin and said, "Playmates at will, I like the feeling of power. In fact I'm going to pick one out right now," she said and led him into a small dress store.

"Hi, Michaela," the salesclerk greeted her.

"I need to use the dressing room for a little while." Michaela reached into her purse and took out a ten to give to the woman.

"Sure," said the woman, taking the bill and slipping it into her bra. "I'll just put the closed sign on the door."

Michaela pulled Mateo into the dressing room and locked the door for a quickie.

Forty-five minutes later they sat at the bar at Biltmore's Charcoal Grill. She had one drink. Mateo had two. She motioned to him, and he threw a twenty on the bar. She took his hand and they made their way to her place, picking up Chinese take-out along the way.

There, he poured some whisky into each of two glasses and laid out the Chinese food cartons on the table.

Michaela was freshening up. He thought of taking a shower, but for now, he liked her scent on him.

He clocked the small, neat apartment. It didn't look lived in. It was nothing like the ornate room she occupied at Claudia's brothel.

Her desk was the only piece of furniture that showed activity. It was strewn with schoolbooks and notebooks and crumpled pieces of paper in the wastebasket.

Michaela opened the bathroom door. "Hey, what about that drink?"

She stood naked, wearing only drops of water that meandered down her statue-like breasts and curved torso. Seeing her for the first time fully unclothed he took his time carrying the glass to her, taking in every inch of her body. She reached out with her hand, entirely comfortable in her nudity, and took the drink.

"I need a few more minutes," she said, walking into her bedroom.

He ambled into the kitchen. Her large purse was sitting open on the chair. Something shiny lay on top. He opened the purse with a single finger. A pearl-handled .38 lay fully loaded atop her things.

He lifted the gun out and found a silencer underneath. He brought it to his nose. *Hmm, recently fired. Son of a bitch, she might have whacked someone before meeting me.* He wiped his fingerprints off and replaced it. *So it's not only guys that get horny after a job.*

They had a marathon of erotic sex. She taught him new ways of receiving and giving pleasure.

Sweaty and naked, they ate the Chinese food and watched Antonio Rocca wrestling on TV. She invited him to stay the night, but he had some apprehension. He thought of her gun. Though not by name, he conjured legends about female buttons and how they'd send guys off after giving them their last whirl in the sack. *If there was going to be a hit on me, it would be after I refuse the offer of being made.*

He was not going to take chances. He told her that he had early morning work to do, knowing she would not question him.

He left for home at three in the morning. Traffic was light. She hadn't let him sleep. As he got out of the cab the scent of her lingered on the outside, but on the inside, he was still haunted by all the choices he had to make. Especially about Marypat.

Mateo lounged on the stoop in front of his house for a while and had a few cigarettes while he thought things through. He liked the fast life and the freedom it gave him. He liked that he did not have to work as a laborer like most people his age who were not connected.

He could have money in his pocket to do what he wished, but after being with Michaela, he began to believe that the world he and she lived in was not secure. He did not like the feeling of sleeping with one eye open or bringing the people he loved into that world of uncertainty, or loving someone he could not trust.

In his room, he found that his mother had starched and pressed his best suit and shirt for his date with Marypat. He was heavy hearted for his mother's hopes. He knew that having someone like Marypat would be a dream come true. He was softening, but choosing Marypat could put him in a dangerous position.

50.

Mateo helped his mother around the house the next morning. She noticed, as they cleaned out the refrigerator, his disposition had changed. A new calmness about him was coupled with tenderness toward her.

"You want anything special at the restaurant this week?" she asked. "Anything I haven't made in a long time? Anything, maybe, that you might want to impress a friend with? Should you choose to invite one?"

He looked at her with love in his eyes. "Mom, everything you make is good."

"Are you all right?" She asked.

"Yeah, why?"

"Well you're acting like a gentleman, and I thought you might have a fever."

"You, Momma mia, are like a tragic Italian opera with a tricky plot and always looking for trouble."

"Well, I haven't seen you this relaxed in a long time. Is it the date with Marypat?"

"No, Mom, it's you."

"Me? What about me?"

"I think the Chinese food I had last night did something to me. I woke up thinking how much I love you."

"Okay, what is it?" she said raising her brow. "You can't make the car payment?"

He hugged her. "No, Mom, it's you," and he gave her a kiss a top her head.

"I love you, too. You're my life."

He knew that he could not go on with Mario and had to figure a way out.

Mateo called in to Mario later in the afternoon to tell him that he made his pick-ups and drops. Then he reminded him about his date with Marypat that evening. Mario wished him luck and told him that they were preparing for camp the next day and needed his help. He knew that "camp" meant a mob war and that they were going to the matt.

That evening Mateo showed up at Casa Filipo to pick up Marypat, arriving at a quarter to seven. Little Vinny and Marypat's father were talking outside, and having a smoke at the front door. They were in good spirits. Vinny spotted Mateo as he walked toward them.

"Hey, look at you all dressed up," Little Vinny said. "You gettin' married or somethin'?"

Filipo put his arm on Little Vinny's shoulder. "Mateo and Mary Patricia are going out for the evening."

"That's nice," Vinny said, trying to act casual about his *faux pas.*

"Marypat's gonna be a little late," Filipo told Mateo. "She worked a bridal shower party that went over-time. Why don't you come in and have a Manhattan, Aldo's specialty, or something?"

Mateo turned to clock the street while opening the door. It had become second nature.

He caught sight of two men dressed in repairmen's coveralls. His spine went cold. Everything slowed down as he saw them pull automatic weapons from a large workbag. In moments, the deafening sound of the guns filled the air. The men only stopped long enough to yell the words, "Die, you *gavones,*" (low classed) and then the bullets would fly again.

Little Vinny took two direct hits to his chest. The force of the bullets sent him flying backwards at the restaurant window that shattered in the hail of rounds being pumped out of the guns. He was dead before he hit the table, sprawled out like a filleted sturgeon in front of an old couple.

Mateo tried to shield Filipo. He felt the burn as lead tore through his side and arm. He was spun around, lost footing and landed flat on his back. Exposed, Filipo dropped straight down as a single shot tore through his heart.

Mateo lay unable to move. His last thought before losing consciousness was *What you sow, you will reap.*

When Marypat arrived, the police had cordoned off the area. It was a chaotic ballet of police, ambulances, medics, and flashing red lights, all performed to the wail of restaurant patrons, some mourning their dead, and some victims of the bullets that indiscriminately peppered through the restaurant's façade.

She started to cross the barricade. A beat cop who knew her took her into the restaurant through the rear door where she spotted Aldo giving a statement to another officer.

"Aldo," she cried, "What's happened? Where's my...?"

The policeman answered, "Marypat. I'm sorry. Your father..." He lowered his head. Marypat fell to her knees sobbing.

Aldo tried to console her. He helped her to her feet. She looked into his eyes, screaming, "Why?" without saying a word.

He trembled. "Little Vinny came to order food and waited outside talking to Filipo. Then that young man, the one who likes you–"

"Mateo?"

"Yes, he came and they started talking with him." Aldo welled up with tears. "Then these two guys just started shooting. I saw Mateo try to save your father, but they shot him, too."

"Mateo. Is he...?" She pushed the words through her sobs.

The officer said, "He's critical, but he may still have a chance. We can have a car take you to the hospital."

"Yes," she said.

Her eyes scanned the scene. Bodies lay in front of restaurant covered in white sheets. Rivulets of blood snaked out from under them. It wasn't the warm home away from home it had been her entire life. She stood mesmerized by the atrocity. Aldo pulled her away. The police officer led them to a patrol car.

* * *

Detective Sergeant O'Rourke entered the Three Feather Bar and asked for Fingers. He sat on a bar stool and waited. A few moments later, Fingers joined him, taking the adjacent seat.

"Three of your people were hit about twenty minutes ago in front of the Casa Filipo restaurant," O'Rourke said.

The mob Captain closed his eyes, rubbed them with thumb and forefinger and asked, "Who?"

The cop replied, “Little Vinny and Filipo are both dead. A young kid, Mateo Patrino, is fighting for his life at Bellevue. I asked to have a couple of guys posted with him at the hospital.”

Fingers thanked him, pulled a hundred from his pocket and slipped it into O’Rourke’s hand. The officer left.

Fingers signaled to Cosmo, the bartender, who came close.

He whispered, “Close the place. Get everyone out. Put a sign in the window that there has been a death in the family and that the place will be closed until further notice.”

Cosmo instructed the wait staff to pack up everyone’s meals to go, and tell them there would be no charge. In ten minutes, the place was empty save the group of men huddled in the rear.

“They hit Little Vinny and Filipo the Chef. Mateo Patrino is fighting to stay alive. Call your wives, tell them that you will be away for a while, and alert your crews to go to the safe houses.”

Fingers’ face was red, his eyes black with thoughts of revenge.

“Cosmo, Paulie, Nicky, Jay,” he barked out. “You guys are with me. Artie and Frank, cover Don Peppino. The rest of you are to go to the houses in Staten Island and wait for my call.”

He handed Cosmo the a key. “Open the box.”

Cosmo unlocked the gun safe and distributed what the men could carry. The rest was loaded into their cars.

“Now, listen,” Fingers said. “You’re not to go anywhere alone, one of you always has to have his eyes moving, covering each other. Be ready to move when you are called. The instructions you receive, follow them to the tee. Mistakes can cost you your life. Anything you had going is cancelled and do not go near your families since you could bring them harm. Listen to your crew chiefs. They have the experience. You hear me? Be careful."

Fingers went to the bar, pulled the phone from underneath and dialed Mario. "It's started. I have two guys coming over. How many you got there?"

"Three," Mario said. Fingers gave Mario the details of the hit, finishing by saying, "Okay, keep them there and don't let Anthony go anywhere alone."

"What happened?" Don Peppino asked Mario, expecting the worst.

"They hit Little Vinny, Filipo and the Patrino kid. The kid is still alive but it doesn't look good. Tell your crew to help Anthony set up some cots and chairs in the basement, and send somebody to Melaina's Pork Store for platters of cold-cuts. He'll know what to get."

"Do we need to get people to the hospital for the kid?"

"No, not now, the cops will keep two guys there for us."

"All right, " Don Peppino said. "Call our people at Con Edison and have repair trucks block the streets out here and post our guys at them. Then call Vegas and Reno and tell them what's going on."

"Boss."

"Yeah."

"I don't know if you care, but we cancelled the used car matter yesterday."

"Okay, good."

Don Peppino went over Fingers' preparations with Mario.

"You see what experience can do? Fingers is a true leader. He crosses the T's and dots the fuckin' I's. That is what I keep talking to you about. You have to be more thorough."

Peppino turned on the radio to hear what was being said on the news. They waited for the broadcast.

"Good Morning New York," the newscaster opened. "Mike Corcoran here. Hot story just in. Mob central is at it again. The Daily News reported that a mobster and two mob associates were gunned down in broad daylight in front of the Casa Filipo Restaurant in mid-town earlier today. The mobster known as Vincenzo "Little Vinny" De Marco was killed along with the Chef of the establishment. De Marco was also one of the men implicated in the death of The New York Mirror's News Reporter Michael Munson a month ago and is believed to be a member of the Pedro Marcoleone crime family, *la famiglia*. The other fatality, restaurant owner and Chef Filipo Calabria, who is suspected of being a mob associate, was DOA at Bellevue Hospital.

"Our sources also tell us that a third victim of the shootings, Mateo "Matty Wheels" Patrino, may be also a mob associate. He lies in critical condition with gunshot wounds to the arm and side.

"More mob news. Police are investigating what appears to be another mob hit yesterday morning at the Save-More Used Car Company on the lower west side. The owner Herbert Cole was found by a customer. The single bullet to his head leads investigators to believe it was a gangland slaying. The police are seeking a young woman for questioning. A passerby described seeing a woman with blond hair, wearing a long red skirt with a ruffled blouse, exiting the trailer office early yesterday morning.

"Cole's wife Shirley refused comment and referred reporters to her attorney who let it be known that Mr. Cole had gone to the police to report a takeover of his business by the mob. A police representative stated that they were sympathetic to the Cole family but have no record of any such complaint. However, they would continue with their investigation."

"Turn it off," Peppino told Mario. "Pay a visit to Little Vinny's family. Assure her that everything is taken care of and she'll be provided for."

Peppino knelt at his safe, dialed the combination, and opened it. He took out a snub-nosed pistol and placed in his suit jacket, and counted out five-thousand dollars.

"This should hold her," he said, handing the cash to Mario. "I'll take care of Filipo's daughter, too. Just assure her that you're there for her and that you will take care of the arrangements."

He closed the safe and returned to his chair.

"What about the kid? How's he doing?"

"Boss, the kid just wound up in the wrong place at the wrong time. He was there to take Marypat on a date. I feel guilty because I encouraged the relationship."

Don Peppino shook his head with sadness.

"Call Dr. Schapiro," Peppino said. "Ask him to get involved as a personal favor to me. Ya know, make sure he gets the best care, private room, all that. And get over to see his mother and leave her some money. Do these things after you make sure to secure our interests on Mulberry, Hester and Mott. Take a couple of Piciottos with you. I'm disgusted. It seems like we have a black cloud over our heads."

* * *

Don Peppino met with Fingers and Birdie later that day. Birdie informed them of the meeting he had with Don Pedro, his underboss Balsamo, and *la famiglia's* Consigliere.

He gave them dossiers, prepared for just such an eventuality, of three men to be whacked. The files included pictures and information about the places they frequented and the times of greatest opportunity. He also told them that commission members were trying to work out a peace.

Fingers worked late into the night with his lieutenants assigning the hits. They also provided the teams of assassins with the support they would need: weapons, money, cars and drivers.

Don Peppino made plans to sleep in a spare room in Anthony's apartment above the funeral parlor. It was watched over by soldiers of *la famiglia* who took shifts guarding the doors.

Birdie and Fingers left together. Fingers told him that he would not go home, since it might be staked-out. He would stay at Matilda's and send his bodyguards to the mattresses in Staten Island, and they could retrieve him in the morning. Birdie told him that he had some work to do at the drug store and then intended to drive to Westchester with the security of two bodyguards assigned by Don Peppino.

51.

Fingers broke *la famiglia's* rule he had imposed on his men by staying at his girlfriend Matilda's house that night, unprotected. It was a costly mistake. Both were found shot to death the following morning, their heads in pools of blood, him by the door and her in the bedroom doorway.

That same morning Carmella made her way to the drug store and browsed while she waited for customers to disperse. She did not know that a war had started. Birdie did not let on when he greeted her.

"Are you feeling okay, do you need medication or anything?"

"Birdie, I need to speak with you alone. What I want to discuss will take some time and I want it to be private."

"Why, is something wrong?"

"I just need to talk."

"My pharmacist will be in soon, and I will come to you."

"I'd rather speak with you in the church garden," she said with a mysterious depth to her voice.

Although surprised, he accommodated her. "Okay, we can go over together."

They met about an hour later and headed toward the church. As they passed the pastry shop Birdie offered to buy a lemon Ice as he did so many times before when they were kids. She reluctantly accepted. They sat for a few minutes eating their ices on a concrete bench at the foot of a statue of the Blessed Mother, which stood serenely in the center of the garden. Carmella spoke first.

"Birdie, I'm getting married."

"Married?" he repeated, amused.

"Yes, I'm marrying Dr. Abramson."

"Abramson? From Canal Street?"

"Yes, and we're going to live in his house in Miami Beach, Florida."

"Wait a minute, let me get this straight. You're going to marry the Jew doctor, and move to Miami Beach? Who's going to run the restaurant?" he asked, shaking his head.

"That's what I wanted to talk to you about. I want to sell the restaurant to you. I know it's been important for you and the boys to meet there over the years and a stranger may not understand your special needs."

He nodded.

"Can't your children run it?"

"Yes, they can but I won't let that happen. I don't want this life for them."

"Well," he asked after a pause, "how do they feel about it?"

"They don't know yet, and never mind how they feel."

"Well why don't you –"

She interrupted and spat, "I don't want your advice, and I don't want them to have your advice either."

"Whoa, slow down, take it easy," Birdie said, holding up both hands in a "stop" gesture.

"I want them free of you, Peppino and Tommaso."

"Why? What have we done to warrant this? We have always been there for you. What you're saying hurts me." His left hand went to his chest to cover his heart.

"Hurts you? What has ever hurt you? You have never had enough feeling to be hurt."

Birdie, taken aback, dropped the cup of lemon ice. He was stunned, as if someone had given him the *Mal'occhiu*–evil eye–then kicked up dirt.

Carmella went on, determined to have her say. "I don't want my son ever to be involved in your business and I certainly don't want my daughter to marry one of your soldiers. I have paid my dues with the three of you since we were children. I stashed your guns, hid your swag and served as your alibi. I was raped by one of your capos and don't want my daughter around people capable of any of that."

Inner rage filled Birdie. No one close to him had ever had the courage to lay judgment on him. His narcissism had always blinded his judgment. He could not believe that she felt that way about him, and had felt that way for so long, too. *She has fooled all of us.*

He rose from the bench standing under the extended arm of the Virgin Mother's likeness and said in a raised tone that quivered with anger, "What do you want from me?"

"I want you to buy my restaurant. I'll sell it to you twenty-five percent under market value. I want you to tell Mario hands off Angie and I want Dominick out even if he doesn't want out."

"I can buy your restaurant and I can give you market value, but I can't tell people, above all young people, what to do with their lives."

She rose to her feet, and waved her clenched fist. "You hypocrite! You order young people to steal. And worse, to murder for you. You really don't have a choice."

"What?" he snapped. "Do you forget who I am? Are you threatening me?"

"Remember when we were kids, how you used to get a kick out of seeing scared expressions on those you bullied, especially the Irish and Jewish kids?" She grabbed his shirt with both hands, her face in his, mimicking his manner when he threatened others. "'This is not a threat it's a promise,' you loved to say. This is how you do it, right?" she said.

Birdie ripped her hands off him. "What are you talking about? You make less sense than Anthony. You can't threaten me."

He grabbed her forearm and squeezed with painful force.

She did not wince. "You see, the beast presents himself. Let go of me, I feel the evil in your lost soul."

"Lost soul?" he flared. "You've really lost it, talking to me like this. *Disgraziata!* (scoundrel) I was the one who cared for you. In fact, all of us cared for you. You were the youngest. We took you to the beach on Coney Island, bought you frankfurters at Nathan's and custard at Elsie the Cow. We treated you like a sister.

"Peppino used to send the dog to wait for you by the school to walk you home. Paolo always had work and he could have had more if he wanted it. You always had medicine for the kids. I don't understand. You baffle me."

She stared at him in silence, then flicked her eyes to look at his hand gripping her arm, then looked back into his eyes. He blinked, and let go of her. She rubbed her arm where he'd grabbed it, took a deep breath and blew it out her nose, then looked directly at him again.

"Birdie, you were a kid then. God knows you may have even had some feelings as well, but you chose your own path and brought darkness into your life and all our lives, too. Out of all of us you where the one with the choices. You had the brains to educate yourself and rise above the poverty and the tragedy of our lives. But you used what God gave you to become a monster, a monster that eats up people's lives."

She paused, taking joy in making him wait. "I prepared a document that names you and others, with places, dates and times. Murders, robberies, extortion. Everything. This envelope is in the hands of people that are even more powerful than you."

His eyes glowed like embers and he bit his lip so hard that he drew blood.

"You don't know much," he said in a raspy voice.

"Well, whatever I didn't know, Concetta-Marie did, and she wrote it all down. If I should come to harm, even if it's an accident, or my children or Dr. Abramson, your ugliness will be known to the world.

"I have despised you for what you did to us, turning us into weak dependent creatures. You ripped the hearts out of wives and mothers, stealing their livelihood and killing their sons and husbands. May God forgive your wretched soul."

She took a breath and wiped the tears from her eyes with her sleeve, before saying, "Even the Cuban girl."

"What Cuban girl?"

"Claudia, who earns money for you from her loins. When you asked me to have her live with me when she escaped Castro. You had the opportunity to help her turn her life around. Instead of helping to heal her, you made her into another money-making monster. Her father sold her body and you sold her soul. That's what you do. You make copies of yourself. You made both her and Concetta into poisonous snakes."

Her words cut him so deeply he could not bear to stand there a second more. He stared at her, his eyes blazing, and veins standing out on his temple.

"This is not over. You'd rat on us?" he said in a low, hard voice. He turned and began making his way to the gate, then looked back and said, "We will talk again, when... my... I could strangle you right here."

52.

The next morning, Birdie fidgeted on the patio while making agitated stirs of his coffee. He'd got a few hours' sleep at best. The pressure of the mob conflict, the loss of men and the affects it had on the loss of business tormented him. In his mind, he went over the advice he had given to Don Pedro and the other bosses questioning if it was sound.

Then he replayed his conversation with Carmella. Anger rippled in his veins. He could not conceive what had prompted her venomous accusations, why she felt an apparent hate for him that had lingered over many years. *This is going to drive Peppino nuts,* he thought. *What triggered this reaction from her? Maybe she was sick or going through her changes.*

His wife interrupted his thoughts. "Are you okay? You did not say a word over breakfast. I brought you some more coffee. Are you worried about Katie and the possibility of her marrying?"

"No, not at all, she seems to be very happy with Kevin and I'm sure that he'll take good care of her. I guess I blew it the other day. I should have let him continue to speak. I just didn't want to say something wrong so I called you."

"I don't know what's going to be," his wife, said. "He needs to return to Europe soon. I think sometime in October. It looks like they are serious based upon what he started to say. I think we should expect to hear something from them soon."

"I guess, we'll see. Right now I need to get to work."

"I put two new lab coats in the shopping bag, and the one you brought home had blood spots on it. I also prepared a bag with coffee and donuts for the men waiting for you."

"What men?" he said, playing dumb.

"Please," she said, ignoring his lie, "be careful."

He kissed her on the cheek, took the bag, and left. When Birdie arrived at the funeral parlor, he was heavy in thought. He passed Mario who stood at the payphone shouting orders, and did not acknowledge him.

Don Peppino was speaking with the funeral director confirming the arrangements for Little Vinny and Filipo the Chef. Birdie sat down in Peppino's glass enclosed office and impatiently waited while Anthony poured him coffee. When Don Peppino came, he gave him the rundown.

"The overnight hits at the Panatela's went as planned. They also snatched Panatela's son as a bargaining chip. We have teams out looking for other targets."

As an afterthought, he asked, "Where's Fingers?"

"He planned to be here early," Peppino said, "but hasn't shown up or called. I'm concerned."

"I have to open the pharmacy. Come with me, we still have more to discuss."

In whispered tone, Birdie told Peppino of Carmella's threats. Peppino's initial disbelief turned to anger as Birdie finished the story. They just stared at each other as if mourning a loss.

Peppino broke the silence, "I had coffee there this morning. She seemed nervous but she didn't say a word to me. I thought she had the horns up. She has to disappear."

"No, forget about that," Birdie said.

"But we don't know what she's got, and how secure it is. She might have gone crazy."

"Take it easy" Birdie cautioned. "I guess she doesn't know us, but we know her. At this point let's give her what she wants. She's been loyal. We buy the restaurant. Peppino, you tell Mario he has to find another girl, and tell Dominick that you don't think he's cut-out for what we do. He knows little. He just made a few drops for us, is that right?"

"Yes."

"So, we can cover by changing the drop places just in case."

"Yes, Birdie. You know, in all the years we have been together I never once questioned or doubted you, but this makes me nervous. We showed Carmella love and protected her. We have done everything possible for her and her kids. She has never wanted for anything. Doctors, medicine – she was always cared for by us. Never did the thought of hurting her ever come into my mind. But we have taken an oath, *'la Cosa nostra,'* – to our thing – there are others we need to consider and account to."

"Cool down," Birdie said. "All she wants is out. We will just make her understand that this works both ways. If we're injured then her children will also be injured."

"We should wait for Tommaso to do this."

"No, let's get this dealt with, we will update him later. We have a lot on the plate."

Don Peppino wondered, *He's always been very careful to include Fingers on important matters. Why not now?*

Birdie's shop attended to, he and Peppino proceeded across the street to the restaurant to Carmella. Birdie let Don Peppino do the talking and lay out the deal. They sat cowboy style, in an intimidating manner, with her at the kitchen table.

Don Peppino said, "I am disappointed with you. Have you lost your mind? I don't understand how you could turn on us. We are your brothers and have always wanted you to be happy.

You did not have to blackmail us for something we would have given you with our hearts."

Carmella just stared as if his words registered no meaning.

Peppino went on to tell her in a scolding tone that she would receive full market value for the restaurant and an additional ten thousand dollars as a wedding gift from them. They expected her to keep up appearances for the sake of their children, family and friends in the neighborhood.

Birdie interjected, "Have your lawyer prepare the contract and deed and leave the buyer's name blank. Our lawyer will fill in the rest."

"I intend to leave the week after Anthony's party, and want all ties between my children and your people broken at once," she said with all the authority of a Capo.

Their piecing looks made their feelings clear.

When they left the restaurant, they found Mario guarding the door, waiting with two other mobsters. Both wore long trench coats concealing shotguns beneath them.

"Why are they here?" Peppino asked.

Mario said, "A precaution, boss." Mario's brow was wet with sweat. He fidgeted.

Peppino asked him, "You look like you saw a ghost. What's goin' on?"

Mario put his lips within an inch of Peppino's ear. "Damn, Boss. They fuckin' whacked Fingers last night."

Birdie, standing near, paying attention to Mario's demeanor, heard the whisper and whirled around.

"No, not Fingers! Dear God. We're cursed."

Don Peppino turned pale as Mario continued with the details, "They hit him and Matilda both. In her apartment."

"Where were his men?"

"He sent them to the house on New Dorp Lane."

"Stupid, stupid. How could he be so stupid?"

"When Sparky went to their door, he found it open," Mario said. "Fingers was lying there shot in the temple with a surprised look upon his face. And Matilda, too. With one in the head by the bedroom door." Mario begged, "Please, Boss, let's get you guys off the street."

The two men hurried to the pharmacy with Mario and the henchmen in tow. They moved to Birdie's backroom infirmary. The henchmen took positions front and back.

Don Peppino collapsed into a chair. Unable to contain his emotions, he cried, lamenting deeply.

"Somebody has given us the evil eye," Peppino cried. "Jesus, it ain't gonna be the same without him. God, I loved him. Our brother. My first and only partner."

Birdie comforted him. But he was not unaffected. His eyes swelled with tears, though not for the same reason.

After composing himself, Don Peppino called the bosses in Brooklyn to report that Fingers was their latest casualty. They gave him their sympathies and orders to hold off with outstanding contracts. Evidently, Panatela's son, their captive, worked out a deal with his mob family and they would get back to Don Peppino later in the day. Continuing with *la famiglia* business, Don Peppino told the Underboss that he needed to ensure that their activities remained uninterrupted and he would make Mario acting Capo.

Birdie went to the door and called Mario. Peppino told Mario, "You have been made acting Capo. You have the opportunity to remain as Capo depending upon how you handle yourself in the cleanup of the war and getting business back on track."

Mario whispered his thanks.

"Remember, you need to focus on details."

"Yes, Boss. Thanks."

With the trademark double kiss, both Peppino and Birdie wished him luck.

"Call Bundles in Vegas," Peppino told Mario. "He will take over as my lieutenant."

Don Peppino hugged Birdie and left with Mario. He knew that the resources of the funeral parlor would be stretched by the war. He had to be prepared.

Birdie had the task of informing Billy and his daughter of Finger's death.

53.

Katie placed Billy in Sister Regina's care and waited for Kevin. Emotionally incapacitated by what she had learned from Carmella, she succumbed to her reality. She was sleepless and riddled with panic and anxiety over Billy's future. She had peeked in at Billy from time to time during the night as he slept, examining his features and almost disturbing his sleep. In a way, she was trying to disprove Carmella's story by observing Billy's face, seeking not to see her father there.

She reviewed the photos of her father with obsessive focus. She scrutinized the shots Billy had taken home from Westchester. She could not deny his likeness. The uncertainty evaporated. She knew he was her half-brother.

Katie whimpered in sadness for him and the deception that they both had suffered. She pledged to herself that she would do everything in her power to shield him from involvement in their father's life. She would keep secret the identity of his real father. She was determined that Billy would not live a life of violence and denial.

Her thoughts went to Kevin. How could she expect him to take on the care of a teenager? That would not be fair to him.

Birdie called the homeless shelter to speak with Katie. Reggie told him that she had taken the day off, adding that she planned to drop Billy off later. Katie's intention was to visit with her mother later in the day. Birdie drove to Katie's apartment. He had to tell her about Fingers before his death was announced as another gangland murder and curiosity for the entertainment of the general public.

When Katie heard a knock at the door, she opened it thinking it was Kevin. Her eyes were red from tears and when her father saw her, he thought she knew what had happened.

"You know?" he asked.

Katie panicked for a moment. She did not know what to answer. *Has Carmella told him of our conversation?*

"About Fingarro," he followed.

The ambiguity gone, she relaxed. "No," she said. "What about Uncle Tommaso?"

"Where's Billy?" Birdie asked.

"He's sleeping."

"Come sit with me in the car, I need to tell you something. I don't want him to hear. Not yet."

She did not know if she were capable of keeping control of her emotions, having such a complex twist of loving and hateful feelings for him now.

In the car, Birdie began. "A terrible thing happened last night. Your Uncle Tommaso. He's dead."

Katie just stared at him, her brain blocked from emotion. She noticed how clinical he was, showing no emotion for someone he grew up with. He was devoid of feeling, but now he was anxious to discuss Billy's future.

"We, your mother and I, could take Billy to live with us after the funeral and raise him. I know that you and Kevin might be planning a future together. It wouldn't be fair to you to be saddled with the responsibility of a teenager from the outset. Your life together should start without that obligation. It could strain your relationship."

What's wrong with him? The body is not even cold and he's making plans.

His concern for the well-being of an orphaned child was reasonable, and common among people mourning the death of a loved one. However, Katie viewed him and his intentions with suspicion now. Birdie did not go into the details but he told her that Don Peppino would take care of the arrangements and asked her if she wanted him to tell Billy.

Katie steeled herself. "I will prepare Billy. I expect Kevin soon. We planned to drive up to Westchester to get my car. I will take Billy with us and tell him at the appropriate moment."

Her father went to hug her, but she withdrew and left the car.

Kevin arrived twenty minutes later. She could only whisper to him, "Billy's father is dead." She was tempted to use the word "murdered," but held it back, as Birdie had, and added, "Billy does not know. I want to speak in greater depth about what happened. How it may affect our future together. But, if it's all right with you, I'd like to get some belongings together and pick up my car and then find a quiet inn somewhere to break the news to Billy."

"Sure, honey," He said with a reassuring hug, "I'll help you pack some things and we'll go. I'd also like to share some things that may, in the end, help."

Then she showed him the envelope and told him that it needed keeping in a safe place.

"I can secure it for you."

"Carmella gave it to me with a grave warning. She said that lives could be at stake if the contents were exposed."

"Don't worry. I have access to a personal safety deposit box here in the city. We could stop there before heading up to Westchester."

"You poor man, what have you gotten yourself into with me?"

He held her, attempting to lighten her emotional burden.

"Gee, I thought I lived an intriguing life," he said.

Kevin called Jack Osborne to inform him that he would be stopping by the US Mission and that he needed to secure something in the safe. Osborne asked if Katie would be with him, since he wanted to discuss a possible position with her. Kevin said that she would be, but that they would also have the teenager with them.

"I think she will be thrilled. But this is not a conversation for today. She's had a death in the family."

"My condolences. Of course, another time. I'll be in all day and I'll let security know to expect you."

Katie heard the conversation and understood that Jack had a position that he wanted to discuss with her.

"Honey, we will get through all of this," Kevin said to her. "I promise I will be by your side whatever you decide. You're strong, you're loved by many people, and my parents are bonkers over you."

She smiled and hugged him, and then quickly packed a small travel bag.

Kevin knew that Malcolm had already spoken to Jack Osborne. The idea of finding a position for her out of the country was presumably his.

Kevin had disclosed the conversation regarding her suspicion that her father and his friends might have mob connections. Malcolm suggested that she and Kevin could leave for Europe together and either wed quietly in New York or in Europe if they wished. He also told him that he could arrange for them to be married at the Vatican if Katie liked. The plan would serve to take them away from the scrutiny of the mob.

As they prepared to leave for the day, Father Tony called. He, like her father, had tried reach her at the office.

"What's going on?" he asked in his favorite telephone lead to her. She spoke to him in Sicilian so, if Billy were to awaken, he would not understand. "My world is exploding, Tony. I just found out that Uncle Tommaso was murdered."

"What?"

"Kevin is here and we were just laying out a plan. I need to tell Billy. My first concern has to be for him. I'm worried about how he will react to the news."

"You have a lot on you. Why don't you guys pick me up and we'll go up to Windom for a night or two? Kevin and I can speak with Billy and give him our undivided attention. We could also try to deal with some of the other things. This has been heavy on my heart, too. I agree with you it would be best to get Billy out of the neighborhood and away from the street talk."

"Yes, that would be good. I also need to sort things out and want to talk to both you and Kevin. Aunt Carmella just dropped a nuclear bomb on me, too."

Katie was feeling the pressure, and she asked Kevin about doing as Tony suggested. He thought it was a good idea. She told Tony that they planned to pick up her car in Westchester, so he offered to drive them to Windom in his car and on return drop them off in Westchester for her car.

* * *

Malcolm, Kevin's mentor at the agency, was a man accustomed to complicated detail, and could empathize with Katie's dilemma. He believed that she found herself in two worlds, one of accomplishment and legitimacy, and the other of hypocrisy and secrecy that was not of her making. Nevertheless, he thought she would be a perfect mate for Kevin. He felt that her background gave insight into the sinister dark side of life, where his young protégé's career efforts nobly centered.

Malcolm had gathered information about her and the people close to her. Her profile showed that she shared Kevin's sense of loyalty and a deep Christian ethic. She, like him, believed in right for right's sake and that good conquers evil. He'd gamble that she would not only support Kevin and his patriotic career but had the potential of overcoming her guilt. She might even be an asset in intelligence. He would approach her carefully. He did not want to endanger her relationship with Kevin in any way.

Katie called her mother to tell her about their plans. Her mother questioned her so Katie told her in Sicilian dialect about the death of Billy's father. She explained that she wanted Billy out of the neighborhood environment before she broke the news to him.

54.

The ride passed rather quickly. Kevin and Tony took turns driving and playing word games with Billy. Billy enjoyed the attention of the men. When they stopped for lunch, Katie bought him comic books, which kept him busy for the remainder of the ride. She rested, preparing herself emotionally for what she had to tell her brother.

She acknowledged the paradox of the difference between her life and the life she saw through the window. The beautiful mountain forests they passed were serene. The trees grew tall, fulfilling their life mission of leaving their seed to co-create with God more trees, sustaining natural regeneration.

On the other hand she thought, Godless humans saw themselves as temporary so they were consumed by self-seeking ambition, and were bent on taking only. They chose paths that gave them superficial gratification at the expense of the suffering of others.

If we could only be like trees.

Upon their arrival at the cottage, Katie and Tony lit the fireplace in the living room. The smell of the burning wood brought to mind the joy and peace she felt with Kevin on their last visit. *Was that just a week ago?* She longed to recapture that mood, but this day it was just a backdrop for an avalanche of bad news.

Before dinner, Kevin took Billy to do some target shooting with the bows. The meal would be a simple one, barbequed hot dogs and burgers with store-bought potato salad and potato chips. Tony lit the grill on the deck, and joined Katie in the kitchen.

He found her crying. Long tracks of tears cascaded down her checks in a torrent that wet her blouse. He held her.

"We will survive this," he said. "I have been praying for guidance since our telephone conversation."

"Tony, they will not get Billy. Promise me that if something should ever happen to me that you will never let them into his life."

"I promise with my life. Go and freshen up. Don't let him see you like this. You're all he has. Be strong."

The sun set behind the mountains. Billy raced Kevin back to the house, laughing and overjoyed that he had won the challenge. He liked Kevin and looked up to him as a role model. He, like Katie, felt that there was something mystical about Kevin's appearance in their life at that time.

As they ate dinner, Billy spoke about his new comic book characters, admitting that Superman remained his favorite.

Kevin and Tony shared their favorites from when they were kids. They compared the unique superpowers of the comic book heroes they favored to those of Billy's. Katie listened, happy to see him enjoying himself with the men while she suppressed her sadness for what she had to tell him.

After dinner, Katie told Billy she needed to speak with him. He responded as he normally would with a challenging grimace, but she sternly took his hand, and led him up the stairs to the room prepared for him. He sat on his bed, and she pulled up a chair and sat facing him.

Katie's eyes started to well as she began to speak, "Billy, you know I love you."

"Yes." His tone turned fearful. "What's the matter?"

"I will never let anything happen to you, and I will never abandon you. You know that, right?"

"Katie, you're scaring me. Are you sending me away or something?"

"No, no. I would never send you away. Never."

She took his hand. "Billy, your father passed away today."

He just bowed his head and took a deep breath in a vain effort to take the sting from her words. After a solemn moment or two, he asked, "What happened to him?"

"Billy, he was shot and killed this morning. They shot Matilda, too."

"Oh, my God, they whacked her, too?" His face crumpled as tears began to fall.

Katie held him in her arms and he did not move. He sobbed on and off, and spoke only once.

"Am I an orphan now?"

"No, I'm your family. We will always be together like brother and sister."

"Will I still live with you?"

"Of course you will, why would you think you wouldn't?"

"I thought that maybe you and Kevin would get married, that's why Cumpari Birdie is getting me new furniture and fixing up the room."

"What new furniture? What room?"

"When you went away with Kevin he took me to the furniture store and let me pick out things. A desk and some other stuff."

"He what?" Katie thought fast. She needed to undo this. "Well, who knows? Maybe he thought, because you're getting older, that he wanted you to feel more comfortable when you visited, so you'd spend more time with them. But your home is with me. Your father wanted it that way. He made me your legal guardian some time ago. I am responsible for you and nobody will ever take you from me."

She held him by the shoulders. "The coming days will be difficult. The funeral and burial will be sad. It's okay to cry if you have to. It's not unmanly. You will see many of your father's friends shedding tears, and you have to allow yourself to mourn. Kevin and I, and Father Tony will be by your side."

Billy nodded as silent tears slid down his cheeks. She put her arms around him.

"This has been a shock for you. Why don't you take your shower and relax in bed for a while? Father Tony and Kevin will come up to spend time with you before you go to sleep. I will be right here all night, only a few feet away if you need me, if you want to talk, or if you just can't sleep and want company," She kissed him and left the room wondering why her father had bought the furniture for Billy.

Father Tony and Kevin sat on the couch with rosary beads in their hands.

Father Tony asked, "How did it go?"

Katie broke out in tears.

"He's confused, and concerned that he's now an orphan. Worried about where and with whom he'll be living. He's taking a shower. I think he'd probably find some comfort in man talk. Maybe you can take turns."

Katie asked Kevin to join her outside. With the support of their prayers behind her, she felt she had the strength to tell Kevin what Carmella had disclosed.

As they walked out into the yard, she turned to face Kevin and said, "We need to talk." As they stood there with their eyes focused on each other's Katie choked out her words.

They sat on creaking wicker chairs under the grapevine trestle, and clasped hands. They remembered how happy they were sitting in the same spot a few days earlier. Life now had plunged a carefree time into intrigue and responsibility.

"Tommaso's death has complicated things for us," she said. "I love you dearly but, in fairness, I can't marry you."

"I thought we covered this already."

She told him what Carmella had said about her father, and all the others, the Hester Street Kids. Kevin tried to reassure her.

"We spoke about this, honey. The only loss to my life would be if you were not in it. I don't want to hear any more about not getting married. I have a story, too. You need to know what you're getting into with me. But I'm sure we can prevail."

She gripped his hand tightly as if holding on for dear life.

"Kevin," she said in a cracked voice, "Carmella told me that Billy is my brother. Concetta-Marie couldn't have children with Uncle Tommaso, so she asked my father to give her a baby, and he did."

Kevin's eyes widened in shock.

"Yes, and I can't leave him in the hands of my father."

"This, too! Dear God, I can't believe it. It's like being hit by three tornados," he said, swallowing hard with sadness for her.

I feel so bad for you. Geez, Katie, I love you, I'm so sorry ... that you had to find out this way." Then he knelt before her and reassuringly took her hands.

"We will get through this, Katie. Carmella told you about Billy, too? This is bizarre." He shook his head in disbelief.

"Yes, it's bizarre, but now it all makes sense. The closeness I have always felt for Billy, even some of our mannerisms are similar and the physical likeness he has to my father and me, I never clicked to it before, but now ... it all adds up."

Kevin tried to help her make sense of it.

"Well, in the end you will have a brother, a fine young man at that. Who, you might have heard, saved my life a while back. That's a gift no matter how you turn it."

She kissed him on both cheeks, grateful for his support, and went on.

"Concetta-Marie, Billy's mother, apparently was in love with my father since childhood and wanted a child by him. Her fear was that Tommaso or my father would bring him into the mob and school him in leadership. She wanted her son to have a straight life ... a good life."

Kevin stood and looked up at the trellis. He inhaled the night air as Katie continued.

"Concetta-Marie asked Carmella to look after Billy, but Carmella realized recently that all she did to keep her children away from them had been in vain. Carmella believes that a drastic change is needed to rescue Billy and her children from taking a dark path."

"Well, hearing all this I have to agree with her," Kevin said. He placed his hand on her shoulder waiting for her to continue.

"The envelope I gave you is insurance for Carmella. The knowledge of its contents, she believes, will force *la famiglia* to release her and her children from their grasp."

"I don't know, Katie. Blackmailing those characters is tricky business. Remember they are the experts with that stuff."

"Uncle Tommaso gave me legal guardianship of Billy so I could take care of any medical or school needs that he has. He never felt comfortable raising him alone after Concetta-Marie died.

My father, the snake that he has turned out to be, almost certainly encouraged Uncle Tommaso to do that so he could be in more control of Billy through me. You know what Billy just told me? My father took him out to buy furniture to set up a room for him in Westchester without my knowledge."

She shook her head, then went on. "I don't know if the guardianship will hold up. I need to speak with an attorney.

I'm not sure if I should tell Billy at this point, if him knowing about my father will complicate his life even more. I have to raise him and I can't expect you to take on that burden with me. You see?" She looked up at him with tears glistening in her eyes.

"Katie, my love, life isn't what we all expect it to be. A large part of it is carrying the cross of injustice like the one Jesus did. The rest of it is mostly mystery. We're both lucky and graced for our ability to choose good over bad. God works in strange ways. Just look at how we met."

Kevin paused with a look to heaven as Katie gazed at him in wonder.

"Even Billy thinks it is a miracle, and I do, too," he said. "It is not an accident. God has entrusted us to each other. For me, Billy is an added joy to complement our love. A love that many people aspire to, but never attain."

Then he kissed her cheek and asked, "Does Father Tony knows this, I mean, about Billy?"

"No, he just knows about my original conversation with Aunt Carmella. I wanted to talk to you first."

"Well, I think we should to tell him. He knows the players and could give us insight to help form a plan. I also need to disclose things to you. I'd like you to meet my boss."

"Your boss?"

"Yes, but let's not get into that now. We need to get Billy through the funeral, and find out how you stand legally with him. I also think we should ask Billy if he would consider marrying with us, being our son."

Katie rose from her chair, throwing her arms around Kevin. "Oh, my dear Jesus, you have sent me an angel. My own special angel."

When they returned to the house, they overheard Tony comforting Billy and let them have time alone.

Billy let down his macho veneer and asked Father Tony to explain heaven to him, and if gangsters were allowed in.

"Will my father get to see my mother?"

Father Tony gave him the consolation by speaking of God's mercy and love. "I believe that people who did bad things could also go to heaven if they were truly sorry and penitent before God."

"You mean confession?"

"Yes, but not necessarily before a priest. That's always best, but in situations where a priest is not available, one can confess directly to God with prayers of forgiveness."

"Wouldn't that be too late?"

"Maybe for some. We know God is merciful but we don't know how He thinks, so it's best to be prepared, and to be in the state of grace, and go to confession often."

"Can I go to confession now? Or do you need to do it in the church?"

"We can to do it if you wish. Let me get my stole."

Billy stared out the window into the night sky wondering about heaven while he waited for Father Tony to return.

Billy sat next to Father Tony on the bed with his hands folded prayerfully.

"Bless me father for I have sinned. It's been two, no, four months ... I don't remember ... since my last confession. I curse a lot. And I make Katie nervous when I don't listen or do my chores."

He squirmed as he confessed stealing hubcaps.

"Yeah, I heard about that," Tony said. "Go ahead, continue."

"I didn't like my father. I was mean to him."

"Why didn't you like him?" Father Tony asked.

"I was afraid of him, and he didn't take care of my mother so she died. I did not feel like I belonged to him, either. He didn't do things with me like a father, and people were afraid of him, too. That's all."

"Well, many of us have similar feelings regarding our parents. Some people even wish them harm, but it does not mean we want it to happen. When we feel those things, it's usually a matter of frustration and anger. It is as if we're blowing off steam. Did you ever hear that expression?"

"Yeah, like I was just mad, right? You mean that if I wished him dead it wasn't a sin?"

"Well, did you really want him to die?"

"No." Billy paused and took a breath, then repeated, "No."

"Did you wish him to be dead sometimes?"

"Yes, a lot of times when I was pissed at him."

"Do you feel responsible for his death because you wished him dead those times?"

"Yes." Billy started to cry. "But I really didn't want him to die."

"I know, Billy, and listen to me - you were not responsible for his death. Other people were, or maybe even himself. He did not die because of your wish. You hear me? Remember, you were expressing your feelings and feelings are neither bad nor good, they just are. We're responsible for doing things, not thinking or feeling things, but those thoughts can lead us into bad actions. Can you forgive yourself for having the bad thoughts?"

"I think so. Yes."

"Then God will forgive you, too. In the future when you have similar thoughts, say a prayer for Jesus to guide and calm you, and follow it with a prayer for those that hurt you.

"For your penance, say one Our Father, one Hail Mary and a Glory Be. Bow your head, ask God's forgiveness and say a good Act of Contrition."

As the young boy began the prayer, Father Tony made the sign of the cross over him absolving him of his sins in the Latin rite.

When Father Tony came back down to the living room, Kevin went up to Billy with cookies and glasses of milk to have together while they played a few hands of hearts before Katie tucked him in.

Kevin and Billy talked awhile about military school and some of Kevin's experiences in the army. He knew Billy admired him and wanted to be a Commando like he had been. Billy talked about his interest in music and that he wanted to learn to play the drums. After a while Billy fell back with exhaustion. Kevin patted his head and promised, "I will be there for you. You know I owe you. If it weren't for you, Katie and I would have not met."

After tucking Billy in and coming back downstairs Katie spoke to Tony about Carmella's more complete revelations. Kevin joined them. Tony's shock was unmasked at the depth and detail of Carmella's experiences, but he admitted that he had come to understand that Birdie and Tommaso were associated with the mob.

"I'm disgusted and angry, but more than that, I'm disillusioned," Tony said.

His elders, including his father, lacked even the basics of morality. The realization made him sick to his stomach. He excused himself. Tony, like Katie, felt that everything he had always thought of himself dissolved into an empty shell that had no foundation.

They both felt detached from their parents and their culture. They were seeing themselves for the first time as victims of defiled identities. They knew that they had to distance themselves from their people and the environment that sustained that culture in order to allow the process of re-building their own self-respect.

They also knew that they had to salvage the best of what their parents were, and what good had come out of their upbringing. Both of them were too deep in feeling and too idealistic to accept what they had learned. A life of truth meant more than survival for them. Moral conviction drove their reality.

In the morning, Father Tony climbed a remote path leading up the side of the mountain and sat upon a large boulder at the edge of a ski slope. From there he had a panoramic view of the mountains and the farm fields that checker-boarded the valley below. He thought about how he had accepted all the benefits his parents' wealth could give him. He never once questioned how they accumulated it, though the evidence and the characters of the people that surrounded him were right before his eyes.

As he began to pray the Litany of the hours, he broke down. *Oh, God please forgive them and me. I've been cowardly. I kept my eyes closed, denying the truth.*

Father Tony walked through the door of the cabin.

"I am ashamed for my parents and myself," he said inside himself. *"I know I will confront them with the hope that they would seek redemption for their souls. May God forgive and have mercy on them. I also know that my life and the way I look at it has to change. I'm not sure if secular priesthood is the life for me. I'm probably better suited for ministering to the poor, maybe as a missionary. I know now that I must seek another direction. However, I first need to support you both, and Billy and Carmella, to see you safely into a new life."*

Tony said Mass on the patio and offered it for repose of the soul of Tommaso. He also asked God to enlighten them with the knowledge of his will. Then he gave a special blessing to the Katie, Kevin, and Billy as a new family, one that would seek truth and justice together.

55.

Tony and Katie dropped Kevin and Billy off at Rye Beach Playland while Katie went to speak with her mother and retrieve her car. Tony followed Katie into the house to say hello to her mother. They found her dozing on the living room couch. Next to her, lay a half-full bottle of wine and an empty glass.

"Mom. Mom. I'm here. With Tony."

The woman woke with a start. "Oh, I must have dozed."

"Mom, Tony stopped in to say hello. He needs to get back to the city to prepare for a novena tonight."

"Hi, Mrs. Burdino, don't get up. I'm not staying." He bent down and gave her a kiss on the cheek, then blessed her. Katie walked him to the door, and thanked him for his support with a lingering hug. Katie watched as he got into his car then returned to her mother.

"Mom, why are you drinking so early in the day? You're not a drinker. Why are you drinking at all?"

"Well, I felt a little under the weather."

"Mom, what's going on?"

"Well, I got depressed about the death of Tommaso and worried about your father, too."

"Mom, why would you worry about my father?" Katie baited her mother. "He's not involved, Mom, is he?"

Her mother didn't answer. If there was any question before, her silence confirmed that she was well aware of Birdie's dealings. Katie became angry. Seething inside she got up and went to her room to pack. Her rage boiled over when she found Billy's room completely redecorated, as if his living there was a foregone conclusion.

Perfect timing, she thought, *the project was completed right on time as if they knew the date Billy would be up for grabs.*

Katie met her mother in the kitchen where she was preparing sandwiches.

"How's Billy handling all this? Where is he?" her mother asked.

"He is with Kevin at the amusement park. I will pick them up when I leave here. Tell me, Mom, why did you and dad decorate the room and buy furniture for Billy without discussing a single word about it with me?"

"I had nothing to do with it. They went out one day and did it themselves. Your father wanted to surprise you."

"Well, he has surprised me, and you have surprised me. How does it feel to be the wife of a major racketeer?"

Her mother flinched, and then stood frozen for a long moment. Then she turned and pointed to a large red envelope.

"Your father left that for you. Tommaso's estate papers. His will and bank account information. The lawyer told him that you had Power of Attorney."

"I bet he wasn't too happy about that, was he?"

"No, he wasn't," she answered in a forlorn manner. "Katie –"

"No, Mom," Katie slammed her fist down on the table. "How could you live life like this? Was it the money? The prestige? The power? All of those things? How could you let his hands touch you? His hands are evil, they drip with the blood of hundreds, maybe thousands of innocent people."

Her mother shook. She put her hands to her face as she absorbed Katie's anger, and tried to answer.

"What was I supposed to do when I found out? I was a young girl with a baby, you! Divorce would have marked me as a loose woman and have you falsely perceived as illegitimate. I did the best I could. I tried to create a world for you. To make you a princess. I did everything I could to keep you away from them." She stopped for a moment to weep, and then asked hollowly, "How did you find out?"

"Never you mind how I found out. I have lived in denial, but not anymore."

Her mother reached out a pleading hand. "Please, Katie, please don't hate me. You have been my only meaning in life. I was a young girl with a shattered dream. I thought I married my prince. Birdie was an educated and worldly man. Who would have ever thought he was anything else?"

She stopped for a moment to gulp some breaths and collect herself, and then said with a sadness as deep as her soul, "If it gives you any peace, I don't think he really ever loved me, or anyone else either. The only one he's ever loved is you."

Katie grabbed the red envelope without a word and walked away.

"Katie!" her mother cried out behind her, breaking into sobs.

Katie took the envelope and the small bag she had packed outside and placed them in the trunk of her car. She transferred her belongings as fast as she could. Her mother came to stand at the door and called in a broken voice, "Please forgive me."

"Right now I don't know if I can," Katie replied, continuing to put things into her car. "And it's not my forgiveness, you should seek. It's God's."

She slammed the trunk closed, got into the car without looking at her mother, started the car, and drove away.

56.

The mob war ended. Concessions were made on both sides, allowing for splits in the construction and garment industry rackets. Reparations where made to the families of those who lost loved ones. Mario took over Fingers' crew and stationed himself at the Three Feather Bar. His first order of business was to meet with a capo of the opposing crime family to work out the details of the new partnerships and territory markings.

They met at Katz's Deli on Houston Street and camouflaged themselves in the noisy crowd of diners. After exchanging their usual pleasantries the two Capos sat together at a table while their bodyguards watched from another. Sam "Sammy the Hook" Campella, representing the Panatela family, spoke first.

"I hate these things when they happen. We lose good men and good friends, for what? Business suffers and it brings down the heat on all of us. Before we get started the boss wanted me to tell you that we did not do the hit on Fingers. He wasn't targeted by us."

Mario stared at him with steely eyes. "Don't bullshit me."

"No bullshit. What Fingers knew about the docks and connections to the Longshoremen's Union was invaluable to all five families. I'm telling you -- the boss exploded when he heard Fingers got it. They went back a long time, had done a lot of work together. He respected him."

"If you're telling me that you had nothing to do with this, who did?"

"We checked it out on our end. Even the others in the commission are not happy and we have taken a lot of heat about it from them.

"I don't want to start anything, but maybe you need to look inside."

Mario exploded. "Are you fucking kidding me? Who of us would want to do that? Fingers was a respected man in the Family! He was fair and honest with all of his men. They made money with him. He never choked them with his cut, and those above him have been his friends since childhood. They are family in every way."

"I don't know what to tell you, but it wasn't us," Campella said. He pulled an immaculate handkerchief out of his pocket and calmly blew his hooked nose. He reiterated, "I don't know what to tell you."

Mario was frustrated. He changed the topic and began to work through the details of the deal agreed to by their bosses. They spent about an hour eating corned beef sandwiches and laying out the new relationship.

After their meeting, Mario was still angry and confused about what he had learned. He drove to the funeral parlor to report to Don Peppino, who he found in front having a cigarette with Anthony.

"Boss," he said, "we have to talk."

Don Peppino saw the urgency on Mario's face. He put his arm around his new capo, and directed him toward the parking lot. Mario told him what the Sammy the Hook had said about the hit on Fingers.

"Bullshit," Peppino said.

"That's what I told him," Mario said. "But he insisted. He said that Panatela was also pissed. That he had gone back a long time with Fingers."

"That's true," Don Peppino said. "A long time."

"He also told me that others in the commission were pissed because Fingers had waterfront connections that were valuable to them."

"That could be true, too."

"They think it's someone inside our family."

Don Peppino started at him for a moment, then said, "Tell me, who had anything to gain from his death?"

"Boss, I thought about it driving over here. His crew was very happy with him. They made a lot of money together, and he protected them. He never busted their chops. None of his Lieutenants had the political or union influence to look for his job. Including me."

Don Peppino nodded. "That's what I thought. When things calm down I will speak to Panatela and confirm this."

Don Peppino instructed Mario to investigate his crew. To find out where they were and who they were with the night of the murder, and see what he could find out. When Mario left him, Don Peppino went to the drugstore to tell Birdie.

Birdie in his usual cool manner responded, "They're lying, but the war is over and we need to go on."

"Tell me something, Birdie. When you and he parted after our meeting, did he say anything to you about any suspicions he might have had?"

"No. The last I saw of him, he was heading for the parking lot. His men were waiting for him. I returned to the store to finish inventory."

Changing the subject Peppino told Birdie that the church would not allow Fingers to be buried at St. Joseph's Catholic Cemetery in Woodhaven because of his reputation as a mobster.

He further explained that Monsignor Scalvo had even offered the Bishop a substantial donation to reverse the decision.

"If he doesn't buy in, we will have to bury him at Greenwood in Brooklyn."

"Yeah, don't push it. We don't need another scandal right now."

His conversation with Birdie left Don Peppino cold. He returned to the funeral home with thoughts rattling in his mind.

Birdie's downplaying anything that has to do with Tommaso being hit.

Birdie had never been a very emotional man, but Peppino thought he could read when things bothered him. Tommaso's death did not seem to. Birdie had little concern for the possibility there might be a traitor in their midst. These observations prompted him to question Birdie's motives.

This is not how someone reacts. They were childhood friends. No feeling?

Fingers had nothing but the highest regard for Birdie and was loyal to him. Don Peppino had never heard him utter a word of disagreement with Birdie.

Peppino decided to put the thoughts aside for a time.

When he arrived at the funeral home, Peppino found Bundles waiting for him in his office. He was sitting in his chair speaking on his telephone. Bundles hung up at once and offered his hand to his boss.

"See that chair you just sat in? You sat in it for the last time," Don Peppino said.

"Sure, boss, sure. I just got in. I wanted to let the wife and family to know I'm back."

"Good. Head over to the Three Feather and let Mario give you the heads up on what's been going on. There are still loose ends. Give your crew the skinny."

"Sure. And let me thank you for the opportunity to serve you–"

"Yeah, yeah. I'm happy to have you with me as my Lieutenant. Make me some money and I'll be fuckin' ecstatic. I hear you did good in Vegas. Good start."

Bundles bowed with respect and left to meet Mario. Don Peppino sat down in his chair and leaned back. He turned on the radio for the news broadcast. He shouted to Anthony to get some espresso.

A few moments later, Sparky came in dressed in his butcher's coat carrying a box of meat.

"Excuse me, Don Peppino. I got some nice stuff here this week, a few roasts, veal cutlets, stew meat, and T-bones."

"Thanks, Sparky. Leave it by the door. Anthony will be back in a few minutes and will refrigerate it. Sit down, how are you doing?"

"Okay, boss. Sure glad they have settled that war."

"Me, too. By the way, you did a good job. The hits were clean and to show our appreciation we're raising your cut at the meat plant. Bundles is taking over for Mario. He will meet with you and the others to give you a heads-up next week after we bury Fingers."

"Yeah, sure boss, we're all shook up about what happened to him. A stand-up guy ... very fair and always delivered what he promised. He got me out of a lot of jams over the years."

"I know. He did many good things for all our men. I know. He was my closest friend, too. A brother. We grew up together. I feel like I lost my right arm." Peppino bowed his head for a moment. "Our work is exciting and we prosper. But we sometimes have our dark moments."

Sparky, did not say anything. He just let his boss vent.

"Is Birdie's meat in there, too?"

"Yeah. I have the package marked. I saw him a few nights ago. He was making for his car on Eight Street."

"Eight Street?"

"Yeah, it was late around eleven. I passed that way to bring meat to my sister after I had a few at Murphy's."

"You sure it was him?"

"Boss, I know him for over thirty years. He patched me up quite a few times."

When Anthony returned, Sparky helped him bring the heavy box to the downstairs freezers and then left.

Don Peppino sat bewildered. *What was he doing there, alone and late at night in the middle of a war? He said he was at the shop doing inventory. Why would he lie? Who does he know on Eight Street?* He searched his mind and it came to him.

Shit. Matilda lives between Eighth and Ninth.

Peppino, with his trust now waning, went to the secure pay phone and called Mario. He instructed him to question the men that were to guard Birdie that evening with discretion. Peppino wanted to know where they were.

"Do this diplomatically, Mario. Don't make it sound like an investigation, and don't ask me any questions. Just report back with what you find."

Peppino hung up, and stared straight ahead for a moment. Then he picked up his coffee cup and hurled it against the wall.

57.

Katie and Kevin brought Billy to A & S's Department Store on Fulton Street in Brooklyn to buy him a blue suit, a dress shirt with a black tie, and shoes for the wake that was starting that evening. He did not like clothes shopping at any time, but shopping for funeral clothes was torture for the teenager. As a reward for his patience, they took him for lunch at Junior's Restaurant a few blocks away, down Flatbush Ave across from the Brooklyn Paramount Theater, where Katie had taken him for Rock n' Roll shows.

Billy ordered his favorite, their Deli-Twin sandwiches on challah bread rolls, one with corn beef and the other pastrami. He topped it off with their famous cheesecake. Katie and Kevin did all they could to make things as comfortable for him as they could knowing he had a rough couple of days ahead of him.

When they arrived at the funeral for the first evening of the wake, Fingarro' s body rested in an expensive mahogany casket surrounded by rows of flowers three deep, with two ornate bronze torchiere lamps positioned on each side of it. The light reflected upon the acoustical tiled ceiling and the imported Italian hand-painted wall. The combined aroma of the floral arrangements permeated the air. The bouquets included roses, mums, lilies, and carnations displayed in shapes to mirror the sentiments of their donors in heart and horseshoe designs.

Katie and Billy lowered themselves upon a velvet-covered kneeler supported by a brace frame adorned with angels posed praying for souls. Fingers lay in a new blue suit with a white dress shirt and black tie. His hands were folded in prayer holding black rosary beads. Above him, leaning against the casket lid, rested a small bronze crucifix and a picture of the Sacred Heart of Jesus.

Billy had tears in his eyes. His father looked like a wax image to him. It frightened him. He had never seen a dead person up close. He clutched Katie's hand while he nervously sped through praying the Our Father and a Hail Mary under his breath.

He forced himself to look at his father. *If you can hear me, I'm sorry for wishing you dead.*

They got up and turned. Birdie and Maryann, Don Peppino and his wife occupied the honored seating customarily reserved only for immediate family. It should have been Billy's alone.

Carmella, with her children, and the Pena's, Father Tony's parents, sat behind them in the first row of folding chairs.

They exchanged hugs, kisses, and pleasantries in muted tones. Birdie made room for Billy between him and his wife. Katie understood the symbolism of her father's actions. He was staking a claim on the boy.

She would not make a scene. She glowered at him and took a seat next to Kevin and Carmella.

Monsignor Scalvo walked in with Father Tony. They greeted everyone. Monsignor recited the opening prayer with Father Tony alongside him. After prayers, Carmella signaled Katie to join her in the ladies' room. Angie, her daughter, stood to join them, but Carmella asked her not to.

Once inside Carmella locked the door. She told Katie she had confronted Birdie and Don Peppino.

"They agreed to buy my restaurant and let me and my kids go."

"I'm so glad. Do you feel you can trust them?"

"I'll have to. Anyway, I'm leaving New York. I'm going to marry Doctor Abramson and move to his home in Miami Beach."

"Marry? The Doctor? This is all too much. I feel like I'm going crazy."

"I know, honey, but it has to be done. We leave right after Anthony's party."

"How did Angie and Dominick react when you told them?"

"They're angry and upset, but I believe they have resigned themselves to the idea. Mario has cut ties with both of them. I offered to give them money to open a restaurant of their own in Florida, if they wished."

Carmella took Katie's arm. "I told them about the envelope. I didn't tell them I gave it to you, of course, but it's safe, right?"

"Yes, very."

Katie was bewildered, but a wave of elation ran through her. *If Carmella can, then Kevin and I can get out. We can be free of them.*

"I will prepare the meals at the restaurant during the wake and afterwards, at the family *pranzu* following the funeral," Carmella said.

Carmella sat in quiet introspection for most of the evening. Looking at Tommaso, her thoughts of them as kids brought tears. Carmella watched as Birdie and Peppino introduced Billy to his father's friends. *Look how they've aged,* she thought. She spiraled back in time to the days on Hester Street. *They were frightened little boys trying to survive in a harsh world without the support of their parents. But there's no excuse for what they've become.*

She remembered the good and bad times. She remembered Billy's mother, Concetta-Marie, a tortured soul who still managed to embrace life. Carmella admired Concetta-Marie for wanting to learn and grow to become a true American, but she was saddened by the memory of the outcome. *She threw her life away. She let her feelings of anger and powerlessness take her away.*

Those bastards used the pain of the abuse she suffered, and enlisted her to become part of their darkness.

She saw plainly that they all had choices, and that they were no worse off than most people of that time. They could have modeled their lives to that of honest people who did not resort to crime, but endured with trust in God. Instead, they left their children an inheritance of secrets and darkness, a lifetime of lies that robbed them of the meaning of life, with only an elusive concept of love.

Carmella whispered to Kevin, "Caterina is a good woman. She has a special loving heart that represents the best of our people. I am proud of you both. Good examples for my children of what is attainable in America."

Kevin held her hand, nodded, and smiled in agreement. Carmella tightened her grip on him. "You need to get her and Billy out from the grip of her father's dominance and that of his *amicone* – cronies."

They endured the first night of the wake. Katie had restrained herself from confronting her father. It made her sick to her stomach to watch how her father assumed a fatherly role over Billy. He introduced the boy to politicians and gangsters alike, as if Billy would eventually be the heir of *la famiglia Marcoleone.*

Katie seethed when she overheard one of Birdie's cronies say, "He's in good hands now." She needed to stop Birdie and Peppino, who tantalized Billy with the promise of material things, trips and cars, and those were only the things she'd overheard. She shuddered to think what they told Billy when she wasn't around.

Katie sensed tension between her father and godfather, but passed it off to the loss of their childhood friend.

Upon leaving the funeral that evening, they noticed plainclothes police officers taking photos. They shielded Billy from the cameras. They were bound for Reggie's quarters at the Center for Billy to play checkers with her and spend the night.

Back at the apartment, physically and emotionally exhausted from the day's events, they decided to unwind. They changed into casual clothes and sat out on the stoop to relax with glasses of wine in the cool night air.

Katie and Kevin exchanged impressions of the day and their respective conversations with Carmella. They were both convinced that the best possible course for Billy was to get him away from the neighborhood as soon as possible. They reviewed their options: how they would marry, where to live, and how they would school Billy.

Kevin went inside to bring out the bottle of wine. It allowed Katie a moment to think. When he returned, she gave Kevin his chance to come clean.

"Are you ready to speak about your life?"

He chuckled. "If you're up to it."

"I think it'll be important. If you're not just teasing me, it will impact the decisions we need to make."

He took her hand, "Baby, I love you with my whole being. Please believe that I'm very willing to alter my life with whatever is necessary to make us happy. My priorities now are you and Billy."

"You're such a salesman. Come out with it already."

"You know that I work in the Diplomatic Corps as a Cultural Attaché and that I play with the Zurich Orchestra."

"Yes," she said with a smile. "You're not going to tell me that you also belong to a secret organization."

"Well ... "

"Oh no! Not really?"

"Katie, knowing that I had to tell you ate me up inside when I considered all you have been through, the shock of what you have learned about the secret world of your father and those close to you, these deaths, especially Fingers'."

"Kevin. Please, honey. Just tell me."

"What I tell you can never be disclosed to anyone at any time, ever. It can put the lives of many people in jeopardy and affect national security.

"I work for the government in Intelligence, that's all I can tell you for now."

"Just what I needed. More words warning of danger," Katie said and started to laugh. "You're real a comedian."

Kevin did not laugh. Katie sobered.

"Oh, my God. You're telling me you're a... spy? You have a secret life too? You, the all-American boy? A spy? Jesus, Mary, and Joseph, my life has turned into a Greek tragedy!"

"Yes, baby. I know. More of an American tragedy. Let's give it some time to set in. I would like us to visit with my boss at the US Mission to the UN. He can answer questions for you with greater authority then I can. Just let it sit until we get through the funeral and Anthony's party. Don't worry. Everything will fall into place."

Kevin reiterated that he'd do whatever she wanted without hesitation to keep them together. They held each other for a long while in the moonlight before retiring for the evening. Her brain was about to explode when she went to bed. He slept in Billy's bed, but could hear her whimpering in her sleep at times throughout the night.

When Kevin awoke the next morning, he found he was alone in the apartment. Katie had left a note for him by the electric coffee percolator: *Good morning. Decided to go to St. Rocco's for early Mass. I ironed shirts for you and Billy. Please have him shower and dress. I thought we'd stop for breakfast at the diner before proceeding to the funeral home. Hope you slept better than I did.*

When Katie arrived at the church, she found five elderly women speaking in Italian wearing black dresses, holding their rosary beads and prayer books tightly in their hands. Their noses were inches away from the ornate aged front doors, and they waited with impatience. At twenty to seven, they began knocking with a fury. The aged sexton came to open the door and admonished them in Italian for their rudeness.

"*Vergogna su di voi, questa è la chiesa di Dio non un carnevale* (Shame on you, this is the church of God not a carnival)," he spat at them in Sicilian dialect. In response, they called him stupid, and boldly told him to shut up.

He acknowledged Katie warmly with old world respect as he welcomed her into the quaint church. The sacred stillness of the empty interior was only broken by noise of the old women groaning as they lowered themselves into the front row pew, claiming it as if it were reserved solely for them.

The sexton raised his hand mocking them and hobbled up four marble steps and proceeded to light the alter candles. Katie sat with her eyes closed, gathering her thoughts and praying for strength. She heard the bell ring announcing the start of the Mass.

Father Tony appeared from the sacristy as the celebrant. He was accompanied by a yawning altar boy. They approached the altar and bowed.

As he began to say the introductory prayers, Father Tony acknowledged Katie with a broad smile. The old women turned back to look at her with indignation, as if they felt slighted by this attention to her.

Tony said the mass in Latin, giving his homily in Italian. Afterwards, Katie sat waiting for Tony to join her. When he sat, they hugged and she placed her head on his shoulder without speaking. The old ladies stayed a while, then they shuffled up the aisle toward the door. They glared at the young priest sitting with a young woman in an intimate posture.

Tony whispered to Katie, "At their next confession, I'll have to insist on a hearty penitence from them for their thoughts."

The comment did not lighten Katie's mood. He sensed her inner turmoil. He admitted to being upset himself and increased his prayer for both of them.

"I've been questioning God about my priesthood," he whispered, as if trying to keep God from hearing him. "Because of my dishonest and hypocritical parents, my life feels like a travesty, and has lost its meaning for me. Everything I thought was true, everything on which I based my choices in life ... " He trailed off, shaking his head, then spoke with renewed energy and conviction.

"Now that the veil has been lifted, I can also see the hypocrisy of Monsignor Scalvo and some others in the church hierarchy. I see how they've profited from the mobsters by giving them the impression that because of their hefty donations, the Church would absolve their wrongdoing."

He pledged to see her and Billy through their grief. He planned to confront his parents and their cronies, after which he would join the Maryknoll community in South America, and live an ascetic life as reparation for his parents' actions and the pain they caused so many people.

Katie looked at him in shock.

"I don't know if I like that. I don't know if I can handle you being so far away. Isn't it dangerous? I feel guilty. Perhaps I should not have told you all I did."

"My sweet sister, I started to see things way before all this fell on you. My ordination party was a farce. That was the straw that broke the camel's back. I had just taken a vow of poverty, chastity, and obedience, and in contrast the celebration was ostentatious and overdone. Jesus came to us as a humble, simple man who taught us the responsibility to love and give.

"I can no longer deny or justify the material world my parents pursued and adopted. Material things became their religion, a religion with a blind disregard for those in need. What is most troubling is that they should have known better, having risen from poverty themselves, and having been raised in the Church."

He sighed, faced Katie, and took her hands in his.

"We both need to make changes. Kevin is God-sent for both you and Billy. For me, I need to find peace by doing meaningful work in the Lord's name."

Katie chose not to burden Tony with Kevin's revelation. He would just be more concerned for her. They meditated in silence for a few moments before walking to the church door. They were both facing another emotionally charged day at the funeral home.

After breakfast at the diner, Katie called Reggie to give her instructions regarding pressing matters at the center. Sr. Regina alleviated her concerns. She had taken care of most of the crucial functions on her own with positive results and would bring correspondence to the wake for her signature later in the day.

When they arrived at the funeral home, they could see Birdie and Peppino in a heated argument out back by the garages.

Anthony was positioned in his usual post at the front door, and he escorted them to the casket for prayer. With tears in his eyes, he spoke to Billy of his youth. Sharing things about himself and Fingers, liked going to Coney Island and the Steeplechase when they could afford it. Adding a flavor of what they experienced together, he told him how they would follow the coal wagon to pick up pieces of fallen coal to heat their homes or sometimes to sell.

"I know a lot of things." Anthony tried to continue, but started to cry and left.

Mario, supported by a podium, browsed through the guest register and waved to Kevin to join him.

"Kevin. I was hoping you could help. We collect and then note the donations and Mass cards we receive, and place them on a stand by the flowers. The money is kept in the safe until the end of the wake, and then we give it to the family with the visitor register, so they can prepare thank you cards. Someone has to be here, you know, for the envelopes."

"Sure just let me know when you want me to stand duty."

Kevin thought, *What a shame. Mario is such a likable guy with class. Why would he choose the life of a mobster?*

One of Mario's soldiers drew Mario away, but Kevin could still hear their conversation.

"The police are out there again."

"Tell me something I don't know," Mario said.

"But Don Peppino and Birdie are out there. The cops could be checking them out big time."

"Look, they have been at it out there for two hours. They know the score. The cops got more pictures of them than

Hollywood's got shots of Marilyn Monroe. I'm not getting involved."

58.

Don Peppino and Birdie had met early that morning at the funeral parlor to discuss *la famiglia* business. They spoke outside at the rear of the property for privacy. After Don Peppino gave Birdie the rundown regarding the resumption of *la famiglia*'s many business activities since ending the mob war, he handed him envelopes bulging with cash, his tribute.

Then Birdie asked about the burial arrangements for Fingers. Don Peppino complained, "The Bishop won't relent. We can't bury him at St. Joseph's so I arranged for interment at Greenwood."

"That's too bad. He liked St. Joseph's. Remember how he enjoyed taking the ride out with us to visit our parents?"

Don Peppino stirred with anger and tried to restrain himself but it boiled out of him. He raised his voice to Birdie.

"You speak of him with such sentiment but there are questions that remain. I feel certain that the Panatelas had nothing to do with his hit and every one of our men have been accounted for. Except, of course, for you."

"What are you saying?"

Don Peppino could hardly speak the words he knew to be true.

"Everything points to you, Birdie. First, you knew where he planned to spend the night. Second, you had your body guards go ahead to your house and you turned up much later. You also knew that he had sent his men to the safe house in Staten Island."

"Has everybody gone completely insane? First Anthony, then Carmella, and now you? Why, I ask you, why would I want to kill one of my oldest and dearest friends?"

"That's the question I am asking! That's what's driving me crazy. He was no threat to you. No one could ask for a more loyal friend or partner. He had tremendous loyalty and respect for you and our thing. You were his older brother. He listened to your every word, followed your demands and orders without question. I'm sure it wasn't money. He was a good earner for us, and we're millionaires, mostly because of his hard work."

Birdie's face flushed with anger, giving Peppino the dead man's look as Peppino went on.

"So, why, please tell me. What made you commit such a despicable act? What made you break the rules we live by?"

"How do you dare to accuse me?" Birdie said through clenched teeth. "I have been your brother. I've always been there for you. You have gone mad! The war, Fingers' death and all the others, Carmella turning on us – it has been too much for you to deal with. You're cracking up."

"Bullshit," Peppino barked back. "You were seen near the apartment that night. What were you doing there? There are no stores there and I know you don't have a Cummata. So, what were you doing there at that time of the night, and why would you send your protection away while we are in the middle of a war?"

"I went there because I got a call for an emergency prescription and dropped it off on my way home."

Peppino answered with a crooked smile, "You're as smooth as a snake, but I don't buy what you're selling. I'm not a damn fool. What's driving me crazy is why you would do it. Out of all of us, you have been the most conservative. We never whacked anyone without them being guilty of something. You were the one who always cautioned us to get the facts, take our time before we struck. You were the one who told us that human life should be treated precious and that we had to think three times before we ended it for someone. And this was Tommaso."

"All right, you want to know? Here it is," Birdie blurted out, "Billy."

"Billy? What does he have to do with this?" Peppino snapped back.

"He's my son," Birdie stated flatly.

"Your son?"

"Yes. *My* son. Tommaso couldn't give Concetta a child. We all know how she always loved me. She approached me one night, and asked me to father her child. Even though it was a moment of weakness, I'm not sorry for it. You wanted to know. There it is. You happy now?"

A stunned Don Peppino spat with disdain on the ground.

"You give your best friend the horns by taking his wife and then kill him fifteen years later to take who he thought was his son, a boy he raised? Is that right? You, who are in line to be the successor to the *family's* boss? You squashed many a made man for not following the commandments. You think you can break them on a whim?"

Don Peppino became dizzy and lost his balance. He stumbled. Birdie reached out to steady him, but Don Peppino pushed Birdie away in anger.

"You know what you did here?" Peppino hissed. "You took away whatever meaning my life has had. Yes, our thing is exciting and we have done well, but what made it that way for me was we did it together. We were a family. We were one before *cosa nostra*, and our home was on a roof in a shelter we made from an old door that we squeezed under together, as a family."

"I know how you feel," Birdie said. "I know you loved him and I feel the same way, too. But think about it. To whom are we going to leave our story and inheritance? You have no children, Carmella took Dominick from us and Katie is a woman, a social worker who will in all likelihood marry that government man."

Don Peppino spat again, "You're mentally ill."

Birdie ignored his remark. "This thing of ours is going to change. We're cash heavy and we have to go legit. For that, we need lawyers and accountants, people that we can trust and that understand money. Corporate acquisitions and the stock market. Do you know anything about that?

I don't know if you realize how much we have. Millions. Perhaps even more than the bosses do. We need someone we can trust, and who is our blood.

Billy is our family. He has the potential and the stuff to carry on our thing into mainstream legal business. He's like us, has a feel for the street, and is tough. Look at our cousins and nephews in Italy. They are goat farmers and always will be. You have no children of your own. You talk about meaning in your life. What meaning would our lives have if all we built was scavenged by *la famiglia*?"

"Does the kid know?"

"No," Birdie said.

"What about Katie?"

"I don't think so, though she's been acting kind of angry around me lately, but I don't think she knows."

"Do you think Carmella knows?"

"Aah, who knows what she knows or thinks she knows? I'm not worried about her. She won't talk about anything because she understands how things work. Her kids are too important for her."

Don Peppino turned again to Birdie. "This is not over. We'll talk after the funeral next week. I have a lot to think about. By the way, the guy who spotted you is a made guy and to protect you he may have to disappear. Think about that. Another good man may be lost because of you."

They turned and entered the back door of the funeral parlor.

Mateo's mother came to the funeral home to pay her respects. Fingarro had been a friend of her late husband. He had recently sent flowers and money to the hospital for her son who was recuperating from the gunshot injuries he'd received at the restaurant.

After Marie prayed at the casket, Carmella introduced her to Billy and Katie. Mario and Don Peppino approached and enquired about Mateo's condition. She thanked them for providing the doctor while restraining herself. She would not show them the contempt she felt.

Marie held Mario responsible for her son's injuries and close brush with death. He would have some paralysis in his left arm and leg for the rest of his life. She mentioned to them that she had just come from Chef Filipo's funeral and that Marypat, his daughter, was overwrought with grief.

"It's so sad. A beautiful young girl without living parents. Marypat has been at Mateo's bedside with me since the day of the shooting, encouraging my son with hope and faith."

Don Peppino pretentiously took her hands in his, the consummate consoling undertaker. "A real tragedy. Let's pray that Mateo has a complete recovery."

Don Peppino excused himself. Marie sat for a time with Carmella who whispered words of hope and prayer. *There but for the grace of God,* she thought.

Marie told Carmella, "I am living with two tragedies, I am watching two young vibrant children full of life being devastated by evil. It's our fault, my late husband's, and mine. We got involved with them out of fear and insecurity. We were young and poor and thought with our stomachs rather than our heads."

Carmella turned to her, "I know we could have made better decisions, but my husband worked hard on the docks and still, they owned us. They preyed on our weaknesses and we bought into the big lie, that they were our protectors. Who could we turn to? The politicians and police were in their pockets."

"Carmella," Marie whispered, "I have to somehow make sure that my son has nothing more to do with them. I don't know if he and Marypat will continue together. It's a lot to ask a young girl to deal with the lifelong infirmity he will have. When I searched for Mateo's baby pictures to show Marypat, I found a key to a locker at Penn Station. I remembered that just a week before he passed, my Marcelo told me to hold on to it, and that someday I may need help. I forgot I had it.

"So, yesterday on the way back from the hospital I went to the station, opened the box, found a leather bag, and took it home. When I opened it, I found it contained close to seventy-five-thousand dollars and a small leather pouch with loose diamonds and rubies inside. I know it has to be blood money and I should give it to the Church for the poor but then I thought of my son and Marypat. With this money, they could start a life together. They could buy Mario out of the restaurant and have a future free of mob control."

Carmella felt chills with what she heard the woman saying. She took it as a sign from God confirming her decision to protect her children.

"Marie, I think you should do just that. Your son earned that money with his pain and losses. Mateo and Marypat have become the poor ones. What future would he have without financial security?"

"I'm so worried about him, Carmella."

"What mother wouldn't be? Just don't tell Mario how much you have, in fact tell him that a relative offered to give you the money. Just ask him what it would take to buy him out and don't agree to his first offer. Let him see that it would be a struggle for you, that you would try and do not tell anyone that you have the money. The diamonds you can sell a few at a time to the Jewish dealers on the Bowery."

They hugged each other and Marie left to comfort Marypat at her home.

* * *

The funeral ended at Brooklyn's Greenwood cemetery. Father Tony shielded Billy from photographers. Don Peppino, with tears in his eyes, glared at Birdie with disgust and resentment.

At the gravesite, after the Catholic burial rite prayers concluded, Billy was asked to place the first rose upon the casket. Carmella broke down as she added her flower and took Billy with her to the car. The rest of the mourners followed and returned to the city, bound for Carmella's restaurant. There were so many people that Carmella decided to serve buffet style and displayed the food in the back room.

Soon after they ate, Katie, Billy, and Kevin began saying their goodbyes.

Birdie asked, "Where are you going? Don't you want to come home with us?"

"We're going to Kevin's parents' home on Long Island." Katie said. "They've been looking forward to meeting Billy."

Her mother's face turned grave, as if she had lost someone, too. Her father stiffened, turned, and walked away.

On their way to Long Island the music on the car radio was interrupted by a news bulletin:

"Captain of crime, Tommaso "Fingers" Fingarro was buried this morning at Brooklyn's Greenwood Cemetery. With the traditional glamour of mob farewells his funeral procession proceeded from the funeral parlor through the streets of Little Italy drawing the attention of pass-

ers-by and shopkeepers. Two flower cars overflowing their capacity and three limousines followed the hearse. The procession stopped for a few moments at the Three Feather Bar Restaurant, his alleged place of business, where the driver of his hearse pinned a floral bouquet to its door. The procession then made its way to Fingarro's home for placement of another floral bouquet. This is a customary Italian farewell ritual.

Mob sentinels guarded the gravesite, as family, friends and Fingarro's Mafia cronies circled the casket and deposited an abundance of multi-colored flowers on top of it. The local church Pastor, Monsignor Scalvo, along with the recently ordained Father Anthony Pena, shared reciting the burial rite prayers of penitence. The young priest's father was also in attendance and is considered by law enforcement to be a mob associate."

59.

FBI agents Calavarro and Murphy canvassed the storekeepers in the neighborhood. They started by visiting Italian-American shops but after weeks of door-to-door inquiries with no success, they began visiting the Jewish storekeepers a little further down where Little Italy bordered on the Jewish quarter.

The first stop was Hymie's, the largest kosher butcher on Hester Street.

When they approached the door, they noticed kids playing stickball. Home plate was a manhole cover. They smiled as they heard them shout with excitement when one of them hit the ball the distance of two manhole covers from home plate, a three-sewer hit and an automatic home run.

They entered the store and were directed to the owner, and waited for him to finish serving a customer. With a tip of his wide-brimmed black fedora hat, which seemed out of place towering over his white butcher coat, he thanked the elderly lady.

"Remember to wash the salt before cooking," he called after her.

Calavarro and Murphy presented their badges.

"We're investigating the murders of elderly women in the neighborhood. Asking residents if they have seen anything of a suspicious nature."

"Yes, yes. Everyone is talkin' about it. The *Talena*, they're all afraid."

Murphy looked at him with curiosity. Hymie caught on.

"*Talena*. It means Italians. Dat's all." He leaned closer across the display cabinet. "I believe dey von't report anyt'ing. Dey're very good about takin' care of dey own."

When they started for the door, they noticed the butcher's twelve-year-old son eavesdropping on the conversation.

"You really a G-man?" the boy asked Tim. Tim smiled and nodded.

The butcher introduced them to his son. "This is Yussel, my son."

Timmy shook his hand and ruffled his hair, tilting his yarmulke.

"How are you doing? Did you hit the homer?"

"No," the boy explained, "it was Morris. He does it all the time."

In order to give the young boy a sense of importance, Colleen asked him, "Did you hear or see anything strange in the neighborhood?"

"No," he said. He squinted as he tried to think of something more to tell her. "The only one I saw was crazy Anthony. He goes food shopping with Mrs. Caputo. He carries her bags."

Colleen and Timmy exchanged glances.

"What do you mean crazy?" Timmy prodded.

Hymie cut in, embarrassed at what his son had said.

The butcher cut in. "He means, slow. Anthony is, you know, slow. But very nice and friendly."

"Yeah," the kid chimed back in. "He plays ball with us sometimes, and he's a good hitter, too."

"When did you last see them together?" Colleen asked. "I mean, Anthony with Mrs. Caputo?"

"Oh, a few days ago or maybe yesterday. Umm, yesterday, I think. We asked him to play. He told us he had to help Mrs. Caputo. He was holding her arm walking to her house."

The Butcher was concerned that his son was getting Anthony in trouble. He said to them, "Ant'ony is a fine man, very liked in the community. He couldn't be involved."

"Where does Mrs. Caputo live?" Timmy asked.

The young boy led them outside and pointed to a house five doors down.

"There. She lives on the first floor in the back."

The butcher came out to retrieve his son. "Don't you have Haftorah studies, young man? Go in, do your homevork, and help your mother."

Timmy and Colleen thanked them both.

Colleen asked the butcher, "You know where Anthony works, don't you?"

"Yeah. At the Italian funeral parlor on Mulberry."

Charged with energy at a potential first lead, they strode up to the woman's house with haste. When they entered the foyer, they found a directory with six doorbell buttons, and located the name Caputo.

They pressed it and waited for response. After trying a few more times, they rang the Super. Immediately a voice came over the intercom. "Yeah?"

"This is Special Agent Cavallero with the FBI. May we speak with you?"

The door immediately buzzed. As they entered, they found the super waiting by his apartment door for them, obviously curious about why they were there. They showed him their identification.

"Does Mrs. Caputo live back there?" Colleen asked, moving toward the apartment at the rear of the building.

"Uh, yeah," the super said.

Colleen knocked on the door. Waited. Knocked again.

"Do you know if Mrs. Caputo is at home?" Timmy asked.

"Celia!" he called into his apartment. "My wife will know."

A woman came to the door dressed in a housecoat, holding a dishtowel in her hands, which she was drying. The husband asked, "Is Mrs. Caputo home? She's not answering her door."

"I don't know. I haven't seen her since yesterday. Sometimes she goes to visit her daughter, but she always tells me."

"Do you have a key? We'd like to check and see if she's okay."

Celia put her hand to her mouth. "Oh my God. You don't think she's like the others, do you?"

"Let's just check to make sure she's not home," Timmy said.

The super unhooked a key ring from his belt. Timmy followed. The door slid open. The security chain was not engaged. Timmy motioned the super away from the door and walked in. Colleen followed close behind.

"Mrs. Caputo?" Timmy called. "Mrs. Caputo. FBI. Just checking to see if you're okay."

Timmy asked the super, who came in uninvited behind Colleen, "This way to the bedroom?" He pointed. The super nodded.

Timmy rounded the corridor and through the bedroom door caught sight of a shoed foot lying on the bed. Timmy stopped and asked the super to wait in the hall.

Both he and Colleen drew their guns as a precaution, and made their way through the bedroom door. There they found the woman lying dead on the bed, nicely dressed, with her hands folded, holding rosary beads.

"There," Colleen said, holstering her gun.

Timmy looked at a note lying on the bedspread.

"Italian," Timmy said.

Timmy picked up the note with his clean handkerchief, and brought it to super in the hall.

"Can you read this?"

"Looks Sicilian. Celia!"

She read it out load: *Senora, I'm sorry I should have told you before you left. Please tell them when you arrive there, in heaven, that you're the last. I have to go there myself soon, too. So, please tell them that they will have to find someone else to do this work.*

Colleen asked to use the super's phone and called in to Detective Inspector Haverty, who said he'd dispatch the task force team at once. A patrol car arrived and two blues were left with Colleen to secure the crime scene.

Timmy made haste for the funeral parlor to question Anthony.

When he arrived at the funeral home, he found a young boy sitting at the desk.

"Is the funeral director here?"

The kid told him with authority, "They all went to a party. I'm watching the place and answering phones and taking messages, too."

"I'm with the FBI. Is Anthony here?"

"No, sir. He's at that the party. It's his party."

"Where does Anthony live?"

"Upstairs, Sir."

"What is Anthony's full name?"

"It's...Stamp...ah...Stampadello, that's it."

He thanked the boy, then without asking used the phone to call in the information to Chief Haverty. He requested that the chief secure a search warrant.

Hearing him, the boy's face flushed red. Timmy reassured him he was okay. They waited until other task force detectives arrived with the warrant. Then he joined Colleen and the others in a search for Anthony.

60.

Earlier that morning Huntington Station, Long Island. The day broke with clear cool air announcing the coming of fall. The sun rose shedding its light through the colonial styled windows. Kevin's parents were already preparing breakfast knowing Kevin and Katie would soon arise for the trip back to the city. Billy awoke adorned in his Captain Video pajamas. He flew down the stairs following the aroma of pancakes.

"Look who's up, Daddy," Kevin's mother said with an excited lift to her voice.

"Hey, Billy, did you have a good night's sleep?" Kevin's dad asked.

"Yeah, but the birds woke me up. You sure have a lot of birds here."

"Yes, we do. All different kinds."

"Are we going on the boat again today?"

"I don't think so. You guys have to leave early for the party this afternoon."

"Yeah, I forgot."

"Billy, you're welcome to come out and spend a weekend with us anytime you want."

"Thanks," Billy said, eyeing the stack of pancakes.

"Daddy, I don't think that Katie would mind if Billy had a couple of pancakes while we waited for them."

Billy's face lit up as he climbed on a stool at the breakfast bar. Kevin's parents had spoiled him in the few days he visited. They tried to compensate for his loss by taking him sailing, shopping for comic books and baseball cards, and making stops for ice cream. He warmed up to them quickly. Lillian's display of dinosaur bones intrigued him, and he wanted to learn to sail. He had made himself at home.

His face glowed as Lillian placed a plate full of pancakes in front of him.

By the time Katie, Kevin, and Billy arrived in the city, the sky had clouded and late summer humidity had set in. They found rubbish cans turned over by alley cats scavenging for food. There were newspapers, advertisements and flyers lying at the door.

"Hey, kid," Kevin said. "What do you say we get this mess cleaned up?"

He and Billy secured the cans. Kevin picked up a police flyer that asked for any information regarding the serial killer of older women, who was still at large. He showed it to Katie. He thought about Timmy and Colleen, and realized he had not spoken to them since the trip upstate.

"They must be really scrambling. Probably putting in long hours. I'll call after the party."

As they readied for Anthony's party, Billy balked about having to wear the blue suit with a starched shirt and black tie again. Katie explained that it was appropriate dress for one in mourning. Her heart was heavy as she quietly shared with Kevin, "I'm happy that this will be our last event in the neighborhood. I'm anxious to meet with the lawyer to discuss Tommaso's will and learn where I stand with Billy's guardianship."

"Well, if you're not too tired after the party, we can review the papers your father gave you."

When they arrived at the four-family apartment building, Katie's mother and father were just pulling into a spot across the street. The men shook hands and Katie kissed her mother. She tried to avoid her father, but he took her aside to admonish her.

"I don't know why you and Billy didn't come to the house after the funeral. We're his family," he insisted.

Sensing that a heated discussion might ensue, Katie's mother suggested that Kevin and Billy go in and let them talk. Kevin was concerned for Katie and hesitated, but decided to follow his future mother-in-law into the building. As she led Kevin and Billy into the building, they could smell the aroma of kerosene mixed with the scent of wine-making. The smell permeated the turn of the century building.

"Ooh, do you smell that, boys?" said Katie's mother. "Kerosene stoves replaced the original coal stoves and it's common for Italian Americans to make wine in their basements."

The first floor hall still had the original white and black mosaic marble tile that showed its age with cracks and chips. A large radiator marked the conversion to steam heat. It sat a few feet from the door supporting men's fedoras like a hat rack. They made their way up the steep first flight of stairs using the thick hardwood banister that was supported by hand-turned spindles.

The creaking steps announced their arrival, sparking a comment from Billy.

"This place is spooky."

Anthony and his friend Vito welcomed guests at the new door leading out onto the roof, a modern replacement for the original window that they used for access as kids.

Kevin remembered that he had promised his mother a call. He asked Anthony if he could use the phone. Mr. Zuppa, the prior owner of the building, offered to let him use his, and ushered Kevin down the hall to his apartment.

His mother answered. "Hello, son. Did you have a pleasant ride?"

"Wonderful, Mom. Thanks again for your support and a great weekend."

"How's the weather there? The radio said that a storm is headed your way."

"Right now it's nice but graying ... I'll call you again later."

"Wait Kev. Don't hang up, I almost forgot. You had an urgent message from Timmy. He needs to speak to you right away. Here is his direct number."

Kevin memorized the number, hung up, and immediately dialed Timmy. A police officer answered.

"Task force. Detective Myers."

"Hi, my name is Kevin Mandrell. Agent Calavarro is expecting my call."

"Yes, he is, Mr. Mandrell, and he needs to speak to you ASAP, but he is in the middle of an interrogation. Can you leave a number where you can be reached?"

"Yes, I can, but I will try to call him back too because we're at a party and the phone is on the other side of the building."

Kevin read the number of the white tab in the center of the dial, and reassured Detective Myers that he would call back in fifteen to twenty minutes.

When he rejoined the party, Don Peppino's wife and Katie's mother introduced him to the Pena's, Father Tony's mother and father.

Carmella rescued him by showing him where they all lived as children, pointing to different parts of the building. Kevin surveyed the large second floor roof. It looked like it had recently been sealed with tarpaper. It gave off an asphalt smell. He estimated its dimensions to be thirty by forty feet.

At the far end, near the roof's edge, a wood platform had been newly constructed. A makeshift table with its top made from an old door covered with a tablecloth and crape paper sat conspicuously by Birdie's old bedroom window. Carmella explained to him how they would all sit under the table to shield themselves from rain, and that she and Anthony would always wind up on an end because they weren't as fast as the others were.

"Birdie, the oldest, used to do his chemistry experiments on the table but eventually it became a clubhouse for us. Our meeting place."

Kevin lost sight of Katie and asked her mother where she might be. "Oh, she's still talking with her father by the car, my guess. I think their conversation is, well, personal. Father - daughter."

"Do you think I should go back down?" he asked.

Before she could reply, the caterers came up the stairs with the food with Katie close behind. Her face was beet red, creased with anger. Behind her Birdie was brandishing heated words.

Their interchange was inaudible over the music and voices of the guests. Katie pushed him back into the hallway.

"You talk about family, you hypocrite," she fumed. "Is it the mob family you help run, or the one built on lies?"

"What are you talking about?"

"You dammed well know what I'm talking about. You hide behind the mask of legitimacy. The accomplished, successful pharmacist who lives in the Westchester suburbs. Who has an educated daughter and a charity-ball wife. What you really are is a mobster. You have the blood and hardship of many people on your hands, and it's all just to satisfy your need for power and money. I will not have you suck Billy into that life."

She stormed away from him, pushing through the crowd toward Kevin.

Birdie was taken aback by her words, which cut him deeply. His daughter was the only one he ever had a spot of feeling for in his entire life. Now he realized she knew the truth of who he was. The wall that he hid behind was crumbling. First Carmella, then Don Peppino, and in the end his own Katie. *Oh, not Katie!* This would devastate him the most.

In his egotism, he viewed her as an extension of himself. She was part of the face he chose to show to the world. Caught by her, all that had remained for him was to react with vengeance.

He had to blame someone so he blamed Carmella whom he surmised had disclosed information about him to his daughter. He vowed, *I will make her and Peppino disappear and take Billy out from the control of my ungrateful daughter.*

He felt that darkness had fallen upon him and he was becoming paranoid. Those he had taken care of had betrayed him under the power of the evil eye. His education did little to dispel his family and cultural superstitions and he saw himself as the victim. Little did he know that a greater darkness was pursuing him.

Kevin saw Katie's agitation and handed her a glass of wine to calm her. He helped Billy prepare a plate of food for himself, and they sat together on wooden folding chairs. They listened to local Italian musicians playing the Tarantella with accordions and mandolins. They watched Anthony visiting with each one of his guests, thanking them for coming, and speaking to them as if he was bidding them farewell.

The guests included neighborhood shopkeepers who were noticeably uncomfortable in the presence of Don Peppino and Mario. They were resentful because they had to pay them protection money, but felt obligated to attend Anthony's party.

They feared retribution if they did not attend, and brought gifts even though the invitation said not to. After making the rounds, Anthony helped himself to some food, filling his plate with his favorite stuffed shells. He made himself comfortable next to his friend Vito who had already begun eating.

"See, Vito," he said as he ate. "See how nice they dance, how they enjoy my party." Then he laughed, "The best is coming."

Kevin remembered that he had to call Timmy again, so he excused himself and asked Mr. Zuppa if he could make another call.

In a minute he was put through to Timmy's desk.

Without pleasantries Timmy asked, "Are you at a party with an Anthony Stampadello? The feeble guy who works at the funeral home?"

"Yes. I'm here with Katie and Billy."

"What's the address?"

"Why?"

"He's the guy."

"What?"

"We're certain he's the funeral killer. Is everybody all right there?"

"Yes, they're eating and dancing."

"We found a statue of Jesus with a votive candle in front of the latest victim, and a stack of funeral prayer cards which included the names of the murdered women. What's the address, Kev?"

"210 Hester Street."

"Okay, try to keep Katie and Billy far away from him. We'll be there in minutes."

Kevin rushed back and found that Anthony had called his guests together on the roof patio to make an announcement. Standing on the wood platform abutting the edge of the roof, which he used as a stage, he thanked his friends for coming. Then he began rambling with flowing tears.

"This is where it all began. This was our real home." He pointed to the table. "There. That was our house."

He called Carmella, Don Peppino and Birdie to join him on the platform.

"Concetta-Marie, Tommaso, rest in peace," he lamented while looking up toward the sky. "My sister and brother, not here." He hugged and thanked Don Peppino and Carmella and asked them to rejoin the other guests.

He turned to Birdie. "You were our father." Birdie smiled, assuming the station and authority he had held for a lifetime.

Anthony smiled and looked at his friends. His eyes moved from one end of the roof to the other. He casually reached into his pocket and drew a pistol. He pulled the hammer down with his thumb and placed the barrel against Birdie's temple. Birdie froze. The women guests screamed. Two men tried to lunge forward, but Anthony yelled, "Stop! Or I'll pull the trigger!" The men looked doubtful, stopped, looked at each other, then at Anthony and Birdie.

"What are you doing, you idiot?" Birdie said angrily.

Birdie moved his hand toward the gun, but Anthony pushed it away and said, "Shut up, Birdie." All the while, the partygoers stood in fear of what they might witness. Anthony turned to the crowd.

"This man standing before you is the father of secrets. He is the father of murder and deceit."

Police sirens in the distance got louder. The sky began to darken with heavy clouds, and rain began to fall. Some of the frightened guests attempted to leave.

"Don't leave!" Anthony cried. "Stay here! Don't move! The best is coming!"

Birdie said, "Put the gun down, Anthony. You're acting crazy and you're scaring your guests, your friends."

Kevin tried to inch his way toward the platform but Anthony caught his movement. In a kind voice he said, "Please, Mr. Kevin. Stay back."

Anthony then spoke to Katie softly.

"Katie, doll, I love you, but God has ordered me to send your father to hell for what he has done."

"Anthony, please he's not worth it. He's not worth it. Please put the gun down now," she begged.

"*Bravo pichotto,*" (good boy) Anthony said to Billy, staring directly into his eyes.

The squeal of tires on the street below informed Kevin that Timmy had arrived.

"This is your real father," Anthony said to Billy, "and the man that killed your grandfather. This is where he threw him off the roof. This is the man who swore us all to secrecy. A curse we have lived with since."

Anthony shook in anger and sorrow. His frail body rattled as he paused for a deep breath.

"It's time. He must suffer the same fate. God has spoken. I must leave, too, because my work is done. I have helped the nasty gray haired ones like my Nonna, Annette Buffa, rest-in-peace on their voyage to heaven with a death of dignity. Not like your mother's father, who he threw down like an animal, rest-in-peace."

Kevin heard Timmy's voice from the doorway. "Mr. Stampadello. I'm with the FBI. Put down your gun, now."

The guests went to their knees, and many went all the way to the floor with howls of fear, and some covered their heads with their arms. Without acknowledging instructions from the police, Anthony continued as if in a trance.

"I sent the evil ones. The ones that gave pain to their children and grandchildren. I sent them to God peacefully, so he could love them, because only he could. I'm tired now, and He wants me to come, too. He told me in my dream that my Nonna is waiting for me. He trained her to be nice and to treat me good." Anthony smiled slightly.

Birdie, knowing that Anthony would not relent, made his move and attempted to wrestle the gun from him. They struggled at the edge of the roof with Anthony resisting Birdie with a strength uncharacteristic of a man of his stature.

Timmy charged at them, Colleen just feet behind. Anthony lost control of the gun. Birdie grinned as he took the grip in his hand, sure he had exhibited his supremacy once more.

Timmy was just three feet from the men when Anthony grabbed Birdie by the shirt and dragged him over the edge of the roof. The party guests who were still watching screamed. There was a moment of silence, and then - the two impacted the cobblestones below head first.

With a flash that blinded them all, and a clap of thunder just an instant later, the skies opened and a torrent rained down on them as if to wash a half century of history down the storm drain with the river of blood that flowed from Anthony's and Birdie's lifeless bodies.

61.

1963

"Kevin," Katie called up the stairs, "We're going to be late for the commencement."

"Okay," he answered, "I'll be right down. Are my parents ready?"

"Yes, they are, my love. They're waiting by the car, and your son is getting restless."

Kevin had gotten in late the night before. He had driven to New Jersey to visit with the watchmaker DiGiacomo who had retired and lived with his daughter. He sold his watch repair shop in Little Italy to a cousin of Don Peppino. The man had entered the country illegally, but no fuss had been made about that.

While there, Kevin presented DiGiacomo with a small velvet jewelry box that contained the antique watch they used to carry microfilmed secrets over the course of many years of intelligence work they shared. The agency gave Kevin the honor of bestowing the time-piece. Now inscribed with, *For Service above and Beyond,* and embossed with the *Presidential Seal* and engraved initials, "*H.S.T.*" *(Harry S. Truman).*

"Thank you, Kevin," he said. "Thank you for the professional care you took in protecting our safety over the years." Then embraced him as a father would a son. He was joyful that Kevin had made a life with Katie, whom he had always admired.

They spent the day reminiscing and basking in the knowledge that they were instrumental in successfully acquiring and transferring information that undermined the Russian missile program.

Seven years had passed. Katie thought back to the first time she visited Kevin's parents and the turmoil that surrounded her at that time. *It's amazing how we survived at all.* She smiled. *If it were not for Kevin's love and support, things would have been much worse. He gave us hope through his love and devotion and helped me to see my value.*

Then she remembered their wedding, a quiet and elegant ceremony with a small family reception held at Tavern on the Green in Central Park. Kevin's parents had the presence of mind to arrange the quick wedding soon after the violent death of Katie's father to counter the devastating emotional toll it had upon her.

It was beautiful but bittersweet, she thought as she recalled the haunting tragedy of that day on Hester Street. She remembered how happy Father Tony was to perform the marriage ceremony in the Lady Chapel at St. Patrick's Cathedral. He simplified the marriage ritual, which not only bore witness to their sacramental joining, but symbolized a promise of healing and a send-off to discover a brighter future, one he felt God had miraculously provided them. Just those close to the couple attended. Timmy served as Kevin's best man, Reggie was Katie's maid of honor, and Billy proudly gave her away.

The others in attendance, Kevin's parents, Katie's mother and Aunt Carmella (now Mrs. Dr. Murray Abramson), were very careful to make the day perfect for her. They knew that her emotions were fragile and that she could not bear another grain of stress.

She flashed back to their wedding luncheon, and how they were spirited off to Idlewild Airport for a flight on a four-engine constellation bound to Europe to start a new life.

It's as if they pushed us into the air. They showed their love and support, like we were baby birds who were ready to leave the nest. They encouraged us to fly for life.

She recalled the first time she saw Kevin's apartment in Zurich. It was situated on a quaint hillside street from which she could see snow-capped Alpine peaks. His friends quickly adopted her. Her first months there were ones of emotional recuperation and rest.

A short time later, Malcolm had arranged an interview as an administrator with the World Health Organization for her, and she accepted the job. She became pregnant with their son whom they named Kevin Jr. after his father.

Father Tony joined the Mary Knoll Missionaries and was stationed in the heart of the Amazon basin at Puno, Peru, where he and many foreign priests worked with Quechua and Aymara peoples.

The CIA recruited Katie to bolster and support Kevin's efforts. Being a couple aided their cover. She became quite good at clandestine activity. She reasoned that she had lived a life of secrets, and now she was keeping secrets for good purposes. Kevin and Katie's relationship remained strong, with the exception of a period of time when the Algerian Ambassador's wife Marisha, who developed an infatuation with Kevin, stalked him through an entire European concert tour. Kevin insisted that he did not encourage her in any way, but she kept showing up, so Katie still held some doubt.

Billy had remained in the States to attend La Salle Military Academy, the *Catholic* boy's private school located on Long Island. When he arrived at La Salle he found himself on a true country estate. It was heaven for him. After a period of adjustment and counseling, he settled down and allowed his competitive spirit to flourish. By age seventeen, he rose in rank to cadet lieutenant colonel and became the battalion commander for the school's cadet corps of three-hundred-twenty-five students. He excelled in intramural sports, learned to play the drums, and played in the Academy's band.

Billy benefited by attending La Salle right after World War II. There were many military people stationed at the school from the First Army. The school served him well because he had a lot to overcome. He learned self-discipline through a highly structured program with a merit system. Katie and Kevin were in constant contact with him and his counselors through his school years. Many of his teachers were born counselors. He had the further support of Kevin's parents who would take him and his friends sailing on their free weekends and holidays.

Today he would graduate summa cum laude with a degree in pre-law and a scholarship to Harvard Law School from St. John's University's new one-hundred-five-acre campus in Queens, NY.

As they drove on the Northern State Parkway into Queens, their spirits were high. They were a family that had become whole. Each one of them in their way felt they had contributed to Billy's success and well-being.

They parked in a designated area flagged off on the lawn. Because the main building was still under construction, the graduation ceremony was taking place outdoors. A carpeted platform would seat the faculty, festooned in academic regalia. The podium, with a Steinway piano behind it, sat center stage flanked by large speakers. The graduates, assembled in their caps and gowns, sat on wooden folding chairs lined in rows on the damp lawn. Their families and friends, seated directly behind the graduating class, fanned themselves with printed programs. Because Kevin made them late, they had no recourse but to sit in the last row.

Katie vented at Kevin, "You, Mr. Diplomat, could be late for your own funeral." Kevin frowned. His mother turned to Katie and said, "What do you expect, Katherine? He was twenty days late when he was born." Then they giggled at him.

Little Kevin spoke up in his defense. "Daddy, are they bothering your feelings?"

"Yes, they are, son, but I know you're on my side," and raised the boy up onto his lap.

"Don't worry, Daddy, grandpa is on your side too, right grandpa?"

"Yes, Kevie, he is my first son."

Their attention was drawn to the master of ceremonies as he approached the podium and made an announcement.

"Would Mr. Kevin Mandrell please come up to the stage?"

"What?" Katie said. "Why are they calling you?"

"I think I'm supposed to play something," he answered her adding. "Billy asked me if I would, but he never confirmed it."

"Oh my God. Go, go," she said. "You were asked to play and you got here late, I can't believe you."

Billy rose from his seat realizing that he did not confirm the arrangements with Kevin. He mouthed, "I'm sorry."

Carmella and Reggie were seated near center. They waved to Kevin as he passed. The master of ceremonies introduced him to the school provost and the faculty and he sat at the piano waiting for his introduction.

"Ladies and gentlemen. Thank you for this wonderful turnout and your support of the University and our graduating class. We're proud of our new facility but unfortunately were unable to have it completed before graduation. However, we will try to move things along because of the hot sun. At this time I'd like to introduce Francis Cardinal Spellman who will lead us in the opening prayer."

After the Cardinal's invocation, he congratulated the school administration and the students. He spoke ten minutes and delivered the underlying message that they, the students, had God given talents, but it was their choice to use those talents or not for the good of themselves, their souls, and humanity at large.

Then the master of ceremonies introduced Kevin.

"We have a special treat for you, Mr. Kevin Mandrell, who is the older brother of honor student Billy Fingarro. He is a renowned concert pianist with the Zurich Philharmonic and has graciously agreed to perform for us today. He will do a fun piece, *De Brevitate Vitae*, on the Shortness of Life, a lighthearted Latin song, and then he will lead us in Pomp and Circumstance for the graduation procession. Please welcome him."

Kevin half-rose, bowed and positioned himself to begin the piece. As he played, students sprang to their feet and sang, unrehearsed, translating the song's comical words.

The graduation ended on a happy note. After flinging his cap into the air with his fellow classmates, Billy met Kevin as he came down the platform stairs.

He embraced him. "Thank you. You were great, as usual."

He introduced Kevin to his friends who also told him how much they enjoyed his music and asked him to sign their programs.

Kevin put his arm around Billy's shoulder. "We are proud you."

Billy in return, confided, "I love you. I always felt that if it were not for you, my sister and I would have been lost. I will be forever grateful to you."

His words brought tears to Kevin's eyes. "Love ya, little brother."

They made their way to the last row. Carmella and Reggie had joined the family after circulating civil rights literature to the graduates and guests. After taking over as the Director of the St. Francis Mission, Sister Regina became a fierce civil rights advocate. She had been arrested twice, so far, for civil disobedience.

They congratulated Billy and complimented Kevin on his playing.

Billy heard a familiar voice calling his name. They all turned to see Don Peppino leaning on a black caddie with Mario at his side. Don Peppino had a powerful aura now. It was unmistakable in his bearing, in the way he held himself.

He had risen to the Under Boss of the powerful Marcoleone crime family. Proving his status, two bodyguards were close by protecting his flanks. He kissed the young graduate on both checks.

"Congratulations," he said while extending his hand to Kevin, who, conspicuously, did not introduce Don Peppino to his parents.

Don Peppino took both Katie's hands and complimented her on how beautiful she looked and how happy he was to see her. He bent down to pinch Little Kevin's cheek. He became emotional.

"Your Cummata and I have missed you. Not a day passes where we don't think of you. You will always be the daughter we never had." He nudged her aside and with more tears said, "I am sorry for all that happened, and what we had all become. But I can't take it back. My life was destined this way."

He stopped to find words and then with a repenting bow of his head said, "I want you to know that you were truly loved by all of us, including your father. We knew no other way. This was our miserable fate. Hopefully, if there is a God, somehow he will forgive us all."

Seeing Carmella standing nearby, he called to her. "Carmella." He waved for her to join him. Reaching for her hand he said, "Carmella, please tell your niece that she was loved. That we all loved her and that was never a lie. She deserves to know that we do have feelings."

Carmella confirmed, "Katie, for whatever it's worth, I believe him."

"You know, Mella," said Don Peppino, "That goes for you, too. It's true. When I look across the street and see you're not there, it's like a knife punctures my heart."

Tears came to Carmella's eyes. She had been softened by her new life. Her underlying Christian belief left open the possibility that God could redeem even a murderer. As they prepared to leave, Mario handed Kevin an envelope for Billy. Then he gave Billy a gift of a soft leather folio with his name engraved in gold leaf. He said, "We're only a telephone call away."

Carmella was relieved when Don Peppino had gone.

"Okay," she said, "I'd like to treat everyone to an early dinner and I will not take no for an answer. I made reservations at a new Italian restaurant on Woodhaven Boulevard, called Villa Mateo."

At the restaurant, Marie Patrino and her daughter-in-law, Marypat, gave the graduation party a tour of the new restaurant. She sat them at a beautiful table set with a floral centerpiece. Bottles of wine were placed on each end. Her son Mateo and his wife Marypat, who loyally supported his rehabilitation, owned the restaurant. Though the gunshots had left him partially paralyzed, Mateo was able to manage the restaurant.

Mario had relinquished his interest in the Casa Filipo restaurant in the city for a nominal amount of money, a gift Mateo's mother came up with to pay Filipo's debt. He let Mateo retire auspiciously because of what they had both suffered and in grateful remembrances of their fathers. Mateo and his mother had recently sold that place to purchase the new one. Marypat was beginning to show, as they were expecting their first child, and she glowed in her anticipation of motherhood.

Mateo, dressed in a chef's uniform, joined his mother and wife to welcome the party celebrating Billy's graduation. They noticed he needed the help of a cane and dragged his left leg, but he was still a handsome and vibrant young man. Standing together with Marypat, you could see the joy in their eyes.

Carmella beheld both couples proudly, so happy that they made it out from under the influence of the mob. They were alive and free. Carmella prayed to God, *Please Lord. Please let my children have similar happiness.*

"Marie, I'm hoping and praying for my daughter. She met a French-Canadian professional hockey player at a party she and herbrother catered in Hollywood, Florida, and they're talking about being engaged. However, Dominick works hard with his sister at their Pizzeria in Ft. Lauderdale and still makes friends with mobsters. I feel that he still has choices to make, but I'm determined to use my influence to keep him out of that world if I can."

The graduation party ended happily and added to the healing for what they all had suffered. However, Billy sought closure for himself. He wanted to visit the cemetery with Katie, telling her that it might be years before they were able to visit again.

62.

Katie had reconciled with the past and agreed to accompany Billy. It was a tradition to visit the gravesite of family members on holidays and momentous occasions. For Billy it was a family history lesson.

Katie briefed him on what she knew about their relatives as they weaved through the headstones. She directed him to their father's head stone, which simply read his name and the dates of his birth and death. Both were silent as they held back tears.

Fingers lay in the plot next to Birdie's. His stone was also inscribed with only his name and his dates of birth and death. Anthony's was the next. Under his dates were inscribed, "R.I. P."

Katie placed a rock upon the headstone, "It's hard to believe that Anthony could have been a serial killer. He had such a gentle heart and demeanor. Look how he remembered you, those things he left you. His precious American Flyer Model trains and his Mickey mouse watch."

Billy rolled up his sleeve and showed her the Mickey Mouse watch. "I wanted him to be part of this today. He loved these occasion things."

* * *

According to their FBI friends, Timmy and Colleen, Anthony had murdered at least twelve elderly Italian women over a period of time that spanned thirty-eight years. His exploits received national and international interest by psychologists, journalists and writers who had contacted Katie for an interview from time to time. She politely refused.

As they drove back to Long Island, Katie asked Billy, "How did Don Peppino and Mario know about your graduation?"

Billy, uneasy, answered, "I visited with him sometimes on family day at La Salle. I also spent a few weekends at his home."

"After all we went through, you stayed in touch with him and kept it from me?"

"I didn't want to upset you."

Her faced flushed red, "That's a lot of crap."

"Well, I guess I'll tell you what's inside the envelope Don Peppino gave me. It's the keys to a brand new Chevy Super Sport that's waiting for me at my dorm. The card had a note that read, "From your father, TF, as promised."

She remembered the day that Fingers made the promise at Carmella's. Katie listened without speaking, feeling somewhat betrayed by him but she knew that they were both stained by their legacy. *I'm going to keep a tail on his ass,* she thought.

However, she held the trump card. The envelope given to her by Carmella was still safely tucked away, and its contents could ransom Billy if needed in the future.

"Billy," she said with an ominous tone, "Mark my words. Choices have consequences. Make the good ones! You're life depends on it."

"A mirror reflects a man's face, but what he is really like is shown by thekind of friends he chooses." Proverbs 27:19-21

Las Vegas Strip 1953 - 3

AUTHORS NOTE

Many of us measure our life by marking our places in time with the milestones we achieve. We define intimate moments, or points of personal awareness of who we are in relation to the greater community in which we find ourselves. Some attain this insight from an early age, some of us only after being tested by the world. We look back and find our place much later on.

In retrospect, I have come to believe that the time that defined me was the 1950s. A dynamic era, one that centered me with a sense of who I am. I was born and raised in the working class neighborhoods of Bensonhurst and South Brooklyn, New York with childhood experiences that taught and molded me. I was an Italian–American, with roots in Catholicism, and an old world Sicilian culture bound by a family history that had spanned centuries.

The melting pot cultures of large cities like New York and Chicago have been the foundation for fulfillment of the American dream for many. My Italian ancestry showed me how to negotiate life, an inheritance that combined old world wisdom with new world vision. I learned how to embrace a dream, reject prejudice, and accept the pitfalls, in order to survive.

My schooling was in an adapted first generation mode of living, which guided me through the contradictions and challenges that emanated from the new world, and by my family's adjustment to them. As I grew, the immigrant Italian community in which I found myself nurtured me through the process of assimilation. I found myself joined to proud people in their journey to find their place in the larger American experience.

We were Americans in every sense of the word, but there were those who did not accept us. They viewed us with the eyes of suspicion and prejudice. There were those among us, fellow expatriates, who capitalized on our innocence and our need for security. These self-serving criminal elements, who brought shame to our culture, poised themselves to subvert our hopes and goals for self-sufficiency and a prosperous future.

I hope that you, the reader, experienced not just another window into the mob underworld, but also heard the voice of the rarely told other story of the Italian-American community, and of our collective human nature and our pursuit of good. The other story of this work speaks to the soul of hardworking, family-loving people, committed to the pursuit of peace and happiness in a new land. People who, like other immigrant cultures of the time, had an appetite for discovery and freedom but with all the responsibility and weight of the choices they made.

They were multi-cultural immigrants who ventured in great numbers to America after the turn of the last century seeking work and education for their children. However, their dreams were sidetracked as they found themselves weathering an economic depression and two world wars. They found themselves in a strange land and in insecure economic times, many without the benefit of knowing the language. The majority settled in large American cities such as New York, Chicago, and others, working as laborers, dockworkers and artisans who were constitutionally bent on building a new life.

To them, America was the land of opportunity. They held the Judeo-Christian belief that if they applied themselves with hard work, anything and everything may be accomplished.

This belief in America and its respect for freedom induced many Italian-American immigrants to enlist into military service. Those that were too old to fight worked in defense plants. They understood the price of freedom and were willing to pay for it. Make no mistake – they loved their homelands. Some had families living in areas targeted by allied forces for bombardment. Many of them had relatives who suffered under the impact of the invasion. Many died.

However, these newly arrived Americans showed a steadfast courage to defend America against global tyranny. They understood, as our founding fathers did, that the freedom and human dignity they sought had to be earned.

In Italy, a fixed class system existed in place for centuries. The poorer classes enjoyed little hope of escape from economic oppression. Only a select minority had the privilege of education and the right to certain select positions in life. America brought hope of a better life and assured a public education for their children. Regardless of how difficult the obstacles of prejudice and internal protectionism were, the immigrants were confident that with the application of their extraordinary talents and skills, they would be recognized and accepted, and take their rightful place in a free society.

History has shown us that the periodic infusion of immigrants into the American populace stirs our patriotism while adding the best part of diverse old world work ethics. Attitudes of complacency never last very long in America. We realize the value of our freedom by the newcomers who revel in it.

As World War II ended and our service men and women returned home, American industry grew in leaps and bounds with untiring energy. New ideas began to arise. The conversion from a wartime to a peacetime economy fostered creative changes. Americans were eager to purchase goods and services which were unavailable during the war. The creation of jobs to supply the demand for business expansion became the norm and marked the fifties with life changing inventions. Inventions such as the silicon transistor and the integrated circuit created the foundation for the high-tech industry we enjoy today. People could take their music with them, in the form of a portable transistor radio.

Many political changes also occurred. The signing of the Immigration and Naturalization Act removed racial and ethnic barriers to becoming a US citizen. The US Supreme Court ruled racial segregation unconstitutional in public schools. Rosa Parks sparked social conscience when she refused to give up her seat on a public bus in Montgomery, Alabama. Transcontinental television broadcasts began. The American Federation of Labor and the Congress of Industrial Organizations merged, making the new AFL-CIO, an organization with 15 million members. The signing of the Federal Highway Act marked the beginning of work on the Interstate Highway system.

America boomed! The baby boomer generation began to take the awkward baby steps that progressively turned into confident giant steps in medicine, communications and space exploration. Dr. Jonas Salk developed a vaccine for polio. Explorer I, the first US satellite, successfully orbited the earth. Then we saw the establishment of the first domestic jet-airline passenger service by National Airlines between New York City and Miami. Alaska and Hawaii became the forty-ninth and fiftieth states.

The 1950s made owning your own home an affordable reality. People could now have their own single-family home in a suburban community like Levittown, NY, built by innovator William Levitt specifically for returning service men and their families. In addition, Frank Lloyd Wright inspired the popular ranch style home.

Fashion designer Bill Blass introduced fun clothing like blue jeans and poodle skirts made of felt and decorated with poodle appliqués. Designer clothing that complemented hairstyles, like ponytails for girls, and flat tops and crew cuts for boys. Teenagers had embraced a new pop-culture with movie screen heroes like James Dean and rock n' roll idols Jerry Lee Lewis and Elvis Presley who revolutionized the music industry and were showcased by Dick Clark's American Bandstand.

The popular toys of the time were hula-hoops and Hop-a-long Cassidy guns and western gear, Davy Crockett raccoon skin hats and Silly Putty. Hollywood produced an assortment of movies destined to be classics: *Twelve Angry Men, 20,000 Leagues Under the Sea, An American in Paris, All about Eve, Bridge on the River Kwai, The Ten Commandments,* and *Vertigo.*

The fifties had its dark side too. The underworld also prospered, riding the shirt tales of human weakness and the blood, sweat, and tears of law-abiding Americans of that era. The post war energy for production and consumerism was channeled into a search for greater excitement. The American mafia was all too glad to provide entertainment in the forms of organized gambling, prostitution, and the drug trade.

Various crime syndicates with infamous leaders like Meyer Lansky and Frank Costello –dubbed the prime minister of organized crime– from New York, and various other mob soldiers and hit men known as *Sgarristas* and *Piciottos*, plus other schemers, were responsible for the continuous growth of the underworld.

The casino became a vulgar, high-volume assembly line, devoted to fleecing tourists for the benefit of faceless corporations, many of which were controlled by organized crime. Las Vegas exemplified the magnitude of cultural change occurring throughout the United States after WWII. In the course of twenty years from the end of the Second World War, the world had changed greatly, by creating and embracing a multitude of postwar innovations.

The Mob invested in Las Vegas with huge amounts of cash and gave a nondescript desert community a glamorous identity. The mafia had come of age. Las Vegas epitomized the scope and skill of a minute percentage of infamous Italian-Americans who provided services that preyed upon human weakness. Moreover, they worked toward imposing themselves on American society, promoting fear of and disregard for their cultures.

So, I hope you enjoyed this intimate journey back in time, a period that defined my family, our community, and me, while we pursued our American experience. This is a work of fiction, underpinned by history with imaginary characters, places and events. Imagination given birth in memories, enriched by a culture of people who enthusiastically embraced the American dream then and now.

MOB TERMS - GLOSSARY

ACTION: Old-time term for illicit profits. Also, sometimes used to refer to the potential for racket income.

ADMINISTRATION: The top members of the Family, usually composed of the boss, underboss, and Consigliere.

ASSOCIATE: Though the usual sense of this word conveys a sense of belonging, in MAFIA-Speak an associate is one who works in affiliation with a Mafia organization but is not an official member.

BABANIA: Heroin, as in dealing.

BABBO: A dope, idiot, useless underling.

BEEF: A quarrel between underworld individuals or groups. Also hard feelings felt by one Mafioso against another. Beefs are generally brought to Mafia higher-ups for resolution.

BLACK BOOK: Nickname for the publicly circulated exclusion lists - generally of racketeers and game-cheats - generated by gaming commissions in Nevada and New Jersey.

BOOK: A gambling racket ordinarily focused on sporting events. The racket is run by a "bookmaker."

BOOKS: Membership rolls of the Mafia families.

BORGATA: Family. The basic structural unit of the Mafia society. The Borgata has an established hierarchy, a body of members or soldiers, and many associates.

BOSS: Sometimes referred to as Father, Godfather or Uncle in the old tradition, the boss is the leader of the Mafia Family.

BREAK: To discipline a Mafia family leader by demoting him in rank.

BUMP OFF: Kill.

BURN: Kill.

BUTTON: A soldier in a Mafia family. A member who can be called upon by a family boss to perform an execution.

BUY: Bribe. A police officer or politician who takes money in exchange for allowing crime to continue is "bought."

CALL IN: The act of ordering - without explanation - a 'made man' to report to his superiors. Mafiosi might be called in so they can be disciplined (murdered). Once the order is received, the 'made' man must report as ordered. Therefore, Mafiosi in trouble with superiors will sometimes drop out of touch to avoid receiving the call.

CAPO DEI CAPI: The leader of all leaders or boss of bosses. The most powerful Mafia boss to whom all others defer. Some know this as the Capo di CAPI or the Capo di tutti CAPI.

CAPO: Originally referred to a Mafia boss but in usage that is more recent refers to a minor leader within a Mafia family, chief of a crew. Also referred to as a captain, skipper or lieutenant.

CAPODECINA: Synonymous with capo, this term designates the capo as a leader of at least ten soldiers.

CAPOREGIME: Synonymous with capo, but often used to refer to more significant group leaders.

CASE: Size up criminal possibilities. Plan a robbery. As in "case the joint."

Clip: Kill. Also to harm in some way. ("Jimmy clipped me of 5 G's.")

COMARE: A Mafia mistress. "Cummari" (slang pronunciation)

COMPARE: Close friend or buddy. Literally, "godfather" in Italian

COSA NOSTRA: Italian for "this thing of ours," the Mafia

OMERTA: The code of silence and one of the premier vows taken when being sworn into the Family. Violation is punishable by death.

COMBINATION: An organized criminal entity including gangs of various ethnic backgrounds. Syndicate. Commission: A ruling representative body serving as the national legislature and Supreme Court of the Mafia network. Commission members are the leaders of the more powerful Mafia families. Each is also assigned to represent minor families.

CONNECTED: A description of a Mafia "associate."

CONSIGLIERE: A translation of this word as "counselor" has led to a mistaken impression about the position's duties (that the Consigliere is an adviser to the boss). Actually, the Consigliere post is intended to serve the family membership, by granting a channel of communication to the boss.

CONTRACT: An old-time term referring to an order to murder an individual.

COSA NOSTRA: To many, this is the proper name of the Mafia in the United States. In fact, it was an effort by some mob bosses to refer to their shared secret society WITHOUT naming it. The phrase translates to, "our thing."

COSCA: Translated "gang," this term is typically used to refer to a Mafia organization in Sicily. Equivalent to "Borgata."

CREW: A body of soldiers assigned to a capo. The crew typically meets on a regular basis at the Capo's headquarters.

CRUMB: Old-time term for a member of "legit" society. A working man.

DO UP: Mafia's 19th Century slang for murder. "Go find Benny and do him up."

DON: A traditional term of respect for a male in Romance languages, which has been corrupted in some circles to refer to Mafia bosses.

DOUGH: Money, especially the ill-gotten variety.

DROP OR DROP-OFF: A pre-arranged location for disposal of goods. Also a holding location where individuals are screened before being taken to an illicit activity, such as a crap game.

EARNER: One who generates income for a Mafia family. Higher levels of income are generated by "big-earners."

FAMILY: The basic unit of the Mafia society. See "Borgata."

FATHER: Antiquated term for the leader of a Mafia family. See "Boss."

FEATHERBEDDING: The practice of assigning more union workers to a project than necessary.

FEDS: Federal law enforcement agents. In pre-Prohibition days, Mafia-feared Feds were agents of the Secret Service, the Federal Bureau of Narcotics and the Postal Inspection Service. During Prohibition, they were agents of the Treasury Department. After Prohibition, the FBI gradually - and reluctantly - turned its attention toward the Mafia

FENCE: One who trades in stolen goods. Or, to sell off swag.

FIX: A situation in which law enforcement has been paid to allow criminal activity. A gangster might refer to such a situation by saying, "The fix was in."

FLIP: To abandon the principle of "Omerta" and begin to cooperate with law enforcement.

FRIEND OF OURS: An introduction in which one Mafia member informs another that a new acquaintance is also a member. It is a means of vouching for the underworld credentials of another person. As opposed to "friend of mine," which, in introduction, means simply what it says.

GHOST PAYROLL: Names of non-existent or no-show employees added to a payroll (typically through a corrupt labor union) in order to funnel money to the Mafia.

GOING TO THE MATTRESSES: Going to war with a rival clan or family. Used in the mafia. It is when a mafia family sends someone out to get some apartments and some mattresses for the soldiers of the family to sleep on while they hide out in safety, waiting for a call to do something.

GODFATHER: Title typically used out of respect and affection. In a Mafia context (particularly in the movies), it refers to the boss. However, no boss in the modern era has been addressed by that title.

GOOMBA: Term of affection and respect.

GREASE: see "buy."

HEAT: Intense attention from law enforcement and/or media. Heavily armed.

HIT: An assigned murder.

HIT THE MATTRESSES: Engage in an underworld feud. Key members of a family quickly move to inconspicuous safe houses. The phrase probably refers to sleeping on a mattress thrown on the floor.

ICE: Another term for murder. Also refers to a delaying tactic, as in "keep him on ice."

JOINT: Older term for prison. Also known as "the can," "the pen," "up the river," "the big house," "stir." A convict in prison might be said to be "away."

JUICE: The shylocking racket.

JUNK: Narcotics. A drug trafficker is said to be in the "junk business."

KNOCK OFF: Kill.

KNOCK OVER: Rob. The term probably comes from robberies of small produce or newsstands, which could be bumped to spill their contents onto the ground.

LA COSA NOSTRA: In an effort to make Cosa Nostra sound more like a proper name, federal agents seem to have been responsible for the addition of the "La." The phrase, literally translated "the our thing," has been interpreted as "this thing of ours."

LAY LOW: Act inconspicuously or stay out of sight.

LCN: Striving for credibility after denying the existence of a nationwide Mafia for decades, J. Edgar Hoover's FBI "discovered" La Cosa Nostra around 1960 and began referring to it with the meaningless abbreviation "LCN."

LEGIT: Legal business endeavors. A distinction applied by members of the underworld to the activities of non-criminals.

LOAN SHARK: See "shylock."

MADE: Formally inducted into the Mafia through a ceremony. Prospective members are called to a meeting without being given a reason. Through an elaborate ritual, they are then invited to join the Mafia. They are typically told the rules of the society, its history and hierarchy, and the general disciplinary measure for disobedience - death.

MARK: A person or place targeted for criminal activity.

MARKER: A notation of a debt. An IOU.

MEET: Meeting.

MEN OF HONOR: An older term referring to Sicilian Mafiosi. The term emphasizes a link between the Mafia and Sicily's displaced old aristocracy.

MESSAGGERO: A relatively recent addition to the Mafia family hierarchy. The job of the messenger is to function as liaison between specific families. Effective messengers can reduce the need for sit-downs and limit the exposure of bosses to law enforcement. New York's Genovese Family was credited with inventing the post in order to coordinate activity with counterparts in Chicago.

MUSTACHE PETE: During the Prohibition Era, old country Mafiosi were referred to with this term. The two most prominent "Mustache Petes" in New York were Salvatore Maranzano and Giuseppe Masseria.

MUSCLE: Intimidate. Also those who function as underworld thugs.

MUSCLE IN: Invade a rival's racket or territory through force.

NUMBERS: A lottery game that has been a moneymaker for American Mafiosi since the US Civil War.

OFF THE RECORD: When a mobster retains all profits from an illicit business venture, without kicking up a share to his superiors.

OMERTA: A uniquely Sicilian attitude calling for non-cooperation with government authority and the settlement of disputes through personal means. Omerta typically refers to the Mafia's strict code of silence with regard to underworld affairs.

ON THE CARPET: The situation that occurs when a made guy's performance is harshly criticized by his superior.

ON THE LAM: Moving secretly. Indicted mobsters, in an effort to avoid arrest, might go "on the lam," changing their address, moving secretly from place to place.

ON THE PAD: Designation for a law enforcement officer who is paid by the underworld to ignore certain criminal activity.

ON THE SPOT: Set up for assassination.

OUTFIT: Chicago slang name for the local Mafia family.

PACKING: Armed with a concealed handgun.

PAPER LOCAL: A chartered union local that has no legitimate membership or reason for existence. Paper locals are known to have played a role in Teamster Union elections.

PIECE: A percentage of profit from illicit business ventures. Also a handgun.

PIECE OF WORK: An assigned murder.

PINCH: Arrest.

POINTS: Interest paid on a shylock loan. Also known as "vig" or "shy."

POP: Kill.

PROTECTION: An extortion racket in which business owners are assessed a tax by a local Mafia group in exchange for assurances that no harm will come to them. Also the money paid by organized criminal groups in bribes to law enforcement.

RAT: To provide information to law enforcement about criminal activities of underworld associates. One who provides such information or who appears likely to give in to law enforcement pressure. See "stool pigeon."

RUB OUT: Kill.

SHAKE DOWN: Obtain money or other concessions from businesses or individuals by using intimidation or extortion.

SHYLOCK: A financial racketeer who loans money at usurious interest rates. Often shylocks arrange payment terms that never reduce the loan principal. Those who fail to make regular payments to a shylock are disciplined with violence.

SHOW-UP TIME: In union contracts, it is the amount paid to employees for appearing at a work site on days when work is not done.

SIT-DOWN: A meeting, perhaps called to settle a "beef."

SKIM: The act of siphoning funds from a legitimate business enterprise to an underworld organization. In addition, the money withdrawn from a venture - such as casino gambling - before income is calculated for tax purposes.

SKIPPER: See capo.

SNITCH: Traitor to the underworld. See "stool pigeon."

SOLDATI: Soldiers. The lowest rank of formal Mafia membership.

STANDUP GUY: An individual who observes the principles of Omerta even when it brings harm to himself.

STOOL PIGEON: Older term for traitor to the underworld. One who "flips" and cooperates with law enforcement by providing information about his former criminal partners. Also known as, "rat" and "snitch."

STRAIGHT: Older term for un-criminal behavior. A man who gave up crime and took a regular job "went straight."

STRAIGHTEN OUT: Resolve a dispute. Formally induct a Mafia member.

SWAG: Stolen goods.

TABLE: A meeting or sit-down.

TAIL: A law enforcement officer who is tracking an individual's movement.

TERRITORY: An underworld jurisdiction. While this is generally understood to refer to a geographic area, it actually refers to rackets officially designated as belonging to a family.

TIMMY GUN: Nickname for the Thompson submachine gun popular with some Prohibition Era gangsters.

UNDERBOSS: Second in command of a Borgata. The Underboss is often selected because he represents a powerful minority wing in the family.

VENDETTA: A pledge of personal vengeance on an enemy. The vendetta is a solemn and secret vow.

VIG: OR "VIGORISH." Percentage of each bet that is retained as income for a bookmaker. The usurious interest charged by a shylock.

WAR: Violent confrontation between underworld organizations.

WHACK: Murder.

WIRE: An electronic surveillance device secretly worn inside the clothing of an agent or a cooperating mobster. Also, the name of a gambling racket involving the transmission of horse race results or other sporting results (as depicted in the movie "The Sting.")

WISE GUY: A "made" member of a Mafia organization.

ZIPS: Derogatory term for immigrant Sicilian Mafiosi operating within the United States. The Bonanno Family in

New York is known to have maintained a working relationship with a crew of Zips.

*Glossary was compiled from free public domain web sites like: http://crime.about.com/od/mafiaglossary/,
http://www.ask.com/wiki/Glossary_of_Mafia-related_words,etc

ACKNOWLEDGEMENTS

I would like to express my deep gratitude to my many friends for test reading this work, motivating me and providing me with constructive suggestions, criticisms, and prayers.

Special mention must be made of my dear friend *Don Kazimir, Author/Publisher Lou Aronica* for their motivation, critique and advice in the writing process, and *Michael Herzog (a.k.a. Mr. Mike) CGI Artist* for his design input and *Merke Baroni,* who helped to structure and proofread the work. Also, my special thanks go to: Author, *Robin Ader* for the initial editing of the manuscript.

And, last but not least, my deepest expression to my editor: *MARY LITCHFIELD TUEL* for making the production of the book possible.

SICILIAN TRINACRIA

The symbol dates back to when Sicily was part of Magna Graecia. People attribute the origin of the Trinacria, to the triangular form of the island, which consists of three large capes equidistant from each other, pointing in their respective directions, the names of which were Pelorus, Pachynus and Lilybaeum.

Sicilian Trinacria is attributed to Greek legends. The head in the centre of today's Triacria was that of Medusa, whose hair was turned into snakes by the outraged goddess Athene.

The Sicilian parliament, which uses the Trinacria as its Flag, replaced the Medusa head with one that is less threatening to the innocent onlooker who, after all, should not be anticipating being turned to stone....

BOUT THE AUTHOR

His first writing project was a non-fiction book about the Apparitions of the Blessed Virgin Mary in the small village of Medjugorje in then Yugoslavia, now Bosnia-Herzegovina. Titled: "Medjugorje, A Pilgrim's Journey." Originally published in 1991; with the forward and collaboration by Author, John Westermann (Exit Wounds). Because of popular demand it was re-released (Second Edition) in 2010. Also, the book is in the process of its Spanish language translation due for completion mid-2015.

He is presently in the completion stage of novel "SCHISM" A fantasy about an unheard of problem in Heaven. He has also written the screenplay adaptions for both "SCHISM" and "THE HESTER STREET KIDS." In the past he has written articles for the National Catholic Register and articles about Marian apparitions for local Long Island, NY publications.

He was awarded a Bachelor of Science Social Welfare with a minor in psychology and a Master's of Science in Clinical Social Work from Fordham University School of Social Service with emphasis on psycho-dynamic psychotherapy.